from despair to where

Loss. Fear. Hope.

OLIVER SMITH

Copyright

Published in the United Kingdom of Great Britain & Northern Ireland and subject to the Laws of England and Wales.

First published 2020

ISBN 978-1-5272-6206-5

Published by Oliver Smith

dystopiannovels.co.uk

For Rebecca, James & Finn

Chapter 1 – Meet Jack

Jack had worked in marketing for about 15 years. He began his career as a salesman, but wrongly thought a career in marketing would be less soul destroying and provide him with the means to buy a nice car, a house, and enjoy the occasional far flung holiday, trinkets. Trinkets that were important to so many people in the world as it was.

As it turns out, the world that it is now, material luxuries and having an in-depth understanding of Photoshop and web design is of no value. Now, of course, being the zombie apocalypse.

Had Jack decided to forego his hazy University days, stayed in his childhood home in rural Yorkshire and chosen a career path in one of the trades; he would have been far better equipped to survive in a world where men with soft, delicate office worker hands were being eaten alive.

Jack, in truth, was quite an unextraordinary person, and probably still is. He would have been described as middle-class, although he hated society's incessant need to classify people into boxes, Jack felt like an individual, on his own. He was about 5 10", early 30s if he was lying, late 30s when telling the truth, average build, handsome to some, but middling to most.

He coasted through school and university and into his work life. Through forged CVs and an ability to sound like he knew what he was talking about, Jack masked his general averageness. He had managed to get himself an above average job, not great, but not bad. It paid him a wage which was the only motivation when it came to his career. He was dancing society's dance.

Having no real purpose was only half the trouble with choosing a career so meaningless; it also meant that Jack lacked any practical skills for survival. A half-finished marketing diploma and understanding how to create a pretty email newsletter aren't exactly in-demand skills come the breakdown of civilization.

In Jack's mind, however, he had been surviving for years. Trudging through a meaningless existence. In stasis. Jack was about to rouse.

Chapter 2 – The Beginning

The beginning for Jack was just beyond the critical breaking point of civilisation. Jack had recently learnt of Earth Overshoot Day: the day that humanity used all the resources that Earth could naturally produce in 12 months, which he was disturbed to find out, fell in August: a four-month shortfall, meaning that sooner or later, Earth, or humanity at least, was screwed. Jack became aware of the outbreak of the infected way past Zombie Overshoot Day: the point where the living could no longer control the dead.

Jack lived in Cheshire, in the North West of England, about 20 miles from Manchester. It was quite populated for the countryside with just over 2,500 people living within a three-mile radius. He lived on a quiet street in a terraced house.

He had been working from home for most of the week, it was 2017 and spring. He was taking a break from the office so he could get some peace and quiet to enable him to write the content for a new website he was due to launch at the end of the month. Which all seems quite laughably trivial now.

Being a marketing man, Jack should have had Twitter open, ready to interact with his company's audience. Jack, however, detested social media so liked to keep away from what he thought were the irrelevant opinions of irrelevant people. If he'd been a little more social himself, he'd have had a lot better understanding of the situation that was taking place all over the world.

The front of Jack's house, number 12, was facing the street, the rear of the house looked out onto back-to-back gardens meaning the building was only accessible via the front; which was once a burden, having to traipse things through the house into his back garden, but now turned out to be a beneficial security feature.

It was upstairs at the back of the house where Jack had his cramped office, which in reality was just the spare bedroom with a desk. He'd been in there for about four days from eight until six trying to finish off the content for his employer's website. On an evening he'd cook something to eat and then either play on his X-Box or maybe, ironically, watch a couple of episodes of the Walking dead.

It was a Thursday when Jack realised something was wrong and that life wasn't going to be quite the same. He'd finally run out of milk and wanted a cup of tea. He thought it was probably best to get some fresh air too. The shop was a two-minute walk away, so he slipped on his New Balance and popped out of the door. The street was quiet, it was about 10:00am and all seemed normal. He could hear the distant drilling and hammering of builders doing something to a house, but paid no attention. He saw a couple of cars speed past at the top of the road, making him a little angry as they were going well above the 30mph speed limit with no regards for the kids that played around the streets; he chuckled to himself as he realised he sounded old.

The way to the shop involved turning left out of the front door, walking to the end of the road, turning right onto a main street, and then going past a hairdressers, pharmacy, and takeaway. There was also a short cut. A narrow alleyway that went behind the row of businesses and directly to the shop. This is the way that Jack walked. Jack entered the shop and wandered around the aisles. It was empty. He got the milk and then browsed the array of sugary treats and chocolate before showing some restraint; he felt like his stomach was growing a little round. He stood at the counter waiting to be served, assuming that the staff were in the back somewhere or having a crafty cigarette. He waited, waited, waited, and became a little impatient. Some coughing. Nothing. He counted his change, could he leave some money, nope, not enough, he'd have to pay with a note. He wasn't going to spend most of his day doing a job he didn't like to just give his money away. He could steal the milk, but he remembered the saying, 'don't shit on your own doorstep', plus they had CCTV. He decided to say 'hello'. A little louder this time. And then a little louder still. Finally, he heard a noise at the back of the shop. It was a banging, not that loud, but on closer inspection it was persistent. He edged past the counter to the last aisle that ran perpendicular to the tills. He knew that the sound was coming from the storeroom or whatever was behind the door next to the beer fridge.

He crept closer, he wasn't really sure why he was creeping, maybe not to scare who was in there. He decided to go to the door and say hello so he could just get out of the oddly quiet shop. It occurred to him that he'd been in there for about five minutes and nobody had come in. It was all a bit odd and Jack was feeling a little uneasy. He got himself out of his daze and picked up his pace to go to the door where the banging was emanating from. As he approached the door he noticed a few specks of red liquid on the floor where the door was slightly ajar. It was a shop, this was the storeroom, items get smashed. Basic logical thinking. No need to worry over spilt ketchup. He pushed the door slightly, it creaked open slowly and the banging from inside began to get more frantic which startled Jack. He regained his composure and began to say, 'he…'

From behind him, he heard the automatic door open and then rushed footsteps. Then what sounded like cans being knocked over and groceries being thrown around. It was a commotion and Jack was now beginning to wonder what the hell was going on. He backed away from the door, where the banging still persisted, and thought he'd just go back home, forget the milk and have a glass of water. He had no idea who was rummaging around the shop only two aisles away and he didn't really want to find out either. Whoever it was, sounded rushed, unpleasant, and not someone he wanted to interact with.

Jack crept away, past the counter and tried to sneak past the remaining two aisles. He tip-toed past the half price Coke display near the door and slipped towards the exit. The door sensor registered Jack as he slowly approached, the door noisily slid open. He was about to leave when from behind him he heard, "What the fuck is going on?".

It wasn't the swearing that made Jack stop, it was the urgency and fear in the voice. Jack turned and saw a man in his 40s with packs of nappies, baby milk and bottled water piled high in his shopping basket. Not wanting to engage with the man who was clearly distressed, Jack responded in an attempted light-hearted tone, "No idea mate.".

The man continued, barely waiting for Jack's response, "What's going on? People are fucking eating people. It's out there, I just drove past it two minutes up the road. Manchester is rioting and the news says it's everywhere."

Jack was now freaking out. *People eating people? Did he just say that?* Jack was now concerned, was this man dangerous, was he in need of help? Jack decided the second option sounded more feasible. With slight hesitation, Jack asked, "What do you mean? Do you need some help?"

"Help? What help can you give me? Do you have a castle? Do you have a gun? Can you tell me what's going on?" He said trailing off with more expletives.

"Look, just start from the beginning, what the hell are you talking about?" Jack said, feeling his irritation starting to build as the man added more confusion to his trip to buy milk.

The man stopped frantically rummaging through the shelves, looked directly into Jack's eyes and had a desperate look of resignation. "People. Are. Eating. People. Have you not seen the news? If you walk out of this shop and walk down the road, you'll see for yourself. Look, I've got to get out of here. I've got my kid and woman in the car."

"Please." Jack said. "Are you being serious. This can't be right. Are you telling me that cannibals are wandering the streets of this village? Are you out of your mind?"

"Just walk out of the fucking door if you don't believe me. I haven't got time for your shit." The man shouted with such aggression that Jack took a step backwards.

On that note, the man looked down, made an unconscious decision that he had everything he needed and made a hasty retreat out of the shop. As he approached the exit, Jack having taken a couple more steps backwards, next to the safety of the Coke offer, the man turned and said in a more reasonable tone, "Please son, take me seriously, get yourself to safety. I'm telling you the truth, I've seen it. Go. Go now."

And with that he ran out of the door. Jack, regained a modicum of composure, slowly left the shop, noting that the incessant banging from the storeroom was still a recurring background noise. As he walked out into the bright sunshine, he heard a muffled scream.

Looking over in the scream's direction he could see a car with a man beating on the window. He saw the frantic man from the shop drop his stolen items and begin to sprint to the car. It dawned on Jack that the screams were coming from inside the car, not one scream: two screams. A woman and a baby.

Jack not being one for confrontation felt the adrenaline kick in straight away. It was never a help for Jack, the adrenaline would make him shake and as a result he'd always involuntarily choose flight over fight. This was probably why he'd never experienced a beating of any sort or struck anyone with anger. Still, he managed to overcome his desire to escape and wandered closer as the man from the shop approached the stranger banging with unnatural coordination on the car window.

To Jack's astonishment, the man from the shop charged the attacker of the car with a fierce shoulder barge knocking the assailant flying so that he stumbled and fell heavily over a curb. Jack got closer and could now see blood on the felled man. He wasn't finished, he was attempting to stand again, like Bambi on ice, ungraciously to his feet.

The man from the shop rushed hurriedly to his car opening the door and caught Jack watching him from the corner of his eye. Leaning on the open door with one foot in the car, the man shouted, "There's your proof son. Take a closer look. This is what I'm talking about, this is what you need to know. Look. Loo-"

A low unnatural moan murmured from behind the car, the person that was knocked to floor was lurching towards the man from the shop. Seeing Jack and the frenzy of overcoming his wife and baby's attacker had made him over confident, his bravado at wanting to prove to Jack that he was in control had led him to turn his back on the man he'd knocked down.

From inside the car, another scream, and a shout, "Mick, it's right behind you…Miiiicccc-"

Mick turned in an instant as the attacker lunged reaching over the open car door, arms outstretched, mouth wide open, saliva glistening in the sunshine. Mick was pressed up against the car as the attacker lurched closer, mouth biting as Mick held the attacker off with one hand pushing the car door and the other pushing the head away as teeth chattered.

The sound of the teeth biting together would stay with Jack. The sound resonated above everything else. The screams of mum and child, and Mick's grunts and exasperations, as he struggled, all faded into the background. Jack's eyes were transfixed to the animal like bite, over and over, teeth against teeth. Bite. Bite. Bite.

As the attacker lurched again, Mick tried to step backwards into the car, he caught his heel on the inside of the door and his foot slipped. He fell back so that he landed on the edge of his seat. The aggressor sensing his advantage scrambled against the door, closing it on Mick's legs. This action seemed to rejuvenate Mick as he kicked the door open, knocking the assailant backwards. Mick sprung to his feet, effortlessly slipping past the open door and catching the staggering enemy with a fierce right hook on the jaw. Jack could hear the crack as something in either Mick's hand or the accoster's jaw broke. The man flew backwards and fell again. Jack thought that he wasn't getting up from that anytime soon.

From inside the car, the woman sternly said, "Mick, get in the damn car. We need you. Get in."

Mick turned once again to Jack, "The name's Mick, but people call me Bulldog. You can come with us while you get your head around all of this. You in?"

Jack stared at Bulldog with a sense of awe and confusion. This man had just floored someone who looked to be foaming at the mouth. This man had told him people were eating people. This man was looking after his wife and child. These thoughts were not helping. He meekly responded to Mick's question, "Err, no, I'm going home."

Mick smiled a toothy smile, "Okay son. Look after yourself. This guy is getting back up. Whatever you do, don't let him bite you."

With that, Mick jumped in his car and made a rapid exit.

Jack, still in a state of shock watched as the car vanished around a bend. He slowly ambled a little closer to the guy who'd been knocked on his arse for the second time. He was murmuring again, a quiet and gentle noise which sounded to Jack as though he was groggy. Unsure what to do, Jack timidly asked, "Are you okay mate?"

With Jack's words, the man on the floor turned his head to look directly at Jack and let out a guttural moan. Jack looked into his eyes and realised that he was no longer a he, it was an it. Rising like a drunk once more, the thing stood up and immediately lurched towards Jack, moaning and biting teeth loudly together.

Adrenaline filled his veins once again; this time Jack let his instincts take over. He turned on his heels and made a run for it. Past the shop, down the side and into the alley, gaining speed as he attempted to process the last ten minutes of his life. He skidded out of the alley and went at full tilt to his front door, frantically rattling his keys in the door to get it unlocked, finally he managed it, turned the key and raced inside, slamming the door shut and locking it for good measure.

Jack put his back to the door and slid down to a sitting position. He put his head in his hands, exhaled a deep breath, and gathered his thoughts. *People eating people? It can't be.*

Chapter 3 – 24 Hour Rolling News

Securely locked up in number 12, Jack began a desperate fact-finding mission. He could feel that something wasn't right. The sincerity of Bulldog, his words, and of course, that thing. Jack rushed upstairs to his office. He checked his email, nothing but automated marketing emails, no emails from actual people in a few days. His phone was in the shop getting the screen replaced so he was without any contact with his family or friends. He did have a landline, but he didn't have a home phone attached to it, the landline was just a necessity for the broadband connection.

A quick check of his personal email showed no contact from anyone that he cared about. He opened another tab on his browser and logged into Twitter. It was the work account and was full of tweets from self-claimed entrepreneurs and assorted 'gurus' offering tips on how to be just like them. Jack couldn't help himself wonder why self-proclaimed social media experts only had 148 followers. The thought quickly passed as he glanced over at the trending topics.

#livingdead

#londonriots

#ManchesterRiots

#eatingpeople

#newyorkterror

The list went on. Jack clicked on #ManchesterRiots and was horrified by what he saw. It was difficult to understand exactly what was happening. Many of the tweets showed blurry pictures of what looked like people fighting. Reading his timeline didn't clarify matters either. Jack clicked on 'Media' to search for useful videos rather than relying on the ill-informed opinions of the masses.

The first video he played was in the Arndale Centre: a shopping centre in Manchester, it was a normal scene for a short while until all hell suddenly broke loose. Screams were quickly followed by mass hysteria as people started to run and push past the person documenting the commotion. It cut off as the person filming decided to follow the crowd and make a run for it, commenting in a monotone shout that there was a terrorist attack taking place.

A terrorist attack. Jack thought about it. Terror had been the nightmare of the time. Attacks were growing more frequent and more ruthless. Even innocent children were targeted. It was feasible that a group of fundamentalists were causing mayhem in a coordinated attack, a coordinated attack across the globe? It wasn't feasible. Jack still had an uneasy feeling. It was that noise again. The biting.

He continued his video perusal. The next two videos he watched bobbed up and down and were the nightmares of people who suffer motion sickness, leaving Jack feeling queasy. The next video, however, was to change Jack's world.

Pressing play, Jack could immediately see that the video was good quality, he was greeted by a face, a woman, perhaps early 40s, red hair, green eyes; the classic English rose complexion. Jack leaned forward towards the screen, transfixed.

She spoke, "My name is Lucy and I'm in an apartment overlooking Portland Street. That's Manchester, England. Before I show you what's going on out there, I want to try and explain some of my observations over the past couple of days."

Jack moved closer to the screen. Her voice captured him. A soft, but confident tone. Lucy's expression was serious, but there was a sense of composure; she was in total control of her emotions.

"I first noticed something was wrong last night. There were screams. Don't get me wrong, I live in a major city centre and there are screams all of the time, but this was different. They weren't the screams of drunk people revelling in the night, they were blood curdling screams. Those that belong in horror films.

"I heard a scream outside and rushed to the window to look down on the street. Below my apartment, a young woman was struggling with a man, the man had grasped the girl's arm and looked to be biting her. I actually saw blood spray from her arm, so I knew it was serious. I opened the window and shouted down to the man to leave her alone. She managed to get her arm free, I could see a dark smear of blood flowing down her arm and staining the poor girl's light dress."

Lucy gulped down her emotions and continued, "I was still shouting at the man, telling him I was calling the police, he looked up towards my voice and I saw the look in his eyes. His dead eyes. It's the only way I can describe it.

"Anyway, a black cab came speeding from around a corner and struck the man at full speed. The man didn't react though, he had turned at the noise of the car and made no attempt to avoid the collision. He was thrown into the air and landed with a crunch. A noise I never want to hear again. The man had to be dead. I ran to get my phone from the bedroom and called the police. To my astonishment, I was put through to some sort of queuing system. I waited for about five minutes before walking back to the window; still on hold. I looked out of the window but couldn't for the life of me see the man who'd been struck by the taxi. On closer inspection, I saw blood stains, a lot of blood. It was as if the body had crawled away, or had been pulled away. I just didn't know. I hung up the phone.

"For the remainder of the night I repeatedly called the police, desperately trying to raise the alarm. If you look through my Twitter timeline, you'll see my attempts to contact them via social media, but with no success. Finally, about 3:30 in the morning I managed to speak to a police operator. The lady who answered asked if I was in immediate danger to which I said no. She then said that I'd have to call back tomorrow as they were busy dealing with serious crimes. She also warned me to stay inside and lock the doors. Repeating not to go outside several times.

"I realise I'm taking my time here, but the point is this: this all happened last night. Yesterday morning, everything seemed normal. Now come with me and I'll show you Portland Street."

With the end of the long narrative, that had captured Jack to complete stillness, the camera shakily made its way to the window. Lucy began to speak again, but her words faded into the background as Jack focused on the images in front of him. From what he could see there was absolute pandemonium on the streets. People were running, bumping into one another, moving down side streets. Two cars had collided and were both trying to manoeuvre away from each other, slowing down their exit as they both blocked one another. Then Jack saw the real focus of the video. At the end of the street there was a group of people all walking with the same unnatural coordination that he'd seen when he'd made his life changing trip to buy milk.

As the camera panned the street, it became clear that there were numerous groups of people all acting in the same peculiar fashion. The camera stopped and began to zoom in to a fire exit where an old man had become trapped. He looked in his 70s and he was surrounded by a cluster of people slowly closing in on him. He was valiantly trying to fend them off with his walking stick, but there were too many. Over the noise of the street, Jack could make out the sounds of a desperate man, weakened shouts that were barely audible. Within a few seconds the first person reached him and overpowered him. The person had leaned in face first. In the struggle, the old man lost his footing and tumbled to the floor. The remaining people, Jack had no doubt that these were no longer people, fell on top of the old man. The camera zoomed closer still. Through the mass of bodies on top of the poor soul, Jack saw glimpses of teeth, flesh, blood, and gore. He paused the video and stepped away from his laptop.

He felt sick. *They were eating him; they were tearing him apart.* He walked into the bathroom and looked in the mirror.

19

He'd always had a habit of talking to himself in the mirror, particularly when intoxicated, but this time it was a counsel he needed for his own sanity.

"They're zombies. I know it." Jack said. He laughed a bitter laugh. He caught himself staring blankly at his reflection and decided to go back to the laptop and continue listening to Lucy. He'd seen enough of the images so went back to the end of Lucy's narrative, pressed play and lowered his screen so he couldn't see the horror.

"I saw one person last night. It's just past 10 in the morning here and look outside. Of course, I've been on the Internet all morning, so I know that this isn't just Manchester. I know this is the world. Look outside, there are hundreds of them. Where have they come from? I don't know, but all I know is that this is a pandemic, and this could be the end of humanity."

Lucy began to speak again, but quickly trailed off. Jack realised that this must have been when she'd zoomed in on the doomed old man. He lifted his laptop screen and quickly paused the video once again. He scanned the tweet and noticed that the date of the tweet was yesterday. Jack clicked on Lucy's profile to look at her timeline, part of him wanting to make sure she was okay, the other part wanting to find out more information.

Sure enough, a post from three hours ago, another video. The video thumbnail was Lucy's face, instinctively Jack pressed play and Lucy began to speak, "Things have taken a dramatic turn outside."

Jack could hear loud bangs and what sounded like machine gunfire in the background of the video. He also noticed that Lucy was less composed and had fear etched into her features. He continued to listen.

"The situation had deteriorated considerably in the past few hours. There were hordes of them. I've seen so many people die, and I feared I would be one of them. The numbers outside my apartment and the strange moans from the corridor had made my thoughts turn increasingly morbid. However, the army has arrived, and they mean business. They got here about two hours ago and created a roadblock on the crossroads of Portland Street and Oxford Street, forming a circle facing all four directions.

"Armoured buses have been gathering those trying to escape the masses of, oh God, I guess I'll call them zombies. It's what they look like. Anyway, I've been watching the attack from my window, but I've since sheltered in the bathroom as I could see the buildings opposite being struck with bullets.

"The important part of this message is that I've learned something. Something that could save you if you're watching this. This following footage isn't live, it's from the past hour and I've stitched together some clips to show you what I've figured out."

The video then flicked to a difference scene, it showed the army as Lucy had described, they'd blocked the road where Portland Street and Oxford Street met and were shuttling people through a cordon onto armoured buses. The hairs on the back of Jack's neck stood up as he saw the vast hordes of zombie like people closing in on those who were trying to escape the clutches of outstretched hands and chomping teeth.

Lucy began to narrate the video, "Try not to focus on the poor souls who are helpless down there. Focus on the soldiers who are shooting the zombies. The stories and films portray an accurate reflection of them. See this one here." A red circle flashed over a section of the screen and disappeared.

"Watch as this person gets shot in the chest. This would kill a normal person, or at least debilitate them. Watch as the recipient of the bullet is thrown backwards. Wait for it." She paused, "Now, see the creature, I can't keep calling them people, watch as it gets to its feet. You can see the blood mark, which would have hit the heart, surely. He…sorry, it, is still going though.

"Now watch this one." Again, a red circle showed Jack where to look. "Keep watching a few seconds…the soldier is a good shot and shoots this one in the head. You can see the awful spurt from the back of its head as the bullet passes through. Keep watching, I know it's disturbing. Watch the lifeless body. This one doesn't get back up. It's the head, attack the head to make them stay down.

"I'll leave the video running and just watch the army's attack. You'll see the same thing over and over again. It's the head. Go for the head."

The video continued to play, and Jack watched a little more to see for himself that Lucy's discovery was true. He stopped the video and spoke to himself, "Thank you Lucy. I hope you get rescued. Stay safe."

-

Jack spent the next few hours reading the constant rolling news on the BBC and Guardian websites as well as other articles posted by various people on Twitter.

The situation seemed grave and looked to be affecting most, if not all, major population centres in the UK and many other parts of the world. Jack started trying to figure out what was happening by attempting to look for the origins of the pandemic that was spreading its web of infection. The news was conflicting, confused and lacking any expert credibility. This wasn't necessarily unusual; 2017 was awash with sensationalist and baseless opinion.

It seemed logical to focus on the consensus and look for eyewitness reports to see what people were saying in common. This proved a useful tactic as some key points surfaced from the plethora of opinion.

The first of which was how this thing was spreading. Many eyewitness statements corroborated each other's stories. They involved people tending to friends and relatives who had been bitten by other people. All accounts mentioned that the victims became ill and developed a fever that furiously burned. They were delirious and those who sought medical help found no medicine that could slow the infection down. Every story resulted in the same conclusion. Death. A temporary death.

The dead would rise again. A short while after passing, a deceased person would reanimate and wake with a thirst for blood. There was no recognition of loved ones, no humanity, no emotion, just a drive and determination to sink their teeth into living flesh. Dead people became the dead.

It occurred to Jack that these people had escaped the clutches of their nearest and dearest to tell their tales. He was sure that countless others suffered a very different fate; caught unaware and full of love and hope seeing their loved ones miraculously come back from the dead. Jack couldn't help himself thinking of the Joy Division song, Love Will Tear Us Apart. He didn't think it was funny as he breathed a long drawn out sigh as the gravity of the situation and the suffering of so many threatened to turn him into panic.

Another bit of information lurched out from people's stories. Bites didn't need to be serious for them to be deadly. As much as that sounded like an oxymoron, the bite would just need to break the surface of the skin for the healthy to become infected. A Doctor from Pakistan, named Dr. Hussain, had prepared a useful video that Jack watched. He detailed minor bites to hands, fingers and even one case of an improbably bite to an earlobe. Naturally, the wounds didn't worry the Doctor and he didn't relate the injuries to the fever that attacked his patients. It wasn't until a nurse pointed out the strange wounds on several of his patients that Dr. Hussain went back to examine his patients more thoroughly. All were bitten, none with life threatening injuries. The Doctor was wrong. They all died. No one survived.

Jack knew about market research and the importance of a decent sized sample, the Doctor's sample was only small, but the fact that everyone who'd been bitten had suffered the same fate sent a chill down his spine. One hundred percent fatality. It occurred to him that this was a disease and it was spread through the bloodstream. He didn't know if this included ingesting the blood or fluids of the infected; but there was still so much he didn't know.

From the limited information Jack had found, he was certain that this disease was like nothing else that mankind had ever faced, it was so severe that the fabrics of humanity were being ripped apart.

He needed to contact his parents, but how? He had no phone, he couldn't even think where the nearest public phone was, if indeed there was one, plus he had no desire to go outside, fear had him locked inside.

A light bulb in Jack's head lit up, an idea. Skype, of course, he could buy some credit and call his family and friends to make sure they were okay. He was grateful Microsoft's services were robust and the payment option was still available. Topped up with £20 credit, Jack proceeded to call his parents. No answer, but then it dawned on him, his parents were touring Scotland in their newly acquired camper van, enjoying their retirement. They usually got Wi-Fi in the campsites they stayed, so he left a video message explaining everything he'd seen and advised them to stay inside and keep away from anyone acting erratically.

Jack then thought he'd call his close friends, he only had a handful of real friends who were like family to him, he needed to check in on them. His heart sank, he couldn't remember any of their phone numbers and unlike his parents, they weren't on Skype. He was so reliant on his mobile and without it he simply had no recollection of the numbers he desperately wanted. His eyes filled up, he wanted to cry, but he took a deep breath, the heavy feeling in the pit of his stomach seemed to consume him.

He'd had enough. Jack lowered the screen of his laptop, stood up wearily and headed downstairs. He picked up a bottle of red wine, opened it, poured himself a large glass and went to take a seat in the kitchen. Exhausted.

Chapter 4 – A Lonely Soul

When someone suffers so much loss in their life, they begin to lose feeling. The everyday joy of life evaporates; most events feel mundane and unimportant. Even disaster and tragedy can be equated to mere trivialities.

This is how Jack had been living his life for the past five years. He was once a popular and outgoing person, enjoyed life and was actively involved in his immediate world. His life became infected with grief and this clouded his thoughts for every aspect of his personal and professional life.

Jack's downward spiral into apathy first began when he lost his mother who had drank herself to death seven years earlier. She was a bitter and unhappy person. When she died, he hadn't been close to her. His mother had left Jack and his dad when Jack was a child, she was a free spirit when his parents got together, and Jack had been an accident that didn't fit in with her lifestyle. She tried to be maternal and strained for three years in an attempt to tame her inner demons and settle into a vanilla suburban routine, but as the strain increased so did the arguments and the loathing at an existence that wasn't planned for. One morning, Jack's mother upped and left without a word. Jack's dad picked up the pieces and Jack had a good life with a loving father and a step-mum, that raised him as her own and whom Jack loved as any child would their biological mother, she *was* mum. Jack's birth mother, *who was not mum,* did stay in his life, flitting in and out, but visits were sporadic and often left him feeling broken when she inevitably let him down. As the years went by, jealousy grew within the woman, whose life had spiralled without meaning, as she looked on at idyllic world that surrounded Jack. Choices in evil men increased her bitterness and the heightened acrimony also correlated with the frequency and quantity of alcohol she consumed. Eventually, she died from severe alcoholic hepatitis. They hadn't spoken for two years prior to her death and it hit Jack hard. He was full of regret having not sought to be the bigger man and build bridges.

Jack suffered for over a year coming to terms with his maternal mum's death. He managed to get through it with the help of his wife, Amy, and their daughter Ruby. They were his rock, his life, his reason for being. He could put up with anything, hell; he'd spend most of his time selling his soul in a pointless job, just to provide for his family so he could enjoy what little time was left with his little trio; his world.

That world ended five years ago. Amy and Ruby were killed on a motorway during heavy fog. A large articulated lorry ploughed through the back of the car when the traffic had come to a standstill. They were both killed instantly.

Since that date, Jack had stopped living, he merely existed. He pushed friends and family away, it wasn't anything drastic, just a lack of communication and effort from Jack. He'd subconsciously stopped letting people get close to him as his care for the world dissipated. Contempt for the world slowly built up. From the outside, he'd seem normal, his friends and family would speak with him, but he wouldn't let them in, everything was small talk, never of any importance. He thought of suicide in the early days, but the fact that it was his job to keep the memory of Amy and Ruby alive, that dark thought vanished and instilled in him a will to survive; a determination that would prove useful.

Jack would go to work, interact and joke with colleagues, but each night he'd return to his empty home, eat, drink, watch TV or play on his X-Box. He'd do anything that would provide escapism from the reality of his losses. He didn't drink excessively, but enough to numb himself. Each night he'd be alone, silently burying his head in the sand, being typically British, sidestepping the brutal reality of his life.

Contempt of humanity had also grown. Jack would find his blood pressure rising as he watched the actions of humanity from the outside. Whether trivial or important, people's carelessness intensified his disdain. It was the one emotion that was a constant for him, the joy and enthusiasm for life had diminished, but he knew he was still alive through his exasperation at society. He'd become angry and bitter, just like his mother.

Jack didn't want bad things to happen to people, in fact, he wanted the opposite. He wanted equality, peace, and a perfect world. His growing disapproval with humanity was at its ability to self-destruct, to be selfish and to make animals look like the civilised occupiers of planet Earth.

Rubbish that littered the streets that people carelessly tossed away, the material nature that made people crave the latest iPhone or the wilful neglect of the environment; Jack despaired at the short-sighted and self-centred attitude of the general public.

Anything would aggravate his mood, for example, at work on social media, he'd find himself looking at profiles where people had written bios stating their passion about digital marketing. Before he knew it, he'd spend half-an-hour wondering why anybody would be passionate about something so ridiculous. *Be passionate about your family, the stars, science, the protection of the white rhino. Be passionate about the Great Barrier Reef, be passionate about eliminating poverty, curing cancer, finding a clean energy source to power the world. Just don't be passionate about digital marketing.*

The worship of celebrities seemed like a vacuous exercise, yet large portions of the population were enthralled by the lives of people like Kim Kardashian, YouTube celebrities and the constant conveyor belt of reality television stars. The Internet had provided anybody and everybody with the opportunity to get noticed, to go viral. Jack loathed it all, but in reality, he was no different, people were looking to escape their daily grinds just as much as Jack.

The state of the world and politics was a mess. Donald Trump was the President of the United States. He was racist, sexist, and homophobic, yet he still had plenty of support and he was still the most powerful man in the world. The UK had voted to leave Europe and with that xenophobia and racism had risen as the voices of experts were cast aside by lies and misinformation. Terrorism was an everyday occurrence. Children and the innocent were targeted by religious extremists. The western world had meddled in the Middle East for so long that the hatred of fundamentalists had intensified to levels which meant no reason could be applied to their will to disrupt and destroy. The world was a mess.

The environment was getting beyond repair too, the world was on the brink of another mass extinction, not of nature's making, but mankind's. Earth's population was out of control, developing nations whose monstrous numbers were churning out more greenhouse gasses to add to those already released from over a century of the developed world abusing their supposed superiority. The ice caps were melting, climate change was happening, but was still being rejected by superpowers whose powerful corporate lobbyists were pulling the strings. It was all too little too late from mankind's point of view.

The gravity of disappointment was all too much for Jack. Since Amy and Ruby had been taken away from him, he couldn't see the good in the world anymore. He wouldn't notice the old couple holding hands in the park or the innocent play of children; he'd be constantly bemused by the negatives. He'd often fantasise about inventing a disease that indiscriminately wiped out 80 percent of the worldwide population, leaving the rest to start again for the good of the Earth; for the long-term survival of humanity.

His macabre fantasy would help Jack. He would often drift off to sleep alone, halfway through a chapter of the latest dystopian novel, many of which would include the very same monsters that were roaming outside, risen from the dead, zombies. From the Zombie Survival Guide to Mira Grant, Jack had read just about every work of zombie fiction, if it could be called fiction in this day and age.

Apathy and bitterness were Jack's weakness in the old world, he grumbled over problems and made no effort to provide a positive contribution. In the new world however, his escape into the world of zombie fiction would help Jack. It wasn't the author's depiction of the blood thirsty monsters that was of help, it was the fact that these books were written by smart people who detailed the likely reaction of survivors. It was important to Jack to stand on his own two feet and avoid the crowd and these books had given him a reference point to make educated plans for survival.

Chapter 5 – Planning

Jack woke about 5:30 the next morning. He opened his eyes, laying on his back, he was feeling relaxed. Then he remembered. This wasn't an unfamiliar start to the day for him. It had been the same most days as he'd wake from a night's sleep with the dreams of making love to Amy or playing with Ruby; listening as she giggled. Waking, feeling good and then the dawn of realisation crushing those sleepy hopes.

He spent the first half an hour of the day writing an email to his friends, James, Andrew, and Scott. They were his childhood friends and although they'd drifted apart, he still held their friendship close to his heart. He explained he wasn't available by phone but could be reached via Skype and email, and for them to please get in touch to let him know they were safe. He knew they weren't the type to be sat by their computer, but he had to try.

He then found himself looking for more news from Lucy. Sure enough, Lucy had posted another three videos. It wasn't good news. The army were gone, but the dead weren't. There were many more and the living on the street appeared to be gone. Manchester looked dead. Lucy, however, was alive and still composed, but appeared to be resigned to her impending fate. She put it simply, stay and die slowly from thirst, or run and be eaten. The options weren't appealing.

The world was ending quickly. Jack had already been convinced that it was the end of civilisation as he'd drank his bottle of wine the previous evening, mulling over what he'd seen and learnt that day. He was surprised by the speed of the transformation depicted in Lucy's videos. He knew that he couldn't sit around and do nothing. Now was the time to make the most of the last remaining evidence of the digital age and come up with a plan so he could survive.

The first thoughts that Jack had were about his modern comforts, the electricity, water, gas and of course his link to news and fact finding, the Internet. This would all be gone, and it would be soon if the pandemic continued the way his gut told him it was going. How long would this take? He felt that he was on borrowed time. There was so much he didn't know.

It seemed to Jack that electricity played a key role. Without this, the Internet would be lost, light extinguished, and water would dry up. He searched the Internet and there were many reports from people, with unsubstantiated qualifications, stating that the power supply would last a maximum of a week. Power plants were complex mechanisms that required scores of people to operate, Jack imagined that the personnel had their own safety and the welfare of their families on their minds rather than powering their nation.

He figured that the situation had become general panic two days previous, although this was guess work as he'd been cocooned for days in solitude with no links to the outside world. He'd liked being on his own only a day ago, but now when faced with the adversity of horror, he wanted to embrace the world and check on its wellbeing. The irony wasn't lost on him, he had pushed away the living and vibrant parts of his life and now that all appeared bleak, he wanted to draw it close and revel in it once again.

Water was Jack's main concern, further desk research explained that for the water to reach his taps, it required electricity to pump it from the treatment plants and of course the treatment plants needed people to operate them. Jack made a mental note to fill his bath and large containers full of water just in case it came to a war of attrition with thirst. This was probably a little bit of an overkill as the North West of England was a very wet climate and would undoubtedly supply all the water he needed, and then some.

Having determined that his utilities weren't going to last very long and that the world outside him was changing rapidly, Jack began to think rationally about what his next steps were. He needed to find his Mum and Dad. They were away in Scotland. This comforted him as he knew that they wouldn't be in a densely populated area and would more than likely be safe. For now, anyway. He was sure that they would have heard about what was happening on the news and figured that they'd probably do what was natural, to head for home. How long would that take? Probably longer than normal.

He also began to think about what other people would be doing. Those living in the more populated areas would either be locked away, eaten alive or attempting to flee. He figured that the last option would be something that many would attempt. This meant that the roads would be dangerously crowded, possibly impassable and could resemble scenes from Mad Max.

He knew his Mum and Dad weren't stupid and that they'd look after each other. They were realists and knew their age and how to avoid trouble. Jack figured that it could take them weeks to make the journey back to Yorkshire from wherever they were in the Highlands. He knew he had to make the trip back to his childhood home and attempt to reunite with his family. His friends were also there so he came to an unexpected decision within an hour of careful thought. He was going home.

Having thought about the masses of people fleeing their home and workplaces, Jack decided not to rush the trip. He needed time to think, time to plan and time to learn. He was woefully underprepared and didn't want to risk his life in haste. If he was truthful with himself, he was scared. So far, he had been rational. The loss he suffered over the last few years was acting as a barrier from the madness, his emotions were still blunt, but he could feel inside himself that they were coming alive.

He made another quick decision; he would leave for Yorkshire in a week. This would provide time for him to get his bearings and ensure he was ready for whatever awaited him.

He would need supplies, he would need more knowledge and he would need weapons and most of all, he would need to find it in himself to fight.

Chapter 6 – Face to Face

It was still only 8:30 and Jack had accomplished many of the tasks he'd set himself to prepare, as best he could, for the unknown wilderness that awaited him. He'd spent an hour looking for articles and instructions containing useful information, using nearly two cartridges printing out his very own survival handbook.

How to syphon petrol, how to hotwire a car, albeit old cars, how to administer first aid, how to start a fire without matches, lists of naturally growing plants, berries and mushrooms that were safe to eat; Jack was attempting to think of every eventuality. He printed vegetable growing tips for a variety of crops and found out where the nearest hunting shops were, both in Yorkshire and his current location. He'd filled his bath full of water along with as many containers he could find.

He was pleased with what he'd managed to do in an hour and a half. Of course, he hadn't absorbed any information, but that was part of his plan for the first week of survival, he'd learn while he waited the week before trekking across the Pennines, back to his family home.

Considering everything that was happening to the world, Jack was bounding around with a positive purpose and could be considered happy. To him, he had a goal, an objective and he was consumed with activity and wasn't thinking about the reality of the situation. He hadn't been this motivated in years; he was surprised as he caught himself whistling a Christmas song that had popped unseasonably into his head, even though it was Spring. To him the world hadn't changed that much, his house was much the same and what he'd seen online didn't really register as being tangible. It was only when he stopped and gave himself time to think that fear would creep in and he'd picture Lucy; alone in her flat, documenting the world falling apart.

Jack hadn't stopped to get maudlin, but he was brought back down to earth after completing a stocktake of the fridge and pantry. He had enough perishable food for a couple of days, however the pantry was bare. He was going to have to sustain himself on tinned food and this was in short supply. He knew what this meant, going back outside and taking a trip back to the shop. Although he'd seen terrible things in the news and from eyewitness videos, his previous trip to the shop, the encounter with Bulldog and the sighting of that thing was what terrified him most.

Today was a day for action not procrastination. Jack had to continue moving forward to keep his mind from becoming consumed with the atrocities taking place across the globe. He decided to get the trip to the shop over with quickly. He wanted to be swift, so he rummaged around in the spare room trying to find a large, traveller style, rucksack. He would stuff everything he needed into it and still be speedy on his feet if it came to that. He also put on two pairs of jeans and multiple shirts as a shoddy form of body armour. The final prep for his shopping spree was to choose a weapon. This was an alien concept to Jack, he'd never been in a proper fight, never been beaten up and had never seriously considered violence an option. He was human, he did think about things he'd like to do to people, but these were just fantasies. Would he be able to attack and kill one of these creatures? Time would tell.

Jack chose his weapon, a hammer. It still had a B&Q label attached to it, having never been called upon to fulfil its purpose. Holding the hammer in his hand, feeling its weight, Jack smiled to himself and said aloud, "I christen thee, Colin."

Amused with himself, Jack went to the front door with his many layers of clothes, large backpack, and newly named Colin the hammer in hand. He paused, took a deep breath, unlocked the door and stepped outside into the spring sunshine.

With his back to the door, Jack stood and listened. All was quiet, the sun was warm, the birds were singing, and he was burning hot in his multi-layered outfit. All seemed normal. There was still an element of doubt about the whole situation. He surveyed the neighbouring houses and couldn't see any signs of life. The road itself had less parked cars than normal. Peering left and then right, there was nobody around. He could see one of the houses further down the road had its windows boarded shut with odds and ends of wood and what looked like an internal door over the downstairs windows. It looked as though someone else had decided to stay home.

Mentally prepared, Jack thought to himself, *let's make this quick, in and out, nice and tidy then back home to relative safety*. He walked to the end of his drive, turned left and began the short journey to the shop. The eerie silence made Jack feel uneasy. Birds sang, but there was no hustle and bustle of human life. He thought he saw a few curtains twitch as he made his way past the dozen or so houses. He went the long way around, past the promenade of shops, avoiding the long narrow and enclosed alley shortcut, and came to the shop without encountering anyone or anything. *So far so good.*

Upon entering the shop, Jack soon realised that much had already been taken. Looted by the looks of the shop. A sense of moral outrage passed through Jack's mind until he realised that he was doing exactly the same. Jack swung his backpack round and began to plunder. He picked tinned fruit, tuna, soup, and anything that looked to have nutritional value. He wasn't above temptation and added a few bars of Dairy Milk for good measure. He was surprised that most of what he needed was there, the beer and wine section had been demolished however. He couldn't blame people for wanting to get pissed to take away the pain of extinction.

Ambling around the shop, a noise burst through Jack's subconscious to the forefront of his mind. It was that banging. Still banging. Repeatedly banging. Curiosity nagged at him; Jack needed to find out what it was. Moving once again to the stockroom door, Jack continued his swift decision making and decided to be brave and investigate further. It was unlike him to be so unfazed by what might be lurking in the back recesses of the shop.

Going further, he pushed the door open slowly, the irritating creak increased the tension that gripped his body. *Why had nobody WD40'd this door?* It was dark, but soon his eyes adjusted to the food in boxes on racked shelves, forever waiting to be consumed. Jack ogled at all the food which eased his nervousness. The ease was short lived however; the creak of the door intensified the banging coming from the dark recesses of the room. His curiosity had got him this far, he wasn't going to stop now. Sense grabbed him as darkness prevented him from seeing what was at the back of the room, he searched for the light switch.

Finally, after some fumbling, much like his early school romances, he managed to find the switch and illuminated the room. His eyes focused on the source of the noise. Someone had hastily pushed the shelving racks together to form a cage and within that cage stood a girl that Jack recognised as one of the shop workers. She was not the girl of his memory. She looked at him, mouth open, hissing a husky noise, pushing her arms through the gaps in the shelving trying desperately to find a way to Jack. Fear took hold; his urge was to turn on the spot and run, but he was transfixed and stuck to the spot, unable to move, like a nightmare.

He remembered this girl, her name was Suzie, he recalled her name tag when he'd frequented the shop on countless occasions. She was a sweet girl, seemed a little dopey, but always had a smile and was very polite. She was very pretty, in her late teens or early 20s and was, in Jack's mind anyway, working in the shop part time whilst she studied for whatever direction her life was going to take her. This was now all past tense. The young and fresh complexion, the youthful optimism and her future had been taken away from her.

From three feet away, Jack could see that she was very dead. She smelt terrible, a mixture of rotten flesh and faeces. Her skin was grey, dark veins etched across her face and arms and her hair was lank. Her eyes were soulless, the whites were bloodshot red, and the pupils were wide like she'd dropped a tonne of acid. Jack thought maybe he was hallucinating. He knew he wasn't though. Being up close to the living dead was everything that Jack needed to confirm the new world order.

This endemic was in his village, it wasn't just miles away in Manchester, London, Leeds and Edinburgh; it was here and had been here for a couple of days at least. He knew this of course having encountered Bulldog, but still, this girl had been infected, most likely, in the village.

On closer inspection, Jack realised that Suzie had been the one to barricade herself in, he could see her phone laying uselessly on the floor beside her and could see how she'd taken provisions from the shelves in a vain attempt to keep her strength up as the infection gained pace and ate away at her until she was dead. Reborn again.

Jack could not take his eyes off dead Suzie, sadness filled him as he thought of the life this sweet girl had taken away from her. The panic that must have befallen her as her lifeless attacker sunk their teeth into her and forced her to flee and build a fortress amongst the goods of yesterday to waste away into darkness. Did she have parents looking for her or sat waiting around at home for their girl to return safe and unharmed? He decided not to leave her like this, he needed to end her rebirth and let her rest in peace. He didn't believe in God, but he knew that if he was ever like this, he'd want someone to put him down permanently. He swallowed hard and took the hammer he had holstered in his belt out. Colin. It seemed so stupid to make light of this world. He chastised himself mentally. He edged closer to Suzie and the nearer he got the more agitated she became. She'd been trying to push at the corners of the barricade which held firm, but as Jack moved forward, he also changed the angle that separated him from the dead girl, which enabled her to push the racking apart. She was getting free.

Fear intensified and Jack lifted the hammer above his head. He knew he must strike hard and quick and remembered Lucy's message about hitting the dead in the head. Dead *in the head, that rhymes*, Jack again had to chastise himself, why was his mind playing stupid games in a time of crisis. He was waiting for the racking to separate enough so he could attack dead Suzie with speed and power and not hit the racking. He counted down, three, two…

Suddenly the lights turned off. Darkness. Jack let out a petrified scream. He was brought to his senses by the sound of the racking scraping on the concrete floor, as dead Suzie moved it further apart. He couldn't do it; he turned and ran towards the light of the open door. He stopped to pick up his backpack, lifting it to his shoulder, as he sped from the shop, his heart racing. He ran in blind panic to safety. Halfway down the alley he realised with increasing terror that he'd run into a narrow ginnel with no escape. *An idiotic mistake.* His fear had removed any reasoned decision-making powers or intelligent choices.

He picked up pace, sweating in his thick layers, holding the heavy bag in the sunlight. He was halfway down the alley when from an opening, he was seized and then knocked sideways as a great weight fell into him. Top heavy with the big rucksack, Jack stumbled backwards and crashed through an age rotten fence panel that lined the alley, stench ridden hands were clumsily tearing at Jack's layers of clothes, the world rolled around him as he fell.

Chapter 7 – Lucy

Lucy had seen the world deteriorate before her eyes. Three days ago, she had witnessed the first girl being attacked; now the situation looked bleak; the streets below her apartment window were awash with people who were infected; the dead.

She had followed the news, read Twitter, and most importantly seen the developments first-hand. She'd made the decision to document the changing world outside, so she could help others, who weren't trapped in a population so dense, and would have hope of survival.

Lucy had sensed that rescue was not that far away when the army arrived at the end of the road that her apartment looked out on. They had fought valiantly against huge numbers of the dead. For long periods, the army looked to be containing the hordes of flesh hungry creatures, fighting them back with wave after wave of bullets. She now knew that the louder the fight, the longer it lasted and the more futile it became. As ammunition diminished and the numbers of the dead increased, with backup seemingly deserted, the army did eventually succumb and the small number that were lucky enough to survive, made a hasty retreat.

Since then the dead ruled the streets. Constant screams, pleads for mercy, and the sound of desperate voices kept Lucy awake at night. She had had little sleep over the previous three nights and her morale had sunk to a new low. She'd contemplated taking her own life, but she knew suicide too well and just couldn't do it to herself. The water in her apartment had dried up, but she'd filled up some pans and was rationing herself. Food was in short supply too, but she knew she could try and loot some of her neighbour's empty apartments.

Lucy was 42 and originally from London. She'd moved to Manchester just a couple of months ago. She was a relative loner due to the fact that she didn't know many people, but she was making friends through her work and was beginning to build a life for herself. She'd made the move because of tragedy.

Lucy had met her soulmate, George, a few years earlier and they were madly in love. It was the sort of love that most couples don't have. They'd spend practically every waking moment together, listening to music and talking through the night. It's not often that a relationship that is years old can still evoke such communication on a regular basis. A year ago, George took his own life. There was no note, no explanation, nothing. This event shook Lucy's world. She couldn't fathom the senseless act that made George feel like there was no escape other than to take his life. George had been a hugely popular person, but Lucy knew that he had suffered from self-esteem issues during his teenage years, but she assumed that he had grown out of it. Just teenage angst. She was wrong, the deep-set psychological problems that affected George were buried and never surfaced until it was too late; Lucy found him naked in the bath with both wrists slit.

She couldn't figure it out, she thought of the conversations they'd last had and nothing could explain why George had committed suicide. From that day, she had felt hollow. But life was beginning to blossom again for Lucy, she'd made the move to start again and rebuild, restart and honour George by living her life. She was a fighter and wasn't going to give up.

That was until three days ago when the uprising started happening on her doorstep. Lucy had witnessed what was unfolding first-hand. From a single woman being attacked to the army fighting in vain, the uprising of the dead had been swift. Her initial response upon seeing the macabre scenes was to help others, but she was gripped by fear, seeing how men much larger and stronger than her had been overpowered by the grasping reaches of the hordes. Her part of videoing and distributing the action from her window was partially to help others, but if she was honest with herself, it was more to be doing something, anything other than waiting to die.

However, for the past few hours, Lucy had sat in silence, contemplating her last few days on earth. She had eventually resigned herself to waiting out the disaster in her flat until thirst took her away. She didn't see an alternative, but reasoned it was a more dignified way to go when compared to the prospect of being ripped limb from limb out on the streets.

The hours passed as Lucy contemplated her life, her friends, George, and the way things were supposed to be. Not this, not the end of the world, not the end of George. Lucy was lost before, but now she was desolate. She gulped down some water, desperately thinking of nothing. Nothing was better than reality. A noise stirred her from her melancholy stillness. It was from outside.

She moved to her window ledge and watched as a group of hooded teenagers ran through the streets. The dead that had loomed motionless sprang to life, zeroing in on the teens as they sprinted down Portland Street outside Lucy's flat. If the world was normal, Lucy would have been appalled at the site of these youths, running down the street, lawless and menacing. But that was the old world, Lucy watched in awe as the exuberant and fearless young men worked their way through the dead. They were organised, quick and deadly. In just a few minutes, scores of the creatures were permanently dead.

One of the youths looked up and saw Lucy, he was laughing. Laughing! He shouted something up at her, but she couldn't hear him. He turned and continued in formation with his friends down Portland Street. Armed with, what looked like a machete, he was dropping the dead with ease. As were the others who had an assortment of blades and bats. These young men were having the time of their lives and making a mockery of the army and all those who had perished in the streets. They worked their way to the end of the street and got into a car and sped off as quickly as they'd arrived.

Lucy moved away from the window energised with what she'd just seen. There was hope. She realised that the army had failed as they'd made a stand with the objective of defeating the ever-growing numbers of dead. There was simply too many to do this. Stand still and die. Move and survive. She made the snap decision. *I need to live. I need to honour George. I will survive.*

She made a quick plan. She needed to get out of the city. The way she knew was south, so south was the direction of her plan. Lucy couldn't walk out of the city, she had a bicycle, but didn't fancy trying to weave in and out of countless hungry monsters. She also knew that when she tired, the dead would continue to pursue her. It was about six miles south to exit the city. She needed a car.

Fate or luck was on Lucy's side. Her neighbour was some sort of financial man who rented the apartment as somewhere to stay when he visited from London. He was rich and Lucy knew that he had a Range Rover parked in the car park under the apartments. She also had a key to the apartment. In Lucy's mind, her neighbour, Lucas, was a player. She knew full well that he had a wife and kids in London, but this didn't stop him making unsubtle advances on her whenever he was in Manchester. She put up with it as he was handsome and she liked the attention, although she'd never have acted upon any temptation. One of Lucas' reasons for visiting Lucy's flat and flirting without shame, was to drop off a key in case the alarm ever went off when he was back at home.

The plan was set. Get the car, get out of the city, and then find an empty house to bed down and determine what the next move would be. For now, survival was a good enough plan for her.

Chapter 8 – Danny

Jack was on his back, hands clawing at him. He'd managed to get one arm across the creature's throat forcing its head back. But the brute was over six foot and had a weight advantage. Jack was fighting for his life. The huge figure on top of him was wild, writhing with anticipation for fresh meat. It lurched forward making Jack lose his hold, teeth launched for Jack's neck, but Jack managed to wriggle sideways. The gnawing teeth connected with Jack's shoulder, he could feel the clench of the jaw as the dead man sought to rip out a chunk of Jack and end his life, either now or through the coming hours with infection.

Jack let out a half scream, half shout, "help me, help me, help me."

He pushed the man again, but it was no use, he wasn't strong enough, he couldn't free himself. He knew he was doomed, his shoulder hurt, and he was close to losing what little resistance he had left. He didn't want to be eaten alive. Fear and sadness filled the pit of his stomach. So much for all his planning.

Suddenly the powerful corpse stopped struggling and all was still. Jack wondered if this was a ploy to get him to give up, but was certain that the dead didn't have the intellect to play dead or trick the living. Lucy had taught him that much from her videos.

The body slumped onto Jack heavily and was then forcibly moved as Jack looked up. Stood above him was his neighbour, Danny. Danny was speaking, but Jack didn't hear, he was lost in the moment, the fear had paralysed him.

Danny repeated, "Were you bitten?" Urgency in his voice.

Jack looked towards the remains of his attacker and saw a kitchen knife protruding from the back of its head, he cleared his throat, realisation hitting him, "It got my shoulder, it got my shoulder. I'm dead, aren't I?"

Danny reached down and pulled Jack to his feet, "Come on. Let's go back to mine. We'll talk about that. You need to sit down, and we need to see your bite. Come on, before more get here."

They walked rapidly back to number 14, the house next to Jack's. Danny had picked up Jack's supplies and pushed Jack forwards as he stumbled with each step, his feet not catching up with his racing mind. *He was dead, he knew it.*

They got in the house and Danny locked and bolted the door behind them. He threw the supplies in the hall and told Jack to take his top off. Jack did as he was told. He needed a second command to take the second layer off. Then further prompts to take layers three, four and five off. Danny came over and looked at Jack's wound. His face gave nothing away.

"It didn't break the skin. You're okay. Jack, you've survived this one. You were lucky."

He paused and then continued, "I should rephrase that; you were well prepared. It looks as though your layers saved your life. Take a look in the mirror, you can see the indents of the teeth on your skin, but it didn't break the surface. You can't be infected."

Jack stumbled over to the mirror and looked at himself. He was sweating profusely. He examined the bite, it was true, the blood thirsty creature hadn't broken the skin. He exhaled loudly and sank to the floor, failing to hold in sobs. He was grateful that he hadn't emptied his bowels, but the embarrassment of crying in front of his neighbour wasn't lost on him.

Danny threw Jack one of his many tops and Jack put it on.

Danny had previously irritated Jack. In Jack's opinion, Danny was just too nice. He was a policeman and his wife a nurse. They were the perfect couple and of use to society, and Jack was a little bitter about this. He didn't know why, it was irrational, it was jealousy. In reality, Jack was jealous of their life together. He always knew that he was in the wrong. Danny was nice, he was a good guy and now Jack felt ashamed for his envy.

Jack moved himself to a chair and looked at Danny, he was embarrassed that he couldn't remember Danny's wife's name, he asked, "Where's your wife?" and then immediately regretted the question.

Sadness filled Danny's face, "Dawn was working at the hospital. I haven't heard from her." He paused, "I haven't lost hope."

Silence filled the room and Jack felt awkward once again. He was no good at small talk, but continued his heavy-footed conversation regardless, "It's not that bad here so I'm sure she's working helping people. She'll be back soon."

Danny smiled, he knew Jack meant well, he said, "It's a lot worse than you realise. I thought you were gone. I hadn't seen you in days, so I assumed the worst. I've been clearing the streets of the dead for the past few days. So far, I've put down over 30. 32 to be precise."

Jack was astonished, "What? How, sorry, I'm thrown a little. I've been locked in at home and I had no idea it was so bad here."

Danny continued, "It's getting worse and worse. When I realised what was happening, we were given a full briefing at the station, I knew I needed to keep the street safe. I want a clear run for Dawn when she gets home. I can't have her getting here and then being jumped by one of those fuckers.

"The way I see it is that we haven't got that much time before things become untenable here."

Jack looked confused, "How so?"

Danny clarified, "Think about it. We're on the outskirts of one of the largest cities in the UK. From the reports I've heard and what I've seen, the rate of infection is high. Let's just take a conservative estimate of 50 percent, we could have 500,000 undead on our doorsteps.

"As the food runs out in the city. The dead will wander, and from what I've seen they tend to follow each other. We could easily have 10,000 stumbling upon us. I swear they sense us too. Any noise, maybe even our smell, seems to attract them."

Danny's face darkened before he continued his impressive situational overview, "It takes about 40 minutes to drive from the centre of Manchester to here. It's been about 3 or 4 days since it really kicked off. I'm assuming that their food will be limited now so that they'll have started wandering. By my guess work, I'd say we'll continue to see more and more of the dead stumble our way in the coming days."

Jack took a moment for all the information to sink in. His carefully thought out plan was unravelling. Waiting a week seemed logical to let things settle down outside, but it now occurred to Jack that he needed to make his move sooner rather than later.

After a couple of moment's silence, Jack said, "If I understand you correctly." Not meaning to sound so formal, "You're saying that we could have thousands of those things in the village in a couple of days?"

Danny looked Jack hard in the eyes, "Hey, I could be wrong, but my assumptions are based on logic and from what I've seen when I've been clearing a path for Dawn."

Danny once again took a pause and looked destitute for just a second. He regained his composure and turned to Jack, "Do you want a beer?"

"Yeah sure." Jack responded.

They spent a couple of hours drinking beer and getting to know one another's lives before the world ended. Jack thought to himself that it only took a small matter of an apocalypse to break down the British social barriers of neighbour interaction.

Jack told Danny his plan to wait it out and then head over to Yorkshire where it was less densely populated and asked Danny to go with him. He knew he'd have a lot better chance of survival with Danny as a travelling companion. He also knew that Danny was never going to leave without Dawn.

Danny was waiting; no matter what the cost.

Chapter 9 – Flee the City of Teeth

Lucy had found the car keys in Lucas' apartment easily. In the fruit bowl in the kitchen. Lucas was so predictable. Why he felt the need to purchase a Range Rover as a second car in a second city was beyond Lucy's grasp of reality, but she was grateful for his opulence.

She also took some time to take a few other items that would come in handy for her attempted city breakout. Lucy's belongings had proved pretty useless for a survival attempt. Silky tops and skirts weren't going to dazzle the zombie hordes into submission. She'd got surprisingly few sturdy items of clothing, other than a couple of pairs of jeans and some flannel shirts that were in a season a year or two ago.

Finding a weapon was also problematic. She saw the machetes and large knives that the teens outside were using, but all she could get her hands on was a four-inch-long kitchen knife that had trouble cutting potatoes, so she doubted it'd be much use killing the undead.

Lucas' apartment proved more helpful to Lucy's quest. Next to the bed was an aluminium baseball bat. A native Londoner, Lucy smiled as she pictured Lucas worrying about Manchester's unwarranted reputation and investing in the bat purely out of paranoia.

Lucy said out loud, "Pussy."

She picked up the bat, enjoying the feel of it as she continued searching. Lucy left the apartment with the bat and a large bottle of mineral water. Together with her own supplies she was ready to start her journey.

Having made one last stop in her apartment to say a silent goodbye to her home, she quietly closed the door and set off, making a conscious effort to not think about the journey that awaited her, the apprehension gnawed in her mind, but she knew she needed to set off rather than find an excuse to stay put.

Passing down the corridor, Lucy moved slowly and quietly. She had no idea if any of the monsters were lurking around in the apartment block. When she was holed up in her flat, the screams and bangs had sounded all around her and she didn't know if they were outside her window on the streets, or outside her door in the building.

Halfway down the corridor, Lucy stopped, annoyed with herself. She was walking towards the lift. The stairs were the opposite direction. She had to get out of the 21st century way of thinking and go into survival mode. Man, or woman, against beast. She was a cavewoman fighting for survival against a cruel earth.

Back past her flat, she turned to smile at her adopted home for one last time, she took her eye off her pace and stumbled over a door mat. She knocked against the wall loudly. From the apartment opposite, something began to pound against the door, low moans accompanied the banging. Lucy stopped and looked. She was safe for now. It was her neighbour's door, Charlie. She'd known him to say 'hi' to, but nothing more, he was quiet but seemed like a nice guy.

Charlie was no more. All that was left of him was a husk of a body, now driven by a burning hunger, that would ultimately end with its starvation, locked in its apartment tomb. Charlie had been bitten a couple of days ago whilst fleeing a group of undead. He was bitten, comically, on his little finger. The smallest of fingers. The smallest of bites. A graze. That was enough for the infection to take hold. He lasted the rest of the day, fell asleep and woke a changed man.

Lucy left Charlie behind the door and made her way to the stairwell, down to the underground car park. She realised she was going to have to deal with the automatic gates. She'd been out of the car park once when Lucas had driven her to the supermarket. It had been raining that day, so Lucy was happy to humour his company. She remembered that there were roller shutters that opened with some sort of fob. She reasoned that there must be a manual way to open them in case of power failure or fire, mentally thanking the world of health and safety.

The car park was pitch black. She hadn't thought of this. She peered into the darkness from the barely lit stairwell. She rummaged through her bag and pulled out her torch. It was now or never. Walking slowly with her bat in one hand and torch in the other, Lucy's heart was beating fast. She heard noises and wasn't sure if they were outside, the building creaking, or worse, something lurking in the shadows.

She had an idea; she pressed the unlock button on the Range Rover keys. Orange lights briefly illuminated the car park as they blinked twice. The car was at the end of the car park. During the brief light she hadn't seen anything untoward and nothing appeared to stir. Still acting on impulse, she knew, to make her escape, she had to attend to the shutters first.

Lucy made her way to the shutters, searching with the torch for a control panel. As she knew, they were automatic, but next to the electronic controls was a sign that read:

In case of power failure, use the hand crank to open manually

"Fuck, fuck, fuck" Lucy muttered as she pondered her next move. All was still quiet in the car park, but far too dark for Lucy to relax and clear her mind to think where the hand crank could be. She knew she couldn't ram the shutters. That would ruin her chances of escape.

Remembering a cupboard just a few feet away along the wall, she shone her torch and located it easily. Cautiously, she knocked on the door. No sound followed. Turning the handle, her luck was in, the cupboard was open. Pushing the door open, Lucy shone the torch and illuminated the small room. It was unoccupied and there at the back, gleaming in the torch light, like a beacon of hope, the hand crank. Pleased with how easy this had been so far, Lucy picked up the crank and marched purposefully back to the shutters.

Placing the crank into the manual opening mechanism, she braced herself. Lucy knew that the cark park was down a floor with an ascending ramp to the street; only 50 metres away. She had to do this quickly and would only get one chance; the dead would hear the noise and hungrily descend to her.

Lucy subconsciously counted down from three and began. With both hands turning, the noise of moving metal echoed in the car park and out into the streets. Dead heads turned to try and locate the new sound, a few stragglers started moving towards the street entrance of the car park.

Every muscle and sinew in Lucy's arms ached and she fought to keep a steady and swift motion. The shutter was about a foot open, she paused to listen, Lucy could hear the low raspy moans of the dead and knew they were coming. She started again and picked up speed, it seemed to take an eternity, at about five feet, she could see movements in the shadows emanating from the street. The damn car was so tall, she needed another couple of feet to make sure she didn't turn it into a soft top in her retreat. She gave everything she had until the dead were close enough to see.

Four of them stumbled down the ramp heading straight for Lucy, she gave the handle one last turn, quickly looked at the shutters and decided that they were high enough. She hoped. The four dead were joined by a few others just a short distance behind. She needed to make her escape. Picking up her bag and bat she bolted for the car, fumbling in her pocket for the keys to the Range Rover. The dead were now inside the car park and following their prey with determined anticipation.

Lucy sprinted to the car with the nearest of the dead only feet away. She had the key in her hand and in blind panic had forgotten that it was already unlocked and struggled to find the unlock button. She paused to shine her light on the key and pressed the unlock button just as the first of the dead sensed her pause and grasped at her from over the car bonnet. The creature fell as it lost balance, grabbing Lucy's coat whilst tumbling to the ground.

Lucy stumbled backwards but managed to stay on her feet. She opened the door, jumped in, shut the door and fumbled for the central locking.

The peaceful solitude of the car was quickly broken as a dead face, that was partially missing, pressed up against the driver side window, hands beating on the glass. The other three quickly surrounded the car. Lucy fiddled with the key fob trying to figure out how to start the car. She looked at the dashboard and saw a start button. She pressed it. Nothing. The dashboard came up with an alert:

Please press down the clutch when starting the engine.

Lucy swore and put her foot on the clutch and pressed the start button once again. This time the engine roared into life followed swiftly by James Blunt singing in stereo. *Christ*, she thought, *Lucas you cock*. She put the car into first and gave the car a nudge forward. The dead grabbed at the car as she slowly manoeuvred it out of the parking bay. The dead banging so hard against the windows she feared they would break.

The car park was tight, but she managed to turn the car with only a little clang. She cleared her throat and added some haste to her escape. Two of the dead tried in vain to claw at the moving car, stumbling as the weight supporting them shifted rapidly towards the exit. Lucy navigated the final curve and straight ahead, was her exit. Coming towards her now were three more of the dead, ambling down the middle of the ramp. She looked up and put her foot down. The big Range Rover was quick and she accelerated into the first of the dead, knocking it back against the wall with the wing of the car. The second of the dead was hit head on. Lucy watched on as if in slow motion. The once living person was hit in the midriff, the force arching the head and shoulders towards Lucy and clattering against the car bonnet with a bang and a dent to show. The impact wasn't enough to kill it, Lucy could see the creature staring directly into her eyes, desperately searching for grip to drag itself towards the windshield. Legs dragging, and gravity against the dead man, the body was pulled swiftly under the car, its head colliding with such force that the skull smashed against the concrete ramp, leaving the monster motionless in a sea of red. James Blunt continued to warble on, *"You're beautiful, it's true"*. Lucy maintained her composure, slammed her hand against the audio off button and continued to the top of the ramp, effortlessly brushing aside the last of the dead.

Outside, in the daylight, Lucy slowed the car down to a gentle roll whilst taking in the vista that awaited her.

"Fuck." Lucy exclaimed under her breath. There were hundreds in both directions littering the wide street. It was now that she started to doubt her idea of escape and envied death by starvation or dehydration. Still, she remained calm. *It's too late to turn back.*

Her plan consisted of heading south, sticking to wide roads so she could manoeuvre obstacles and turn around quickly if needed.

"Slow and steady wins the race." Lucy spoke to herself to calm her nerves as she turned left and slowly weaved cars, debris, and the growing numbers of dead, rolling over many, bones crunching audibly. Lucy's heart raced as she slowly ploughed forwards.

Chapter 10 - Make Haste, the dead Are Coming

The morning after spending some time with Danny and listening to his experiences and predictions, Jack decided he was going to make haste with his planned trip across the country. He was planning to leave the next day.

He was practically ready, practically, as in supplies. His near-death experience had left him frightened and shaky on his feet and the thought of making the trip filled him with trepidation. Jack knew he needed to pull himself together and throw himself in at the deep end. He needed practice.

A thought hit him. He needed things to survive. He needed warmth for the winter, he needed more practical clothing, ropes, weapons, and a host of other things. Just on the outskirts of Manchester was an outdoor activity shop called Adventure Island that would provide Jack with everything he needed. *I will go to Adventure Island.*

Jack knew the risk. It was just on the edge of Manchester so the numbers of dead would be huge. He reasoned with himself that he could go and get as close as he could. If it was too bad, he could turn around. The purpose of the trip was as much for practice as it was for supplies, so reasoned that the short trip should give him plenty of experience to take across the country. It helped keep him brave having a goal. The thought of obtaining a nice sharp ice axe built up Jack's shivering courage that hid somewhere deep inside his stomach.

Searching the house for his car keys, Jack decided he'd go light, taking Colin, the Hammer, as his only weapon. Colin was yet to taste action other than to cling to Jack's belt and bruise his leg as he was toppled by the marauding dead man. A bottle of water, some walking boots and many, many layers of clothing completed Jack's survival kit.

Jack nipped next door to see Danny with the hope that he would volunteer to come along. The gardens of both houses were next to each other, so rather than go out visibly around the front, Jack just had to lift the fence panel and duck through. It was a great idea, Danny's idea, not Jack's. Jack felt woefully underprepared for everything around him, whereas Danny was willing and able to throw himself into every challenge effortlessly. For all Jack's bookish preparation, he had achieved nothing other than just staying alive, thanks to Danny.

Knocking gently on windows, as not to make much noise, there appeared to be no sign of life. Jack could see through the open plan living area and couldn't see Danny. He threw a few pebbles to the upstairs windows, still nothing. Danny was out.

I'm on my own then. Jack was determined to explore this new dawn and find out if he had the mettle for the fight. Swiftly through the house, Jack peeped through the small window in the front door and saw that the coast was clear, he shut the door quietly behind him and quickly got in his car, a small Citroen, not the ideal all-terrain vehicle. Creeping out of the drive and down the street, everything was quiet. Evidently Danny had done a good job of clearing up the dead.

It was soon apparent how wide Danny's radius was. Just a short drive past the shop and following houses, the village became more dispersed with sweeping corners and narrowing roads. Two of the dead could be seen in a farmyard wandering around trying to locate the noise of Jack's car. He could see that the dead were penned in by a fence so were going nowhere. Approaching the first bend, Jack slowed the car down, almost to a standstill. On the adjacent corner was a crumpled wreck of a car wrapped around a tree. A mangled body lay half out of the windscreen. The flesh had been gnawed off, leaving sinew, muscle, and bone curdling in the spring sunshine.

Jack turned his head and felt his stomach turn. He began to retch but managed to control himself before he vomited. Driving on, glass scattering the road and other bloody wrecks became a common sight. Jack swore he saw movement in the back of one crumpled vehicle, but carried on like a determined and frightened missionary.

The journey Jack had chosen was slightly further than the quickest route. That route featured main roads and built up areas and he wanted to avoid populated areas until absolutely necessary. The journey he chose featured country roads, one main road and then most worryingly for him, the motorway.

The country roads were mainly clear. There were cars every now and then, but easy to navigate. Some of the fields were occupied by cows or sheep. Another field told a different story. It reminded Jack of a scene from Dances with Wolves where the white man had obliterated the buffalo. The entire field was a sea of sheep carcasses; accompanying the deceased sheep was a small group of dead, feasting with endless hunger.

Handfuls of the dead scattered the road at irregular intervals. Normally in groups of two or three, they tended to amble carelessly down the road until they caught sight or heard Jack's car. This would stir them and they'd pick up pace, but they were easy to get around in their small numbers. An idea, a practical idea, hit Jack. Most of the dead he came across were heading towards Jack's home, having been drawn towards the sound of his car with what little cognitive cohesion remained in their brains. Jack's idea involved passing the dead and then slowing down and drawing them to follow him, away from home.

Jack was pleased with himself. A great idea and it felt safe. He imagined that this might be how a lion tamer might feel, safe but not safe. Jack laid himself as bait two more times, drawing seven of the dead away.

About a mile down the road, Jack saw a lone figure walking towards him. Instantly Jack knew that this person was living. The way he walked was normal, perhaps a little erratic, but there was a definite coordination that the dead lacked. As the car pulled closer, Jack could see that the man was in his late 50s or early 60s. He was short and small framed and looked like he was going out for a walk in the country. He had a ski pole, small ruck sack and was dressed like a rambler. Jack slowed the car and wound down the passenger window to see if the guy needed a lift.

As the car pulled to a stop, the man leaned in the window.

"My name's Stanley" He said and paused for what seemed to be an age.

Jack waited for him to continue, but nothing came so he responded, "My name's Jack. Are you okay? Do you need a lift anywhere, there's about seven of them coming this way about a mile back?"

"No son. I'm fine." Stanley spoke again and then said nothing.

Jack waited again. This man wasn't exactly talkative. It reminded Jack of seeing a vague acquaintance in the street and stopping to realise that neither has much to say. The silence hung in the air when Stanley continued, "I see you haven't been judged yet."

Confused, Jack asked, "Judged by who?"

"Whom."

"Judged by whom?"

"By God of course. It's judgement day or is it judgement month? I don't know."

Jack almost snorted, "What has God got to do with anything?"

This fired Stanley up, leaning further into the car with one finger pointing towards Jack, he said, "What has God got to do with anything? What hasn't God got to do with? He's tired of us humans and he's called Armageddon. What did we expect though? Gay marriage, Muslims, bloody women bishops, war, famine, paedophilia…"

With Stanley mid-rant, Jack lost his patience, and spat out, "Paedophilia? You God botherers would know all about that. Don't come at me with your mumbo-jumbo cult bigotry. God is a way to control societies, what is happening is nothing to do with God."

With that, Stanley lost his temper, pulling up his ski pole towards the open window Stanley incoherently stammered, "You little shit, I'll judge you myself."

Jack had heard enough, he slowly accelerated away to get rid of the crazy old guy. Stanley held on, but eventually let go of the car at running speed. The man still had some sense.

A few feet away, Jack stopped the car and stood out of the door and shouted, "Look Stanley, sorry it got heated. Get off the road, you can see them coming, there's seven of them."

Stanley gestured with his hand whilst mumbling something and continued towards the dead that Jack had lured away from home.

Jack got back in the car and continued, glancing in his rear-view mirror to check on the welfare of Stanley, the bigoted Christian. He saw Stanley hobble over a wall and into a field. The dead couldn't scale anything over their tipping point so had no chance of making it over the wall to feast on Stan.

Smiling to himself, Jack thought that bumping into Stanley wasn't a complete right off. He was a country boy at heart, and he knew that the UK was covered in fields with separating walls and hedges that would slow down or stop the dead, depending on their numbers. *God bless you Stanley*.

The rest of the country roads followed a similar pattern, minus Stanley, there were quite a few scares for Jack on the main road and motorway slip-road however. He had seen about 30 dead on the country roads in total, but the main road had many more scattered about. Driving through the dispersed crowd, Jack could only guess that there were hundreds of them. The little Citroen was like a magnet and the zombies like iron shavings. From all directions the dead clambered, hobbled and dragged themselves towards the car.

The road was also full of smashed and abandoned vehicles. He could get past the vast majority by slaloming through the obstacles, but this also narrowed the chances of avoiding the dead. Jack was conscious that he couldn't plough into the dead at any great speed as the car would be knackered in no time, if that happened, he'd have no chance on foot with so many dead around.

Jack was beyond reason now, if he would have envisaged this scenario when coming up with his half-baked plan, he would have said that now was the time to turn around and call off the trip. Adrenalin pumping and the false security of his car, wild eyed and scared, Jack pushed forwards around crumpled cars and around the flailing arms of the dead.

Near the entrance to the motorway, three creatures blocked Jack's path, instinct started to take over in the still air of the car. He slowed and crawled into them pushing them backwards. It took just a few steps backwards for the three dead to lose coordination and tumble to the floor. Jack turned the wheel sharply left to avoid going over all three. The car jolted to a grinding and sudden stop. *Shit.* Two of the still writhing bodies were pushed and then wedged under the front of the car. Jack accelerated and the wheels span trying to find grip. The left tire caught traction on an arm, the spinning wheel tore flesh ripping it from the bone as the car jolted forwards, climbing over the torso of the still moving creature. The fleshy part of the stomach gave the tires more grip, ripping the creature's gut apart as the car jolted over the last body. With both front tires on the road, the car attained maximum grip to continue Jack's merry jaunt.

The slip road onto the motorway was unobstructed. It looked as though something had cleared a path as several cars were pushed aside. Jack remembered the army from Lucy's video and wondered if they'd come this way. He couldn't even think where the nearest army base was. Whoever had cleared the path didn't really matter; it lifted Jack's hopes of achieving his goal.

The motorway was depressing. There were lots of cars, but they weren't closely packed together, and most had been pushed to the side of the road by whatever had cleared the slip road. There weren't hordes of dead either; just stragglers ambling around like a plague of sleepwalkers. The upsetting thing for Jack was seeing cars packed with belongings; toys, photo albums and other items, useless for survival, calling out to a world that no longer existed and the lives that were no more.

The road, without other careening cars, made Jack think of films where they shut down part of a city to make it look deserted, but as he continued down the motorway taking care to avoid sharp debris, other vehicles and the dead, he knew it was very real. He was concentrating on keeping damage to the Citroen at a minimum, it was vital for his retreat.

The motorway widened and separated into three lanes going to Manchester and two that joined the ring-road. It wasn't as bad as Jack had feared it would be. The road into Manchester was surprisingly deserted. Thinking logically, Jack shouldn't have been surprised, how many people would have wanted to make their way into a densely populated area where people were rising from the dead and becoming hollow husks with a hunger for meat?

Jack continued along the motorway until it changed to the Princess Parkway, which led into the centre of Manchester. The road passed under the M60, the ring road around Manchester, and beyond that, on the other side of the road, separated by a central reservation, was Adventure Island. Jack was close and had come so far. The journey, which can't have been more than 10 miles, had taken about an hour and a half, but it seemed to Jack like an eternity.

It was upon entering the first suburbs of Manchester that the abandoned cars and debris became too congested to pass. The store was only 200 metres away. The numbers of dead were nothing like Jack had expected, he could see a handful of small groups. Nothing more. He decided he was going to take the last part of the journey on foot and taste some action. Jack was running on pure excitement and adrenaline, it almost felt like a game. He had never been so reckless in his life, he was always quite passive and avoided conflict and this new fight exhilarated him, he wondered if he'd get an extra life in this game?

Jack turned the car around on the motorway to face the way he came, just in case he needed a speedy retreat. He made his way out of the car, grabbed the hammer, and set off. The two nearest dead were about 50 feet away and ambling towards him. He made off and decided to jump the central reservation onto the other side of the road. Weaving in-between cars, Jack was light on his feet and trying to be quick. A bang on the window from inside a car nearly made him soil himself. Trapped inside its tomb, one of the dead clawed at the window. It was a girl, maybe 12 years old. Her weak pounding was no match for the car windows. The driver, presumably the girl's mum, lay half eaten across the steering wheel with blood smearing the windows. The sight sickened Jack as he continued to a break in the cars that made for an easier passage and avoided more of the dead.

About 100 metres from Adventure Island an overturned truck and a host of smashed cars blocked the way. It looked as though the truck had decided to speed through the traffic jam, whether this was during the evacuation, Jack didn't know. It was tight, but he could see a rough route through the wreckage with only a little climbing. Jack made his way forwards past a couple of cars.

A hand from an unfeasibly small space grabbed Jack's ankle, he was off balance and fell headlong. The hand lost grip but Jack landed with his face peering through a broken window to a grotesquely mutilated form, still animated, only inches away. The creature no longer looked human, crushed, and bent beyond recognition, the bloody mess was missing most of its cheeks and lips, but broken teeth still crunched together as prey landed in front of its hungry and still active brain. The dead person lifted its arms to seize Jack's head, but as its shoulders moved, the arms hung limply: shattered bones, a result of the thundering truck, meant the creature's arms and hands were useless.

Jack had seen enough, he pushed himself up and jumped over the car, he could now see the end of the pileup. He hurdled the remaining obstacles and found himself standing in front of a more able-bodied monster. Without thinking, Jack took the hammer from his belt and swung with his right hand from right to left with all his might. He caught it on the temple, a terrible sound, as the hammer sent the dead man falling to the floor. Lifeless.

Jack was out of breath and could see about 50 or more of the dead in close proximity. *To hell with it.* He started to sprint to Adventure Island. He knew he'd draw them there, but he could wait for them to disperse or he could escape quietly out of the back if his way in became too congested. The thought of being inside and away from the dead was something that appealed to Jack as he approached the door to find it unlocked. *Thank Christ.*

With his shoulder holding the door shut, Jack looked to find a lock or bolt as the dead made their way to the store. Two bolts on the top and bottom secured the door. He turned around and found the store empty. He was surprised; with the chaos outside he would have thought people would have sought refuge here. Maybe they did, but there was no sign of disruption. It was dark with most of the windows covered with branded slogans wasted on unintelligent zombie brains.

Failing to bring a torch had been an oversight and Jack searched clumsily around the partially lit till area until he found a display of torches, the extreme sports person's impulse buy. He picked one up and began to rummage around the shop for essentials he could take with him. He found a rucksack and started to fill it with more suitable clothing for survival. To Jack's dismay there weren't any useful weapons, he was expecting ice picks, axes and all sorts of other things, but no such luck. The shop appeared to be appealing to the vanity of outdoor pursuit rather than actual extreme sports enthusiasts.

Jack packed some rope, waterproof and warm clothing and was ready to leave within a few minutes of arriving. He took a drink from the warm fridge and greedily gulped down some of the sweet orange energy drink. He could see the dead covering the door he'd bolted; he would need to leave via the back.

He went to explore the rear of the shop when he heard a scream.

Chapter 11 - The Government

The UK Government had been one of the best prepared regimes in the world when it came to the rising of the dead. Incredibly, they had practiced drills and written up contingency plans for a zombie like outbreak. They had been mocked heavily in newspapers with many questioning the use of public funds for such bizarre and unnecessary procedures. The ranting agendas of newspapers such as the Sun and Daily Mail no longer mattered, if they ever did. Their reporters eaten, their offices empty, the huge printers motionless, collecting dust.

The Government no longer had cause for concern about media backlashes to bumbled politics or Boris Johnson offending half the world with oafish comments. They could operate without recourse, no public outrage, no social media criticism, and no dividing party ties. However, the Government was completely cut off from the people it was supposed to be governing and with that, could be seen as just another group trying to survive the harsh realities of post-apocalypse living.

The only rules governing the people of the UK were those of survival; mankind's basic needs guided by individual moral compasses. This of course created issues as hunger and disease, combined with the grizzly horror of each day, added to the distressed and panicked state of Joe Public. Survivors were sacrificing right for wrong, forcibly taking what they needed, people were beaten, deceived, and even killed for food, cars, and other possessions. There were still people helping others, sharing, and even taking those in need into their care and shelter. Strangers stood together fighting to keep their domains safe and dead free. The trouble with helping people is that it adds more risk to existing. Sticking your neck out was more than just an inconvenience, it was a potentially life-threatening action.

Charles Darwin said, *'It is not the strongest of the species that survives, nor the most intelligent that survives. It is the one that is most adaptable to change."*

He couldn't have been more accurate. Those who were trapped in the social boundaries of the old world were being eradicated either by their own good deeds going wrong or by others who had adopted more aggressive tactics in order to survive. People who were naturally open and experienced to violence had an easier and more successful chance of survival. Someone who was willing to punch a fellow human being in the face would have no hesitation about clubbing a dead monster over the head. Of course, the biggest influence on a person's survival was circumstance. If you were living in a remote location, the chances of even encountering the dead in the early days were slim. If you were unlucky enough to find yourself in the middle of a city when the outbreak reached its pinnacle, then the odds of survival were minimal, unfortunately for the people of the UK, urbanisation was on the rise and the vast majority of the population lived in cities and towns.

The UK Government: no longer headed up by Theresa May who had been infected by one of the hired help within 10 Downing Street, was a mishmash of Labour, Conservative, other parties, and various high-ranking members of the armed services. They were at a classified location planning and plotting.

The Government had been well informed in the build up to the disaster. They had caught and contained many small outbreaks before anything was in the news. This only gave them a day or two head start. Intelligence from other countries showed the potentially devastating effects of the disease. They ran advanced simulations showing the predicted infection rate, watching with grave faces.

Plans were put in place, but they made public announcements too late. Containing the infection was no longer a viable option so all other choices other than to go public were off the table. They put out messages online, on television and radio. The official statement read:

Public State of Emergency:

We are facing an emergency on a national scale. There is an outbreak of infection that is spreading rapidly across the world. The infection has a very high rate of mortality. It is spread through the bloodstream with most cases of infection being as a result of a bite.

We stress that an infected person will ultimately die, but their corpse will reanimate. They will come back to life. When this happens, that person will no longer be capable of reason; they will try to bite anyone who is uninfected. Once bitten, you are infected and hope of survival is bleak.

Avoid contact with anybody acting strangely, this includes family members and friends. Stay indoors and barricade yourself in. Do not let anybody into your place of shelter who has been bitten or is acting strangely. Conserve your food and fill up containers with water. We cannot guarantee continued utilities.

If you are approached by someone who is infected, you will need to either avoid contact or fight them off. Someone who is infected will feel no pain, the only way to stop them is by damaging their brain so you will need to attack the head in the event of a confrontation. Please note that the best possible action is to flee and get yourself to safety.

We will be issuing updates when we have them and will advise you on the next steps.

Remember:

1) Do not approach the infected

2) Stay indoors and barricade any windows

3) Do not let anybody who is infected or bitten into your home, even if they are friends or family

4) In the event of confrontation, the only way to destroy the infected is to attack the head.

5) Avoid contact with the DEAD.

The statement lacked the usual clarity and tone of Government communications. None of the senior press officers within the Government had been seen for days and the office junior had painstakingly tried to write a statement that covered everything in a language and urgency that would resonate with the public. The office junior could not get an authorised sign off on the statement as ministers were either missing or focusing on other more pressing matters so released the statement anyway.

The office junior would be left high and dry come the Government's relocation to their classified and secure location. He attempted to retreat home to his parents, but would only last a short while before being torn limb from limb still fully conscious, as teeth and hands clawed at him, slowly taking his life painfully away.

The Government plan was simple. Release a statement to tell people to stay indoors and sit out the pandemic. There were not enough resources to go into every city and fight off the infected, they had tried and failed in this approach. They would concentrate on securing utilities. They knew that if the power failed or water stopped people would leave their houses in greater numbers and ultimately perish. Power stations and waterworks were all secure workplaces and required only military guard to increase their security. The workers were briefed of their duties to their country and small specialised military units were sent out on missions to bring the worker's families to the power plants and waterworks. Not ideal living conditions, but the value of the worker's expertise meant that all stops were pulled to keep them powering and watering the country.

This was why the power and water lasted as long as it did. Whilst the streets were awash with the dead, hundreds of thousands of people waited inside with their provisions and water, waiting on word from their Government. Not often lauded, the powers that be had saved many lives and had avoided doing what the United States had done: bombing major population centres and sacrificing the survivors in a bid to contain the dead. Unsuccessfully.

Several smaller military units were stationed in remote bases all over the UK as part of the Government's survival plan. The thought behind the web of stationed troops was to be in position when the timing was right to suffocate the infection and bring it down from all directions. Before any fight however, the Government and military were to wait for the worst of the infection to die down and the opportunity to become apparent to begin the eradication of the dead.

After years of mollycoddling the General Public, the Government had put in place a plan that would truly empower them, giving total freedom to their destinies. The plan relied on resourceful and good people surviving and building small communities. When the time was right, the Government would come out of hiding and work with the small communities to rebuild the country and defeat the remaining dead.

Like most Governments, the UK's was out of touch with the people, the statistics and simulations could not accurately predict how people would react to total anarchy. The regime had proven their incompetence at understanding the population, Brexit, years of underfunding the NHS, and the general discord with austerity all proved the disconnect. Could people go from a rule driven existence to a life of need and action? Could people forgive a Government that had left them to fend for themselves? If humanity ever dug itself out of its current mess, the powers that be would need all their best PR spin doctors to work with a rabid society. Would the living become more dangerous than the dead?

Chapter 12 - Gangs

Manchester has been associated with gangs for over 140 years. Dating back to Victorian Manchester, in 1870, The Scuttlers, a neighbourhood gang from working class areas of Manchester and Salford, were running around with a furious love of fighting; horrifying civilised society. Fast forward 140 years and the gangs have remained the same, society however, was certainly not so civilised.

One appeal of gang membership was the bond between members, a group looking out for each other, normally in a lawless pursuit of their wants. Cut off and ostracised by society for generations, a typical gangster's contempt for outsiders was high and empathy towards others non-existent. The breakdown of society was positive for many gangs. Normally accustomed to hiding in the shadows and away from police, gangs were organised, strong and quick. Other gangs would still be a threat, but the police were no longer there to keep law and order so, other than the hordes of dead, life was a little less complicated.

Of course, gang members weren't superheroes, many were bitten and turned, or simply eaten, but the fact that these groups, mainly young men, were resourceful, meant they had a far superior survival rate compared to 'civilised society'. Gangs had secure hideouts, were generally armed with at least a knife, and were in top physical condition. They had years of experience sneaking around, and of course, were adept with violence and fighting.

Lucy was unaware of Manchester's gang history as she slowly made her way south. She had been in a state of zen, pure concentration on the streets ahead, looking for gaps to squeeze the increasingly scratched and dented Range Rover through. She'd had a few run-ins with large crowds of dead whilst trying to vacate the city centre, managing to find the four-wheel-drive setting to test the car's horsepower as it pushed its way slowly through a concentrated mass of bodies all scrambling towards the prize inside the car.

Lucy's route south, out of Manchester, avoided the problematic roads that were always congested in the days of the living, such as Rusholme, and used the wide streets of suburbia. She was approaching South Manchester; an area Lucy knew well. It was a nice part of Manchester and she'd often bike there to visit the few friends she'd made since moving to Manchester. The plan was to zigzag her way through Fallowfield, Withington and Didsbury, using the back streets to bring her to the M56 which led out of the city and into Cheshire; where she was planning on finding a place to crash for a night or two.

Lucy's plan was working. The car had so far stood up to the challenge and navigating the roads had become less and less concerning the further she got from the city centre. Arriving in Didsbury, turning down Park Field Road South and over a bridge crossing a tram line, the corner turned right, a blind corner. Travelling speedily, Lucy stepped on the car's breaks as a hooded man with his hand outstretched came into view. Instinct told her in the blink of an eye that the man was alive which, luckily for the hooded figure, stopped her careening into him. Pulling the car to a stop, Lucy looked around and could see a few figures appear, emerging from crouched positions behind parked cars. They were all hooded and armed with bats and knives. Lucy was cautious but reasoned that these people were surviving in the suburbs of the City, so needed to be prepared for action. She wound down her window a crack.

The man in front of the car said with a thick Mancunian accent, "Alright. Nice wheels."

Lucy was anxious to be off, she responded, "Can I help you?"

The man pulled down his hood. It wasn't a man, but a boy. He must have been 17 or 18, lean and tall, almost whippet like. He said, "We can help you. We have a safe place and we're helping people survive. It's not far from here."

"That's nice of you. Thank you. I don't want to stay in the city though so I'm getting out of here." Lucy said as she relaxed a little.

"It's blocked love. The Parkway is blocked. Too many cars, too many of the dead. We're your best bet. We'll protect you." The man smiled, but the smile didn't look sincere.

Lucy then heard one of the men at the side of the road sneer to his companion, "Dibs on this one first. That posh MILF would love the taste of my cock."

The man in front of the car shot a look of death at the person who had spoken and rapidly made his way to Lucy's side of the car. Lucy had seen and heard enough. These people did not seem the charitable type and she feared being raped more than walking into the embrace of the dead.

The boy tried to open the door, but it was locked. Lucy fumbled for the window up button, but the man grabbed the partially open window with his fingers to bring it down. He snarled, "You're fucking coming with us and we'll have your Ranger too."

The window shattered as the man pulled it towards him. Lucy, let go of the break and stepped on the accelerator. The boy stepped aside as the car lurched away, through the rear-view mirror, Lucy could see the gang scrambling to get into cars. They were up for the chase.

Disregarding her cautious approach, Lucy sped around a corner and careened head on into two of the dead. They crunched with force into the car's radiator and bonnet, blood smearing the windscreen. She found the wipers and spread the blood, limiting her view, but ploughed on regardless. A warning light flashed on the dashboard. The car was damaged. *Please not now.*

The car continued on. It was leaking fluid from the engine and would eventually overheat and grind to a stop, but it continued forward like a brave injured steed, valiantly carrying its master to safety.

Lucy turned onto Barlow Moor Road and headed for the Princess Parkway, which turned into the M56, her hopeful escape. Behind, she saw three cars turn onto the road in pursuit, she had a few hundred feet head start. Barlow Moor Road was chaos, cars were upturned, dead roamed and the passage was frustratingly slow and painful for the car as it haemorrhaged more fluid with each collision. The Princess Parkway intersection was in sight and Lucy, heart racing, could see lots of the dead and what looked like a tangle of vehicles. *No! He was telling the truth. The road is blocked.*

Desperation hit her, but she had no choice but to continue forwards.

She reached the intersection and had to stop. In a split-second decision, Lucy bolted out of the door with only her bat. The dead were scattered around her, too many to count, but there was space to dart. She remembered the youths outside her apartment window and the speed at which they moved. *Were they the same gang as my current pursuers?* The only option was to stick to the plan. Head south. The Princess Parkway was unpassable to cars, but she could scramble over the wreckage. Several vans, cars and trucks had attempted to squeeze through with no space to do so and had created a vehicle bottle stop for the road.

Running left and right, ducking grasps and using all her senses, Lucy made her way towards the roadblock as the first of the chasing cars pulled up. Four youths got out and immediately started bringing down the dead with efficiency. The crowd had grown denser on Lucy's arrival, so she had gained some distance to the gang of four fighting their way through the crowd, still in pursuit.

Scrambling over cars and around taller vehicles, Lucy broke through the roadblock into a clearing of about 100 metres, the other side of the clearing was also blocked; a truck had tried to plough through the stationary traffic causing devastation. She could see about 50 of the dead crowding around the doorway to the Adventure Island store, they were occupied so she continued to run. She loved to run in her previous life. She could run for miles and did it as much as a form of meditation and reflection than for fitness. It was her personal therapy. Running through the dead and away from the gang was a different type of running, her mind on overdrive and her senses alert, Lucy made for the wreckage on the other side of the clearing to scramble over.

She didn't know that one of the gang had broken away from the others and had closed in on her. He grabbed her shoulder as they both ran. In an instinctive swing, she turned, with the bat in both hands and caught the man in the ribs. He recoiled and fell to the floor struggling to catch his breath. Still in motion, Lucy stumbled to a stop.

A cold hand grabbed Lucy's wrist and caught her off guard, she uncharacteristically let out a scream.

Chapter 13 - Awkward Silence

The commotion outside had drawn the dead away from the entrance of Adventure Island. Peering through the now cleared window, through the tangle of slowly moving uncoordinated bodies, Jack could see a woman was being attacked by one of the dead, as more approached her.

The woman had snatched her arm out of the grasp of the creature and stepped backwards away from it. Jack could also see a man slowly getting to his feet, feeling his ribs as he pulled a long blade from his belt. The man was alive too. He made his way towards the woman and, to Jack's astonishment, started to grapple with her. She managed to pull up her baseball bat and with the butt end caught her attacker square in the face, breaking his nose. She ran behind the monster that had held her arm and pushed it towards her assailant, before continuing her sprint towards the wreckage at the far end of the clearing.

Jack, perplexed at the situation unfolding, exited the shop and went in pursuit of the woman in a bid to aid her escape. She'd drawn the dead away from the door and had their focus, so Jack slipped out to the left of the shop to cross the barrier of crumpled traffic from the opposite side to the woman.

They both crossed the vehicle remains at the same time, the curve and height of the crash hid the two from each other. Jack came through without trouble into a clearing. The woman did not. She jumped over a grasping hand and landed face to face with four of the dead blocking her path. It was time to fight.

Jack ran to where the woman was holding her own, outnumbered, he knocked one of the dead around the side of the head, but not with enough power, it went down, but was getting back up again. The three others pushed the woman back to the wreckage. Jack approached the closest of the dead and brought the hammer down hard on the top of its unguarded head. With a crunch and smattering of blood, it fell to the floor. The woman responded to the help by smashing a skull on the side of the head with full power. Its neck breaking and skull shattering as the aluminium bat shattered the neural network powering the dead being. Jack finished the third with a similar blow to his first as it dithered about which of the living to attack. The woman then finished the last one as it struggled to its feet. She brought the bat high above her head with both hands and hammered it home, turning the dead creature's head concave.

The woman then turned and swung wildly at Jack. He ducked backwards and stumbled over onto his backside. She approached him with her bat extended, pointing at him.

Jack stuttered, "You're Lucy, aren't you?"

"How do you know my name?" Lucy shouted back, stepping closer with bat extended.

"I watched some of your videos. I was just in Adventure Island when I heard your scream. You got them away from the door, so I was able to escape to try and help you. My name's Jack" Jack managed to spit out as he began to worry that Lucy had lost all senses since he saw her on Twitter. *Is she going to kill me?*

Lucy softened and lowered the bat to her side and said, "I am Lucy. I'm being chased, I need to get going. Thanks for your help. I guess I was screwed."

"I've got a car just over the other side of the road. It's ready to go. I can drive you out of here and drop you off somewhere safer." Jack said, he knew immediately that he wanted to invite her back home but thought this was probably a bit of a taboo subject, having just met the woman. It was as if he was star struck having watched her videos and already built up a mental persona for her.

Staring as if in deep thought, Lucy considered the offer; she looked Jack up and down for the first time and decided he didn't look like the gang did and, although he seemed to have an unusual amount of clothes on, seemed fairly normal.

She said, "Sure, I was planning on heading that way and finding a place to lay low until I figure out what to do next."

Jack smiled and suggested they made their way to the car, he added, "I've got a place in Westerlyn that's fairly safe at the moment, you're welcome to come with me to figure out your next steps."

Lucy didn't answer as they worked their way through debris and the outstretched arms of the dead, who were ambling over in growing quantities, to the car. Jack unlocked the car remotely and they both got in.

-

Lying on top of the overturned truck, a member of the gang watched on as Jack and Lucy fought off the four dead. He listened as Jack gallantly offered a place for Lucy to stay. He smiled and turned to watch his gang of 10 finish killing the 50 dead stranded in the clearing between the two crash sites. Beyond the other heaped wreckage, the dead had gathered to impassable numbers, the way back into Manchester was blocked by a wall of monsters. He jumped down to the clearing as the gang of youths walked towards him; blood smeared their clothes and weapons.

One of the gang stepped forwards and asked, "What the fuck are we going to do now Dale? There's no way back."

Dale calmly walked towards his inquisitor and put his arm around him, half hug, half headlock, smiling he said, "Shut the fuck up Naz. I've got a plan."

Dale let go of Naz's head and walked between the gang. It was obvious that Dale was the authority figure among the group. The rest looked on with obsequious anticipation waiting for Dale to continue.

"That bird got away. She was helped by a man. He looked like a pussy. I heard where they were going. He said it was fairly safe. It's not far, but we've got no wheels. We should be able to pick some up from somewhere." Dale paused to see if there was any discontent. There was none. The tired youths were weary having fought for what seemed like an eternity. Their frequent and dangerous excursions were physically and mentally draining and had taken their toll on the group.

He continued, "It makes sense, these people are rich in Cheshire. Anything we want we can have. Lamborghinis, swimming pools, mansions. It's all for the taking. There's less of the dead so it should be easy pickings.

"Before that though. I've got the scent of a fit as fuck red-headed milf that I want to make squeal. We're heading to the country lads. Let's get rich. I'm sure you want a little action too Richie?"

Richie nodded, he had a cracked rib and broken nose following his encounter with Lucy. He desperately wanted some retribution. A short stocky man, at 28, he was at least ten years senior to the rest of the group, he was unintelligent, had psychopathic tendencies and didn't understand or relate to feelings of remorse or guilt. Richie was born for this world, one step up from the dead.

-

Lucy and Jack worked their way along the M56 and spoke infrequently. Jack was still frozen, and star struck, desperately pleading with his mind to break the ice, but the more he tried the tenseness in his stomach increased leaving him cursing himself for being so pathetic at small talk.

Eventually, Lucy spoke, "So why are you out here if you've got a safe place in the country?"

Jack was quick to answer, thankful for the question, "I was out here for supplies and practice."

"What do you mean practice? Where were you when all this happened?" The questions started to flow from Lucy as she started to embrace being in contact with another living person who wasn't out to sexually assault her.

"Well…where to begin. It sounds a bit sad, but I'd locked myself at home for a few days to get a website done for work. My phone's knackered and I was also trying to avoid social media and email to keep away from distraction. I sometimes do this…I guess I'm now doing it permanently." Jack laughed half-heartedly at the poor humour. Lucy didn't laugh.

"Anyway, basically I had no idea what was happening. I found out when I went to the shop. Someone I bumped into told me about the whole end of the world, which I didn't believe. I then saw one of the zombies and ran home to lock myself away and find out more. That's when I watched your videos. I should thank you for your eyewitness accounts, they were brilliant."

Jack was cringing inside. He wasn't painting a good picture of himself. He'd ran away and hid, not very heroic or masculine, then he'd started to act sycophantically towards the videos. *I must look like a sap.*

He continued, "Anyway, I've got parents and friends over in Yorkshire and I need to get over there to check on them. My step-mum and dad were up in Scotland with their campervan, so I've got to assume they'll make their way back home. I'm planning on making the trip in the next day…or two. I figured the population is lower over there, so I reckon I've got a better chance of survival the other side of the hills.

"This jaunt out was to prepare for what could well be my last ever trip."

Lucy smiled at Jack's use of the word jaunt, as if he was out for a picnic. She began to warm to him and told him about her journey out of Manchester. Jack was all ears. Coming to the end of the M56 after a weaving and careful drive, Jack said to Lucy that he was leaving the motorway and heading into the country and asked if she was okay going that way.

She agreed and sank down into the seat, her feet pushed under the chair, knees pointing up with the bat resting between her legs. Jack glanced over and could see she was taking stock of her amazing escape from the city.

Jack was hunched over the steering wheel, consumed with fear whilst navigating through the wrecks and dead stragglers, when Lucy spoke softly, "If it's okay with you, I'll take you up on your offer of a roof over my head for a day or two."

Preoccupied, Jack didn't answer until the words made their way past his unconscious mind, into consciousness, eventually he said, 'great', and explained that he had a spare room, attempting to sound nonchalant, hiding his pleasure at her acceptance of his offer.

There were a few scares and close calls during the remainder of the drive, but once they got onto the country roads it was plain sailing. The dead that Jack had lured away, or maybe different ones, were turned around back in the direction of home, so much for Jack's practical ideas. Lucy and Jack sat in silence. Lucy reflected the past few hours; the hours had seemed like days and had left her exhausted. Jack sat there in an awkward silence, should he say something, could he even think of something to say. Jack continued the rest of the journey this way, feeling awkward about the silence. Lucy on the other hand had sunk into a contented silence with her new friend.

Jacked inserted a CD into the car stereo, The National's Blood Buzz Ohio came on and they sat in silence listening to the haunting and melancholy music while staring thoughtfully out of the window.

Things will be okay.

Chapter 14 - Two's Company

Lucy and Jack arrived at number 12 about 3pm. Jack showed Lucy around the house and to her room. He left her there as she gathered her thoughts. She'd left her carefully packed bag in the Range Rover when she was on the run. She had no possessions other than the clothes on her back and her bat, which she had grown rather attached to.

Jack was waiting for Lucy in the kitchen when she came downstairs, he said, "You must be hungry, let me rustle something up for us. The gas is still on so I can make us some pasta."

Lucy smiled, "You read my mind, I must admit I am famished, but I'm off carbs." She laughed as did Jack, she was feeling a little awkward in Jack's home, but was happy to be there.

Jack set to work and Lucy sat down at the kitchen table and watched on. She was eager to change, she had the day's sweat and the dead's blood on her, she said, "I left my bag behind when I fled from those arse wipes, I don't have any spare clothes. I don't suppose you have anything I could wear?"

Jack stopped placing pans on the hob and paused. After a few seconds he said, "Yes, I think I can help you with some clothes." He went upstairs and left Lucy sitting there without saying another word.

A few minutes passed and Jack appeared in the lounge holding a pile of clothes, "They should fit you; she was a similar size to you." He looked sad.

Standing up from the kitchen table, Lucy walked towards Jack and touched his arm. She asked, "Where is she?"

Jack smiled; he knew she was thinking that his wife had been lost in the current climate of things, he said, "She died five years ago. These might be a little faded and dusty, but they should be okay. I couldn't throw them away."

"I'm fine in these clothes if you don't want me to wear them. I can get some more somewhere else." Lucy said, still touching Jack's arm.

"Please, make use of them. Amy would have wanted me to help you anyway, so please don't argue, you need clothes and I have clothes. Please, no more, get changed and we'll eat. I've got some wine!" Jack tried to lighten the mood with the promise of wine.

Lucy grabbed the clothes and headed upstairs. Jack returned to the kitchen to make some pasta. He had some tomatoes that were just about spent, some onion, garlic and a few herbs and spices. He put the tomatoes in a small pan, added some olive oil, balsamic vinegar and Worcestershire Sauce and covered them over a low heat. He cut an onion and the garlic and fried them with some olive oil while boiling water for the spaghetti.

He was still preparing the food when Lucy returned. She wore some tight-fitting jeans and a shirt with swallows printed on them. Jack had always liked that shirt on Amy and he pictured her walking into the lounge calling out with joy in her voice, "Where are my two-favourite people?" He began to choke up, tears welling in his eyes. The vision and memory stirring great sadness inside, he tried to shove them aside. It wasn't Amy, she was dead. This was Lucy.

She called through to the kitchen as Jack had moved away from watching her, "That smells great. You must have been a chef."

"I wish. I was selling my soul in the corporate world dancing to the capitalist tune. I was in marketing, not that useful now I can tell you." Jack responded cheerfully; finally getting a grip of his emotions as Lucy walked back into the kitchen.

"How do I look?" She questioned with a smirk.

"Beautiful." Jack said and immediately regretted the choice of word. It wasn't the word itself; Jack thought Lucy did look beautiful; she was stunning and was like a ray of sunshine. It was the situation, a man and a woman, alone, Jack using romantic terms. He didn't want to give Lucy the wrong impression.

Lucy blushed, sensing Jack's discomfort, and sat down as she said, "What was that about wine? I feel I've earned a drink today."

Jack pointed to the work surface behind him, "There's a bottle open there, the glasses are in the cupboard above, please help yourself. Mi casa su casa."

They greedily ate and enjoyed a bottle of wine together. Lucy had been in purchasing for an online fashion business. Originally from London, she was new to Manchester. She didn't give much about her life away, but was able to talk freely about things like music, TV and art. Jack and Lucy had liked many of the same things, such as going to gigs, reading and people watching. That was the old world though.

Lucy was everything Jack had envisioned and more. She was wise, kind, intelligent and funny. Jack was enjoying himself and enjoying the company. Was it the end of the world or was it the person? He'd felt a longing for the old world upon learning about the worldwide catastrophe, so maybe this feeling of happiness was a result of this yearning, rather than being close to someone of the opposite sex. Still, he felt more alive than he had done in many years.

It turned out that the next phase of Lucy's plan wasn't so simple. She didn't know what to do. She was from London, but by all accounts, London was a no-go zone. Too big and out of control, the City was awash with the dead. Escaping a city the size of London would be an impossible task. She had made peace a couple of days ago with the fact that her London friends would have probably perished. Her parents were already dead, before the dead started rising, and she had no immediate family. She was truly alone and when this realisation dawned on her, her face darkened immeasurably. She was alone and had nowhere to go, but she remained composed and committed to her survival.

Jack stared on in wonder. *What a woman.* They continued to chat, sitting at the kitchen table like old friends, when Lucy said with whispered urgency, "Jack, there's a man at the kitchen window!"

He swung his head around quickly and relaxed and waved, "Don't worry, that's Danny, he's my neighbour." Adding in a hushed tone, "He's the one who's been keeping the street free of the dead, he's clearing it for when his wife returns home."

Lucy grimaced and Jack understood the look. He got up and opened the back door letting Danny in.

"Danny, this is Lucy, she's a friend and staying here for a couple of days. Lucy, this is Danny, my neighbour." Jack did the introductions.

Making his way to a cupboard, Jack got another bottle of wine and opened it, getting a glass for Danny. The three of them talked, joked and laughed together through the remains of the afternoon and into the evening and night. Danny had been out doing his errands in the day and seemed impressed with both Lucy and Jack's tales of adventure. He had lots of questions about the city and the general state of how things were. He listened gravely as Lucy spoke about how she'd been pursued by the gang and the sheer numbers of the dead that were currently barricaded behind crumpled pileups.

Danny and Lucy seemed to be getting along famously. At times, Jack felt like a spare wheel as the two of them joked with one another. The old feeling of envy and jealousy filled him, but this time is wasn't a general life thing, it was jealousy over a woman. He'd felt a warmth from Lucy and had been feeling like a schoolboy with a crush, he had been trying to push the alien feelings down, but Jack was smitten with Lucy and he hadn't been like this since Amy. He didn't like himself for feeling this way, but he knew Amy would be happy about it…she'd probably have teased him about it if she could talk from beyond the grave, but she would have wanted Jack to be happy. Perhaps not in a world filled with the walking dead.

All these thoughts were wasted anyway. Lucy's warmth was just part of her personality. She was showing it to Danny as she had to Jack and Jack had to make sure his stupid crush didn't ruin things between the three of them. They were the only living people he knew, and he cherished every moment he spent with them. How times had changed, his outlook on human interaction had turned on its heels, he now wanted to be as close as possible to the people he cared about.

The night came to an end as Danny decided he'd drank enough wine. They'd polished off four bottles between them and they were all quite inebriated. He kissed Lucy goodnight on the cheek and shook Jack's hand and left out of the back and under the fence panel.

Lucy and Jack were left alone. Lucy smiled and said, "He's a really nice guy. A policeman too, a hero now and a hero then."

"He sure is." Jack answered trying to hide the jealousy in his voice.

"You can see it behind the smile though. There's desperation there. I think he knows Dawn isn't coming home, but he can't give up. I don't know what would be left if he gave up. I felt I had to spend the whole night making him smile trying to keep his hopes up. I really hope he finds her."

Jack looked at Lucy smiling. Her warmth and compassion were pulling at his heartstrings again. She'd seen through Danny's mask and into his soul, something Jack had failed to notice. She was taking extra care of Danny this evening as he needed it more than anybody.

Jack spoke, "You're a very special person.

"I should go to bed before I fall over."

"I should join you…well, you know what I mean, I should go to bed too." Lucy said, blushing for the second time that day as they both headed upstairs.

They said their goodnights and went to their rooms.

After 15 minutes, Lucy couldn't sleep; she was drunk and decided to see if Jack was still up. She knocked on the door and called out, "Are you asleep yet?"

Jack had been lying there thinking about Lucy and wasn't asleep, he gently called out, "No, come in."

Lucy tentatively pushed the door open; it slowly swung open as Lucy seemed to float into the room. She lightly tiptoed over to the side of the bed and sat down. She was wearing one of Jack's old t-shirts that he'd laid out on her bed for nightwear. Jack could see her silhouette and contours of her body as the moon shone through the open plantation shutters.

"Can I spend the night with you? I don't want to be alone." Lucy asked meekly.

The calm and warm exterior was making way for a more intimate and tender side to Lucy. Jack sat up in bed and hesitated. He hadn't had this sort of connection or intimacy with anyone since Amy. He was nervous and apprehension was catching his tongue. Lucy leaned closer and said, "I lost someone before all this started happening. It's okay, I understand."

She stood up and looked rueful, Jack spoke up, "Please don't go. I don't want to be alone either."

Lucy turned and started to lift the bed covers when Jack remembered he was naked, in a panic he sat up and blurted out, "Wait! I'm naked I should put some underwear on."

Lucy didn't stop; she continued to pull the covers up and slid into bed. Jack immediately felt the warmth of Lucy's body from the other side of the bed. She turned on her side and faced him, her hands lying flat on the pillow under her face, and whispered to Jack, "Just so you know, I'm not in the habit of slipping into bed with boys I just met."

With heart pounding, Jack smiled and lay down again and turned to face Lucy.

"Nobody is watching any more, society can't judge. It's just you and me." Lucy said, she leaned closer and kissed Jack with a tender kiss. Jack's whole body lit up as years of living in an emotional wilderness were swept aside with feelings of romance, passion and lust. He kissed Lucy back, but it was clumsy and half-hearted having been caught off guard and battling the guilt that still wrangled in his gut.

Lucy turned, facing away from Jack and said, "What does a girl have to do for a cuddle around here."

Jack slid over the bed, conscious that he was naked and had a stirring that could be a little awkward. Lucy lifted her head and Jack put his arm around her. She smelt sweet considering the day's exertions. He leaned in and pressed his chest into her back making sure to arch his body to keep his erection from ruining the tender moment. He knew he wanted her and was 99 percent certain she was interested, but that one percent weighed heavily on his decision making. Jack wasn't even sure he was capable of sex anymore; he was a little out of practice.

Gently holding Jack's hand, Lucy wrapped his other arm around her and let out a contented sigh. She then began to push her hips backwards into Jack; she was naked under the t-shirt. Frozen, he held his breath as his heart reverberated through her body. She moved her hips closer and the gap between them closed as the feeling of skin on skin sent lightning bolts through his body. Slowly she began to seductively push her delightfully perfect rear into Jack's arched groin. Jack could no longer control his desires, he put his hand on her hip and worked it up under her t-shirt, tracing the contours of her body and pushing himself firmly against Lucy's silky soft skin, she twisted her upper body and they kissed passionately, he span her around, the feeling of her against him was electrifying, they continued to kiss exploring each other's bodies with an eager animal passion, their hips rhythmically tempting each other further.

They looked at each other and Lucy smiled. Jack was transfixed, she was so beautiful, and this moment felt perfect. The whole world had ended but he was happier now than at any other point in the last five years. He leaned forward and affectionately kissed her. They made love slowly to begin with, but soon left any sense of nervousness behind as they both lost themselves to their carnal desires, both moaning in ecstasy as their self-imposed celibacy came abruptly to an end.

They drifted off in each other's arms happy to share something beautiful in a world of atrocity.

-

Jack awoke to pouring rain. It was light outside and he dreamily recollected the previous evening's pleasure with growing relish. He then realised that Lucy was not in bed with him. Getting up, he put a pair of boxer shorts and a t-shirt on. Searching the rooms upstairs, she was nowhere to be seen. Going downstairs, she wasn't in the lounge or the kitchen. He moved into the kitchen and looked out of the window.

Outside, on the patio, completely naked, stood Lucy in the rain. The vision in the morning light, darkened by the heavy rain clouds, was breath taking. Tall and lean, Lucy had the body of a runner; she was sleek and incredibly sexy. She washed herself with some shower gel in the rain, the soapy foam running down the patio. She looked up and smiled and motioned for Jack to come and join her.

He went outside and joined Lucy. She kissed him passionately and took his t-shirt off. He was quick to remove his boxer shorts and kick them away. The rain was cold, but the thrill of the moment took any unpleasant sensations away. She applied some shower gel in her hands and started to wash Jack's chest and back; gently kissing him every so often. Jack was in a state of pure arousal.

He pressed up against her, kissing her passionately. She took his hand and led him to the lawn and smiled, "I've always wanted to do this."

She got down on the grass and pulled Jack with her. Naked on the lawn, they continued their carnal passions from the previous evening as the cold rain heightened the exhilaration as they lost themselves to lust.

Jack was like a teenager again. He was smitten beyond all reason. He felt as though he'd known Lucy all his life. Pulling her close and kissing her, he said, "You're making this world worth living."

Lucy's smile vanished from her face. She looked sad and pushed Jack away, half running to the door, stooping to pick up her clothes before making her way, still dripping, through the house and upstairs.

Well done Jack.

Chapter 15 - Good and Bad

For the rest of the day, Lucy avoided Jack, which was a skill in such a small house. Jack tried to talk to her, still confused about the mood, but only got short answers and no warmth. He was tormenting himself: did she just want a little bit of pleasure in a world turned bad; did he say too much? Was he too emotionally involved already? Had she sensed this and recoiled from his foolish hopes? They'd only met the previous day, but Jack had watched the videos and felt as though he'd known her already, she on the other hand had met a man who wasn't exactly Brad Pit and certainly didn't have the sparkling wit of a comic genius.

Jack continued that way for a couple of hours. He was attempting to work through the road atlas planning possible routes for his trip to Yorkshire. After the events of the previous day, Jack had decided to revert to the original plan of waiting for a week. The roadblocks were stopping most of the dead escaping the city, so he figured he'd have enough time to wait it out. Of course, a major part of this decision was down to wanting Lucy to come with him, although he hadn't actually admitted that to himself yet. He also hoped he'd see Danny's wife, Dawn, return safe and sound so that they could both join the trip too.

Walking into the kitchen to grab a bottle of water, Lucy didn't speak to Jack as he sat at the kitchen table. He was tired of his internal torment so said, "Please Lucy. Sit down. Talk to me."

She hesitated but relinquished the urge to walk away and took the seat opposite Jack. She began, "Did you mean it?"

"Mean what?"

"That if I wasn't here, you'd stop trying? You'd give up."

"I didn't say that, did I?"

"You implied that you didn't know if you could go on if you hadn't met me."

"I didn't mean that literally. I'm not used to opening up to people anymore. It was meant as a compliment. I was just saying that you've made my life better."

Lucy paused and for the first time throughout all of the struggles that Jack had seen her face, her eyes started to fill up with tears, "I'm sorry, I overreacted. I just...I couldn't see that again."

Jack moved to the seat next to Lucy and rubbed her back gently, "See what again Lucy?" Jack felt great just saying her name, he needed to stop being so love struck.

"I didn't tell you how I lost my partner." She choked in a sob and continued, "My partner and I, George, were very much in love, but he had a few issues. He committed suicide just over a year ago."

She wept openly. The intimacy with Jack was the first time she had given herself over to anyone since George had died and she had drunkenly instigated it. She was feeling guilty and this guilt manifested itself into thoughts and memories of George and their life together, and ultimately finding him in the bath soaking in his own blood. Jack's unfortunate choice of words in his intended compliment had awoken these feelings and as such she wanted to avoid all contact with him in an attempt to erase her infidelity to George.

Jack put his arms around Lucy and let her cry, he said it was okay and that he was sorry. He realised that he had so many questions, but these weren't questions you could ask or expect an answer. He said nothing and continued to hug Lucy until the tears died down.

She looked up at Jack and smiled, "I'm sorry, I feel like an idiot. Here I am bearing my soul to someone I met only yesterday and worse still, I'm sobbing like a damn fool.

"Look Jack, last night and this morning were the best thing to happen to me in a long time. You've been so kind to me…Hell, you saved my life from the minute you met me. But-" Jack hated that but, "you've seen what I'm like. I'm still grieving, and I was thrown by the whole end of the world thing. I don't know what you want from me, but I'm not ready for anything serious."

Lucy began to laugh, "Sorry again, I'm not laughing at you; it's the whole situation. Here I am in what can only be described as a zombie apocalypse and I'm sat with a guy I had amazing sex with last night who is really quite a lovely chap. And here I am saying it's not you, it's me, like we're on the set of a Hollywood movie. Is this a romance or horror flick?"

The teenage feeling of rejection hit Jack hard; he was so out of touch with the world of romance that his emotions had regressed into the extreme highs and lows of adolescence. He managed to restrain his out of control reactions and avoided burying his head in the nearest cushion and wailing, he smiled and said, "Please don't apologise. You have nothing to apologise for. I completely understand, I've been living in stasis, cut off from the world, for five years.

"I'll level with you. I feel like I've known you all my life and I really like you. Last night and this morning were amazing and will be a memory I'll cherish."

Embarrassed by the words coming out of his mouth, Jack continued his out of control ramblings, "I really like you, but I understand your reluctance for anything else. It's taken the end of the world to make me realise that I want to be part of the living again. You completed my final step, the freeing of my shackles…of…of anger. I know I'm still grieving, but not like I was before, I'm now grieving the world and its wonders, the realisation of this zombie thing hasn't fully dawned on me yet. My emotions are all over the place, I'm like a love-struck teenager, but most of all, I want to be your friend and I want you to be safe. That's enough for me. You are warm and wonderful, and you make me feel wonderful too. It might be selfish, but I want you with me, romantically or not."

Lucy lifted her head and gently kissed Jack on the cheek. He knew what it meant, last night was last night, now is now.

Jack continued, "Look, I'm going to cry in a minute, so I'll ask you this. Will you come with me to Yorkshire?" He didn't wait for an answer, he was on the full sales pitch, "I know you don't have a plan and I enjoy your company. I would worry, without hope of helping you, if I go and you stay or do your own thing. Please come with me."

She weighed up her options and looked at Jack and said, "I'll come with you Jack. We need to do something first though. We need to help Danny find his wife or help him get some closure."

-

Jack and Lucy spent most of the morning hunched over a map plotting possible routes. They reasoned that they'd need quite a few contingency plans and a list of possible destinations to crash as many roads could be impassable, so the journey might not be accomplished in a day. The two of them made a good team, Jack had more knowledge of the area, but Lucy used her brain and logic much more efficiently so effectively made the plans based on Jack's familiarity with the roads. They wished for Google Maps and street view, so they could zoom into any location to check out the layout of the roads. That was the old world though.

Using the experience of the Adventure Island excursion, they decided it was sensible to stick to country roads and avoid built up areas. This proved a tricky assignment, but they'd done their best to limit routes through urban areas. Happy with the plan, Lucy went to see Danny, the back way, to talk about going to find his wife.

She returned quickly and despondently, Danny wasn't in.

They ate some hummus, pitta bread with some carrots, the perishable food was getting thin. Sitting in a comfortable silence together, a noise from outside made them stir, they looked at each other.

Jack rose to his feet and ran upstairs to peek out of the shutters without being seen. Lucy was quickly behind him. Outside, a woman in a dressing gown was pacing down the street, she was sobbing, carrying something in her arms. Jack didn't recognise her from his street.

Lucy said, "She's alive, come on, she looks like she needs help."

Turning around and running down the stairs, Lucy was out of the door before Jack could reason with her to stay inside. She slowed her pace as she approached the woman in her nightwear and called out, "Hi, are you okay? Do you need some help?"

The woman didn't answer, she sobbed quietly, shuffling her feet as she moved. A tiny arm shot out and retreated from the bundle the woman cradled. Lucy realised that it was a baby; a poor little child born into a cruel world. This infant wasn't supposed to face a future filled with carnivorous humanoid ghouls, it was meant to grow into a world of uncertainty that's for sure, but trivial unknowns, like robots taking all the jobs or the pressure of growing up in an ever-connected world of social media; what sort of future could this innocent being expect now?

Lucy put aside thoughts of the baby's future and asked, "Do you need anything for the baby?"

The woman still didn't answer, she shuffled forwards still sobbing. Lucy put her hand on the woman's shoulder. The contact made the woman swing around violently. In her arms the baby looked up. It was turned; grey and blue in colour, its eyes so bloodshot they looked black. The baby would have been three months old and growing, but now the little monster was permanently stuck as an infant with a thirst for blood. It clawed at its mother, instinct making it snap at her hands and arms, but with no teeth, its hunger could not be satisfied. The mother held the baby close, forcibly stopping it thrash.

Lucy let out a yelp and stepped back upon seeing the dead baby. She turned to Jack with a look of horror and motioned for him not to look. Jack didn't heed the warning, although he wished he'd listened. The sight sickened him.

"Can we help you?" Lucy repeated.

"Too late, it's too late, too late." The woman garbled back incoherently.

Jack and Lucy watched on. What could they do? She was in need of help but had clearly lost her mind. There was no way she was letting go of the baby and both Jack and Lucy were certain that it was not coming in the house. They watched on, unable to move or think how to help, as the woman continued to shuffle slowly down the road as she clutched her dead infant.

From the alley at the side of the road a fat woman appeared and wrapped her arms around the woman and dead child. The fat woman was no longer living and she took the robed woman by surprise. Wrapping her bulbous arms around the now struggling and screaming woman, the fat zombie sunk her teeth into the woman's neck, pulling her mouth away breaking the skin and arteries with a spray of blood as the three of them toppled to the floor, the baby bouncing out of its bundle.

Jack immediately ran to the woman and kicked the obese monster in the head. Its grip on the woman, whose dying struggles became weaker, was so strong that Jack's kick barely moved the huge beast. From behind him, Lucy appeared with bat in hand, with a high swing, Lucy brought the bat down, crushing its fat head. Jack managed to roll the large dead woman from the injured lady with all his might. The woman in the dressing gown lay there bleeding to death. Incoherent ramblings still echoed from her mouth, her life slowly slipping away.

Gripping Jack's shirt sleeve, Lucy pulled Jack a step backwards. The dead baby was on the road, naked and grey, slowly crawling to the pool of its mother's blood, dipping its mouth into it. Feeding.

Lucy and Jack held each other, both wanting to throw up, to cry, to wake up from a nightmare. The woman on the floor was gasping her last breaths as her offspring drank her life force. Jack looked at Lucy and weakly said, "She's going to turn soon."

He knew what he had to do, but didn't have the courage to volunteer for the job. Jack wasn't a violent man and had never had a proper fight. This was all too much for him, but he was aware he couldn't ask Lucy to do this. It wasn't a macho thing, it was a human thing.

Bounding over a fence a few yards up the road, Danny appeared. He had heard the commotion and had come running. He walked over and checked that Lucy and Jack were okay. He looked emotionless as he surveyed the terrible scene. Looking up he said in a monotone and robotic voice, "Go inside. I'll deal with this. Go now."

"But what about the b–" Jack couldn't finish his sentence.

"I'll take care of this. Just go, I don't want you to see this. Go now before she turns. I'll come over tonight"

Jack and Lucy left Danny in the street. The pair were torn, every part of them wanted to leave Danny to this heinous task, but that didn't make it right for them to leave him to it. They left him anyway; relieved and guilty.

The household that afternoon and evening had a sombre atmosphere. Jack and Lucy studied the pages of instructions that Jack had printed out when he still had power. The two of them were close, they rarely left each other, but that night they both slept in separate rooms, both waking regularly from dark dreams.

Danny didn't visit them that evening.

Chapter 16 - Worse

The following morning, Lucy and Jack woke early and were still consumed with the previous day's events. Lucy walked across the hall to Jack's room and knocked on the door. He smiled to himself at the formality that had built up so suddenly following the first day's passion.

"Come on in." Jack said in a mock chirpy tone.

"You're in a good mood." Lucy responded rubbing the tiredness out of her eyes.

"Not really, can't get yesterday out of my head. I'm putting on a stiff upper lip attitude." Jack said.

"Can I get in with you? Don't try to jump me this time!" Lucy cheekily remarked.

Jack laughed, "If I remember rightly, you seduced me. I can't blame you though, you're only human."

Lucy laughed this time as she got into bed and pulled the covers over her. It was chilly for the time of year and she was a little cold. Putting her cold feet on Jack, he pulled away and yelped. She laughed again.

"I think we should both go over and see Danny this morning. I'm feeling really ashamed for leaving him yesterday. Did you see the look on his face? He was emotionless." Lucy said, half burying her face in the duvet.

"Sounds like a good idea to me. He seemed completely out of it."

Jack continued, "Do you think we care too much for this new world? I don't mean Danny; like with that woman outside, we can't help everybody we meet, but I'm not sure how I'd feel about myself if I just hid in the shadows and did nothing to help people." Jack was pondering out loud.

Lucy was quick to respond, "I don't know. All I know is that while I'm a sentient living being, I want to keep hold of some essence of innocence and moral decorum."

Jack sniggered, "Moral decorum? What about that redhead I saw frolicking in the mud yesterday morning?" He immediately regretted saying that; the flirty nature of their initial conversation had passed onto more serious topics.

Lucy wasn't fazed though, she retorted, "I do believe my good sir that being sexually liberated is to be more enlightened, you ought to try it sometime, Mr. Frigid."

They both laughed enjoying each other's company and grateful for something light-hearted to talk about.

She continued, "Seriously though, Danny. I'm worried about him. All of this 'clearing the streets' must be taking its toll on him. You read about PTSD and things like that. Just look at the woman outside yesterday, she'd cracked mentally, we can't be letting Danny get into that state.

"We should call on him this morning and make him come out with us to search for Dawn. It'll give him something to focus on and distract him from killing dead folk."

The words revolved around Jack's head. He knew what Danny was doing but hadn't really stopped to consider the effects to Danny's mental wellbeing, this combined with the fact that Dawn had still not come home was troubling.

Jack got up, he was naked again, Lucy didn't look away however, she followed him with her eyes as he rummaged in the wardrobe for something to wear. He looked round and caught her looking, she smiled and looked away. He stopped himself from making a comment and quickly dressed and turned to Lucy and said, "No time like the present, Danny is always up early anyway."

Lucy jumped out of bed; her t-shirt lifted as she scarpered out of the room giving Jack a glimpse of her wonderful behind. His loins stirred, and he cursed himself that he might have missed an opportunity to be close to her again.

Lucy was quick getting dressed and joined Jack on the landing. She gave his hand a little squeeze and grinned at him. His heart melted a little more. She motioned for him to follow her and they headed downstairs, out the back and under the fence panel to Danny's backdoor.

Rapping on the door didn't produce any effects from inside. Lucy tried the door handle, it was open. She pushed the door open ajar and called, "Ooooo oooo, helllloooo."

She turned to Jack and grimaced at herself and said, "Too chirpy, maybe you should go in and wake him. It's only 6:30 so he can't be out already."

He hesitated before stepping through the doorway, Lucy behind him almost clinging to his back. There were no signs of life in the kitchen and living room. The layout of the house was similar to Jack's, but most of the interior walls had been knocked through to create an open plan living space. It was immaculate. There were no pots and pans in the sink, no dust, it was an OCD paradise. Jack called out to Danny, but there was no answer again.

"Just go and wake him. I can't do it; he might get the wrong idea." Lucy said.

"How do you know I might not give him the wrong idea?" Jack said smiling.

Quick as a flash, Lucy laughingly said, "You're not masculine enough."

Jack feigned a hurt look and went upstairs. Lucy waited downstairs in the lounge.

On approaching the master bedroom, the same room as in Jack's house, he saw a note taped to the door, it read:

Jack & Lucy

Read this. Do not enter.

Jack called down to Lucy and she raced up the stairs, hearing the urgency in his voice. She approached and he ripped the note off the door and handed it to her. He then went to try the door handle, but she held his arm and showed him the note.

Read this. Do not enter.

Lucy handed the note back to Jack, he opened it and read out loud:

Dear Jack and Lucy,

I don't know either of you very well, but I thought you deserved an explanation.

After seeing you yesterday and disposing of the dead you encountered I set off determined to find Dawn. I made my way to the hospital, but it was impossible to get in.

I then went along the 3 routes that she could have taken to get home. Eventually I found her. I saw her car and there she was. She was dead. Mercifully, she had died in the car and not become one of those soulless creatures. She'd crashed head on to a van and looked like she hadn't suffered.

Anyway, I've decided I'm going to join her in the next world. I'm nothing without her and cannot continue to live like this.

Please do not come into the room.

Let me rest in peace for eternity with Dawn.

Remember me as a good person and one who loved God and his fellow man.

I bid you goodnight. Farewell.

Danny.

Silence filled the air. Jack looked up to Lucy who was on the verge of tears. He held her and they both sobbed quietly as Danny lay on his bed, stone cold and dead on the other side of the door. He'd arrived home late the previous evening, had taken a bottle of whiskey and all of the painkillers he could find upstairs with him. He wrote a few notes, discarded them and settled on the one that Jack and Lucy had found taped to the door. Danny had drifted off to sleep hoping to see Dawn once again.

-

Lucy and Jack didn't speak much for the rest of the morning, they had returned to Jack's house and sat around studying print outs of instructions again. Lucy was deflated and low, but Jack was finding it difficult to think of anything to lift her or his own spirits, so they sat in silence.

Around lunchtime, Lucy lifted her head that she'd been resting on the arm of the couch and said, "We need to bury Danny. He deserves that after what he did for us yesterday and for saving your life."

Thinking of the physical logistics of digging a hole and moving Danny's heavy frame to the garden were Jack's first thoughts. Angry with his own selfish reaction he wondered how long it would be for Lucy to realise that he wasn't that good a man. He responded, "You're right. We should do it sooner rather than later though."

Sensing the need to be chivalrous after his self-regarding thoughts, he continued, "After lunch I'll go in there and cover him up in a sheet, you don't need to see him like that. I'm probably going to need your help to carry his body, but before we do that, we're going to need to dig a hole.

I'll sort Danny out and then we can dig a hole. I've got some old wood from when I had my staircase done so we can mark his grave."

Lucy walked over to Jack and kissed him tenderly.

Chapter 17 - Next Door

Jack put off seeing to Danny's body straight away, he couldn't face him yet so decided to concentrate on digging the hole. Lucy was quick to help and they both dug in silence as they worked tirelessly on a task neither of them would have been able to comprehend doing just a week ago.

The day had turned out to be warm with the sun breaking through the sparse clouds. The soil was still wet and heavy from the rain and the task was arduous. They dug on in silence, the laughter and flirtation between them had vanished as they both wallowed in the harsh realities of the world they found themselves in.

The hole took a couple of hours to dig and they were both physically exhausted. Jack got a bucket of water, which he'd filled in the rain, a sponge and some shower gel. He took hold of Lucy's hands and began to wash the mud off them. He couldn't seem to lift her spirits, but she let him wash the mud away with a distant look on her face.

They rested for half an hour in the warm spring day. Birds flew overhead and could be heard chirping, unconcerned with humanity's struggles. Jack decided it was time to face up to the task he'd been avoiding and make Danny presentable so that Lucy could help move the body without seeing his corpse in the flesh. It was stupid really, Lucy had driven through thousands of corpses on her escape out of Manchester, but Jack felt as though this was different and was more personal to her recent history. He ushered Lucy inside, made her a drink and told her to rest while he went next door.

Gingerly making his way upstairs in Danny's house, Jack paused outside the door and counted down from five. He had used this technique since he was a little boy, he remembered taking a bath before school and always counting down from five to get up out of the hot water and into the cold. This time the countdown was far more serious.

Opening the door slowly, Danny's image started to appear, he was fully clothed including boots lying on top of the covers. The duvet had been cast aside to the corner of the room. It appeared as though Danny had considered everything and positioned himself in the middle of the bed ready to be wrapped in the sheets should someone take the time to bury him. Jack remembered his previous perception of Danny and the irritation that he used to feel when faced with Danny's niceness. What a fool he had been, Danny was too nice for Jack that was clear.

Jack walked over to the side of the bed and looked down at Danny. He looked peaceful; he could have been asleep were it not for his grey pallid complexion. Sighing loudly, Jack said, "Danny mate. You could have survived; you could have come with us. I understand though. I hope there is an afterlife and I hope you found Dawn and you're both happy. Thank you Danny."

He reached for the corner of the bed and pulled the sheet out from under the mattress, he did the same with the other corners. He folded the top and bottom of the sheet over Danny's head and feet and then stood on the left side of the bed and folded the sheets over the lifeless form. He tucked the sheets under the body and rolled Danny over twice to wrap the sheets around him. Jack had zoned out through the entire process and let his mind drift to avoid the stark reality.

Looking down once again at the mummified body, Jack was satisfied that Danny was ready to be moved. He was about to go and get Lucy when a screech of tires stopped him in his tracks. Rushing to the window, Jack looked down and saw a BMW stopped outside his house, four hooded youths were out of the car and making their way to the front door.

One thought screamed out in Jack's head. *LUCY*.

He ran past Danny's body and downstairs two steps at a time, when he saw Lucy closing Danny's back door. She was carrying her bat and raising her finger to her lips in a shushing motion. Lucy ran towards Jack, grabbed him by the arm and pulled him upstairs.

They moved into the spare room at the back of the house and she whispered, "It's that gang from Manchester. I recognised the little stocky guy through the window in the door."

"How do they know where we are?" Jack asked, panic setting in.

"I don't know, the last I saw of them was shortly before I met you. It could be coincidence."

Jack raised his eyebrows in doubt.

Lucy continued, "There was four of them, they didn't hear me leave, I locked the patio door behind me, there's no way they could guess we're here. We should just wait it out."

Amazed at the clarity of Lucy's mind, Jack gazed at her in wonder; he would never have thought to escape out of the back, let alone remember his hammer or to lock the door behind him. He agreed with Lucy and they sat nervously listening to the banging as the gang began to kick at the front door.

-

Richie kicked at the PVC door with a furious look, his features crinkling around his large nose, as he grunted with each blow. One of the door panels collapsed inwards and Richie crouched to reach around for a key. He found it hanging in the lock on the other side where Jack had left it in case of the need for a speedy exit. Richie pulled the key out of the slot and handed it to Naz.

Unlocking the door, Naz, followed by Richie and two others, swarmed in. Naz commanded, "You two check upstairs, me and Richie will take care of down here. We want the woman, remember, yeah?"

The two men followed their orders and ran upstairs wielding an axe and machete. Naz and Richie did the same downstairs. A quick sweep of the house saw that it was empty. The two from upstairs joined Naz and Richie in the lounge. All eyes were on Naz.

Naz looked down at the coffee table where two road atlases were cast down. Richie made his way to a shelf and picked a picture up, asking, "Is this the guy Naz?"

Looking at it, Naz snarled, "How the fuck should I know Richie you thick cunt. Dale saw him, not me. Fuck knows why that lazy bastard stayed in the fucking mansion."

He stopped to wipe the spit that had exploded out of his mouth as he roasted Richie pedantically. Richie stood there, his body language showing nothing as his mind raged with fantasies about crushing Naz's skull with his own hands. Naz continued, "Take the photo and show it to Dale. It's the same type of car outside alright."

One of the others picked up an open map that lay on the table. Highlighted routes were all pointing to the same destination. Eastloch in Yorkshire, he studied it and said whilst handing the map to Naz, "Looks like we've missed them, they were planning a trip."

Rolling his eyes in annoyance, Naz spoke again, "Fuck me. Am I the only one with any brains around here? Why the hell would they go on a trip like this and not take their maps? I bet they're out getting supplies.

"Come on let's get the fuck out of here and see if this is definitely the fuckhead we're looking for."

On that note a bang at the front door followed by a phlegmy moan got the four men's attention. Richie stepped forward with a smile, taking a large hunting knife from a sheath in his belt, and said, "Mine."

He opened the door and grabbed the dead man by the neck and pushed the knife forcefully into the creature's ear, pushing through skin, bone, and eventually brain. The dead man went limp, but Richie continued to hold it by the throat as he twisted the blade back and forth, causing a nauseating wet sound.

"Fuck's sake Richie. Put him down you sick fuck. Let's go, yeah?" Naz said. Deep inside he feared Richie, but he couldn't back down to him or let him see his fears. He watched Richie drop the body and stepped past the deranged stocky little man, stepping over the limp sack of skin that fell over the doorway. The others followed Naz as they got back in the BMW and left with the same urgency as their arrival.

-

Lucy and Jack heard the gang leaving and sneaked past Danny's body to see the car drive away from the bedroom window. They went back to Jack's house and saw the body in the doorway. Jack was quick to pull it outside and shut the door. He locked the door and managed to bend the forced door panel shoddily back in place. Turning to Lucy, he said, "We need to leave, now. It's not safe here, they'll come back, I know it."

Surveying the room, Jack swore.

"What's wrong?" Lucy asked.

"They've taken a picture of me and Amy. Why would they want that? It was my–" He cut off, not wanting to finish his sentence. It was a picture that was important to Jack and was, without cloud backup, lost. In the early months after the accident, Jack often spoke to Amy through the photograph and pleaded with her to come back. It was the light in the photo that made her sparkle, showing her smile, kind eyes and sense of fun.

Seeing the look on Jack's face, Lucy knew what he meant and didn't question him, she stroked his arm sympathetically.

126

She had left her memories of George in a storage unit in London. She couldn't get to them, but knew they were there and that one day, if the time was right, she would be able to get them back. This was a comfort.

"Okay, let's do this now." Lucy made the call.

Chapter 18 - Highwayman

It took less than an hour for Lucy and Jack to get their stuff together and the car packed. It would have been quicker, but one of the dead wandered down the street and hung around for a little too long. Neither of them wanted to go out and deal with it so they'd silently and individually made the decision to let it wander off.

Jack had taken a plastic jerrycan from the garage and snuck next door to Danny's car. He'd had to get the keys from inside Danny's house to open the car's fuel cap and had felt guilt whilst rummaging around the recently deceased man's house.

With his hose pipe, jerrycan and 'how-to syphon fuel' printed instructions, Jack managed, after some difficulty and a rancid petroleum mouth, to fill up the jerrycan. He made a mental note to take a bottle of water, to swill his mouth out, with him next time. He took the petrol, and with a funnel he'd found in the kitchen, topped the Citroen up. He went back to Danny's car and filled the jerrycan up once again and secured the lid. Extra fuel for the trip, just in case.

The two of them had reasoned that it could take up to three days to make it over to Yorkshire, so they packed food and water for the trip. The hammer and bat would ride in the front with them along with the maps. They were going to share driving and navigation, but Jack was driving first.

Jack looked at Lucy and said, "We're all packed, the car is fuelled. Are you ready?"

"One last thing, then let's go." She replied and got a pen and piece of paper and sat down at the kitchen table and began to write a note. Lucy left out of the back door, under the fence and came back soon after.

Turning to Jack with a smile, her eyes teary, she said, "I know we can't bury Danny, so I wanted to leave something nice for him."

"What did you write?"

"Just the truth. He was a good man."

Jack didn't question further, he took Lucy by the hand and gave it a little squeeze. They quietly left the house, Jack locking the door for the last time. They drove down the road, Jack leaving behind his old life: Amy and Ruby, the years of happiness and the past five years of simply existing. Watching out of the rear-view mirror, he choked down shuddering sobs and swallowed hard.

The car moved away from the house and from Danny. A folded note lay on top of his body and read:

My name was Danny. I was loved as a husband, a son, and a friend. I am with my beautiful wife Dawn and we are happy.
17/05/2017.

-

The route they had chosen was over 300 miles and zigzagged avoiding major roads and built up areas. The pre-apocalypse route would have been about 100 miles, so they'd added a lot of distance for their own safety.

They were still in the village heading out, driving slowly to conserve fuel, Jack had wished he'd syphoned more petrol as the car was a little over half full. A mile down the road, Jack slowed the car down to a crawl, a dead man staggered across the verge and towards the car, Jack said, "Fuck me, that's Wes Brown."

"Did you know him?" Lucy asked with compassion.

"No, err no. He used to play for Manchester United, he's a footballer, he was a footballer. I think he lived around here." Jack responded, the surreal nature of seeing someone he'd seen play football at the highest level; now a reanimated corpse was just too bizarre for him to comprehend.

They drove on concentrating on the task at hand, a mile further, around a long and blind corner there were four cars blocking the way. Once again, the car slowed to a crawl, Lucy spoke, "They weren't here last time."

Jack nodded and made a concerned sound. He thought for a moment and said, "We need to get through, we can't go the other way it's too populated."

Lucy nodded in agreement. They made a plan that Jack would get out of the car and push one out of the road while Lucy drove through the roadblock.

Neither Jack nor Lucy was stupid and the coincidence of the gang appearing at the house and now this roadblock didn't escape them. Jack cooked up a contingency plan should anything happen during their forced manoeuvre, he'd described a back road for Lucy to drive to and wait for him should he not be able to get back to the car. She reluctantly agreed, she would wait there and Jack would make it on foot over gardens and fields if anything bad happened.

Surveying both sides of the roadblock, Jack couldn't see any of the dead. Those that they had passed before the sweeping bend had followed them for a short while, but became distracted by a horse in a field, safe behind walls and hedges, for the meantime. He couldn't see any sign of the gang either. Getting out of the car, about 50 feet away from the roadblock, Jack jogged over ducking down to try and stay inconspicuous. He looked at the cars and decided that an old X-reg Ford Focus was probably the easiest to move. The door was unlocked, he bent in and released the hand break. The car was at an angle so would roll straight back which was good as the steering wheel lock clicked into place as Jack grabbed it to start pushing. The car picked up momentum after the initial struggle to get it moving. Aided by a slight decline in the road, the car was pushed aside quickly. It was all going well, Jack smiled and waved Lucy through, play acting like he was a traffic officer. The car crawled through the tight opening and Lucy pulled to a stop to wait for Jack to get back in the car and continue their journey.

Jack opened the door and with one foot in the car a hand reached over his shoulder and pulled him forcibly around. Stood in front of him was Richie, the gang member who Lucy had beaten twice, who'd also been in the house earlier that day. He didn't hang around, Richie got hold of Jack with both hands and threw him into the parked cars with effortless strength. Jack flew tumbling backwards into the parked car, taking the wind out of him. Richie pulled out his hunting knife, smiled demonically and said, "I'm going to gut you."

Richie may not have been academically gifted, but he had a knack of knowing how people would react in certain situations. It wasn't Jack he wanted; it was Lucy. He wanted vengeance for his broken nose and ribs, he wasn't interested in sex, he was in it for the violence. He knew that if he were to try and get Lucy out of the car she could just drive away. By attacking Jack, he could draw Lucy out and get what he craved.

Like clockwork, Lucy was out of the car with her bat in her hand. Jack could see her and he longed to shout for her to drive on, but cowardice caught his tongue at the sight of the hunting knife in Richie's hand. Richie's plan had worked, but he hadn't counted on Lucy's remarkable will and drive, she was brave, strong and decisive which made her quicker than he anticipated. Turning to try and catch Lucy off guard he was surprised to see Lucy right behind him swinging her bat, she caught him in the ribs once again making him recoil in pain. The already cracked ribs felt the full impact and he crumpled into a wheezing ball.

"What's wrong with you, you complete dick!" She roared, "Did mummy not love you enough? Uncle Gary fiddle with you? Or are you just a fucking psychopath?" Lucy was angry and shouting at the felled man without much comprehension about the words leaving her mouth, she wanted to be cruel to Richie. Finally, she calmed down and looked at Jack and made eyes for the car. He was quick to understand and staggered to his feet. They turned to the car, but it was too late, they were surrounded. The rest of the gang, whose numbers had been depleted in their escape on foot from Manchester to just six, had surrounded them and were brandishing weapons, one had a pistol and Jack's eyes locked on it. *Was this the end?*

"Princess, how nice to see you." The gang leader named Dale said. Turning to Jack he said, "Fuck off. We want her. You, fuck off."

Jack stayed where he was. He didn't know what to do; he wasn't cut out for this. The only time he had been faced with someone of Dale's ilk was when he was a student and had been mugged. He had willingly given over his money and wallet to avoid a beating. The giveaway wasn't so easy this time round.

He found the courage to speak, "Just leave us alone, we're going away, we don't threaten you at all."

Looking furious, Dale said, "Leave now. We want her, she's the reason we lost five brothers, she's the reason why we're out here in the sticks and she's the reason why our brother Richie is holding his ribs."

"I won't let you take her." Jack responded in a desperate tone.

Dale pulled up the pistol he was holding and held it to Jack's head. He got close to Jack's face and snarled, "I gave you a choice and you blew it. It's time to die."

"Please, no…Jack just go, leave me, just go." Lucy spoke up.

"Speak when you're spoken too bitch." Dale hissed not letting the pistol drop. "I've had it with this pussy, any last requests?"

Jack swallowed, he realised that this was it and calmness hit him. He looked at Lucy and thought, I must try, for her. He did a very quick mental countdown from three and made his move.

BANG!

Red was the colour. An explosion of red. Blood, skull and brain mixed into mulch. Lucy let out a cry as she looked on at Jack, blood smearing his face. The body of Dale fell to the floor, the back of his head gaping open.

All eyes moved to the rear of the ugly scene. Stood there with rifle cocked and aimed was a man walking cautiously towards the group. He shouted over, "You with blood on your face, go over to the girl, the rest of you, stay the fuck where you are."

One of the gang made a sudden movement and the man fired again, this time missing, but showing his intent. The gang member who moved and two others let instinct take over as they bolted through the trees lining the road, leaving Richie, who was still winded, and the other gang member, Naz, alone to deal with the armed man, Jack and Lucy's saviour.

As the man approached, Jack recognised him, it was Bulldog. He got closer and saw Jack and smiled and said, "I thought you'd be dead by now."

Lucy looked confused and asked, "Do you know him Jack?"

Jack nodded and said, "This is the guy I told you about when I went to the shop and began to realise what was happening to the world."

"Bulldog, pleased to meet you." Mick said in Lucy's direction smiling, looking her up and down.

Lucy waved and said to Jack quietly, "We need to get moving again, those other three might come back."

Still in a state of shock and covered in the contents of Dale's skull, Jack looked on and waited for her words to sink into some sort of comprehension. They eventually did and he nodded.

"These two will follow you. Do you have any rope, we could tie them up?" Mick said, still pointing his rifle between Richie and Naz.

Lucy and Jack looked at each other, it made sense to slow them down and put some distance between these evil men and themselves. Jack turned to Lucy and whispered, "Go to the meeting point, I'll meet you there, it'll take me no more than 15 minutes to run there. I'll be alright with Mick"

Lucy didn't want to leave him, but she could see the determination on his face so reluctantly agreed. Jack went to the boot of the car and took out some rope. He held Lucy at arm's length and said, "I'll be 30 minutes max. Promise."

Looking past his grotesque face paints, Lucy grimaced a smile and mouthed 'hurry' and got in the car and drove off.

Mick walked over to Naz who had been stood there looking for an escape to no avail. Mick quickly brought the butt of his rifle up and knocked Naz spinning to the ground, unconscious. Walking to Richie and after two attempts with the rifle, knocked Richie out cold too.

Jack watched on, concerned by Mick's wilful violence, Mick called out, "That should make it easier to tie them up."

They both struggled with the two bodies; Richie was considerably heavier than Naz. They'd decided to lock them up in one of the cars making up the roadblock to give them a fighting chance should any of the dead come stumbling over. Eventually, they secured the two unconscious gang members, Mick thanked Jack and asked, "Which direction you heading?"

Jack pointed in the direction Lucy had driven, even though he was going to go through gardens and fields to shorten the trip and avoid the dead. He was anxious to get back to Lucy and make sure she was okay.

"My car's just around the corner, come on I'll give you a lift." Mick said smiling.

Hesitating, Jack felt exhausted and was in no mood for physical excursion after digging a grave and his run in with the gang, "Thanks Mick, I feel I owe you so much already."

"Don't mention it, good things will come my way. By the way, that woman, well done, she's lovely." Mick grinned.

"Her name's Lucy." Jack said with a smile, still caked in blood. He wondered what had happened to the woman and baby that he'd seen Mick with the first time they'd met, but he didn't make the same mistake he made with Danny, he left the question unasked.

Walking to a blue pick-up, Mick enquired, "Where am I taking you?"

"Do you know Ancoats Lane? There's a layby there that you can drop me at. Do you have any spare water? I need to wash my face." Jack had walked in front of Mick.

"JACK!" Mick called.

Turning to face Mick, the last thing Jack saw was the butt of the rifle as it struck him. Without time to react, the butt connected with Jack's jaw, knocking him out sprawling to the floor.

Mick got in his pick-up and headed to Ancoats Lane.

-

Mick pulled up to Ancoats Lane to find Lucy waiting. She was puzzled and then distraught as Mick explained that one of the gang members who had escaped came back and shot Jack in the head. He painted Jack as a hero, saying that he pushed Mick out of the way and saved his life. Consoling Lucy, Mick convinced her to come back to meet his girlfriend and baby to rest a while.

Lucy followed Mick in Jack's car, she was in a hollow dream, floating aimlessly. The stability she had found through Jack had gone. Lucy was spiralling into a pit of despair; the walls were slick with grease and the light fading.

Mick's house was along Ancoats Lane, a small cottage down a narrow track, she could see smoke coming from the chimney which she thought a little odd considering it was a warm spring day. Approaching the house, several outbuildings were scattered around, she could see dead pheasants hanging in one of them.

Unlocking the door, Mick held it open for Lucy to enter first, saying, "You are a guest at Bulldog's house."

Walking into the dark living room, curtains drawn, Lucy could see a woman kneeling by the fire, she appeared to be cooking some type of meat by the smell. The woman looked round and saw Lucy, the woman's face didn't change, she just dropped her head and turned to carry on cooking.

Mick locked the door behind him and said, "Lucy, this is Jen." He went off and locked the rifle in a cabinet and took his coat off whilst walking into another room.

Jen turned to Lucy and looked manic, in a hushed tone she said, "Run!"

Chapter 19 - Stockholm Syndrome

Lucy sat for a couple of hours in Mick's living room in a state of alertness. Jen had terrified her, but since the single word, the woman had remained mute, busying herself with various tasks and seeing to her baby. A baby girl! The sight of the child had raised and then crushed Lucy's hopes; the joy of a baby and then the realisation of what her life might become, if she survived, in this cruel new world.

Knowing there was a baby living in the house made Lucy relax, a little. Mick had spoken to her a few times, but the conversations weren't exactly two way. He had a strange way of talking and referred to himself in third person quite often, he spoke in disjointed statements rarely listening to the other person. Lucy wasn't in the mood for talking anyway, her mind drifted to Jack and she wallowed in an unhappy stupor.

It was late afternoon when Bulldog said he had to go out and run some errands. He left with his rifle and locked the door behind him. This action prompted Lucy to pace the house and explore, she found that there was one door out, the locked front door, and the downstairs windows all had bars on them. The bars looked as though they were in place long before the end of the world. She was stuck in the cottage unless she wanted to jump from the upper floor. Returning to the sofa, Lucy sat down heavily and sighed. A nagging thought persisted at the back of her mind: had she willingly become an accomplice to her own kidnapping.

With the baby sleeping upstairs, Jen came down and sat next to Lucy, she attempted a smile, but it was forced and unnatural, "You need to get out when you can. He. He-" She struggled to continue.

Lucy leaned forward and placed her hand on Jen's, "Tell me, please."

"He takes what he wants, and I know he wants you; I've seen him looking at you."

"What do you mean, he takes what he wants?" Lucy knew the answer already.

"He feels we owe it to him for keeping us safe. He says women are the most precious thing left and he vowed to keep me and my baby girl safe."

Lucy put her head in her hands. Her situation seemed bad, but a thought troubled her, Jack. Had Mick killed Jack to get his hands on her? The thought frightened her and she struggled to contain her anger, she grew angrier still when she pictured her baseball bat sat on the passenger seat of the car, parked just a few feet away.

Turning to Jen, she asked, "How long have you been with him?"

"I was with him for a couple of months before this all happened. He was sweet, but loved a drink and a fight. We moved in together as I needed a place to stay and he was happy to have me. Even before the dead started walking, he had changed though. He sometimes confiscated my phone and was controlling. Since all that outside stuff happened things have got worse with him. He does and takes what pleases him. I'm trapped here." Jen was emotionless as her thoughts rambled out of her mouth.

"Your friend might not be dead." Jen's words hung in the air.

"Jack, what do you mean?" Lucy questioned turning to look seriously at Jen.

"He's not all bad. I don't think he's a cold-blooded killer. I doubt the gang killed Jack; how would Mick have escaped unscathed? I think Mick thought he could look after you better so took action to make that happen."

"Are you saying he's locked me in here for my own protection? Without my say so. He's a hero?"

Lucy paused, feeling her blood boil, "Bollocks, not a killer! I saw him blow a man's head off." Lucy was getting frustrated and angrier at Mick and his perverse sense of chivalry and with Jen who seemed on one hand deeply scared, and on the other, besotted with the controlling man.

"If I were you, I would toe the line, do as he says and build up his trust. He doesn't usually lock me in, he knows I'd never run. Make him believe you are happy here and you'll be able to escape." Jen was an unusual woman, completely devoid of emotion as she spoke, and this made Lucy feel uncomfortable in her presence. She also noticed holes in her story, one minute she was trapped, the next she could leave freely. *Something is not quite right about Jen.*

Mick returned a couple of hours later in the evening light. Rain clouds had darkened the spring day and it reflected Lucy's mood, a pathetic fallacy, a pathetic situation. With Jen's words still echoing in her mind, Lucy decided to deceive Mick.

He was bringing in bags of items he'd looted while out on his errands. Whistling a tune while he worked, the man seemed happy. He unpacked tinned goods and from another sack pulled out a machete, an axe and a couple of hunting knives. Turning to Lucy who had approached him he said, "Not a bad trip, these'll come in handy."

Lucy looked down with worry at the array of barbaric weapons and said, "They are a good find. Look Mick can I ask a favour of you?"

"Anything pretty lady, Bulldog would walk on water for the fairer sex." He was almost theatrical in his speech.

"If it's okay with you, can I stay here for a week or two? I just need somewhere to get my head around everything that's happened and to help me grieve for my friend Jack, I know-"

Not letting her finish, Mick continued his infuriating trait of not listening, and said, "No need to explain darling. Stay as long as you want. Bulldog is standing here because of your friend Jack so I'm indebted to him to keep you safe."

"Thank you." Lucy paced with a burning rage inside her, Mick handed her a bag he'd taken from Jack's car. It was her belongings.

Lucy glanced up at Jen, who sat on the sofa, they both exchanged a knowing look.

Chapter 20 - Awakenings

The sound of Mick's car moving slowly through the roadblock woke Richie from his enforced slumber. He opened his eyes and immediately felt the blinding headache from two heavy blows to the jaw. Looking in the rear-view mirror, he saw that he was caked in his own blood. He tried to move, but his hands and feet were tied. Looking over to the passenger side he could see Naz in a similar condition, although he was still unconscious, but breathing.

Richie tried to loosen the ropes, but they weren't budging. He reached for the door handle with both arms tied together. Opening the door, he closed his eyes and rolled his weight out of the car. Landing painfully on his broken ribs, Richie let out a quiet curse. Lying on his side he surveyed his surroundings. He found what he was looking for under the car he'd been tied up in. The hunting knife he'd been holding when Lucy hit him had fallen under the car. Her words were still echoing in his aching brain and he longed to squeeze the breath out of the woman.

With a grunt and more shooting pains in his chest, Richie managed to get a finger to the knife and drag it to him. Picking the knife up with both hands he cut through the rope around his ankles. Placing the knife between his battered old Reebok trainers, he sat up and began to run the blade of the knife across the rope around his wrists. After a short while the rope gave way and with a rub of his wrists, Richie slowly rose to his feet. It had started to rain.

From inside the car, Naz stirred. Richie picked up his knife and took shelter in the car again. He looked over to Naz who was now taking stock of his situation. "Fucking hell Richie, I think I might have brain damage."

"My head hurts." Richie responded.

"You had brain damage already so you should be fine." Naz snapped with his usual contempt aimed at Richie.

Richie fumed inside and picked his knife up, looking at the blade. Naz gulped regretting his words and said, "Just banter Richie."

Lifting the knife, Richie smiled and turned his gaze to Naz. Bringing the knife down swiftly, he cut away the ropes around Naz's wrists and then instructed him to lift his legs so he could cut the ropes around his ankles.

Without a thank you, Naz got out of the car into the rain, walked around it and looked down at the body of Dale, "Have you found his gun?"

Richie shook his head. Naz continued, "I'm in charge now. We need to find the fuckers who ran away. Cunts. Come on brain dead, let's go." Naz couldn't help his vehemence towards Richie, it was habit.

Richie got out of the car once again and walking close behind Naz, he pulled Naz's arm and turned him round with some resistance.

Naz scorned, "Get the fuck off me Richie, no. Richie, no-"

Grabbing Naz by the throat and squeezing it, Richie pulled the knife back and forced it into Naz's chest and through his heart. Pain and shock showed on Naz's face as his eyes narrowed, staring on into the dark eyes of Richie, the last thing he'd ever see. Richie watched with interest as the life drifted from Naz's body, he fell limp, but was still held by Richie's powerful grip.

Dropping the body, Richie muttered to himself, "That's done. Good." He walked past the roadblock and followed in the direction he'd heard the car heading off in. He was every bit the blood thirsty monster as the dead.

-

The raindrops were big and full. They were cold too. Blood stained trails of water flowed onto the road from Jack's face. The refreshing precipitation was his saviour, waking him in time to see the feet of a shuffling dead person preparing to crouch and eat. His subconscious took control before he had a true understanding of what was happening, as the dead creature dropped its weight towards Jack's face.

He rolled over barely escaping the grey hands with broken and ragged fingernails. He crawled himself to a move, using his feet and hands to scramble further away until he managed to struggle to his feet. Breathing hard, the world span around him as he tried to steady himself and gain some understanding of the situation. He couldn't think straight or remember exactly what happened. *Lucy. Where was Lucy?*

The dead thing, slow to react to Jack's movements, landed teeth first, breaking its top left incisor on the road as it tried to fall upon Jack. It was slowly raising itself once again, three others were close, blocking the way back home. Jack had no weapon and no choice, he began to run, giving in to the adrenaline which was helping to ease his aching head.

Running through the roadblock, Jack saw the body of two gang members and his memory came flooding back to him. Bulldog had hoodwinked Jack and gone to get Lucy. *Holy shit, where are they? They could be anywhere.* Seeing Dale's body, Jack remembered about the gun, when Dale had been shot the gun had been thrown into the hedge at the side of the road, somehow he remembered seeing the gun fly through the air as if in slow motion as he had been mentally preparing to fight or die. With 10 metres now between the dead and him, Jack made a beeline for the approximate location of the gun. He saw it straight away, the luscious green of England's spring contrasted the gun metal, living against death. He picked it up and ran until the dead were no longer visible.

Jack needed a plan. He saw a large house to his right that was protected from the outside world by a high wall and gate, without hesitation or much thought he started to climb over the gate. He managed to grip the flat tops of the stone pillars that supported the gates and pulled himself up. From his elevated height on top of the pillars, Jack could see the dead still wandering in his direction. He threw the gun in a bush below and began to lower himself down. He did so painfully, scratching his chest against the pillar as he ungraciously lowered himself. Landing with a stutter, he looked at the house in-front of him, it was a giant house, it looked newly built with a mixture of timber and brick. He was secure in the front garden, gated off from the road, so he had a bit of time to figure out how to get into the mammoth house.

It occurred to Jack that somebody might be hiding away in here. It was a fortress really. He'd do the courteous thing, he'd use old-world rules and knock on the front door, not before holstering the gun in his belt under his clothes. He didn't want to look like a bandit, he was also worried about the gun, he'd never seen a gun, never mind hold one. He didn't know where the safety was or how to reload it, he was a novice and he didn't want to shoot himself in the backside accidently.

Ringing the doorbell, Jack sighed, it didn't ring as there hadn't been power for a couple of days. He knocked on the door loudly and waited. Nothing. He knocked again and went to look through the windows to see if there was any movement. He saw his own reflection in the window and gasped in horror, his jaw was swollen and his face was a mixture of mud and blood, he looked up into the pouring rain and began to scrub frantically with his hands, desperate to remove the other man's blood from his face. The horror made him more resolute to find a way into the house, get out of the rain and make a plan.

Jack knew that Mick must live close by, although with nothing other than that to go on, it could take months to track his house down. He had to believe that Lucy was well, but he needed a better plan than randomly searching around. His immediate plan was to get in the house in front of him and hope and pray for some inspiration.

Searching the rear of the house, there were no open windows or doors, Jack would have to smash his way in. The doors looked too sturdy to force so he opted to smash one of the large glass panels of the bi-fold doors that spanned the back of the house. He found an intricately carved stone plant pot that weighed a lot, with a struggle he lifted it and began swinging it back and forth to build momentum. Suddenly

Jack heard an engine. The momentum of the stone pot was too much, he let go and it shattered the glass and carried its journey into the open plan kitchen and dining area.

Jack turned around and headed for the front garden again, running as the engine sounded louder, as if driving down the road outside. He jumped onto a low wall that connected with the stone pillar holding the large wooden gates, and scrambled up the pillar, holding himself up looking out onto the road. It was Mick's blue pick-up truck. He'd come back. Jack watched.

The truck slowly moved past the house Jack was hiding in and passed the four dead that were still milling around. Jack watched as Mick turned the car around and parked facing the way he'd come, a few feet away from the dead. *Does he know I'm here?* Mick jumped out of the car wielding a fire axe with his rifle slung over his shoulder. He was quick on his feet for his age, Mick attacked the four dead with speed and relish. The first he sprinted on and powerfully put the axe vertically through the creature's skull. With a couple of severed arms and cracked skulls, Mick's fighting was impressive. As a coup de grâce, he performed a pirouette whilst swinging the axe and decapitated the last of the dead. The head flew a few feet and landed with an absurd hollow clonk on the road. Mick raised his arms in the air, still holding the axe, and let out a battle cry, "Bulldog is Mick the Warrior!"

Reality seemed to hit Mick as he lowered his arms and surveyed the surroundings, looking a little embarrassed at his outburst. Jack ducked as Mick peered over at the house. Peeking over the gate pillar again, Jack saw Mick walking over to the roadblock. He rummaged around the bodies and the rest of the scene. From Jack's distance he couldn't make out any details, but could see that he was looking for something. It occurred to Jack, whilst watching on, that Mick didn't go and check on his welfare, Jack had been knocked out just down the road and Mick had no intention of seeing whether Jack lived or died. Jack was angered by how little consideration or respect this man had for his life; he was a mere nuisance to Mick.

Mick eventually finished searching the site and did go to check on where he'd left Jack. The rain had stained the road red, the blood caking Jack's face when he had regained consciousness. The blood stain had satisfied Mick, he assumed Jack had been bitten and was now one less worry in his mission to keep his women alive. He went back to the roadblock and made one last search before heading off into the trees in the direction the three gang members had escaped. He disappeared from Jack's view.

The inspiration came to Jack in a flash. He was grateful for his slice of luck, or Mick's stupidity in coming back to the scene of the crime. In a perfect world, Jack would sneak into the back of the pickup and hide under some tarpaulin, but the back of the pickup was uncovered and empty. No hiding place. Jack decided he'd have to follow Mick and find out where he lived so he could rescue Lucy.

He went around the back of the house and stepped inside through the broken window. He didn't really know what to do next or what he was looking for. If he followed Mick in a car, he'd be spotted, after all there wasn't much traffic these days, but he needed to follow him somehow without being seen.

Rummaging through the kitchen drawers he took a large knife. He heard a noise from inside the house, he looked up and stood in the kitchen door was a little girl, staring at Jack. No more than seven years old, the girl was grubby, she held a teddy close to her as she asked, "Who are you?"

Jack was taken aback; he hadn't really taken the time to notice the mess around him in the kitchen, he put the knife he was holding back in the draw and said, "My name's Jack, sorry about your window. Where are your mummy and daddy?"

"Daddy left to get mummy and hasn't been back. Do you know my daddy?" The girl asked.

He knew that daddy or mummy wouldn't be coming back and that this girl was alone, he lied, "Yeah, I'm a friend of your daddy, what's your name?"

"My name is Chloe, I'm seven." She then started to cry.

Jack walked over and picked her up and cuddled her. She smelt terrible; she'd been living in her own filth for some time. This was a problem for Jack, he couldn't look after himself, how could this girl look after herself? He wondered whether she was his problem or if it really was a dog eat dog world, but he quickly put that thought to one side.

The girl's sobs died out, so he put her down. He asked, "Does daddy have a bike I could borrow. I need to go out, but I'll come back and check on you later today."

The girl pointed to a shed in the garden and asked, "Did they get in past the gate?"

It hadn't occurred to Jack that this girl might be aware of the zombie apocalypse, he responded, "No, no, there aren't any out there now. You're safe here. Stay here and I'll come back for you."

"You promise?" She asked peeking through the teddy she held covering her face.

"I promise." Jack didn't know if he was lying or not.

With promises made, Jack ran to the shed and found a mountain bike. He wheeled it round to the front of the house and thought about how to get the bike over the gate. He tried the gate handle and surprisingly it opened lightly. He cursed his own idiocy for not trying the gate in the first place and pulled the gate shut behind him. Peeking out of the drive, Jack looked left, he saw Mick's pickup and then looked past it, Mick wasn't coming back yet. Getting on the bike, Jack peddled hard and quickly came to a junction in the road, the road turned right to where Jack had agreed to meet Lucy. He didn't come across any of the dead, but couldn't shake the feeling of being watched. A car was conveniently parked on the corner of the junction that he could hide behind with the bike. Here he waited to see which way Mick went.

After 10 minutes hiding, Jack heard gun fire. Three sharp bangs at long intervals. They weren't that close, but sounded like they came from the direction where Mick had vanished into the trees. More time passed and Jack heard the now familiar engine. It was Mick.

The car turned right down the road; Jack had made the right call waiting at the junction. He waited for the car to pass and move into the distance before revealing himself and mounting the bike. Mick was travelling slowly, no more than 30 mph, but Jack had to peddle hard to keep the pickup in sight. Every corner that he turned he caught a glimpse of the pickup as it vanished around another corner. With thighs burning, Jack continued, he evaded a dead woman in leisurewear, her headphones still over her head, and continued. He got to the entrance to Ancoats Lane, where he was supposed to have met up with Lucy, but he'd lost sight of the pickup. He made a quick decision to head down Ancoats Lane, he was left-handed so quite often chose left when given a random choice.

Jack's luck was in again. After peddling around a chicane, he saw the pickup in the distance, Mick must have been half a mile or more in front, but the narrow lane was long and flat, so Jack could see the top of the pickup over the hedges. Standing on the pedals and pushing his body to the limit, Jack couldn't get enough speed to close the gap, but saw the brake lights flash on and thanked Allah, Buddha, Jesus and all other deities he could think of, the truck swung left into a lane and drove into a dip and vanished from sight. *Bingo!* Jack thought, he was onto something, he cycled to the small lane and proceeded down there with caution.

A cottage came into view and Jack stopped, jumped off the bike and threw it into the open field next to the track, the young crops were not tall enough to mask its presence. Creeping through trees and bushes, Jack stealthily made his way closer to the cottage to get a better look. He could see Mick who was unloading some large bags from the back of his pickup. Mick's mission into the woods must have borne fruit. Jack watched as Mick unlocked the door to the cottage and stepped inside, he left the door open and Jack could make out Lucy sat in the front room unhurt. He was beyond relieved, but he didn't really know what to do next. Drawing the gun from his belt, he looked at it, he was going through the familiar countdown, he was going to rush the house.

The front door shut, and Jack heard the rattle of a key as Mick locked the door behind him. Surveying the rest of the house, Jack could see bars covering the bottom windows. He couldn't storm the house now; one failed attempt and Mick would be aware of his presence and Jack already knew that Mick had a keen aim with his rifle. His hopes of a reunion with Lucy were dashed for now. Wrestling with his emotions, Jack had to leave the cottage and come back early in the morning, he needed Mick to open the door before he made his move. His moral conscience reminded him of Chloe, he had promised her that he'd return. He made mental pleads with any and all of the Gods to keep Lucy safe and out of Mick's clutches, not feeling happy with his decision to leave the woman who he'd grown so close to in the hands of a deranged lunatic.

Jack cycled back to Chloe with less gusto. He was tired, and he was down. The end of the world was less than a week old, but anarchy spread amongst the survivors like wildfire and Jack didn't like what he'd experienced.

He was going to help Chloe, for her, but more for himself. He needed her innocence to remind him that the world had some good left in it.

Chapter 21 - The Next Day

Chloe had been waiting in the kitchen for Jack to return. The temperature had dropped with the rain and it was cold in the room. The little girl wore a princess outfit, some Disney character that Jack didn't recognise, and shivered in the fading light. She was a very trusting child, and this worried Jack, he loved her innocence, but he was sure that this trait could get you killed out there in the wilderness.

That night he took care of the little girl. There were lots of bottles of water in the grand pantry and the gas hobs still worked so Jack made some pasta with tinned tomatoes, onions, and garlic. It wasn't the most ingenious of dishes, but Chloe gulped it down with relish. Jack looked on in astonishment at the amount of food the girl ate, it seemed to bend all logic. Inspecting the house, the bathroom was a mess, the natural order of bodily movements was stinking the top floor out from the toilet. Jack had seen some buckets outside that had filled with rainwater. He carefully poured one of the buckets down the toilet and cleared the mess. With the remaining water he filled up the sink, found some soap and called down to Chloe who was playing in the lounge.

She came bounding up the stairs and Jack asked her to get a spare change of clothes and for her to wash herself in the water he poured. Chloe didn't look happy at this and said, "It's cold."

"Look, you don't smell too great and you need to get those grubby clothes off. I'm going to bring a special lady to meet you tomorrow and want to make sure you look your best. Now wash and get changed and I'll read you a story" He said, not really knowing how to communicate with children anymore, he feared he was too direct? It worked, and she began to undress. Feeling awkward, Jack went downstairs and lit the fire, that was already made, using matches he found on the mantelpiece.

Chloe joined Jack in the living room, he had arranged cushions from the sofas into two makeshift beds and brought two duvets downstairs. They were bedding down in the sitting room. The little girl looked at the surroundings and her face showed delight, she said, "It's like a slumber party." She was carrying a copy of Roald Dahl's George's Marvellous Medicine, one of Jack's favourite books as a child.

Jack smiled at the girl and sat down on the remaining sofa with cushions on. Chloe jumped next to Jack and nuzzled in. She was looking up at Jack and said, "Mummy and daddy aren't coming back are they? They're monsters now aren't they?"

He didn't know what to say and wasn't ready for a question of such directness, stumbling for the right words, Jack knew the answer already, but instead said, "I don't know Chloe, anything is possible, they might have got stuck somewhere."

The answer didn't suffice and she continued, "Will you look after me now?"

"I will." He kissed her head and opened the book where a homemade bookmark kept the girl's place in the book safe. Looking at the homemade bookmark he imagined Chloe sitting with her parents having fun creating it, sadness filled him, and he wanted to cry.

Chloe fell asleep 15 minutes into the story. He placed her on the makeshift bed. Jack fell asleep shortly afterwards while sitting on the sofa thinking about Lucy, praying for her wellbeing.

-

Lucy's evening would have been quite entertaining under different conditions. If she were not mourning for Jack and a prisoner in a remote cottage with Bulldog and his brow beaten girlfriend. She had lost hope of Jack's survival and was melancholy. There were some mercies to being trapped in the cottage, it used a water tower, so they still had running water and by some miracle Mick had managed to keep the boiler running so Lucy could take a hot shower. Mick had also looted some expensive wine from his day's escapades and the three of them drank. In the beginning, he was charming and odd in equal measures, sensing Lucy's mood, Mick was putting on a show for her. He woke the baby frequently with the noise of his theatrical tales, each time Jen silently slunk out of the room to attend to the baby's needs.

The more Mick drank, the more animated he became. He was all over the lounge, pacing here and there, telling incoherent stories, swinging arms around wildly. The more he drank, the more he stared at Lucy. She began to feel claustrophobic in his intimidating presence. As the night wore on, Mick became more touchy-feely with Lucy, eventually taking a seat beside her on the sofa. He put his hand on her leg. Her whole body tensed at the touch as the hand just lay there. He began to say something when Jen stood up and grabbed Mick's hand and said, "Come on Mick, I've got a surprise you're going to really like. Plus, I think Lucy could do with some sleep, she's had a hell of a day." She winked at him.

With that, Mick rose to his feet with gusto, "Bulldog likes a surprise. Lead the way baby!" They both disappeared upstairs.

Lucy thought that Jen had sacrificed herself for her. Jen made it clear that Mick would have wanted Lucy more and more until his advances went past flirting to a very dark place. Lucy thought of Jen closing her eyes and sucking Mick's cock; keeping him satisfied and his hands off Lucy, but for how long?

"I'll go and get the bottle, you get undressed." Lucy heard Jen call as she came back downstairs. She moved past Lucy and picked up half a bottle of wine and turned to her, "You need to leave tomorrow; it's only a matter of time before he tries to sleep with you, he wants you pregnant."

Gasping, Lucy mouthed the word 'pregnant'. She was confused.

Jen said, "He wants to repopulate the world. He's father and we're all the mothers, all roads lead back to the daddy. Bulldog."

"I'm getting lonely." Mick's voice drifted down the stairs. Jen hurriedly went to join him.

That night Lucy stayed in the spare room waking frequently, her thoughts drifting from Danny, to Jack and back to her sorry situation. Every creak of the old cottage made her heart miss a beat as she expected the door handle to turn and for Mick to appear.

-

Jack woke as the sun was rising. Peeking out of the heavy and expensive curtains, he could see that it was shaping up to be a beautiful day. He guessed it was about 5am. Walking groggily into the kitchen, he checked the clock on the wall, it was 5:05am. It was time to put his plan to action. He'd slept fully dressed and ached from the sofa, stretching he thought that he needed to write a note to Chloe to let her know he was going to get Lucy and that they'd be back for her today, he wasn't sure a seven year old could read and tried to remember back to being seven but couldn't stretch his imagination back that far. *Surely she could.*

He rummaged through the pantry and found a loaf of bread that was still semi-fresh. Taking out four slices, he buttered the bread and added some strawberry jam. Leaving two slices on the table for Chloe with a miniature bottle of Tropicana he'd also found.

Eating two slices of jam on bread, Jack wrote a simple note:

Gone to get Lucy. We will be back <u>today</u>.

I've made you some breakfast, make sure you eat it and drink the orange juice. It is on the kitchen table. Also drink lots of water today.

See you later.

Jack xx

Surprised with how easy it was to fall back into the parental mind set after five years made Jack sad. The end of the world was like therapy for him, it had given him closure, he could

158

say goodbye to Amy, to Ruby and to the old world. The introduction of Chloe had thrown him and now he was in danger of wallowing and eventually apathy. Shutting down the negativity, he focused on the bread he was eating and looked at a blob of butter that was slowly making its way off the crust as gravity begged it to fall to the plate. Looking at the butter he just couldn't stop the feeling of despair, he wondered if he'd ever have butter again, or yoghurt or fresh ice-cold milk? He loved dairy produce and he hadn't printed out any instructions for how to make extra mature cheddar or banana choco-flake yoghurts. He was working himself into such a state, tears were forming.

"For fuck's sake Jack, pull yourself together, come on three-two-one let's go." He said to himself in an attempt to shake the trepidation about his rescue mission from his bones, which was also a major factor towards his current mood.

Taking the note back into the front room, Jack knelt by Chloe and placed it next to her. He was tempted to wake her, so she didn't worry when she got up, but she looked peaceful and cute; her bed warm red cheeks and blonde hair ruffled by a night of tossing and turning.

He retrieved the gun that he'd stored in a kitchen cupboard, at head height and out of Chloe's reach. Tooled up and ready, Jack wheeled the bike around the front, poked his head over the gate pillar to look out for any of the dead, and left through the gate when satisfied that the coast was clear.

Jack checked the gate was properly closed three times to ensure Chloe was safe and set off on the bike as quickly as possible. His body ached from the previous day, he had

159

scratches up his chest from needlessly scaling the gate pillar, back pain from being thrown into a car, his head still ached and he feared he had a cracked tooth from taking a rifle butt to the jaw. For the first time in Jack's life his hands were workmanlike, rough with callouses; they were transformed from the soft skin of his previous life sitting behind a desk all day.

Carrying on through the aches and pains, Jack reached the cottage in 15 minutes. He'd cycled past three of the dead, but left them behind so didn't worry about them creeping up on him whilst he undertook his stakeout. Taking extra care to hide the bike this time, Jack made for the bushes that he'd watched Mick from the previous day. Seeing that all was quiet, he crept to the cottage and waited around the corner of the wall adjacent to the front door.

It was too late to back out now, he was operating on pure fear and adrenaline, heart racing at a million beats per minute. It was two hours before Jack heard anything, the first signs of life came from the drainpipes as water flowed from the house down into an underground network of pipes. Jack had become complacent in the two hours of waiting, boredom taking over from the initial panic. The sound of flowing water was a wakeup call and he stood from his sitting position and held the gun purposefully in both of his hands like he'd seen on TV.

After another two hours of waiting, Jack had sat back down and listened intently. Noises were ever present in the house, plates being moved, muffled voices and other household noises echoed around. He kept his fingers crossed that Mick wasn't choosing today to be lazy and rest at home. Mick wasn't the type of man to sit around doing nothing and before long Jack heard the key in the lock. It was time for action and Jack waited with his back to the wall, gun held pointing up against his chest while he concentrated on his breathing, long deep breaths.

The door didn't open straight away, Jack heard Mick call something out to the house, then the key turned and the door opened. Without waiting Jack turned the corner with gun outstretched and placed it against the back of Mick's head.

Mick froze as Jack tried and failed to sound commanding, "Don't move."

Not one for following orders, Mick turned around to face Jack, the gun pointing at his forehead now. He smiled, "Jacky boy. How nice to see you. I see you found the gun, I wondered where it had gone."

The plan wasn't going to Jack's liking, he had expected Mick to do whatever he said, not this cockiness, "You left me to die out there.

"LUCY, it's Jack, come on, I've come to get you."

"Bulldog was testing you dear boy. I want to keep that wonderful woman safe and I wasn't overly impressed with you so had to take things into my own hands to keep my women safe." Mick spoke calmly still smiling at Jack.

"That's not your decision to make." Lucy's voice came from behind, it was a broken voice, wobbling through emotion.

"Lucy, are you okay, did he hurt you?" The anger was boiling up in Jack as he heard the pain in her voice.

"Relax Cowboy. I've been a perfect gentleman. Lucy, I think your man wants you, come on out here. I apologise Jack, I've underestimated you and Bulldog is feeling generous. I know you'll keep her safe, so I won't bother you anymore. You're obviously more equipped to survive then I thought. Good job son." Mick said, his words were patronising, but his face came across earnest.

A scream came from inside the house as Jen came downstairs to see Jack pointing the gun at Mick's head. She begged, "Please don't hurt my Mick. He's all we have, we need him."

"It's okay love, Jack's not going to do anything stupid, are you boy?" Mick said.

"Move away from the door and let Lucy out and then, you" nodding in Jen's direction, "throw her the front door key."

Mick moved away from the front door and Lucy stepped out into the late morning sunshine. The sun reflected off her red hair, her skin looked flawless, she was more beautiful than he'd remembered. Jen threw the keys to Lucy who caught them, she was looking at Jack, a solitary tear slowly traced down her cheek, she said softly, "I thought you were dead. Oh God, look at your face, what did he do to you?"

Butterflies fluttered in Jack's stomach as emotions tangled. The pleasure of seeing Lucy was tarnished with fear and panic as Jack was now operating without a real plan, just pure instinct. Seeing the Citroen in his peripheral vision, Jack asked Lucy, "Do you have the keys for the car?"

"No, Mick has them." She said surprising Jack by using Mick's name.

"Give me the keys to the car, now." He demanded of Mick.

Mick took the key from his trouser pocket and threw it to Lucy, "Luce (he'd never called her that before), please get in the car."

Turning to Mick he continued, "I should shoot you here and now. You're going to come back for us and I can't let you endanger Lucy again. I should do to you what you tried with me." Jack's grip on the gun tightened and for the first time he could see fear on Mick's face.

Jen came running out of the house and stood next to Mick and pleaded, "Please we need him, my baby needs him, don't hurt him. We'll die without him."

"Jack. No. It's not you." Lucy stood with the car door open looking at him with a look he'd never seen before.

"Look son. Bulldog is a man of his word. You've proved yourself to me. Just keep her safe and you'll have nothing to worry from me. In this new world, we don't need men, we need women. Just one man is enough, but I guess two is fine. You keep her safe and we're all good. I give you my word." Mick spoke with clarity and conviction and Jack, despite himself, believed him.

Taking no chances, Jack asked, "Does this place have a back door?"

"No, it's an odd cottage, one way in, one way out." Mick responded.

"Will you be able to get out if I lock you in?"

"Pain in the backside, but yes."

"Good, now you two get inside the house and stay by the window where I can see you. Move and I shoot. You come looking for us Mick and I will kill you. That is a promise. We'll be out of the area today, so you don't need to worry about us."

Mick nodded and then moved inside the house with Jen and stood at the lounge window. Jack could see them both looking out, Jen terrified, Mick unmoved. Lucy threw Jack the front door key and he quickly locked the door, leaving the key in the lock, and ran to the car. Lucy and Jack got in the car and sped out of the yard.

-

Jen watched on and thought to herself, *I got rid of her, he's not going to leave me now.* She was pleased with herself having deceived Lucy by spinning a web of lies about Mick and his likely rapist tendencies. Mick would never have raped any woman, he put them up on a pedestal. Upon seeing Lucy, Jen had worried that it was only a matter of time before Lucy became as attached to Mick as she was. Mick had often expressed the need to repopulate the human race and believed he could cope with numerous wives and kids to spread the gene pool enough to grow a clan of his own. Jen didn't have to kill Lucy now; she could just carry on living her life with her knight in overalls.

-

Jack and Lucy drove, she was turned on the seat looking at Jack, tears in her eyes as she took stock of the fact that he was very much still alive. Avoiding the dead on the road, now

164

five of them, Jack turned to Lucy and asked, "Did he hurt you?" Still not convinced.

"No Jack, honestly, he didn't touch me.

"I've never been so happy to see you. You are my hero."

The rescue mission was like one of Jack's dreams in his teenage years where he'd stop some group of aggressors at school and save everybody, including the girl. This was real though and he felt nauseous as reality started to hit him.

Lucy looked concerned for a minute and with a serious face asked Jack earnestly, "Were you going to kill Mick?"

"No, well, I didn't want to. I wanted him to be scared, to make sure he wouldn't come looking for us. I don't think I scared him though."

"Good. I didn't want to think of you like that." Moving on swiftly, she asked, "Where are we going, what's the plan?"

"I've found a place to crash tonight. We should go tomorrow morning and get some distance between this place; I think we both need a fresh start! I need to show you something first however."

Lucy didn't respond, she sunk back into the seat and held Jack's hand on the gear stick as they drove the short trip back to the house where Chloe waited.

-

Impressed with their temporary and secure home, Lucy smiled at Jack as he shut the gate behind him, "My, you've gone up in the world." The sparkle in her voice had returned.

"You haven't seen anything yet. You wait." Jack was regretting not telling Lucy about Chloe, but he'd gone this far, too late to change the surprise. He led her by the hand around the back of the house and in through the broken window.

"Hi Jack. You must be Lucy." Chloe said sat at the kitchen table amusing herself with some crayons and paper.

Lucy looked at Jack in wonderment, stuck for words. Regaining her composure, she turned and smiled at Chloe and said, "I am indeed Lucy, what's your name?"

Chapter 22 - Expected Departure

Chloe, Lucy, and Jack got acquainted during the day. Chloe was an open and affectionate girl and took to Lucy straightaway, taking her by the hand and showing Lucy her collection of dolls. Lucy took to Chloe straight away too; she humoured the little girl and was led around the house by the hand; showing interest and joy in everything that Chloe pointed out to her.

Jack had expected to have a serious conversation with Lucy at some point that day. He was expecting her to express fears about how they would look after a little girl and make it across the country. He expected some resistance to their initial plan with Chloe, the spanner in the works, complicating matters. No concerns materialised though, Lucy had of course had these thoughts, but kept them to herself. She knew why Jack was helping Chloe and she was doing the same. They couldn't abandon her. Lucy listened to the girl talk about her parents and seen the girl's frankness when she explained she didn't think they would be coming back and that they were probably monsters anyway. Chloe's childlike honesty left Lucy in no doubt that the girl was her responsibility now, she chose not to think about what this meant and the dangers it would create. For now, this little girl needed Lucy and Jack.

In the afternoon, Jack and Lucy sat Chloe down to talk to her about the planned trip to Yorkshire. The little girl knew where Yorkshire was, she was bright. She listened as Jack laid the maps, mercifully salvaged from the recovered Citroen, out on the table and went through the plan like Chloe was an adult. She listened and didn't ask questions. It turned out that it only took the mention of there being less monsters over in Yorkshire to convince the girl to come along, not that Jack nor Lucy would have left her behind.

Jack started to run through the rules of the trip. He needed to make sure that the girl had her eyes open to the dangers ahead: the dead and the living. Lucy was quick to stop him mid flow and told him that the two girls would have some girl time to talk about all this. Chloe was excited to have another girl in the house and smiled while clasping her hands together at the prospect.

Watching with a broad grin as Chloe led Lucy upstairs, Jack sat back and relaxed. He decided he'd enjoy his last night in the magnificent house with the two new women in his life. Life moved quickly before the end of civilisation, now it was careening at lightspeed.

-

Lucy and Chloe played dress up in the master bedroom, Chloe wore shoes too big for her and put on jewellery, the two of them laughed together as they had girly fun. Lucy sat down with Chloe and delicately explained the danger of the trip whilst they played and was struck with how much the girl knew, which made Lucy feel easier about the daunting trip, her confidence in Chloe grew when the girl said she would run from living and dead, trusting only Jack and Lucy. They meticulously packed a bag for Chloe and Lucy, Lucy having left her previous clothes in Mick's spare room. Chloe was demanding about what to take with her, insisting on bringing all her worldly possessions, but was told in no uncertain terms that she could only take what would fit in the bag. After much deliberation she settled on an array of clothes, not really suitable for the trip, but Lucy acquiesced to the decision after so much trouble getting her to decide the final shortlist.

Chloe, stood on a stool she'd painstakingly pushed across the room, picked out a black dress from the wardrobe and asked Lucy to put it on. Lucy didn't want to wear it, so said she'd put it on later, but the girl persisted saying, "Please, my mummy used to look so pretty in it. I'd really like to see you in it. You're pretty like mummy."

Knowing Chloe would never see her mum again, Lucy didn't have the heart to say no. She undressed to her mismatched underwear and inspected the dress, it was Prada, and this excited her, she knew the dress well having worked in retail, it was a Prada crêpe dress and retailed for over £1,000. She had owned some expensive dresses, but nothing quite this extravagant. Remembering happy times shopping, she decided to cherish the moment as it might be the last time she could afford the time for luxuries like this. Slipping the dress over her head, the material felt cold and wonderful against her skin. It was an amazing fit, like the dress was meant for her. She looked in the full-length mirror and did a twirl. She hated to admit it to herself, but she looked good, the dress was elegant, dropping at the front around the cleavage, hanging over both shoulders, the straps fell into an elegant arch across her back.

Chloe smiled and gave her thumbs up, "You look like a princess."

"Thank you, but not quite as beautiful as you." Lucy responded looking at Chloe with affection, who was wearing a mishmash of clashing colours that once belonged to the girl's mum and swamped her little body.

"JACK, JACK, JACK." Chloe began to call.

"No Chloe, please don't." Lucy was embarrassed and opened a wardrobe door and hid behind it. It was too late; Jack came running up the stairs, alarmed at Chloe's calls.

Running into the room Jack asked in an alarmed tone, "What's wrong Chloe?"

"Nothing! We were just playing dress up." Lucy answered still hiding herself behind the open door.

"Show him!" Chloe demanded.

Gingerly, Lucy closed the wardrobe door and stepped out. Jack stood there and was speechless, his mouth hanging open as he looked Lucy up and down. The dress complimented Lucy's frame, hugging her hips and cupping her breasts, her red hair flowed over one shoulder and the black contrasted her English Rose complexion to perfection.

The silence was all too much for Chloe, she demanded again, "So?"

Knocked out of his silence, Jack remembered a poem by Wordsworth that he'd learned off by heart as a kid to try and, fail to, impress a girl at school, he recalled the words of a verse and said them out loud,

"And now I see with eye serene
The very pulse of the machine;

A Being breathing thoughtful breath,
A Traveller between life and death;
The reason firm, the temperate will,
Endurance, foresight, strength, and skill;
A perfect Woman, nobly planned,
To warm, to comfort, and command;
And yet a Spirit still, and bright,
With something of angelic light."

Lucy blushed, but didn't take her eyes off Jack. They both stood there, acutely aware of each other. Chloe chirped up joyfully, "Kiss her, kiss her, kiss her!"

He didn't think about it, walking over to Lucy who didn't move, he put his hand to her face and delicately kissed her, her soft lips touched his and the tenderest of kisses flickered quickly between them.

The kiss ended and they stood transfixed with one another, Lucy let out an involuntary sigh and blushed, saying, "Right young lady, we better see about getting something to eat for us all."

-

It was pasta yet again that evening, Chloe once again eating greedily. They made a great team and spent a happy evening playing snakes and ladders, snap, and charades in candlelight. Chloe drifted off to sleep around 8pm in Lucy's embrace, Jack watched on wishing they could stay here, wishing the world was different. He got up and excused himself, he decided to freshen himself up with the bucket of water he'd left in the bathroom. When he got back to the lounge, Lucy had moved Chloe to the makeshift bed of cushions and was softly speaking to the girl to get her back to sleep. She then went to leave the room taking a candle with her and blowing the others out.

At the door Lucy turned to Jack and said, "We'll leave her to sleep, we need to talk about tomorrow.

"Can you give me five minutes to change for bed? I'll be in the master bedroom; we can talk there. You may as well bring that bottle of Champagne in the pantry with you; we should celebrate our reunion, I'd hate for that bottle to go to waste, it looks expensive." She winked at Jack and scampered quickly upstairs.

Jack watched Lucy go and smiled to himself, he said goodnight to Chloe in a whisper and shut the lounge door making sure the latch clicked so it couldn't be pushed open should anything wander in through the broken window in the kitchen. Getting the bottle of Champagne and two glasses, Jack waited at the kitchen table and watched the clock as the five minutes took an eternity to tick by. He couldn't bear being away from Lucy any more, even though they were in the same house, he wanted her close, he wanted to look at her, to feel her warmth and to keep her safe from the evils of the world. She had already attracted more criminally insane people than Jack had encountered in his 37 years of living. She was worth it and then some.

Finally, five minutes passed, he stood and hurried upstairs.

Opening the door slowly, Jack could see the light flicker as the draft caught the candle, he walked into the room and saw Lucy standing there in the dim light. She was wearing the Prada dress once more, Jack was mesmerised, the glasses in his hand rattled as he nearly dropped them to the floor, Lucy smiled and said, "I thought I'd give the dress one last outing, it seemed to have a positive effect on you last time. Now put the bottle and glasses down before you drop them and come here."

He put the glasses and bottle on a dressing table and walked towards Lucy. He felt as though he were in some period drama, the lady of the house was summoning the servant, he was in jeans and t-shirt whereas she stood there, barefooted in that black dress looking like the personification of elegance. Reaching her, he was no longer able to control his desire, instinct was becoming his ally after all the years of flight and subservience, he was taking control. He kissed her gently and then passions boiled over from them both, the sexual flirting and their first night together had lingered in both their minds. He pushed her up against the wardrobe and moved his hips against hers, she could feel him harden through the soft material of her dress. Kissing her neck, she nibbled on his ear and whispered, "I'm not wearing any knickers you know."

He looked at Lucy and smiled and let out a groan of ecstasy. She took his t-shirt off and he unbuttoned his jeans, sliding out of them eagerly, she pushed Jack back and he fell onto the bed, he was quick to take off his socks trying to be smooth, but failing. Edging back on the bed, Lucy followed him and straddled him, she leant over him, her hair brushing against his chest, the sweet smell of her body making him tingle. Gently, she kissed him and looked into his eyes, lowering her hips she was teasing him, he could feel how wet she was, but she wasn't giving over all too easily, she rotated her hips teasing him further, he pulled her hips down, but she wasn't giving in that easily, she was having fun with him, building anticipation. She continued to gaze into his eyes, a wicked smile over her face as she relished the control of the situation. Finally, she gave way to her own desires and lowered herself, he was inside her and they were moving rhythmically lost in each other's embrace. All of Jack's aches and pains evaporated as their union climaxed together quickly, but with satisfaction painted on their faces. Lucy collapsed onto Jack and they lay there sweating and breathing heavily. She raised her head and kissed Jack once again and said, "You're stuck with me now you know."

"You're stuck with me too." He replied smiling, wishing he had said something more poetic or witty.

-

Sitting up in bed together they talked, they had grown close and neither of them really knew if what they felt was real or the by-product of being thrown together in a global catastrophe, the question wasn't one that either wanted to answer or say out loud, this world was made for living in the present.

They made plans to leave early the following morning, most of Jack's stuff was already packed in the car, including his trusty hammer, they just needed to load Lucy and Chloe's bags and then do a sweep of the house to see if there was anything useful that they could take with them.

By 10pm the two of them were shattered, surviving was taking its toll on their stamina. With one last kiss they bid each other good night and slept naked, intertwined together carrying their closeness into sleep. They woke twice that night and sleepily made love, both embracing their sexual reawakening.

-

The next morning, the newly formed family packed up their belongings, scoured the house for useful items and began their journey.

Jack had suffered nightmares through the night, the shattered remains of the dream still haunted him as he made himself busy, he looked on and worried for Lucy and Chloe's welfare. He wasn't a psychic, they were just dreams.

Chapter 23 - Expedition

In their morning sweep of the house, Jack and Lucy found some useful items: a wood cutting axe, bottled water, a camping stove, and some more tinned food. The car was bursting from the seams and Jack wished he'd taken the time to take a neighbour's car, there was a four-wheel drive just up the road.

The planned route had changed since Lucy and Jack had drawn out their initial idea, they took steps to avoid Ancoats Lane, where Mick lived, and drove around it on the main road to join back up with their original plan at a later stage. The main roads were more dangerous, but it was a risk they were willing to take, the dead were not as unpredictable as a man who liked to refer to himself in the third person by his absurd nickname.

The plan for today was to navigate through country roads and make it to the hills, the Peak District, where they would find a place to rest the night away and set off again the following day. Jack was concerned with a couple of points in the plan, firstly, finding a place to stay that was safe, and secondly and most worryingly, he was concerned that the route would take them past densely populated areas. It was too late; they'd been through the map countless times and this was the best way. He had to swallow his fear and continue.

The numbers of the dead had increased noticeably, clusters of them loitered menacingly. The numbers could still be navigated, but if they continued to surge then it would cause issues.

Chloe sat in the back and covered her eyes every time the car passed a dead man or woman. Jack recalled a scene from the Walking dead he'd watched not that long ago, it featured a young girl who had become psychologically damaged and started to reason with the dead, she'd ended up killing her sister and had to be put down because of the danger she caused to the rest of the group. It was a chilling episode and one that Jack wished he'd not remembered at that precise moment. He glanced in the rear-view mirror and wondered what effect the rising of the dead would all have on the young innocent girl. She had lost her parents, probably, which would affect her immeasurably and he wasn't sure if she still had hope for them. In an attempt to help her through this trying situation and provide her with optimism of a reunion, he had left a note in Chloe's house addressed to her parents telling them where they were taking Chloe and that she was safe. Jack knew deep-down that this was a waste of time, but wanted to keep some hope alive in the girl, whether this tact was wise or honest, he didn't know.

Thoughts drifting from fiction to reality, Jack decided to attempt to ease some of the nervous tension that filled the car, "You know girls, it might surprise you to learn that I'm not just the debonair, sophisticated guy that you've come to know. I'm a bit of a geek at heart, I used to love zombie books and films. You're with an expert so you're in safe hands."

Lucy laughed; Chloe looked confused, Lucy responded mockingly, "Did you hear that Chloe? Jack thinks he's sophisticated. We both know you're a geek at heart, that's why we both like you, you're our comic book nerd."

"Shit…err sorry, I mean shoot." Jack said correcting himself in the presence of a youngster, Chloe giggled.

Lucy looked concerned, "What's wrong?"

"I can't believe I haven't thought of this. The radio, the car radio! We should be scanning the airwaves for news out there. I'm an idiot, the radio features in just about every story like this and I hadn't thought to check it out."

Flicking on the radio, Lucy smiled and said, "You've had your hands full. I think you can give yourself a break."

Shifting through the FM frequency the radio filled the car with static. Jack pressed buttons randomly and managed to finally change the frequency to AM and set it so Lucy could manually find anything out there. His eyes were shifting from road to radio in anticipation of news from others.

After carefully scanning the airwaves, Lucy found something. It was faint and crackly, but it was definitely a voice, frustratingly though, they couldn't get the signal strong enough to hear what the voice was saying. Lucy looked hopeful and said, "When we get higher, we can listen again, hopefully the signal will be stronger on the hills." Jack and Lucy smiled at each other, Chloe had stopped listening and was busying herself with two dolls in the backseat.

The journey was arduously slow, debris and abandoned cars littered the roads, the dead also proved troublesome as the Citroen developed dents and scratches making its way. Jack worried about the damage, not because it was his car, but because it needed to last the journey. He was also worried about fuel, he knew it was a stretch for it to last the entire trip, but he kept his worries to himself and concentrated on the task at hand.

The drive itself was causing a lot of anxiety for Jack. The end of civilisation was still very new to him and the visions of horror were all too frequent, blood stains, bodies, car crashes and the walking dead were around every corner and Jack's sensitive soul struggled with each sighting. While he was safely locked up at home, Jack had his eyes closed to the stark reality of the world. The short time he'd been out in the wild, he'd nearly died twice, and he'd been running on adrenaline, but now with time to reflect behind the wheel of the car, the damning truth of his existence began to nag at him and fill his gut with doubt. Doubt about everything, the trip to Yorkshire, their chances of survival and his own nerve to make it in a lawless world filled with flesh eating corpses. He glanced at Lucy and then in the rear-view mirror to Chloe, it didn't help his fear. A girl and a woman he'd just met, both he'd developed a strong bond with, he felt he'd die for them, but still he reasoned with himself that he didn't know either of them. It was a ludicrous situation, but then again, he thought about the logic behind the dead coming back to life, everything was ridiculous. *Am I going to wake up soon?*

"You okay Jack?" Lucy could see the anxiety etched on Jack's face.

"I'm thinking too much." Jack said without any other explanation.

Lucy smiled sympathetically and seemed to understand. She had been staring out of the window looking out for danger. Her mind was set, alert and determined. Lucy was strong and she was ready for a fight, she looked at both Jack and Chloe and knew that it was her job to keep them together and keep them safe at any cost. Lucy had never bought into the male chivalry idea and felt every bit as responsible for the lives of Jack and Chloe and would not hesitate putting her body on the line for those that she cared about. Worries and macabre thoughts filled her, but she wouldn't let them control her, to Lucy, the mission to travel the 300 miles would be a success, they would make it together unscathed.

-

The first troublesome part of their journey came as they reached Alderly Edge; it was a small affluent town known for opulence and extravagance. Footballers lived in the area along with successful businesspeople who lived in the large mansions and drank in champagne bars. Jack had hated the place before civilisation broke down due to the fact that it had no diversity, it was just a place for people to gather and outdo each other with their expensive trinkets: cars, jewellery, designer labels and Botox, it was hell on earth as far as he was concerned. He liked it even less as they came to cross the main road to see it blocked by a pile up of expensive cars. The dead were in abundance too, milling around or just stood motionless, there were at least 100. As the car approached, heads turned in their direction.

Seeing the road blocked, Lucy and Jack looked at each other, trying to keep their worries silent to avoid Chloe noticing. Jack turned the car around and drove to a clearing they'd passed half a mile up the road.

In hushed tones, Lucy and Jack began to formulate a plan to get across the road that blocked their route. It had taken nearly 45 minutes to drive four miles; a different route could prove just as troublesome and would take them to more densely populated areas. They had to get through the blocked road.

Jack said, "We need to draw the dead away and then move a couple of the cars so we can pass, just like we did earlier, but without -" He hesitated, not wanting to recall the surreal events of the past couple of days, "Well you know."

"Did you see the cars though, they're wrecked, and we won't be able to push them." Lucy responded, her eyes looking up as though deep in thought.

Not knowing what to do, Jack sat there in silence. Chloe was speaking in the back seat, but her words were lost as the two adults considered the options available. A bang on the back window brought them around. One of the dead was pressed up against the rear window, its mouth and mutilated face smearing up against the glass. Jack accelerated and left the dead creature falling to its face as the car catapulted away. Driving without thought, Jack turned left into a road and sped down a narrow street.

Lucy shouted, "Jack, stop!"

The car skidded to a stop. Lucy turned her head around and pointed, "Look, that Honda over there. It's abandoned, the door is open, we could use it to push the cars blocking the road out of the way."

"What about the dead?" Jack said.

"Monsters!" Chloe screamed.

"Don't worry about them, you're safe with us Chloe." Lucy said with kindness, but uncertainty.

Now hushing her voice and turning to Jack, Lucy continued, "I'll draw them away, when the coast is clear, take that car and clear the road."

Jack sat in silence letting Lucy's words sink into some sort of comprehension, finally he said, "I can't let you do that. It's too risky."

With annoyance painted on her face, the second time Jack has seen that look, Lucy responded sharply, "Do you have a better idea? I'm quick and I can run forever if needed. Plus, you're bent out of shape due to the past couple of day's excursions. I'm not asking, this is what's going to happen." She softened a little and continued, "I know you're worried about me, but we don't have a choice, I have to do this, and you have to push the cars out of the way.

"Look, this is the most plausible plan." Lucy hushed her voice further, "You need to keep Chloe with you, she's more important.

"First of all, we need to check that Honda to see if we can get it going. If we can, we'll all drive it closer to the blocked road, leaving your car here, which we'll come back for later, I'll then create a distraction and get those beasts to follow me. Once you've managed to move the cars, drive back, pick up the Citroen and head to the layby we passed up the road, I'll meet you there."

She paused still thinking about the plan she was cooking up on the fly, and then said as an afterthought, "I'll be careful, I can escape over walls, so they won't be able to get me."

Jack looked crestfallen, his male pride hurt, but he knew she was right, and her tone told him not to argue. He nodded and felt like a coward.

"Good, now Chloe, did you understand what I said? We're going to get in the other car, you need to do exactly what Jack tells you to do. I'll be back soon to meet you both." Lucy said, firmly taking control of the situation.

The little girl gripped one of her dolls and didn't say anything. Being out of the house had turned her into a mute, but she didn't argue or cause a fuss.

"Before we set off, Jack and I need to check that car over there. We'll just be outside, but we need you to stay in the car and out of sight while we see if it still works." Lucy continued her instructions.

"Stay here, out of sight." Chloe repeated with a worried smile.

"Good. Come on Jack, let's make this quick." Lucy got out of the car with her bat and shut the door quietly behind her. Jack was quick to follow, turning around to Chloe before he got out, smiling at her, and affectionately ruffling her hair.

The two of them walked over to the car, one of the dead had seen them at the end of the road and was making its way towards them. They both spotted it, but it was a distance away, so they had time to check the car. It was a Honda CR-V, the door was open, and the keys were in the ignition, the owner must have left it in a hurry. Jack got in the driver side door and tried to turn the car over, but nothing, no lights on the dashboard, the battery had died over time, the internal light draining the power.

"The battery's dead." Jack said.

"We can push start it. Do you know how?" Lucy asked.

"I think so, I did it once with friends when we were younger, we need to get moving though that thing is getting closer." Jack said looking in the direction of the creature swaying its way towards them.

Without a word, Lucy jogged towards the dead being.

Half-heartedly, Jack shouted in a hushed voice, "Luc-" but stopped himself as she carried on anyway. He looked on with apprehension as she approached the dead man. It was now groaning with arms outstretched, it looked relatively fresh and normal, with no visible bite marks. Lucy skated around it with grace and managed to get behind it, with a swing of the bat she hit it hard on the head and knocked it down. It continued to move on the ground as Lucy once again brought the bat up and swung with all her might. Jack heard the crunch of the skull and saw the body fall limply to the ground.

Lucy jogged back to Jack and told him that she would push and to get in the car. He was feeling a little emasculated, but Lucy's mental strength was something he secretly liked and cherished, he felt safe with her, but desperately wanted it to be the other way around. Jack obeyed her orders and got in the car, racking his brain to remember how to push start the car. It came to him: turn the ignition to on, put it in second, clutch down and then when moving, release the clutch and press the accelerator.

Pushing the car was made easier by the slight decline of the street and Lucy soon had the car moving at jogging pace, Jack released the clutch and pressed the accelerator, with a spurt the car sounded into life. He breathed a sigh of relief as the fear of letting Lucy down and not being able to get the car started vanished. He brought the car to a stop, being extra careful to take it out of gear to avoid stalling, Lucy got in and they made their way back to the Citroen.

As they reached the car, Chloe clambered out of it and came running up to Lucy and gave her a big hug. She looked at Lucy in awe, "I saw you kill the monster." The girl said whilst burying her head into Lucy's chest.

Lucy picked Chloe up and told her to sit in the front and stay with Jack until they all met up again. Lucy got into the back of the Honda looking pensive. Jack reached around from the driver seat and handed her the spare key to the Citroen and the gun, "Take the gun, fire it when you're at a safe distance from the crowd, to lead them away. I also brought the spare key for the car, if you end up here or need to get to the car, take it and meet us at the layby, if the car's gone when I get back, I'll know where to find you."

They drove the short distance back towards the blocked intersection, as close as they could get to let Lucy out of the car and draw the dead away. The dead had scattered a little and some had made their way down the road towards the car, having been lured by their initial arrival. Nervous energy filled the car, every part of Jack wanted to change Lucy's mind and come up with a different plan, but he stayed silent, unable to think of anything better.

"Here will do." Lucy said, she leant over the front seats and kissed both Chloe and Jack on the cheek and opened the door.

"Please be careful." Jack said, tears involuntarily forming in his eyes.

"I'll be with you again in no time. Get us through those cars." Lucy said, and with that she shut the door behind her and weaved in and out of the dead that had broken away from the main clump by the crushed cars. Jack reversed the car around a corner and hid out of sight so that Lucy could do her part.

Lucy ran hard. She had her trusty bat and had already caught one of the dead around the side of the head as she made her way to the blocked road. When she got past the first cars, she began to shout, "You miserable lot, come and get me. Fresh meat."

Heads turned, bodies scrambled, and the dead started to gather en masse, heading in Lucy's direction. At the crossroads, she had decided to turn right up the main road and draw them away and out of sight from the blocked road that Jack was to clear. She wanted to run with all her might, but she knew she had to be steady and keep within spitting distance of the pack, to ensure they carried on their hungry pursuit. First, she had to navigate the entrenched area, full of the dead, all gathering into a cluster to sink their teeth into her. Some of the dead had been rotting in the spring sunshine and the air smelt putrid and she wanted to vomit. It made breathing hard.

The dead were in greater numbers than she'd anticipated. The 100 or so that they'd seen near the crumpled wreckage of the intersection were joined by many more along the main road. Climbing over a car bonnet, she was surrounded and began to panic, the dead were closing in on her and getting too close. One of them grabbed her arm and pulled her sideways and off balance, her momentum pushed her into the waiting arms of a giant man wearing a tattered suit. Lucy managed to pull her bat up, and with the butt, pushed the reeking face backwards, but more were on her, she had no escape.

Lucy wasn't prepared to die just yet, she ducked and then dived and rolled under a four-wheel drive car. She panted, thinking what the hell to do next when she saw the feet and legs of the dead gather around the car she was under. One by one they crouched, fell, and crumpled to the ground all sensing that their feast had arrived. Hands clawed at her clothes and she felt like she was going to be sick. Pushing hands and snarling faces away with her bat, she clambered flat on her front to the back of the four-wheel drive and came out ahead of the pack. Carrying on moving, getting to her feet as she crawled, Lucy saw that she was out of the main pack and had only a few of the dead in front of her. Looking back, she saw just how many had gathered behind her. Banging her bat against a car to get the horde's attention, Lucy began to speed walk up the road as the hungry crowd gave chase.

Half a mile up the road, Lucy came to a small cul-de-sac called White Barn Road, she slowed her pace and shouted to the crowd who were about 50 meters away from her. Turning the corner, she walked down the road and waited for the first of the dead to follow her. Like an obedient group of puppies, they started pouring into the little road. Lucy took the gun out of her jacket pocket and pointed it into the air, she hesitated and then brought it down and aimed at the nearest one's head. Without hesitating she gently squeezed the trigger letting the gun fulfil its destiny. An almighty bang filled the air, making Lucy's ears ring, she had stood firm and resisted the kick back and watched as the bullet struck its victim to the left of its forehead and continue its journey into the ensuing mob.

-

Jack heard the distant gun fire and put the car into first gear and drove to the blocked road. The dead were gone, and the scene didn't look half as bad as he'd remembered. Surveying the area, he could clearly see the path they needed to take and that he'd have to push two cars out of the way. They weren't up against each other, it was two separate crashes, one was Jack's side of the road, the other was the opposite side. He drove slowly up to the first car and pushed the front end up to the rear half of the crumbled wreck. His idea was to push it from an angle, turn the wreck around and then push it from the front where it should be easier to move. Chloe had moved herself into the footwell of the car at Jack's request and remained silent, shutting her eyes out of fear.

The two cars were moved relatively easily, and Jack breathed a sigh of relief as he saw a clear a route through the once blocked crossroads. The whole operation was noisy and more of the dead were wandering over sensing an opportunity to ease their never-ending hunger. Happy with his part of the plan, Jack slowly reversed the car through the roadblock, turned around and headed back in the direction they'd come to get to their car and back to the meeting place.

Trepidation filled Jack's entire body and he thought of nothing but Lucy, even Chloe's questions faded into background noise as he concentrated on his worries. The gun shot had eased his fears, but it sounded so far away, and the dead seemed to be coming out of the shadows in increasing numbers. They'd been on the road for a couple of hours now and they'd only made four miles progress. Worry was overwhelming Jack.

The road where they'd left the Citroen was no longer deserted, three of the dead roamed menacingly and Jack was concerned about transferring between the cars, particularly Chloe who seemed to freeze upon seeing any of the monsters that terrified her. He lured the dead away by driving slowly up the road to ensure they could swap cars without drama.

Having bought some time, Jack parked the car next to the Citroen, which was still there, meaning Lucy hadn't made it back before them. He instructed Chloe to jump straight into the passenger side. Jack turned the Honda off and left the key in the ignition, should Lucy need it, hoping it would have enough juice in the battery to start a second time. He joined Chloe in the Citroen and set off for the meeting place.

Arriving at the meeting point, Jack couldn't see Lucy, he slowed the car and pulled into the layby, from behind the hedge, Lucy appeared looking traumatised. Jack seeing the look of despair on her face felt his spirits sink to new depths.

Chapter 24 - Fake News

The survival rate at the beginning of the zombie outbreak was greater than many experts feared. The popularity of zombie fiction, be it television programmes, books or comics meant that a good percentage of the western world were familiar with the potential outcome of the dawn of the dead.

Huge population shifts were evident in the United States of America. Those who were lucky enough to escape the sprawling cities travelled by road, rail and even on foot to the countryside. A population shift took place similar to that of the first settlers in the once great nation. Disputes over land prevailed and many lives were lost over infighting between families and clans that worked selfishly rather than together. Those who were left in the major cities were to play a waiting game from inside their homes only to be let down by their Government who took the extreme measure of bombing large sections of cities in order to control and reduce the numbers of dead. This tactic was short-sighted and detrimental to those who had fought to survive. Many of the armed services failed to deliver their payloads out of guilt, but the steady supply of dutiful soldiers meant that the living didn't have to wait long for the bombing to start.

Those who still survived in the cities after the bombing ceased were stranded, roads were blocked and the chances of escape were minimal, meaning they would have to adapt quickly to a life of scavenging or perish from thirst or hunger.

The people who made their way to the countryside were faced with similar problems to the towns and cities they left. Huge populations were gathering and with frequent infection, those who made their way from cities faced everyday outbreaks. With less secure accommodation, sleeping in makeshift shelters, cars, and tents, it was easier for the dead to attack in the darkness of night. Humanity spread like locusts, eating their way through the country to find a place to stay, but it was a move that lacked any thought of their long-term future. Many continued their journeys to keep out of reach of desperate people ready to fight for whatever they could steal in order to keep their loved ones safe.

The common thought throughout most of the western world was based on misinformation. The UK had been told to stay indoors and stay safe until the infection died down and order restored to some sort of normality. Normality of course is relative, normality as people knew it, no longer existed. As food and water diminished, people started to panic and began to make a late dash in search of safety. Fear gripped those who were left to fend for themselves in the world of rotting corpses and the walking dead, it was natural to fear the dead, but there was also huge concern for disease spread by the sheer number of bodies that were decaying. It was a misconception that was in fact not true. The World Health Organisation had issued statements that fell on deaf ears. Bodies dying from trauma did not pose a threat to spreading disease, but as the air began to fill with the foul stench of death, people panicked and began their desperate getaway from the cities and towns that they had once called home.

It didn't take long for people to start making their moves. On average it was approximately seven days after the outbreak that people began to flee their homes and attempt half thought through plans to get to islands, hills, and the countryside to seek a new life and a better chance of survival.

The movement of people caused the second biggest fatality rate, almost as much as the initial outbreak. Less than ten percent of those trying to break out of the cities made it out alive. Most of those that did make it out were on their own and fending for themselves. Many of those who died were in groups of friends or family; looking out for each other slowed them down and forced them to take more risks which ultimately got them killed. The exodus also added many more walking corpses to the already swelling numbers, and those cities that had been barricaded shut by the army to stop the flow of dead escaping, were being opened up, letting a steady stream out into the unknown.

Unfortunately for those who were still living, the fear of disease sweeping city streets forced many into the hands of the dead. With no Internet or ways to locate information of use, hearsay and misinformation were equally as responsible for many deaths as the infection itself. Very few had access to useful information, had they stayed put and allowed the great hordes of dead to disburse, the chances of survival would have been far greater. The lack of knowledge about the spread of disease wasn't helped by outbreaks of gastroenteritis and food poisoning from eating out of date and unrefrigerated food. Fear and panic about disease intensified and ultimately made people leave their shelters.

Disease did rear its head in parts of the UK, and this was nothing to do with cadavers. Poor sanitation and not having anywhere to properly dispose of human waste saw a sharp increase of many infectious diseases including cholera and typhoid, but these cases were infrequent and weren't spread throughout the living due to the living rarely coming in to contact with each other. The spread of diseases, or lack of, was aided by the fact that those who contracted them were weak from malnutrition and didn't have access to medical support so often perished alone.

The UK Government who were holed up with power, facilities and enough food and water to keep them operating for years were trying their best to communicate via radio transmissions, but this was a one-way communication link with no feedback into them. Their main goal was to keep as many people safe as possible by keeping them inside, it was an oversight not to warn people that dead bodies were not going to spread diseases and that the major issue facing the population was hygiene. Having done a good job keeping survivor numbers up in the first weeks of the outbreak, the Government failed with the finer details, which might have stopped people from going insane, locked up with nothing but worry. This lack of information had inadvertently undone their early endeavours. Just how much the survivors would have listened is hearsay, but a little information might have gone a long way.

Chapter 25 - Slow Progress

Jack jumped out of the car and rushed to Lucy's side, she was upset, and he was petrified, he said in a rushed mumble, "Are you bitten?"

"No, but I think I've killed them." She said looking destitute.

"Who?" Jack questioned.

"I drew the dead down a cul-de-sac and did as we planned and fired the gun. One of the houses down there had a family waiting inside." Lucy shook her head.

"A man came out and called out for me to get in, he was fighting the dead to help me. I told him to go in, but he wanted to help me. They overpowered him and they got him. He left the door open and I couldn't get across the sea of bodies.

"They got in the house.

"There was nothing I could do."

Lucy struggled with the words and was visibly shaken, she of course had no idea what would happen and couldn't control the actions of others, but she was acutely aware that she had drawn the dead down the little road and straight into the family who had been safe until she turned up.

Jack held Lucy as she sobbed, guilt eating her, like the dead had eaten the man who'd attempted to rescue her. She had shot as many of the dead as possible, but with only three bullets it was in vain. She had waited and tried to help, but the dead were everywhere, and she had no other choice other than to escape over a fence and circle back round to the meeting point.

A low moan from the road brought Jack and Lucy back to their senses, seeing it was only a few feet away, they both hurriedly got in the car and set off, she picked Chloe up and sat the girl on her knee, giving her a cuddle. The sensitive and intuitive child hugged Lucy, sensing her emotions as Jack drove away.

"Did you clear the road?" Lucy asked, muffled through Chloe's hair.

"We did, yes." Jack said, but he looked worried.

"It's worse than we thought isn't it?" Lucy was thinking the same as Jack.

Jack simply nodded his head as he concentrated on the road, his face grave as the growing numbers of soulless creatures sauntering the streets ate away any confidence he had.

Chloe crawled into the back; she had been subdued ever since they began their journey. All the little girl wanted to do was hide and pretend everything was a dream, so she lost herself in her dolls and stared down to the safety of her lap, playing make believe with two plastic figures with normal jobs, normal names and normal lives.

Lucy retrieved the map that was lodged in the compartment in the door and began to study it while Jack approached the now unblocked roads. Taking her eyes off the map and still lost in culpability, she surveyed the road and saw that it was passable.

The car moved through the narrow path and pushed past a couple of the dead still ambling around, they banged on the car windows as it passed, making Chloe gasp and duck in the back. Smears of grease and filth lined the windows from unwashed dead hands. They made it through the intersection and Jack drove up the hill that exited the town, lining the road were large houses of the rich, hidden behind tall walls and gates, they would have been perfect places to lie low, but they were on a mission and stopping now was not on the agenda. As they left Alderly Edge, they also left the dead behind, at the top of the long hill, the rows of large houses ended, and the countryside sprung out. They all separately and independently let out sighs of relief as the luscious green of spring mixed with blooming flowers changed the atmosphere in the car.

A short distance down the road, Jack pulled into a car park that was usually packed full of people who visited to walk in the countryside and visit, the Edge, which was a rocky cliff overlooking the town they'd just past. Today it was abandoned by both living and dead, Jack had a theory that the long and sharp hill acted as a deterrent to the dead. It seemed to him that the dead opted for the path of least resistance, he didn't know if his theory held any weight behind it, but to Jack, his logic seemed like something to remember and gave him hope for heading to the hills of the Peak District.

"Lucy, you did well, you couldn't have known what would happen, I would have done exactly the same and I was part of the plan too so I'm as culpable as you are. We need to stick together and keep each other safe, it's the world we live in and there are things we cannot control." Jack was attempting to shake Lucy out of the stupor that she'd fallen into since returning to the car. He was annoyed with himself at being so patronising and wondered how he would react had someone spoken to him so callously after accidently causing the death of an innocent man, and maybe his family as well.

Lucy did want to react to Jack's words, but not in annoyance. She knew he was trying to share the responsibility and remind her that they both had Chloe to keep safe. It didn't help the empty feeling and the helplessness of being unable to do anything, it was exactly the same as with George, she had no answers and even if she did, they wouldn't provide any satisfaction. Lucy had to do what she had been doing for the past year, carry on regardless.

Lucy gave a half-hearted smile. Jack was concerned about her, the spark had vanished and she was no longer certain and in command which worried him, not only for her mental welfare, but also in his ability to make the right choices, considering his track record of nearly getting himself killed.

"I've got to pee. Do you girls need the loo?" Jack enquired.

"I do." Chloe chirped up and the sound of her voice relieved some of the tension that had been mounting in the car.

"Okay, maybe we should have some lunch too, it's nice on the Edge and it looks quiet, so perhaps we should take a breather." Jack said.

Getting out of the car, Jack packed his rucksack with the tinned meat sandwiches he'd made earlier that morning and they headed off into the woods. Lucy took Chloe behind some bushes to relieve themselves and Jack found a tree and alertly did his business.

The three of them walked cautiously to the Edge, Jack and Lucy were both silently wondering if it was a good idea, but they wanted to be out of the cramped car and were eager to enjoy the vista and attempt to think of nothing.

The Edge was deserted, they approached the large stone surface that looked over miles and miles of Cheshire countryside, ice age glaciers had forged large planes eons ago and Jack mulled over his limited knowledge of the ice age and thought that if life could continue after such upheaval then it could again. The views of the green fields and the distant hills on the horizon filled him with hope and he looked at Chloe and Lucy as they both seemed lost in the view. Climbing down rocks, they settled on the edge of a large flat stone, dangling their legs over the side, ravenously eating sandwiches, quenching their thirst by sharing a large bottle of water.

"This was a good idea." Lucy said reaching over to squeeze Jack's hand, Chloe was smiling and enjoying swinging her legs.

"I came here with Mummy and Daddy and played hide and seek with Daddy up there." Chloe said, still smiling.

Lucy put her arm around Chloe and gave her a squeeze and kissed her on the head. They were like a little family even though they'd all been together for no more than 24 hours.

It was about 2pm and they'd been on the road for a few hours and had only managed about five miles, but they were making progress, even though it was slow going.

Getting up to go; a rustling of leaves and the sound of breaking twigs made Jack and Lucy freeze as Chloe continued unaware. At the top of the rocks, that the trio had clambered down, a large man appeared, he was dead. He spotted Chloe first and his phlegmy groan stopped her in her tracks, he lunged forwards and tumbled down the rocks, she panicked and ran in the opposite direction, heading for the overhanging rocks that they'd dangled their legs from. Jack managed to wrap his arm around Chloe just in time before she plunged in her frenzied state to her death.

The creature had fallen 20 feet and landed on its feet, but the fall had broken its legs making Jack wince as the bones shattered and the legs buckled and snapped. The dead man continued to crawl forwards using its arms.

Lucy picked up Chloe from Jack's grasp and they climbed up a nearby rock out of reach of the monster. She set the girl down on the rock and crouched down to face her, "Chloe, you can't just run like that, you nearly fell. These monsters are slow and stupid, and you need to be clever to avoid them.

"That one down there just fell because it wanted to get to us. They can't run and they can't climb so we can easily get away from them if we're careful and don't panic.

"I know they scare you and that's okay because they scare me and Jack, but we just can't run at the sight of them, we need to use our brains and be careful. Do you understand?"

Chloe nodded slowly, she was crying quietly, but she turned to look at the dead man who was now at the bottom of the rock clawing helplessly at the stone breaking its fingers nails.

"Does it feel anything? It looks sad." Chloe said in broken whimpers.

Jack answered, "I don't think so, I think it's almost like a robot just doing one job, it doesn't know anything. It isn't a person anymore."

"I know it's not a person, you can tell from their eyes." Chloe said looking earnestly at him.

"If we see more of them, we just need to leave quickly. Climbing over walls will help too. You just can't run without a plan; you need to be careful and make your way around them safely. We'd like to keep you away from the monsters, but you also need to be aware that they are out here, so you always have to be alert." Jack said trying to make her understand that it wasn't safe, but it wasn't hopeless. He had no idea if she understood, but he felt like it was necessary for Chloe to see the stark reality of the dead.

"Come on, she's seen enough and it's time we got going again." Lucy said while she climbed up the rock and reached around for Chloe's hand, pulling her up. They made their way through the trees and back to the car without seeing any more of the dead and set off on their journey once again.

-

Progress was still painfully slow, impassable roads and, to Jack's embarrassment and annoyance, going around in circles meant that they'd travelled less than 10 miles in seven hours.

"I think we should find a place to stay for the night and continue early tomorrow." Jack conceded.

"I think it's probably for the best, who knows how long it'll take to get to the hills and we're short on time today." Lucy agreed, sensing the despondency in Jack's voice.

They were still in an affluent area with large houses sporadically lining the leafy and elegant road, it was quiet and would have been a place for the wealthy to retire and enjoy their success surrounded by their peers. Jack pictured men going to play golf and women getting pedicures and manicures to fill the void of not having to waste their lives working for the man in meaningless jobs, perhaps his mind was still stuck in the world that it was, but a little bit of envy still lingered in the back of his mind.

"That one is massive!" Chloe screamed excitedly from the back of the car, Lucy and Jack were stirred from their own musings and looked to their left and couldn't argue, the house that Chloe had spotted was impressive, the garage was as big as Jack's house; the mansion was three stories, and to make it even better, surrounded by high walls, it looked perfect.

"Well spotted Chloe, it looks like you've found us our accommodation this evening." Jack said smiling at the girl who grinned back looking pleased with herself. The run-in with the dead man at their picnic area had an abnormal effect on her, she was more relaxed and had been a lot more vocal since.

Pulling up to the tall dominating gate, Jack got out of the car and tried to open it. It wouldn't budge, going back to the car he asked Lucy to get in the driver seat and wait for him to return, he wanted to ensure the coast was clear and there was a way into the fortress looking house. He instructed Lucy to drive away should any of the dead approach and to come back when the coast was clear.

The car was idling away with Lucy and Chloe sat waiting, Jack jumped up on the wall and over to the other side. It was clear and the house looked even more impressive the closer he got, it seemed more like a hotel than a home. Jack turned to check the gate, it was automated and looked like it slid open, he found the mechanism and saw that there was a manual override, but this needed a key to function.

Looking around the outside of the house there were no signs of life, Jack walked up to the front door and knocked. He put his ear to the door and listened, but the door was thick, and he couldn't hear anything. Knocking again, he waited, but there was still nothing. Learning from his previous scramble over the gate of Chloe's house, without first checking to see if it was open, he turned the door handle and, to his surprise, it was unlocked. A vast expanse of a hallway greeted him. A huge staircase dominated the far end of the hall, with eight doors, all shut, leading to different parts of the house. Jack took the hammer from his belt and started to explore the mansion, taking the doors to the left first. Each room was impressive, not to Jack's taste, minimalist and expensive, it looked like a showroom. He checked the hallway more thoroughly for the key that would open the front gate, but was unsuccessful. Conscious that he needed to speed up his search to get Chloe and Lucy in the house and away from danger, Jack picked up his pace.

He walked towards one of the large doors and carelessly knocked his shin painfully against a heavy marble coffee table that accompanied a sitting area in the hall. He cursed loudly. As expletives exploded from his mouth, a loud banging sprang to life from the door in front of him. He had no doubt what waited behind the door and knew he was going to have to deal with it. He was tired and couldn't keep dragging the girls around all day, he'd felt a disappointment to them so desperately wanted to give them this house as compensation for his incompetency and his failing plan.

Jack walked over to the door where the banging continued, it sounded loud and powerful against the sturdy timber frame. He placed his hand on the doorknob and could feel the door shake with each thud. Counting down from three, he turned the handle and pushed, it was wedged, but he knew what was keeping it from swinging open. Putting his shoulder to the door, he pushed with more force, and it opened.

"Fuck me." Jack exclaimed as a giant of a man stumbled backwards unsteadily. It must have been over 6'7" and weighed twice as much as Jack, it was muscly and would have been a monster of a man, Jack wondered if the creature had been a heavyweight boxer.

The dead man lurched forward having regained its composure, forcing Jack backwards, he tried to swing the hammer, but caught the creature on the shoulder, it was too tall for Jack to get a powerful strike to the head. He backed off into the hall as the giant strode forward, quicker than any of the dead that Jack had encountered. He turned and ran up the staircase, partly out of panic and partly hoping for a height advantage. The monstrous brute was struggling with its coordination whilst attempting to climb the stairs, it missed a step and fell forwards landing awkwardly face first onto the hard-stone steps. Jack sensed his opportunity and as the dead man began to get to its feet, arms lifting the gargantuan form, he swung the hammer down on the giant's crown. It wasn't enough, it continued to rise. Jack pulled the hammer up again and this time slammed it down with everything he had. The hammer landed with full impact and buried itself into the creature's skull, with a splash of red, it fell face down, lifeless. Jack fell backwards and sat on the stairs, breathing heavily.

Getting to his feet, Jack needed to act quickly so he could get Lucy and Chloe inside. He first needed to sweep the rest of the house and ensure there were no more undead monsters lurking in the shadows, he then needed to move the body and mop up the blood, and finally, he had to find the key to the gate.

The house was clear of further dangers, in the kitchen however was the carcass of a dog. It looked as though it had cowered in the corner, away from its once master, and hadn't stood a chance locked in the kitchen with the infected giant. From the remains, Jack couldn't tell what type of dog it was, but the sight depressed him more than many of the human remains he'd seen.

Diverting his eyes from the grisly sight, Jack checked the kitchen drawers and found an array of keys, he put them in a plastic bag and jogged to the gates to get them open and let the girls in.

He stood by the gate mechanism and went through each key until he found the correct one. Unsure exactly what to do, Jack used the key to operate the manual override, he took a quick peek over the gate to see what was waiting for him. The car sat where he'd left it, still idling away, beside the car lay two bodies; evidently Lucy had been busy whilst Jack had been running around inside the mansion.

Jack dug his heals into the gravel and began to pull the heavy gates open. His body still ached, and the pain felt like a permanent thing now that life's luxuries had been taken away from him. With the gate open, Lucy was quick to pull the car in.

Lucy and Chloe jumped out of the car and stretched, happy to be out in the open, Jack glanced at Lucy and then at the two lifeless bodies on the road and raised his eyebrows, Lucy shrugged.

Closing the gate and turning the key to lock the manual opening, Jack said, "Can you two just stay outside for half an hour. There's a few things I need to take care of before you can come in."

"Do you need a hand?" Lucy enquired, she made a face as she knew something was wrong, she could see spots of blood on his face, but kept her concerns to herself to spare Chloe from worry.

"It's okay, you two relax a little, I won't be long."

-

Walking back into the house and closing the door behind him, Jack looked at the giant body at the foot of the staircase, he groaned at the thought of its weight and decided to take a short cut. Rather than drag it outside, he would leave it in one of the downstairs rooms along with the remains of the dog.

Retrieving a sheet from one of the seven bedrooms upstairs, Jack set it down at the bottom of the staircase and wrapped the body in it. He dragged the heavy remains into a small snug, the nearest room. Taking another sheet, and some rubber gloves he found under the sink, he wrapped the body of the dog and left it with the human body. Finally, Jack cleaned the blood on the staircase and in the kitchen, and got a duvet and covered both bodies, disguising them as a lump under the covers just in case Chloe found them.

Sweaty and generally knackered, Jack mustered up the energy to push a large cabinet in front of the door where he'd left the bodies, one final security measure to keep Chloe from seeing the mess of the world. He breathed hard and summoned what little energy he had left.

Opening the front door, in mock grandeur, he announced to Chloe and Lucy, "Ladies, if you'd please like to make your way into the house, I have been expecting you and am delighted you could join me in my humble abode."

Chloe shrieked with joy and ran in the house, Lucy followed slowly, weary from the day and her traumatic experiences. She stopped by Jack and he put his arms around her, pulling her close to him and hugging her tightly. She hung there in his embrace breathing slowly, grateful for the warmth and empathy.

"There's a lot I've got to show you in here, we've hit the jackpot." Jack said warmly as he lost himself in the embrace.

Chapter 26 - Nostalgia

That evening, rather than discuss the escapades of the day, Chloe, Lucy, and Jack ate mezze style, using jars of expensive pickles, olives, flavoured peppers, and cured meats. Jack made some garlic ciabatta on the hob bringing back to life some stale bread. Chloe enjoyed copious amounts of Coca-Cola and Lucy and Jack found a bottle of 1983 Chateau Musar in the huge wine cellar, which they drank with relish, knowing from the date of the bottle that it must have been expensive and far grander a tipple than they'd ever had the pleasure of quaffing.

While the girls were still eating, Jack went to explore the house and came back to the kitchen a short while later to lead the two girls to a cupboard with a grin on his face. Inside was a series of hooks with an array of car keys. Porsche, Lamborghini, and Bentley logos gleamed at them as they looked on.

"Wow, where are they?" Chloe exclaimed excitedly, she was quite the tomboy and loved cars and recognised the symbols of the prestige brands.

"Come with me young lady and I'll show you." Jack said ruffling the little girl's hair.

He led them to the garage at the side of the house; a massive two-story structure with an office on top, it was almost as impressive as the house. Opening the door, the light shone through to six cars parked on an angle like a showroom, the waxed paintwork gleaming from the light that stole through the door opening.

Chloe ran inside and pressed her face against the window of a Ferrari, the girl gleamed at Jack and said, "This is a Ferrari 488 GTB and it can go over 200 miles per hour and can get from 0-60 in less than three seconds."

"You're quite the petrol head young lady, I'm sorry you've had to slum it in my Citroen." Jack said, feeling the joy of the girl spread to him. He'd never really been materialistic and knew very little about cars, but seeing the girl's enthusiasm and wonder made him happy.

"Why don't you have a sit in it." Lucy said as she grabbed the key from Jack and tossed it to Chloe who caught it with one hand.

"I think we'll upgrade the Citroen and I think this beast will do just fine." Jack said as he gestured theatrically to a sunburnt red Bentley Benteyga.

Lucy walked over and inspected the car, but she didn't say anything. The events of the day still weighed heavily on her conscience. Jack had been worried about her ever since they met up again after her ill-fated diversion. Finally, she spoke, "This is great Jack, it'll do. It'll do very nicely."

"I've checked it out, it's got a full tank of fuel. Once we're in the hills, it will be better. I promise." Jack was desperately trying to lighten Lucy's mood, he'd noticed that she'd drank the wine at dinner, not because it was a nice bottle, but out of necessity.

"Sounds like a plan." Lucy responded with little enthusiasm while inspecting the car.

"Come with me, I've got something to show you upstairs too." He said, leading her by the hand.

"Chloe, I've left the keys to the rest of the cars on the stool over there, knock yourself out, have a play. Just don't start any of them, we don't want to attract any attention to ourselves with the noise." He called to the little girl who was busy, sitting in the driver seat of the Ferrari, imagining racing the car at high speed.

"Okay." The girl called back absentmindedly.

Leading Lucy up the steps of the garage to the first floor by the hand, Jack opened the door and marched her over to an enormous metal cabinet, he fumbled for a key and found the one he was looking for. With a clank, he swung the two doors outwards to display its contents.

"Christ almighty." Lucy said as her jaw dropped open, her hand involuntarily moving to her mouth.

In the cabinet, neatly hung with labels detailing each item, was a series of guns, including shotguns, rifles and what looked like modified handguns with extended barrels. In the drawers under the guns, labels showed where ammunition for each weapon lived: shotgun cartridges, rifle bullets and a larger draw marked simply with .22.

"Who lived here? A gangster?" Lucy enquired as she picked up a pump action shotgun and held it against her chest, posing like she was at an NRA rally, "Does it go with my outfit."

"Sexy, I was always one for watching women in bikinis fire machine guns." Jack joked, bringing a laugh from Lucy and filling Jack with pleasure, seeing her smile again.

What neither Lucy nor Jack knew was that all the guns were legally owned by the house owner. His name was Jordan and he'd made a fortune through cyber currency having sold an IT business and invested heavily in both Bitcoin and Ethereum. With his new-found wealth, Jordan had invested in lots of toys to fill his time, this included his fascination and love of guns. Jordan had joined a gun club and gone through countless measures to stockpile his arsenal, this included police interviews, home visits from the local authority, criminal record checks and thorough research as to what type of guns were legal in the UK. With his keen eye for detail, Jordan had learned that he could own semi-automatic firearms, if the bullet didn't exceed .22 inches in diameter, and he could own pump action shotguns if they didn't hold more than three cartridges. He'd also learnt that, although handguns had been illegal since 1997, someone could own long-barrelled pistols with a fixed counterweight rod, which essentially was a handgun, but looked like someone had modified it. All of this information and a lot of cash had meant that over a few years, Jordan had built an impressive and expensive collection of guns. The guns however, hadn't helped him when he was attacked and bitten whilst trying to grapple his dog out of the hands of one of the dead, the irony being that he ended up eating his dog anyway.

"I'm not sure about these, Jack. It seems…it just seems wrong. Dangerous." Lucy said as she put the shotgun back on the shelf.

"Hey…I'm not a gun lover, I hate the things. Week after week you'd see another shooting in America and think how crazy it was that pro-gun lobbyists would argue that the reason these shootings were happening was because people didn't have enough guns. They are terrible things, but look at us, the world is a terrible place." Jack paused a moment fearing he was ranting, but he continued.

"Look at what's happened to us already, Bulldog, that gang of pricks, who knows who else is out there, not to mention the dead. If the guns help to act as a deterrent and let us escape quickly, then its good news for us all, Chloe and you especially."

"Okay, I'm just a little uneasy about this, but I understand and agree. We need to be careful to keep them out of reach of Chloe, I don't want her shooting herself or one of us by mistake." Lucy said still hesitating.

"Alright, when Chloe's asleep we'll load up some of the guns and bullets into the boot of the car, she'll never know that we have them. We can take a couple in the front with us…just in case." Jack said trying to quash Lucy's worries.

-

Jack and Lucy had some difficulty dragging Chloe away from the array of performance cars in the garage, darkness and tiredness finally won its battle and they settled the exhausted little girl in the master bedroom in a bed that would have fitted 20 clones of her. Lucy sat with Chloe for about five minutes until she fell asleep.

Walking downstairs, Lucy joined Jack in the kitchen, and he poured her a drink. They were both tired, but neither felt like sleeping.

"Fancy going into the garden? It's a beautiful evening." Jack asked.

"Sounds wonderful." Lucy wanted to be in the fresh air.

They wandered outside and Jack saw a giant hammock on the decking, pointing at it, he said "Come on, lets swing ourselves to a drunkard stupor, I see you've got the bottle."

He handed Lucy his drink and ungraciously tried to mount the swinging hammock, bending his torso onto it, and then kicking his legs wildly, wriggling himself up and turning around, just avoiding tumbling over the other side.

"There's that sophisticated man you were describing earlier." Lucy said with a chuckle.

Lucy told Jack to move over, putting the drinks and bottle down on the floor, she sat on the edge of the hammock, waited for it to stop swinging and graciously pivoted her legs over and nestled in next to Jack.

"I see you've done that before." Jack said with a grin.

"Once or twice.

"Tell me, what happened in the house earlier for you to take so long? I saw the blood on your face."

"I met the owner. He was dead unfortunately, maybe luckily, he might have shot me if he was still alive. He was big! Maybe 6'8" and it was a struggle, but I got a bit of luck when he tripped on the stairs." Jack decided to leave the part about the dog out of it, he didn't see the point of making an unpleasant situation worse.

"Good God, you must be careful. I need you, we need you." Lucy turned and kissed him gently on the cheek and Jack tingled instantly forgetting the traumas of the day.

"I could say the same of you. How are you after today? I know it's taken its toll on you, I can see it in you."

"I can't stop thinking about that family. I could have gone further, just led the dead down the main road and jumped over a wall or something further down the road."

"You were trying to get them off the main road so they wouldn't stumble back on me and Chloe. I'd have done the same and I'm not just saying that to make you feel better. I really mean it."

"I know, but it doesn't ease my conscience.

"What are we doing in this world, it's just the beginning, things will get worse." Lucy was down and the conversation wasn't helping, she decided to change the subject, "What was your favourite gig you've been to?" She looked sombre again and added, "I guess there won't be any more gigs."

"Don't write off humanity just yet." Jack responded desperate to raise her spirits. "To answer your question though, it's a tough one, can I have two?"

"That's not really answering the question, but as you've got a bruised face and you're still my hero, then I guess I can grant you two favourite gigs." Lucy said smiling again.

"That's very gracious of you. So, my first would be the Super Fury Animals at the Reading Festival in 1997. I was so young and idealistic, but very drunk. I was at the front of the crowd being stupid. It was a ridiculously hot day and the security were passing water out, but we kept stealing the water and throwing it over everyone. It was fun, but I think it was that feeling of being young and surrounded by likeminded people and the feeling of utter positivity and that my whole life was ahead of me and that my opportunities were endless.

"My second was not the most cultural, but again a lot of fun. The Courteeners, you may not have heard of them not being a Manchester girl, but they are big round these parts. It was a Christmas gig and I think after the release of their first album. It was a big crowd for not that big a band, but the crowd knew every word, including me, and the noise of the crowd singing drowned out the band. I remember leaving and everyone was still singing in unison. It was a wonderful moment." Jack was smiling at the thought; a tinge of sadness filled him knowing he'd never have that again, he pulled himself out of it and returned the question to Lucy.

"I see you're an indie kid then. Those are two obscure bands" She said smiling, "I've always had a soft spot for an indie boy, tell me you play the guitar."

"Err, I'd like to lie to you now to impress you, but, no, I'm not that musical. Anyway, stop evading the question, what's your favourite gig?"

"Okay, I was going to say the Spice Girls in 1997, but then I fear I'd lose my street cred."

"You are joking, aren't you?"

"Don't worry, that was a joke. My favourite gig was recently after I moved to Manchester and I managed to snag a free ticket through work to see the Pixies at the Apollo. They were so loud and so good, but at the end they let off so much dry ice it just crept out from the stage and filled the entire place while the band still thundered away. It was both surreal and breath-taking, literally too with all that dry ice."

Jack laughed and looked at Lucy and kept his gaze.

"What will you miss from the old world? I'm not talking about the obvious." Lucy asked, the obvious referring to friends and family that hadn't made it, those topics were conversations they'd not broached with each other, apart from their losses before the outbreak of the walking dead.

Jack pondered for a while and in a sombre tone said, "The people I didn't know."

"What do you mean?" Lucy asked turning onto her side as they got a little deeper with their conversation.

"I used to work from home quite a bit and often I'd sit in the living room near the window and watch as people went about their business. I'd see the same people walking past living their own personal routines. Families, couples, people on their own, young and old. I'd watch them and make assumptions about their lives and in my mind those assumptions were real. I'd feel as if I'd known them, their lives, where they were going.

"For instance, there was this one guy who always looked a little rough around the edges and wore leather gloves no matter what the temperature, I used to refer to him, to myself

I'll add, as the murderer. Then there was Walkie McWalkerson, an elegant tall lady who used to go for brisk walks. There'd be couples I'd see in love and then one day they'd be on their own and would no longer be with their other half. I know it's stupid, but those strangers used to keep me company when I'd locked myself away from the world."

Lucy put her arms around Jack and pulled him closer and squeezed him tightly, "It's not stupid at all. You're so sweet."

"Sweet! That's just what a guy wants to hear from the girl he's crazy about. You'll be telling me I remind you of your friend's little brother next." Jack laughed.

"Sweet and sexy I should have said, plus I always had a thing for the younger man." Lucy said mockingly.

"Toy boy, I could get used to that."

Lucy relaxed into Jack and he held her with her head resting on his shoulder, she looked up at him, "Do you think that if we get settled somewhere, we'll stop being so close. Sorry, that sounded cold, I mean, we've known each other less than a week and here we are in a world that's broken, flirting, sharing and very much together. I'm not saying it feels wrong or anything, but, I don't know, do you know what I mean?"

"Don't worry, I've thought the same, but I'm not worried about us and to be honest I'm not thinking of the future. Right now is what's important. It's the moment we are in that matters.

"I've told you before and I'll tell you again now, I feel like I've known you all my life. I think you're an incredible person; I also want to rip your clothes off every time I see you." Jack and Lucy were both smiling and enjoying the warmth of their bodies pressed together. "If, or should I say when, we make it to a place where we can relax and be safe, who knows what will happen, maybe we'll both need time to grieve the world and our previous lives, but with everything that's happened I know I'm ready to move on and start living, and right now all of me wants that to be with you."

"You make everything seem so simple. I see you doubting yourself at times, I've noticed it, but you shouldn't; you see things with clarity and that makes me feel safe and I think that's very sexy…not sweet." Lucy laughed again and kissed Jack once more, she whispered to him, "Right now is what I need and right now, you are what I need. I'm taking your advice and living in the present and you are my now."

They spent a couple more hours talking and getting to know each other, they knew their characters and were interlinked because of their recent experiences, but they knew very little about one another. They talked about the old days, things they liked; jokingly arguing over the pros and cons of Sex In the City and the traits of Carrie Bradshaw and whether she was a feminist icon or self-infatuated egomaniac; they both enjoyed chatting inconsequential shit and not worrying.

They didn't have sex, but they slept together, holding each other close. Inseparable. Intimate.

Chapter 27 - The Hills are Alive

The following morning, Jack was startled awake by a clap of thunder in the throes of another nightmare. The weather outside looked and sounded terrible and was a pathetic fallacy of the images in his head. The expensive wine was lingering heavily on his brow. He slid out of bed and left Lucy sleeping; peeking his head into the master bedroom, he saw that Chloe was still fast asleep laying horizontally across the giant bed.

Checking the time on his newly acquired Rolex, courtesy of the previous owner, it was 5:15am, he'd finally become a morning person. He tucked the watch in his pocket as it was far too big for his slight wrist and pondered whether time would lose meaning and if it was just a throwback to more civilised times. Rubbing his eyes, he got a bottle of water and decided to make a start on packing the car rather than contemplate the meaning of time. First things first, he'd get the guns.

Walking back into the office above the garage, Jack pulled out the key and unlocked the gun cabinet, having secured it the previous evening just in case Chloe had gone wandering without his knowledge. Staring at the guns he made quick decisions, conscious that he needed to get them loaded into the car before Chloe saw what he was doing. Looking at the labels and without any real knowledge, he decided to choose based on two criteria: short range and long range. He reasoned that the only times he'd need to use a gun were to fend off the dead when their numbers were too large to fight by hand, scare the living away and use a rifle from distance to help people who were surrounded. He picked the following guns:

1 x Benelli M4 pump-action shotgun,

1 x Pump-action Mossberg 500 shotgun,

1 x Ruger 10/22 semiautomatic rifle with telescopic sights,

1 x Remington Model 700 bolt-action rifle with telescopic sights,

2 x GSG 1911 long-barrelled pistols.

Resisting the temptation to load gun after gun, he moved on to ammunition. He had no idea which bullets were right for each gun so referred to the labels that the fastidious Jordan had printed and stuck in place. The shotgun cartridges were obvious, so he picked two boxes. Opening a draw that had a .22 label on it, Jack sighed with relief, gun enthusiast Jordan had labelled the draw into two sections, rifles, and pistols. He took three boxes of each making sure he remembered the different brand names, luckily for him the rifle bullets were Remington, R for rifle, easy to remember. Jack then made three trips back and forth to the Bentley loading the guns into the recess of the boot. He took the Benelli shotgun, one of the pistols and a box of ammunition for each and put them in the passenger side of the car.

His next job involved moving the supplies from the Citroen into their new car. It didn't take long to move the water, food and bags across, but in the few trips across the drive, he was drenched to the bone and shivering in the cold rain. He was cold and wet, so decided to get some soap or shower gel from the luxurious bathroom and give himself a good scrub.

Jack was washing himself as fast as he could, wincing in the cold rain when he caught Lucy smiling at him from the door in the kitchen. He had his back to her and was extremely grateful to hide his shrinking appendage as it retreated in the cold, he became self-conscious, and covering his dwindling modesty, made his way hurriedly to the door to get the towel he'd left there.

"I've seen it all before you know." Lucy said, amused at Jack's behaviour.

"It's pretty cold out here if you know what I mean." Jack said feeling his cheeks redden.

Lucy laughed out loud and held out the towel, shivering with one hand still covering his bits, the towel was yanked from his grasp as Lucy teased him, greatly amusing herself. Jack jumped in the house and grabbed Lucy and pulled her close to him and pressed his cold and wet body against her. He kissed her and the contact brought some life back into his manhood and he relaxed.

"You're freezing and now I'm wet!" Lucy cried out, "I'll have that towel after you please."

Lucy undressed, and Jack watched on, stopping drying himself, transfixed as she quickly whipped off her clothes and jumped outside with a squeal, the cold rain splashed down in large droplets making her body shimmer. He wanted her with all his might and was about to drop his towel and join her when he heard Chloe, "It's rude to watch you know."

"Yes, you're quite right, sorry about that." Jack responded with guilt. He put on a dry t-shirt and walked into the hallway with his towel wrapped around him to put some underwear and trousers on, away from Chloe. Returning to the kitchen he saw that Chloe had gone outside in her knickers and was being washed by Lucy, wincing at every drop of rain. Jack rushed to the bathroom and got two fresh towels from the large cupboard and ran downstairs to leave them by the door. He then explored the kitchen, taking any non-perishable food he could find.

-

While the girls got ready to leave, Jack looked at the maps once again to reacquaint himself with the route and after a good night's sleep he was optimistic about navigating through side streets and suburbia to get to the hills.

Having spent 10 minutes trying to get the garage door open, Jack finally managed to pull the car into the drive. He got a little emotional saying goodbye to the Citroen, running his hand over the battered bodywork as he bid a farewell to his trusty steed.

Lucy helped Chloe into the back of the car and looked surprised when she saw the pistol and shotgun in the front seat, but didn't say anything. Jack checked that the coast was clear over the wall, unlocked the gate and opened it, he drove out and decided to shut the gate behind him, thinking it was better to keep the place secure should they, or someone else in need, require refuge.

The trio all looked back at the big house as they set off on their journey again, hoping for an uneventful and more productive day on the road.

Turning back onto the road they'd traversed the day before, the way was clear, many of the dead had been drawn off the road by wildlife. Car crashes and debris still made the driving slow, but Jack wanted to take it steady to conserve fuel so wasn't concerned.

Lucy tried the radio once again and the signal was there, but still weak with the words undecipherable. They were more relaxed after a night's sleep and chatted away as though they were going on holiday. They were becoming acclimatised to the scenes outside and deliberately chose to avoid looking directly at the more gruesome sights to keep their spirits up.

Before they could reach the hills, more towns and suburbs awaited them and the number of dead increased dramatically, Jack felt as though his mind was on autopilot as the car weaved in and out of devastation. He hated every stressful second of the journey. His mind ventured into itself and he found himself thinking about driving in the old world, the morning rush hour and having to deal with the inconsiderate actions of others. He'd often get infuriated with BMWs and Audis cutting him up, switching lanes and trying to take shortcuts to save 10 seconds in their daily commute. He remembered most mornings, cursing as people would drive millimetres behind him even though the row of traffic in front of him meant they couldn't have gone any further. Or people who would get on the motorway and immediately traverse to the middle lane and drive there no matter what was going on around them, unaware of their own bad driving. He used to think that if everyone drove sensibly, gave each other room, and stuck to the lanes they were supposed to drive in, then everyone would have benefited, and traffic jams would have been far less severe. This mutual consideration didn't occur to most people at the time and it was 'every man for themselves' on the roads. He hated the commute, but would have settled for a lifetime of rush hour now that his vista included death and sadness around every corner.

"Left Jack, take this left." Lucy called with urgency as Jack bounced over a curb and managed to steer the car in the right direction. They'd all been silent as they'd tensely navigated through suburbia all concentrating on getting out of the built-up areas and into the countryside. They had made good time, dodging the main towns by sticking to the outskirts and had begun their assent to the hills through a small town called Bollington. The town was heaving with the living dead, as the roads were lined by walls and terraced houses creating a funnel for them with nowhere to go, other than the road itself. The car took some battering, Jack was forced to drive slowly and push his way through, as gruesome forms banged against windows and clambered on the bonnet, but he carried on regardless.

They made it through Bollington unscathed and with the steady assent, the numbers of the dead reduced until the road was empty. Buildings and the remains of civilisation were replaced by rolling green fields. The air seemed sweeter and the scene more inspiring as the bright yellow of oil seed rape contrasted beautifully against the dark rain clouds. The trip gathered pace and the three passengers breathed a little easier as they all started to believe that the journey across the country was going to succeed and give them a better chance of survival.

The world seemed normal again, only a couple of car wrecks on the narrow road showed signs of disaster, but they were sporadic. The clouds were breaking up and the sun was beginning to peek through, giving the countryside and spring bloom an optimistic feel.

"Look over there, he's hunting!" Lucy said pointing at a man in the field with enthusiasm in her voice. The man had turned as he heard the car and waved as they slowly drove past. Chloe sat in the back smiling and waving back.

"It's the first signs of life we've seen since leaving." Jack said feeling good.

"We haven't seen any monsters for ages." Chloe said joyfully.

They agreed that they would pull over to relieve themselves and eat the last of the perishable food taken from their two temporary homes of the previous evenings. It would be tinned food from then on.

-

Lucy spotted a road that led into a national park, so Jack pulled down the single track and then drove off road, parking behind some bushes to stay out of sight. They were still on edge, even though they'd not seen any dead in a while, but with their encounters over the past week, they were equally as weary of the living, so were glad to be hidden.

Taking Chloe by the hand, Lucy led the girl into some trees so they could do their bodily functions. Jack found a nearby bush and quickly relieved himself and then set out their lunch on the backseat for the girls to devour when they returned. He was anxious when they weren't with him and watched and listened, like a meerkat dosed with amphetamines, for any noise or movement in the surrounding trees.

The pair came back whispering and giggling together. Smiling, Jack handed some humus and crackers to Chloe and they ate with relish, silently enjoying every morsel. Clearing the food packaging, still in conservation mode and not wanting to litter the countryside, Jack asked if anybody needed the toilet again to which there were shakes of the head. Getting ready to leave, they were stopped in their tracks as the sound of a diesel engine approached.

Jack moved to the bushes in front of the car and was quickly followed by Lucy and Chloe. Peering through the gaps in the leaves they saw an army truck with a trailer pull down the track that led right past them.

"It's the army." Lucy whispered.

"Let's just watch, we don't know who they are, they might have stolen the truck." Jack said feeling tense.

The truck bounced down the uneven track and turned a corner out of sight, but they heard the engine cut out a short distance away. Men's voices soon followed, carried on the wind towards them.

"Did you ever see 28 Days Later?" Jack asked Lucy and she nodded her head.

"I'm worried that if there are small groups of military men left without proper leadership then they might start acting in a similar way. Basically, doing whatever the hell they want to." Jack said, seriously stressing.

"Can we go?" Chloe cried.

"Not just yet, they'll hear us leaving, we're better hiding and waiting for them to leave." Jack said.

"Come on, we should go through the trees and see what they're doing. Be quiet though, we don't want to be spotted." Lucy said as she held Chloe's hand and walked the way they had previously gone to relieve themselves.

Jack followed quietly, watching the floor trying to avoid standing on twigs. They slalomed through trees, keeping low, until they found a spot behind a tree overlooking the army truck.

Down below, five men dressed in army fatigues, carrying assault rifles, gathered around the back of the truck they arrived in. Another man came out of the woods, who had been surveying the area, and announced in a loud and commanding voice, "Right lads, live training starts now. Leave your guns in the cab, you will only be armed with your army issued blade."

A distinctive grumbling could be heard as the men proceeded to place their guns in the truck and then moved back into formation around the man who had spoken. He then began to speak again, but the words were lost as Lucy and Jack strained to hear. He had told them to stand 10 feet towards the back of the trailer. The spying trio watched as the men walked to the back of the trailer all standing a few feet apart, each holding a knife purposefully in their hands.

With a running jump, the leader of the troop, jumped onto the truck bonnet, walked over the roof, and leapt onto the top of the trailer, which looked more like a horse box. Banging on the roof fiercely he shouted, "Right then you horrible lot, come get your fresh meat."

He unlatched the back of the trailer and pushed the door down which noisily crashed to the floor. After a brief silence, infected corpses started to stream out of the trailer and down the sloped door that had transformed into a ramp upon opening. Jack, Lucy, and Chloe watched on as at least 20 creatures ambled out of the back towards the five men who stood motionless waiting for the dead to attack. The army men were outnumbered, but it was evident that they had been trained for this eventuality. They all stood waiting as the first of the dead lunged for the nearest soldier who was quick; he reached up and grabbed the creature around the neck with his left hand and with his knife wielding hand lodged the blade into the side of its head dropping it with ease. The rest of the soldiers joined the fight as the dead approached, sensing the living and breathing flesh in front of them. Each soldier was engaged with differing success, a couple faced three of the dead attacking in unison, where others had only one to fend off. One of the smaller soldiers had three large dead creatures attacking him and had dispatched one of them only for his knife to become lodged in its head, he was desperately trying to remove the blade when the other two lunged at him forcing him to fall backwards with the two dead on top of him, gnashing their teeth as they tried to force themselves on him. The soldier lost his trained composure and shouted, "Fucks sake Sarg, do something."

Jack and Lucy watched on, not wanting to reveal themselves, but feeling helpless as the soldier looked doomed. They watched as the man on top of the trailer unsheathed a pistol and fired two quick shots, the two infected creatures on top of the felled soldier toppled left and right, taking direct hits to the head with the precisely fired shots. The rest of the struggle between living and dead didn't take long, the soldiers worked together bringing down the remaining creatures.

The Sergeant, who had jumped down from the top of the trailer, gathered his men around for a debrief. The soldier who had been knocked down managed to retrieve the knife that was still lodged in the head of the walker, and joined the group, he was covered in blood and his body language made him look like a defeated man. The leader talked to each man pointing out the pros and cons of the fight, but he seemed to be congratulating them on a successful exercise. Looking directly at the crest fallen soldier, he said loudly so that Jack and Lucy could clearly hear, "A valuable lesson was learnt today. You've got to be quick, use your brain and move around them. They are slow and clumsy and easy to bring down. Knock them down and you buy time. What you definitely do not want to do is panic. You panic and you become more like them, relying on instinct rather than trained intelligence and that is what will help you survive. Panic is not your friend."

Murmured agreements drifted on the wind as a couple of soldiers patted the disgruntled man on his back in an attempt to console him. Orders were given and the troop quickly clambered into the back of the truck, departing quickly, leaving a tangle of mangled bodies in their wake.

Lucy turned and smiled at Jack, "The army are still running drills and training. That's got to be a good thing. Right?"

"It can't be a bad thing. Would you have gone with them if they saw us and invited us to tag along?" Jack said, wondering if the two girls would be in a better position with men who were trained and prepared.

"You're stuck with us Jacky boy." Lucy said smiling, touching his arm. "Besides, I want to see your family home and some goofy pictures of you as a boy." She continued, laughing.

A low moan rang through the trees and they all looked through the wooded area and saw one of the dead stumbling through the roughage towards them.

"Come on let's go." Chloe urged.

Jack and Lucy didn't need a second invitation as they speedily made their way to the car and set off again.

Seeing the army prompted Lucy to try the radio again and this time they had a signal strong enough to listen to the broadcast that repeated itself over and over. It was a short message and it was from a Government broadcast explaining that the army were dotted around laying low for the initial wave of infection to die down and that people should stay inside and stay safe until instructed otherwise. It said that plans were in place to suffocate the disease at a later date and that resources were too stretched to rescue people. The broadcast also gave a brief overview of how to kill the dead in case there was no alternative.

They listened to the broadcast three times until Lucy turned the radio off, "They have a plan, but we're on our own until then."

Nobody responded, silence filled the car as they each contemplated the message and what it actually meant. Jack was sceptical, but there was an element of hope in his gut that humanity might survive this disaster.

-

The journey after running into the army wasn't plain sailing for the trio in the expensive Bentley, a few wrong turns and unpassable roads ate into time and left their progress hampered. As 4pm approached Jack and Lucy were both getting twitchy, wanting to find somewhere safe to stay and avoid travelling through the night.

Lucy was now taking her first stint driving and was enjoying the feel of the powerful car, while Jack searched the map looking at the highlighted markers that they had earmarked as potential safe havens, "There's a place called Dove Holes, I think if we get past there we get to some quieter spots; we can sleep in the car and set off again at first light. We need to turn right somewhere along this road."

The road ahead was breath-taking with sweeping corners, dipping hills and views that stretched miles into the horizon. Lucy couldn't help but slow the car down to a crawl so the three of them could look out onto the rolling green hills and breathe in the natural wonder that they'd taken for granted, she stopped the car and got out and crawled up the grass verge to soak in the vista. Jack and Chloe followed, unsure what was going on, but did so anyway, happy to be out of the car once again.

"We should be getting on." Jack called up to Lucy, but she didn't say anything, she beckoned them up the verge to take in the view.

"It's funny, I'm over 40 years old and I've never driven down a road so small and been so isolated in this country. I imagine that this place hasn't changed a great deal since…well you know.

"We haven't got far to go today so we might as well take five minutes to take in the view. Look around us, there isn't a soul around. It's a shame we can't just stay here, I feel wonderful right now." Lucy reached for both Jack and Chloe's hands and held them as she smiled into the distance, the grand view bringing tears to her eyes.

"It is pretty. It reminds me of Lord of the Rings." Chloe said who also looked to be lost in the wonder of nature.

They stood in silence for five minutes, grateful for peace and tranquillity, the silence comfortable between the newly acquainted family.

"Come on, let's get cracking before we do stay here forever." Jack said, skipping down the verge.

They continued down the narrow track and turned onto another road called Lesser Lane, which was no less beautiful. After about three miles, signs of civilisation began to materialise, a house here and there, then turning into a full-blown street at a crossroads. The car pulled up and, to the occupant's astonishment, a couple walked down the street towards them holding hands, the man waved and smiled.

"What the hell is going on?" Lucy asked.

"I have no idea." Jack said opening the window as the couple approached.

"Hi there, nice car." The man said.

"Thanks, we kind of borrowed it. Are you guys safe here?" Lucy asked.

"Relatively safe love. A few wander over, but we've been managing quite well." The woman answered pleasantly.

"Are there many of you living here?" Lucy continued her questioning.

"Aye, quite a few of us, silly really, but it's really brought the community together." The man answered this time giving the woman a little squeeze around the hips.

"Listen, I don't mean to be insensitive, but we're looking for a place to stay tonight, do you know if any of the houses are empty?" Lucy was thinking on her feet.

"All of the houses are full apart from Mrs Hambleton's house. She's in there though, but she didn't make it, she's stuck in there and none of us wanted to deal with her. She was a real dear." The woman spoke this time, it was like they were in some sort of relay.

"Go to the pub love, Maggie will help you out. I'm George and this is Cathy" The man chipped in.

"Nice to meet you both, I'm Lucy and this is Jack and Chloe." Lucy said pointing at the two others in the car as they both waved and smiled in unison.

"Will Maggie really help us?" Lucy asked feeling paranoid due to her experiences of the past week.

"She's a gem is Maggie, she'd love some youngsters around, most of us are getting a bit old in the tooth." Cathy said with a wink in George's direction.

"Just turn left here and you'll see the pub just up the road, you can't miss it, it's the Beehive Inn." George said continuing their bizarre way of following each other's sentences. Lucy thought that the couple must have been together for eternity by their behaviour.

"Thanks a lot for your help, we'll go and see Maggie. Maybe we'll see you later." Lucy said with a wave.

"We'll be in the pub later playing dominos in the corner, come and say hello." Cathy said as the couple continued walking down the road.

"What do you think?" Lucy turned to Jack.

"They seem like decent people and I'd much prefer to sleep in a house rather than in the car. What do you think Chloe?" Jack had made his feelings clear, but wanted to include the girl in the decision, she had as much right.

"I liked them. Maggie sounds nice, plus they'll have Coke too." Chloe said, excited at the prospect of going to the pub.

"Sounds like we've got our decision then." Lucy said, as she drove the car in the direction that Cathy and George had pointed.

Parking out the front of the pub, they disembarked the car and as they got out, Jack ensured he hid the guns from sight as not to scare the community, the pub door opened and a large lady stood in the door frame grinning towards Chloe.

"Hello there, you need some help?" The woman called cheerily.

"Hi, we just bumped into Cathy and George who said you might be able to help us out with a place to stay tonight." Lucy said taking the lead once again.

"Those pair should not be walking around without a care in the world. We've warned them about it, but they won't listen the old buggers…oops pardon my French young lady.

"My name is Maggie by the way and yes I'd love to help you out. We could do with our average age bringing down around here." Maggie was a talker and a charmer. Lucy, Jack, and Chloe took to her straight away.

Chapter 28 - A Solitary Person in the Shadows

Hooded, slow and determined, the solitary person walked through fields and over walls. Often with a couple of dead only feet behind for company, the person walked through rain, sunshine, and wind without slowing pace. Accompanied only by a bag, map and compass, the person walked, heading north-east.

The person wanted nothing to do with the living and felt a bond with the dead, not a need, but a want for blood. Mercy and compassion were no longer part of the person's soul. A life of misery had befallen the person who was half raised by a mother that showed no love. Their father had been abusive from a young age and the only memories of the man revolved around heavy beatings as a four-year-old, cowering in the corner of a dilapidated house while the father kicked and beat the innocence and happiness out of the child. The person was a man who had never been shown love, had been deprived of any good and through abuse and torture had little education or intellect to escape the perpetual spiral of sin and depravity.

The destruction of the man's childhood was completed by his mother's addiction to heroin. With little time or care for the child, his mother would sell everything in order to satisfy her stimulated needs. All she had left to sell was herself, and wave after wave of indecent men would enter the house. Some of these men would take a fancy to young boys and any bright future for the child was wiped away with despicable actions from despicable men. The man's mother died from an overdose when he was just eight year's old and he was left in the house with the corpse for two weeks, eating cereal and drinking water to survive. Social services had never been able to locate the mother and child, the former having moved around Manchester several times, renting houses using pseudonyms and paying cash; the child was left defenceless.

He was eventually found by one of his mother's punters who belonged to a gang. This man had also supplied his mother with heroin and had been owed money so broke down the door and instantly recognised the smell of the dead. He had also recognised that taking a child so young could prove a useful asset. Children had many functions for his gang, theft without consequence and acting as a mule. The biggest asset of a child joining his troop of criminals was loyalty. By providing for the child and stopping the abuse, the child would do anything that was asked. The abuse stopped and loyalty grew. For the child, life was changed and a new direction was provided, taking and doing as he pleased with the approval of his new family, he was no longer abused physically, mentally, or sexually, under the wing of his new brothers.

As time went by, the child grew into a man, short, but powerful and with a wanton desire to destruct society, a society he blamed for his upbringing and the atrocities that he lived with on a daily basis when he should have been safe and enjoying his childhood. The gang changed over the years as the child grew into a man, the first leader got sentenced to a long jail sentence, but others stepped in and the fact that he had become part of the fabric of the gang, his standing and protection remained. With the passing of time, a man named Dale took over the gang, young, but intelligent and ready to lead, he knew the potential of the rescued child, now a man. The man's name was Richie and Dale saw that his eyes held no fear and recognised that he was a killer in the making. Dale put Richie to work, eradicating rivals and heavy debtors. Richie relished the work, taking pleasure in extinguishing lives, with each life he took, he felt a little more whole and it helped wash away the unpleasantness of his upbringing. Richie lived side by side with the gang, but didn't like the majority of them, he swore vengeance every time he was wronged, but never acted out of the respect he had for Dale and the togetherness of the group.

The death of Dale had released Richie from the gang and in taking Naz's life had freed him completely of any loyalty. For the first time he was on his own and making his own decisions. His decisions were based upon revenge and retribution. As a young man he had vowed to act against any person who wronged him and took great pleasure in plunging the knife into Naz and watching him die.

He now had vengeance as his sole reason for being. Lucy's words still rang in his ears, his mother, his abuse, she didn't know her words of fury were so accurate as she lost her temper shouting at her tormentor, but the words hit home and Richie was made to relive his early life. He also felt the constant discomfort in his ribs from Lucy's bat, whilst replaying his last meeting with the fair skinned redhead. Bulldog, Jack, and Lucy. They must all die.

After murdering Naz, Richie wandered the area looking for Bulldog, he was certain that the man, whose name he didn't know, was local and was confident that he knew where Jack and Lucy were heading to, so his natural instinct was to find

Bulldog first. Eventually he returned to the mansion that the gang had taken refuge in and found two of his former gang members dead, each shot through the head. He felt nothing seeing their bodies, instead, he searched the house for their weapons, but found none. It was evident that the man he was looking for had been back and killed the two men and taken the weapons. He spent a long time searching the area, but couldn't find any sign of Bulldog and had a nagging doubt in his mind that if he was to find the man he sought to avenge, he'd be outgunned. With reluctance, he decided to leave Bulldog until a later date and make a trip across the country to North Yorkshire, to the place he'd seen highlighted on the map in the house the gang had ransacked, Eastloch.

Richie was prioritising and his priority was hearing the pop of Lucy's trachea when he crushed the life out of her.

Chapter 29 - Old Ways

Maggie seemed genuinely happy to give Lucy, Chloe, and Jack a bed for the night and rolled over backwards to accommodate them. She had two spare rooms and offered one to the girls and the other to Jack. Both rooms were made up and Jack and Lucy wondered if the people these rooms belonged to were gone. They didn't ask.

To the delight of Jack and Lucy, but not Chloe, who had revelled in the lack of washing, the pub had hot running water thanks to Maggie's late husband who was an engineer and had rigged the pub up with solar and wind power long before the collapse of the UK's infrastructure. The pub itself was old and had its own water tower. A member of the community had recently installed a pump to keep the water topped up from a nearby stream that ran from the hills. The electricity worked, but was a limited supply so was reserved for refrigeration and hot water, the pub still had a working gas supply too. Maggie welcomed them to take a shower, but told them not to be any longer than five minutes each, Jack was tempted to combine their time and jump in with Lucy, but thought it might be a little rude considering they were guests and that Lucy probably wanted the shower to herself anyway. Jack and Lucy gratefully accepted the offer and savoured the five minutes; Chloe on the other hand had to be convinced, but did seem happy when she was given some banana scented shower gel.

After finishing getting ready, they made their way downstairs into the pub following the smell of bacon and eggs. Maggie awaited them with a big smile to match her warm and large frame, "Come and sit down, I've made you an egg and bacon butty, I bet you could do with some real food."

Chloe eagerly ran to the table with a grin on her face. Lucy smiled back at Maggie and said warmly, "Thank you Maggie, you have been so kind to us already and now you're using your meat, you should save this for yourself."

"Nonsense dear, we've got chickens laying eggs, we have pigs, cows for milk and some sheep. We'll not starve here, we're all working together sharing everything we have with each other, pulling together for our community." Maggie said, beaming with pride.

"It's nice to meet such good people. We've had a bit of a rough run of luck with some of the folk we've run into." Jack said looking serious.

"Aye, we've had a couple of, shall we say, undesirables come through from the towns. Most have just been scared and left without much trouble, but Frank, you'll meet him later, he frightened a few of the more determined off with his 12-bore, you hear that fire and you run for your life." Maggie said with a chuckle, unconcerned about what these 'undesirables' could do to an elderly community.

Lucy decided to move the conversation on to a more positive note, "How come you have hot water, running water, and I've seen a couple of lights on, you have electricity?"

"The lights were on? I must turn them off." Maggie said to herself, she continued, "My Eric was a bit of a whiz with all of the technical things, I've no idea what it all does, but we've got solar power, wind power and a water tank that fills up from the stream out the back. It's a wonder that was designed to save us money when the pub was struggling, but it's even more miraculous now. Luckily for me, his friend Frank is also a sparky and helps out if anything stops working.

"Fortunately for Eric, he passed away 14 months ago so he didn't see any of the awful things that are happening. There are about 30 of us in the village and we all have our jobs. We tend to eat together in the evening in the pub and then we each go about our business in the day. Some of them are avid gardeners so are setting about planting fruit and veg, others are trying to get the materials together to turn the village into a fortress to stop the dead from wandering in, but that's some way off becoming a reality, they can't make up their minds about how to do this. The others keep us safe from the dead, we're well hidden so not many pass through and are quickly tackled before they can cause any harm. You met George and Cathy, they were on lookout, but they're like a couple of lovesick teenagers, always bonking."

They all chuckled at the use of the word 'bonking', Jack and Lucy smiled at the thought of the old pair and their randy habits.

"It's impressive how organised you've become in such a short space of time." Jack said in awe of Maggie and the community as a whole.

"We had a gathering in here when it became apparent that the living were losing the fight. We've got some sharp minds here and they were the ones who got us organised, we were happy to have a plan and keep our community ticking over.

We've lost most of the village, there were over 150 people living here, but most didn't come back. Many of the people who are still here didn't lose anyone as they're all mostly retired so hadn't ventured out of the village. It was the younger ones who went to work or did the school run who weren't so lucky, the poor souls.

"A couple of people don't come in the pub much because they did lose people, so we leave them food and visit them regularly to check up on them. There's not much we can do for them other than let them know we're here when they are ready." Maggie said as she lost her big smile for the first time.

"Anyway, enough of the sad tales, you'll meet most of the people in the village in a couple of hours when the grub is served. I hope you like beef stew as that's on the menu tonight. The poor vegetarians have had to change their diets." Maggie continued with a chuckle obviously not approving of the vegetarian lifestyle.

"I've got to finish preparing tonight's meal so please make yourself at home, help yourself to drinks, beer, wine, anything you want."

"You are too kind. We can't thank you enough." Lucy said, holding Maggie's hand.

"Think nothing of it dear. It costs nothing to be nice." Maggie said as she disappeared into the kitchen at the back of the pub.

Lucy and Jack left Chloe eating crisps and drinking coke playing with a set of dominos and her dolls and went to explore the pub. They found five chest freezers full of food, it looked as though someone had raided a nearby supermarket, there were also four fridges brimming with fruit and vegetables, they were well stocked and the fact that they were already planting a variety of crops and rearing animals filled both Jack and Lucy with a great deal of hope about surviving in a world without the luxuries they were used to.

-

In the evening, around 7pm, people started streaming into the pub filled with anticipation for the meal that awaited them. Some brought bottles of wine and beer and a couple of older gentlemen brought guitars. The average age must have been close to 60 and there was almost a joyous expectation from those filling the pub. Jack thought that this must have been what it was like in the old days, before the Internet, television and social media had introverted society. It was a throwback to togetherness and the pub was the hub of the community once again.

Maggie was out of the kitchen and had handed over the reins of finishing the meal to another couple who oversaw the final preparations. She weaved in and out of the group, warmly spreading kisses on cheeks and greeting everyone with open arms. She was a fine hostess and was quick to introduce Chloe, Lucy, and Jack around. She took Chloe to meet another little girl, the only one in the village, who was called Alexa and they ran around the pub playing. Jack and Lucy were introduced to Frank, who was a big, yet gentle man with a knowledgeable way of talking.

Before long, beers, wines and spirits were flowing freely among the group as the noisy chatter echoed around the room. George and Cathy came over to say hello to Jack and Lucy and continued finishing each other's sentences whilst never separating their hold of each other. Jack and Lucy were both worried that the noise would attract the dead; Maggie saw the anxious looks they gave towards the door and windows and assured them that the look outs would be watching and warn us should anything come uninvited into the village.

Dinner was served and kept the room quiet for a short while as the hungry people of the community devoured their food with great appetite. After the meal, people began to circulate the room and introduce themselves to Jack and Lucy, they met quite a few of the village, some were dull, but some were interesting and insightful, the people they met included:

Frank: A master of electricity and engineering, he was also brave having been out to the more populated areas to stock up on supplies to keep the power running in the pub. Frank explained to Jack how to set up and construct renewable energy sources into the mains and made detailed notes for Jack to take with him.

Alice: A dull bore who spoke of missing playing Candy Crush and the fact that she was stuck on level 345, but had nearly mastered the level and was upset that she would no longer be able to complete it. Maggie was quick to see who Lucy and Jack were talking to and whisked them away. Lucy had been growing angry listening to the woman complain about such trivialities and was close to blowing her lid and causing a scene so was grateful to be pulled away.

George: The man eventually left Cathy's side and sat down to talk to Jack and Lucy about the state of the surrounding towns. He'd been keen to go on supply runs and check on surrounding villages. He told them that there were other communities around the hills that weren't faring so well, many were losing members on a daily basis and weren't as organised. He told them about two villages called Hope and Dove Holes that weren't far away. The dead were in the streets and people weren't working together to keep their communities safe and as such they were starting to panic and had begun to slowly succumb to the growing numbers of dead. He had tried to talk to people to help them organise, but they were only concerned with their immediate family and friends and weren't prepared to change their habits. He also told them about trips to Buxton and Chapel-en-le-Frith that were practically no-go zones, although he had been there earlier in the week in a modified tractor to get supplies. He said he hadn't seen any living and had a lot of trouble getting through the growing crowds of zombies. It was this information that speeded up the community's decisions to try and fortify their village.

Susan: She was younger than most, in her early 50s and a project manager in her previous life. She was heading up the fortification of the village. She had mapped out the houses closest to the pub and centre of the village and wanted to use the structures of the houses as the main parts of the walls. She was organising a team of 10 to come up with a quick way of building a strong barricade around the rest of the village. They had machinery thanks to the farm equipment and a ready supply of red diesel, to dig foundations, but they lacked the materials. Bricks and mortar were too slow to construct so she decided that they needed two sets of chain-link fences and was currently using the supply runs to source these.

Maggie: Although Jack and Lucy had already got acquainted with Maggie, it turns out they'd only scratched the surface of her amazing character. Not only was she warm and kind, she was sharp and a natural leader. It was her that had brought the community together after studying the news on the TV and radio, and had quickly realised how badly the situation could escalate. She had saved many of the people in the community by her conviction to the cause and kept them from venturing out to look for those who had perished. She had called the initial meeting and had led the discussions about the grim outlook and had organised people into groups with tasks and objectives. It was by keeping the community busy that had brought them closer together.

Jack had often thought that the idea of communism was essentially a good one, but that it was let down by the greed and corruption of humanity. People had really believed they were better than animals, but when it came to the crunch, people would often seize the opportunity to make for the top to the detriment of anyone who was in the way. It was common in the animal kingdom, lions fighting to become the dominant male, territorial animals fighting over their patch of land, humans showed the exact same characteristics and that they weren't that much more evolved. What Maggie showed Jack was that the principles of Marxism could be achieved, namely a utopian society that is both classless and stateless, in a smaller community, committed to their basic needs of survival. There was no evident envy or need that was not fulfilled by the group.

It occurred to Jack that it was still early days and that discontent could grow, especially if something terrible were to happen in the community, but he also thought that the more elderly and wiser group had relinquished their need for material items and status long ago and realised the true beauties of the world, he was doubtful that a group of younger people would be so cooperative and peaceful with each other.

-

The night went on and Jack put Chloe to bed around 9pm after her eyes started drooping, she still resisted, but was quickly asleep when placed in the soft bed. Returning downstairs, Jack heard the strum of a guitar. Walking into the bar area, he saw Alan and Winston sat on stools, preparing to play a few songs. Walking over to Lucy, she leaned in, kissed him on the cheek and cheerily said, "This is a fantastic place with wonderful people. It gives you hope. It really does." She squeezed Jack's hand and watched on and listened with pleasure as the two men played a couple of songs that neither Jack nor Lucy recognised.

After the second song stopped, Alan called over in Jack's direction, "This is a long shot son, but I don't suppose you know the words to Highwayman? Three of us do, but we need one more to complete the set."

Jack immediately blushed as this was one of his favourite songs and one he knew well. He was going to say no, because he wasn't much of a singer and didn't want to embarrass himself, when Lucy looked and smiled, whispering in his ear, "You know it, don't you?" She was beaming.

Jack did an involuntary nod in Lucy's direction and stopped himself before he gave the game away, it was too late though, Lucy called to Alan with joy etched all over her face, "You're in luck Alan, Jack knows this one."

There was a cheer from the on-looking group and Jack grimaced and turned a brighter shade of red, he turned to Lucy and said in a hushed tone, "I'll get you back for this."

She winked at him and whispered, "I'll make it up to you later, I promise."

Alan beckoned Jack over and he walked slowly, with his head down, to the two guitarists and other man, named Malcolm, who were getting ready to sing the other three verses. Alan asked, "Which verse do you want?"

"Um, I'd like Waylon Jennings's verse if that's okay with you gentlemen?" Jack asked and they all nodded their approval.

"Good stuff lad." Alan said and immediately started to play the opening chords and was followed by Winston.

Alan sang the first verse as the crowd provided the percussion by slapping hands on the tables and clapping,
"I was a highwayman
Along the coach roads I did ride
With sword and pistol by my side
Many a young maid lost her baubles to my trade
Many a soldier shed his lifeblood on my blade
The bastards hung me in the spring of twenty-five
But I am still alive"

Malcom was next,

"I was a sailor
I was born upon the tide
And with the sea I did abide
I sailed a schooner round the Horn to Mexico
I went aloft and furled the mainsail in a blow
And when the yards broke off they said that I got killed
But I am living still"

And then it was Jack, who breathed hard and missed his cue, but was given a quick nudge by Malcolm to start, he quickly caught up and sang in a deep voice,

"I was a dam builder
Across the river deep and wide
Where steel and water did collide
A place called Boulder on the wild Colorado
I slipped and fell into the wet concrete below
They buried me in that great tomb that knows no sound

But I am still around

I'll always be around and around and around and around and around"

Finally, Winston sang, and they'd saved the best till last, his voice was silky smooth and perfect,

"I fly a starship
Across the Universe divide
And when I reach the other side
I'll find a place to rest my spirit if I can
Perhaps I may become a highwayman again
Or I may simply be a single drop of rain

But I will remain

And I'll be back again, and again and again and again and again"

The music stopped and the crowd cheered happily. Jack made his way back to Lucy with a few people giving him a slap on the back. Lucy greeted him, put her arms around him and kissed him tenderly. He melted.

The kiss lingered, and he heard in the background from a man, "Hey, they're as bad as George and Cathy, get a room." This was followed by laughter from those that heard.

The night went on, Jack had stopped drinking as he wanted a clear head for the morning, but Lucy continued, revelling in the atmosphere of the remarkable community. It was getting late, but Jack didn't want to appear ungrateful and stayed up and talked with the group past 2am. When people started making for the exit, he was relived to make his excuses to hit the sack and asked if Lucy was coming. She was quite drunk, exhausted, and ready for her bed.

They both checked on Chloe, who was sound asleep and then went into the room that Maggie had laid out for Jack, it was a single bed, but that didn't stop them wanting to spend the night with each other. The evening had been full of meaningful glances, playful touches and lingering closeness, pressing themselves close feeling the electricity between them grow. Jack and Lucy were ready to tear each other's clothes off by the time they reached the bed. They were both naked within seconds and Jack was harder than he'd ever been, before they knew it, their bodies were pressed up against each other and they were kissing passionately, their hands all over one another. The passion left no time for foreplay and Jack pushed Lucy up against the wall, he lifted her and she wrapped her legs around his waist as he pushed deep inside, she made a loud groan of pleasure and bit down onto his neck as the cold wall on her back and the thrusts of Jack's lust brought them to climax quickly, both exhausted. They stood there for some time, gently kissing one another, naked pressed together.

They sat up in bed together for a short while, happy. Lucy turned to Jack and lay her head on his chest and said in a soft voice, "We can do something similar as these people when we get to your mum and dad's. They are an inspiration and have given me hope of a future that could be more beautiful than the world we've left behind."

"You're right and I couldn't have put it more eloquently. I feel like I can do anything when I'm with you and would move heaven and earth to give you the future we all want." Jack said feeling Lucy's warmth. She didn't respond as she had fallen asleep. He spent the next 10 minutes watching her in the candlelight. Finally, he managed to shuffle down the bed without waking her, blew out the candle and drifted off into a contented sleep of his own.

Chapter 30 - Hordes

2015 figures showed that the population density in the UK stood at an incredibly crowded 268 people per square kilometre. That's 1,000 metres, by 1,000 metres. In England that figure jumped up to 420 people and in Scotland it fell to just 69. In short, that made England like an incredibly dangerous sardine can.

During the first week of the outbreak, around 85 percent of people perished. The first few days, when news spread about the global catastrophe, survival figures were much higher, with 52 percent enduring the uprising of the dead, but that still meant 48 percent of people died. Take London for example, the population stood at 8.8 million people in 2016, 48 percent of that number equates to over 4.2 million people. Not all of the poor souls who died were turned into flesh eating zombies, but many did.

The second wave of deaths came as the dead grew in numbers and began to congregate and follow the living en masse. Many people had followed warnings to stay inside, especially in the big cities, this decision had been made a lot easier with the sheer volume of blood thirsty monsters on the street. However, when food and water ran out, people were forced to flee with many falling victim to the hands and teeth of the dead.

Those living out of the cities fared a little better in the beginning. Much like the village Jack had lived in, the numbers of dead were manageable for one or two people willing to halt the steady growth. But, again, much like Jack's village, they were idyllic in their appearance but were perilously close to densely packed populations. Many of the places that people sought refuge were not far enough away from the large towns and cities and this turned the commuter belt areas into sitting time bombs. Danny, when still alive, was wise to predict the influx of the dead, but he was in a small minority with the foresight to see things clearly.

Food began to disappear in towns and cities and with less of the living to feed them, the dead began to wander; they followed cats, dogs, pigeons and even rats; anything living. Hordes as big as 100,000 slowly moving bodies gathered in London, in Manchester and in Birmingham and they were like a plague of locusts; devouring everything in their sight. The people who were locked away and had the misfortune of attracting these crowds were soon overcome as their barricaded windows and doors could not withstand the constant barrage of combined force, eventually letting the dead in to eat their victims alive.

The roadblocks that the army had quickly put together in the major cities began to shift and scrape open as tonnes of crumpled cars were swept aside as a mass of bodies combined their strength in numbers to pursue whatever had sought safety the other side of the roadblocks. It wasn't long before blockades were no longer fulfilling their purpose and the dead were streaming into the countryside like ink slowly spreading itself on blotting paper.

Fields with livestock helped to draw the hordes deeper and deeper into the countryside, the walls and hedges keeping the stragglers at bay were no match for the force of the dead as they marched on. Soon the people who had felt relative safety were being devoured in their homes and on the road. Villages close to the major cities were torn apart by the hordes. These large groups were like a symbiotic organism, acting as one, working together for their next meal.

The worst affected areas in the beginning were around London, Birmingham, the North West, West Yorkshire, South Yorkshire and the North East as large towns and cities merged into each other to create mass urban areas. It was the villages and rural areas that were close or sandwiched between these urban sprawls that felt the full force of the largest hordes. The hordes were so big that they toppled buildings with the weight of their numbers and those unlucky enough to be caught in the earliest and deadliest of crowds were mostly ripped limb from limb, surrounded without hope of escape.

The hordes didn't follow any particular pattern in their movement, the places they stumbled upon were down to chance, sometimes they were drawn by the living, other times it was simply following the path of least resistance. Roads and railway lines drew the dead along, as if some sort of semblance of their past made them traverse along the country's transport links, in reality, these were just paths for the dead to follow. Some communities evaded the hordes by chance, some act of God, or fate or luck, diverted crowds, as people sat out the disaster in their homes; unaware that they narrowly avoided hell dropping into their front yard. Because the UK was so small, it was only a matter of time before luck ran out for those that managed to escape the masses.

The best way to survive being in the middle of a horde of the dead was to remain unseen, make no noise and hope and pray that it moved on and didn't stop to wait it out. The dead have an endless supply of patience and can wait an eternity for their supper. Escape wasn't out of the question either, although again, this relied on luck. Many people on the coast took to the water in boats, zombies can't swim, and their brains need oxygen to function so avoided water. Many people who had the experience and access to boats, set off for islands in sunnier climates looking for a new life away from this deadly outbreak.

People were learning fast or dying. The need to adapt to the new world was a necessity. Only the most adaptable survived. Maggie and the rest of the community in the Peak District had age and wisdom on their side and had adapted to their new surroundings well. Were the close-knit and organised community strong enough in the face of a horde to survive? Time would tell.

Chapter 31 - Hit the Road Jack

The morning after the party, or the nightly ritual for the elderly community, Jack, Lucy, and Chloe set off again aiming to complete their trip that day. As a thank you to Maggie, they left her with one of the rifles and a box of ammunition, she protested and questioned what she'd do with it anyway, but eventually took it with thanks. They left details about where they were going and said that any and all of the community were welcome to join them if they ever ventured further north. Maggie had warned them to circumvent main roads and to avoid the bigger towns around the area as they were swarming with the dead. Jack and Lucy had already planned to avoid them anyway and aimed to head as far east as possible before driving North. Jack's plan was to get close to York and then wing it from there where he was familiar with the roads.

They still had to clear the rest of the Peak District and then zigzag the country roads to avoid the main towns, but they were setting off with renewed hope having spent the evening surrounded by good and inspirational people. Jack felt hazy from drinking a little too much, but Lucy was in a worse condition. She wore sunglasses that were too big for her, attempting to shield her eyes from the agonising daylight. Jack and Chloe joked at Lucy's expense and she laughed half-heartedly with them, but even through the nagging headache, Lucy was ready and alert.

The journey was long and at times, arduous. The previous evening's festivities had made them relapse into their old ways and every gruesome sight was as disturbing as the first time they witnessed the frequent horrid scenes. Chloe, who had come out of her shell while playing in the pub, becoming an outgoing and noisy little girl, had shrunk back to a frightened shell and sat in the footwell; speaking infrequently and busying herself in a make-believe world of toys. Lucy was envious of the girl's ability to switch off to her outside environment, but knew she could not afford such luxuries, Chloe's life depended on the actions of both Jack and Lucy.

Travelling across the Peak District was almost pleasant, the roads were quiet and obstruction free, only a couple of dead were spotted in miles of travelling. The journey was more complicated when they came down the hills and made their way around Sheffield and Rotherham. The dead were in larger numbers and several roads were blocked causing more miles to the journey. The Bentley was getting beaten out of shape having to force the dead and obstacles out of the way.

The journey took them over bridges crossing the M1 and A1 motorways and the views from their elevated positions wiped away any of the joyous feelings of the Peak District and the previous evening's revelries, reminding Jack and Lucy about the stark reality of the new order. The traffic on the motorways was end to end, vehicles were upturned, and many cars looked abandoned with doors wide open, these sights were paled into insignificance by the dead. The numbers, thousands littering both carriageways, a sea of grey, a nightmare with the colour washed out. The smell came through the car vents and made the atmosphere putrid. From both sides of the bridge, heads lifted, the ghastly hum from the thousands of dead hung in the air, penetrating deep into consciousness, and made Chloe whimper with despair. Lucy held her hand as they continued their journey, elevated above immediate danger.

Heading east, the route took them between Scunthorpe and Doncaster before turning north, the Vale of York began to extend itself across the horizon, the flat expanse was green and pleasant, but the dead were never far away. Jack, in a lapse of concentration, hit one of the dead at 30 miles an hour; with a crunch and a splash of blood, the car took the full force of the blow and was drifting to the left. Jack was frightened that the damage would force them to ditch the car and attempt to make it on foot. Lucy, fearing the same, had managed to figure out the shotgun and had loaded cartridges into it, ready for an escape on foot, the action of doing so easing her fears.

The car motored on; the tough Bentley was made of sterner stuff than Jack, who was in full-on panic mode, the fear about leading Chloe and Lucy to the unknown consumed him and his doubts were exacerbated with each shudder of the steering wheel. They limped to York and skirted around the city and continued north until they broke onto roads that Jack knew well and the nostalgia of his youth came flooding back, tinged with sadness. He knew that the kids of today weren't going to enjoy the idyllic childhood that he'd adored.

"We're almost there." Jack said smiling as they entered the village of Great Ouseburn. The village was quiet and there weren't any dead to be seen, but there was no living either. It could have been a summer's day in the early hours of the morning, before anybody stirred, but it was 4:30pm and there should have been people milling around.

"Brilliant!" Chloe cried from the back seat, she'd moved out of the footwell and was stretched out on the big leather seat desperate to stretch her legs having spent over seven hours cooped up in the car. Jack and Lucy were feeling much the same and were exhausted from the forced concentration of driving through a hostile territory.

"Where are your keys Jack?" Lucy asked, eager to prepare for getting in the house quickly.

"They should be in the backpack next to Chloe, the black one." Jack said as Chloe passed the bag over to Lucy.

"We need to be quick getting in, Chloe, we don't know what it'll be like, so when we park, wait for me to get out and then hold my hand and follow my lead." Lucy commanded to Chloe as the scenes of the day lingered on her mind.

"Okay." Chloe said sullenly.

The car pulled into Eastloch at 5:25pm and they rolled into the village. It was quiet, they'd past a couple of the dead up the road, but the village appeared empty. Driving past the small primary school, Jack felt emotional as memories flooded in waves and his mood turned sombre, the hope of seeing his mum and dad seemed slim and it was now coming to the crunch. He'd blocked all thoughts about them and his friends in recent days as he'd been busy concentrating on staying alive.

Memories of Jack's childhood were stirring his emotions and he was now speeding through the village to get back home. Lucy didn't say anything, she was aware of how he must be feeling and looked out of the window as curtains twitched when the car sped past, what was inside those houses, she didn't know, but kept quiet and focused on getting the three of them safely inside.

Jack pulled into the drive of his childhood home and sighed loudly as he saw it was empty with no sign of his mum and dad's campervan. He turned off the car and got out and ran around the side of the house to the gate that led to the back garden. Tension had built up and he was at the edge of his nerves, carelessly leaving both Chloe and Lucy behind to fend for themselves. They were quick to follow; Lucy didn't forget her responsibilities. In Jack's rush he hadn't taken the keys with him. The back garden was secure, surrounded by a high wall so was safe from the wandering dead. Lucy caught up to Jack, who was peering through the windows of the house, half crazed, his composure gone.

"Here are the keys, let's get inside and have a look around." Lucy said trying not to antagonise Jack who was clearly acting through fear and panic.

He didn't respond for a minute, lost in his own thoughts, he saw Lucy's outstretched hand with the keys and the words sunk in. He snatched the keys and unlocked the door and rushed inside. Lucy and Chloe waited in the hallway as Jack whizzed around the house, passing them several times as he searched. Finally, he didn't come back, so Lucy told Chloe to wait and went to find Jack.

Finding him slouched on a couch with his head in his hands, she approached, and he spoke through tears, "They're not here, they haven't been here."

Lucy sat down beside Jack and held him as he sobbed, she looked for the right words, but none came. After some time, she managed to string a few words together, "It will take them some time to get back from Scotland. We may have beaten them here."

"Yeah." Jack said doubtfully, pulling himself together. "I'm sorry you had to see me like this. I don't know what I expected, I was optimistic, that's all."

"Please don't apologise, you have nothing to be sorry for. You've got us here in one piece and we can start to think about a future now." Lucy said touching Jack's face gently.

"I think you were the one who got us here, I merely facilitated it." Jack said with a half-hearted laugh. "I can't tell you how glad I am that you came with me. I think I love you." Jack had let the emotions boil over and saw himself from afar for a minute and wanted the ground to swallow him up.

Lucy didn't speak and was relieved to see Chloe walk into the room.

Chapter 32 - Lazy Day

Jack spent most of the morning moping around, lost in despair as he thought of his parents out there in the wild. He wasn't prepared to be as morbid as his lingering doubts wanted him to be, but even so, he wasn't much fun to be around. He was short tempered and snappy. Lucy didn't hold his mood against him, she gave him a wide berth and spent time with Chloe, playing games and talking.

The house still had running water and the gas hobs were working which meant they could all shower, albeit in cold water, and heat up the tinned food for their meals. The garden was surrounded by a tall wall meaning that they could enjoy the spring sunshine without fear of being ambushed by the dead. It was idyllic, spring flowers were blooming, thanks to the loving care of Jack's parents' green fingers, the place was peaceful, and swallows swooped in and out, busy with their own tasks, unaware of humanities woes.

To keep out of Jack's way, Lucy boiled pots of water and spent at least an hour pouring a warm bath for her and Chloe to enjoy. She was eager to relax in the soapy suds and have some time to just lay and think. Since she'd met Jack and Chloe, life had been a whirlwind and there hadn't been an opportunity to digest anything. Deep down, she knew dwelling on things was probably a bad idea, but she was all too aware that not facing up to problems was far worse. Unselfishly, she let Chloe have the bath first and rushed her through it so she could enjoy the warm water for as long as possible, she had found some paper and colouring pencils and left them on the kitchen table for the girl to entertain herself while she soaked away her troubles.

Lucy drifted off into thought with the warm water wrapping around her body, she looked at her legs and arms and saw she was covered in scratches and bruises. The water stung a little, but she leaned back and relaxed and began to think of things, of life, of Jack, of George and the future.

It was impossible not to feel melancholy and her thoughts drifted off to her time stuck in her apartment waiting to die. She had been watching videos trying to get a better understanding of just what on earth was happening and she stumbled on a few clips of pranksters who had been all the rage at the time; craving attention and fame by playing cruel tricks on their friends and strangers. These clips had irritated her in the normal world; they were always so banal featuring people with carefully coiffured hair, they had to look their best for their followers. These pranksters hadn't changed their tact with the rise of the dead, they saw social media was more alive than ever and spotted opportunities to increase their exposure. She had watched several videos of well-known social media 'celebrities' taking their jokes and cameras out into the world of chaos and destruction with the intention of their own self-serving agendas. One clip showed two brothers, they'd caught one of the dead and tied it to a chair and tied the dead thing's shoelaces together. One brother then released it to chase the other brother who they'd wrapped in bacon. Another showed a guy running down the street with old-fashioned custard pies slamming them into the faces of the dead. Lucy grimaced at the stupidity of their actions and how utterly pointless and selfish these people were, wasting their time for popularity when they could have been helping others.

Her thoughts moved away from social media to her own witness accounts outside her apartment window, she thought proudly how Jack had recognised her from her videos and that she may have helped other people survive through her accounts of the situation. She still couldn't get the images of the streets of Manchester out of her head, the army retreating, the early days of people running for their lives, chilling screams and then the streets left with nothing living, just the dead.

Lucy was all too aware of the evils in the world before the breakdown of civilisation, but hadn't been consumed with them. Although she had suffered great loss through the death of her parents and more recently her lover George, she was still committed to seeing the good in the world. Upon moving to Manchester, Lucy had volunteered for Manchester Action on Street Health, or Mash for short, a charity organisation that helped women who worked in the sex trade. Here, she helped support the Sexual Health Nurses by talking to women who worked as prostitutes on the street or in massage parlours and provided them with free condoms and needles. Many of the women who visited the drop-in centres had suffered tremendously; domestic violence was a common theme as was mental health problems and drug addiction. But even through the tough facades on the faces of the women that came to visit, she saw light and brightness in many of them, just by visiting the drop-in centres, these women were one step closer to seeking the help to get them away from seedy men, the wrong crowds and the desperate cycle of depreciation. It was a tough volunteer gig, but she went to each session with relish, desperate to help as many people as possible, much of the time her efforts were in vain, but she did witness the team helping some of the younger girls to turn their lives around and to begin new lives with hope. But now, as Lucy lay in the bath, thinking about these women, she knew that many of them would have been the first ones to have perished, left vulnerable on the street with no protection. Many would have gone seeking heroin after the breakdown of civilisation looking to satisfy their addiction, leaving whatever safety they'd holed up in to go in search of their vice, only to fall into more immediate perils.

Her thoughts moved on and settled on Jack; she felt a little happiness for the first time since settling in the warm water that was now cooling rapidly. She already knew before he had blurted out his declaration of love the way he felt for her, she could see it by the way he looked at her and how he worried about her. Part of her recoiled at the prospect of someone loving her in such a short space of time, particularly the absurdity of their entire situation, contrary to the recoil, she also cherished being loved, even if she didn't know if it was real or not. She did feel strongly towards him, but knew they were in some sort of weird honeymoon period, time being warped by the intenseness of living in a world of the dead. Guilt about George nagged at her when she thought of Jack, but her thoughts of George were being left behind, like Jack, she was feeling a sense of closure forced upon her as her old life, the world's old life, had been wiped away like a shaken Etch-A-Sketch.

She was also a little concerned that Jack was showing signs of being clingy, but reasoned with herself that it was natural with the current order of things. He was a man and society had bred men to feel the need to look after women, it wasn't a bad thing, but he had shown quite a few signs of panic and had been rash at times when her cool head would have been better equipped to deal with situations. Contradicting her own thoughts, she remembered how he wouldn't leave her in the face of certain death with a gun held to his head and that he had risked his own life once again to rescue her from Mick's house. She also liked the fact that he wasn't a cocky arrogant man, he was conscientious, sensitive and caring and, although he didn't talk a great deal, he was funny, intelligent and resourceful considering he was from a similar background to Lucy: having no discernible skills for survival. She was also concerned for him, since they'd arrived at his parents' house, he had withdrawn into himself and pushed both Lucy and Chloe aside, it was natural, of course, as the disappointment of finding the house empty must have been a huge distress and disappointment. She also knew that he'd spent many years in turmoil and self-imposed exile following the death of his wife and child and worried that their current situation would leave him listless and unable to move forward. For the sake of Chloe and herself, they couldn't afford to carry a passenger for long. Lucy cursed herself for being so callous, but knew her thoughts were true and she knew she had to shake Jack out of his stupor so they could figure out what to do next.

-

As Lucy bathed herself, Jack had sat and thought, lounging in a large sofa of soft cushions. He was tired from constant travel and worry, but didn't want to sleep. He thought of his Mum and Dad and tried to remain hopeful. Like Lucy, he sat and thought about the world and let his mind drift off to Amy and Ruby and a time they had spent in the Lake District in a little cottage. It had rained all weekend and the three of them had spent the weekend stuck inside their little cottage. It was complete bliss. He was almost grateful that neither Ruby nor Amy had lived to see the way the world had turned out, but was angry that he couldn't have gone with them. He didn't believe in God or Heaven, but would have preferred to go with them rather than go on alone. He lay on the sofa in tears, desolate.

Jack finally managed to pull himself together, as he realised he'd been alone for too long and hadn't seen Chloe or Lucy for some time. The now familiar sense of unease struck him, wiping his eyes, Jack stood and walked out of the room to go looking for the girls. He walked down a corridor, past the laundry room and hovered by the door that led to the kitchen, he leaned on the doorframe and looked into the room, sat at the round table at the far side of the room was Chloe, with a towel on her head, the way women wear them, occupying herself with some colouring pencils and paper, she hummed happily as she drew. He watched on and the realisation hit him that he needed to pull himself out of his wallowing mood and focus on the future. The three of them had come so far and seeing the girl's innocence drawn out through play made him get a grip of his own pathetic self-pitying. He walked into the kitchen and Chloe turned and smiled, "Hi Jack, do you want to come and draw with me?"

"Sure kiddo, that sounds fun." Jack said with a smile, his eyes still red from his tears. He felt that warmth in his stomach that often followed a bout of tears.

"What are you drawing?" Jack asked as he approached the table.

"It's me, you and Lucy." Chloe said holding up the piece of paper proudly.

"It's brilliant, you're very talented." Jack said and he wasn't lying. The drawing was good for a seven-year-old. She had drawn herself in-between Lucy and Jack holding hands with each other, they were all smiling in a sunny setting. It was beautiful to Jack.

"Thanks, I made it for you and Lucy. I'm glad you rescued me." Chloe said looking seriously.

"We're a family now aren't we." Jack said, not as a question, but more of a statement, giving the girl a little cuddle as he sat down next to her.

"I think so, I know you're not, but you're like my mummy and daddy now." Chloe said, looking sad.

The statement of frankness from Chloe threw Jack a little and he had to pause to gather his thoughts, finally he spoke, hoping to say the right thing, "We are, and we'll take care of you. Do you want to talk about your mummy and daddy? We've not really spoken about it and I want to make sure you're okay."

"Me and Lucy speak about them. I miss them, and it makes me sad. I should have made them stay home with me; I could have stopped them going out." Chloe said.

"You couldn't have known; nobody knew what was happening. It's not your fault and you shouldn't blame yourself for anything." Jack said holding her hand.

"They might come back, even if they're monsters, they might get better and see the note you left and come looking for me." She said hopefully.

"They might just do that. It's good to hope. My mum and dad are out there somewhere making their way back here too." Jack said smiling, "Shall we draw something together? What would you like to draw?" He moved the conversation on as he didn't want to give the girl too much false hope.

"Can we draw some horses in a field on a farm? I like horses." Chloe began to draw before she'd even finished talking, the choice of muse was chosen.

-

Lucy had been listening from the dining room and smiled to herself. She thought to herself that she didn't need to pull Jack out of his mood, he'd done it himself, or Chloe had. She had listened to the two of them talk and her heart had melted a little and felt tears form in her eyes, through sad happiness. Maybe she was falling in love with Jack, she didn't know, but she liked what she saw.

-

That evening Chloe slept in the room next door to Jack and Lucy. Lucy and Jack made love slowly and wrapped themselves together once again. The closeness growing stronger with each intimate moment they shared. After they had exhausted themselves, they lay in bed in the darkness and talked.

Lucy asked, "What should we do now?"

"I'm tired so might go to sleep." Jack joked, knowing Lucy wasn't talking about this precise second.

"You know what I mean." She said with humour in her voice.

"My friend lives in a village called Greyholt a few miles from here. He's got a farm and the means to grow things on an industrial level, plus the knowhow which is a big bonus considering I've killed every house plant I've ever owned.

"I'd like to go over there tomorrow and see if he made it. I'm certain he will have, he's tough." Jack said thoughtfully.

"Okay, shall we come with you?"

"No, I don't think so, it's not far and I know this area like the back of my hand so if the car finally stops working I can leg it over the fields and come back here. It'll be better on my own and I know you hate me doing this, but I'd feel better if you two stay here."

"Leg it over the fields? You're back in Yorkshire five minutes and you're already talking like it." Lucy was smirking although Jack could only sense it through her voice as he couldn't see her in the darkness.

She continued, "You don't have to look after me you know. I'm perfectly capable, although I do appreciate everything you've done for me, I'm here for you too and I want to protect you and Chloe."

"I know and I'm sorry, but I just can't help myself. Call me old fashioned or a chauvinist pig, I'm not really like that, I just, you know, I care about you and I selfishly lose my head when you're in trouble. I can't help it."

"I know and I'm only partly teasing you. I think you're quite wonderful, but we need to work together as a team if we're going to survive. You and me need to take care of Chloe and that means we'll both have to take occasional risks."

"Okay, deal, but I still won't like it. And, by the way, quite wonderful? I'm fully wonderful don't you know."

Lucy laughed, "I'll give you that, but that's only because I've just had my wicked way with you and I'm high on endorphins, we'll see how I feel in the morning."

Jack laughed this time, "I'll just have to make sure we find a way to keep those endorphins topped up tomorrow then."

They drifted off leaving the melancholy of the day behind them with thoughts locked firmly on the future.

Chapter 33 - The Farm

The following morning Chloe, Lucy and Jack ate tinned fruit for breakfast in the garden, it was warm, and the birds were singing. The air was fresh, and the world seemed like a better place than it did the previous day. The three of them were more relaxed having had a night's rest. There was little to concern them with the outside world as they sat locked away in the secure garden, the front of the house had all the curtains drawn so they were oblivious to any threat. Jack explained to Chloe that he was going to see a friend and that Lucy and she were going to spend the morning in the house together. Lucy had laid out flour and yeast on the table and told Chole she was going to teach her how to make bread.

At about 10:00am, Jack said his goodbyes and went around through the back garden, checked over the gate for any lurking danger and climbed over it rather than leaving it unlocked. He'd done that trick quite a few times as a teenager for no other reason than the joy of climbing the gate. He walked to the road and glanced left and right to see if there were any dead, there were none, so got in the car and drove off, worry rising in the pit of his stomach as he left the two girls alone.

Driving out of the village, Jack didn't see any dead, he did notice curtains twitching again, but no real signs of life. It struck him that his childhood home hadn't managed to salvage the community spirit that they'd encountered in the hills, but this didn't surprise him. When he was young, the village was full of colourful characters, aging characters who were brought up in the area and lived and worked all their lives in a short radius of their homes. As house prices went up and the older generation died off, the village turned into a commuter belt, younger generations couldn't afford houses, so it became filled with affluent middle aged families who wanted an idyllic setting not too far away from the large cities and towns. The once thriving community spirit died with the generation before it.

To get to Greyholt, Jack needed to skirt around a little town called Strongborough, it was where he went to high school and held many memories for him, he passed his friends parents' house along the way and wondered about their welfare. Upon reaching the outskirts of the town, the dead started to be visible again and he shuddered at the sight of them, once again reminded about the state of the world. The car wasn't faring well either, its steering was becoming increasingly erratic and it pulled to the left considerably, so he tried to avoid collisions at all costs. He took the bypass which ran parallel with the A1 motorway, to dodge Strongborough town centre, and found it was quiet. Before he turned down the bypass he had to pass over the A1 and looked down at the carriageways and saw the familiar sight of cars strewn across both sides of the motorway with several hundred of the dead ambling around the vehicles, all heads looking up to the sound of Jack's car.

Jack continued the journey in silence, weaving around abandoned cars and the dead. Looking in the rear-view mirror he could see that quite a few of the dead had climbed the verge of the motorway and were stuck at the fence between the bypass and the A1, he was careful not to attract any more on the way towards Greyholt, the last thing he wanted to do was jeopardise his friend's safety.

The roads leading to the small village were narrow and abandoned and as he entered the village, it looked pretty much the same as he remembered. A little further in, he saw mounds of mud at the sides of the road, they looked like they'd been dumped there to form a barrier. Further in still and he found that people were working on various projects, they stopped what they were doing and looked up to the car, all staring with suspicion towards Jack entering their space. He decided he'd continue on regardless and not speak to any of them. He came to his friend's house and drove past it and parked a distance away out of habit; not wanting to alert any of the dead to his presence. He knew it was pointless as there obviously weren't any lurking around with the men and women working a short distance up the road.

Walking into his friend's farmyard he looked upon the expanse of fields and saw that everything looked how he remembered. It was a good sign and he was hopeful that his closest and oldest friend was safe and well. A diesel engine started noisily from the nearest barn and he walked over and saw a JCB idling and recognised the driver instantly.

"Hey, James!" Jack shouted, but James didn't hear him as he shifted the JCB into gear and started to reverse.

Jack ran into James's eye line and waved. James glanced back with a look of annoyance, but the recognition hit him, and he smiled. Stopping the JCB, he jumped out of the cab and said, "Fucking hell Jack. I thought you were a goner. I tried to call you, but your phone was dead!"

James grabbed Jack and pulled him close for a hug, "It's fucking good to see you mate." James rarely spoke without cursing.

"It's a long story, but I'm still here and made it out of the west to come back home. How are you? How's Beth?" Jack said, again wincing at himself, he hoped he hadn't put his foot in it like he had with Danny.

"Beth is good, she's getting big now, but she's still as bossy as ever!" James said with a smile patting his friend on his back.

"Are you at your mum and dad's house? Are they okay?" James asked.

"I am, but they're not there. They've been up to Scotland in the campervan so I'm praying that they're on the way back now." Jack said attempting to sound positive.

"Come on, come inside and let's have a drink. Let's catch up. Fuck, I thought you were dead man. This shit is crazy." James said as he bound over to the JCB leaning into the cab and turning it off.

-

Beth was tearful when she saw Jack, like James she'd assumed that he'd perished and hugged him tightly, she was five months pregnant and was big for how far gone she was. They sat at the table and Jack told them all what had happened and about Lucy and Chloe.

276

"She must be some woman. It's the end of the world and I haven't seen you smile as much as this for a long time. Crazy bastard." James said, teasing Jack about Lucy.

"She's amazing." Jack said blushing.

Beth and James looked at each other and laughed.

"What's going on here then? I saw those guys working outside, are they anything to do with you?" Jack asked.

"We've got big plans and I'm fucking amazed at how quickly we've grouped together. As you know I've always been an esteemed and important part of this ageing community." James laughed at this thought and continued, "Well these old bastards called a meeting the first day that the situation looked really bleak and the whole of the village, or the ones that are still here, got together. We had a projector, all sorts of stuff, 21st century tech in this backwash of a village. Anyway, Roger, remember him? You and me did a waiting service for a big party of his when we were kids. Anyway, he did a whole presentation about how bad this shit was going to get and that we'd be fucked if we didn't all pull together. He was compelling, and roped me in to lead this lot of old codgers. We've got a plan for survival here Jack and it all revolves around the farm. Who'd have thought that the farm would be the hub of the community once again? No more producing food for cattle for me, I'm going upmarket. Anyway, Roger made a lot of sense and I think he's got a point, I saw the footage of the cities and how bad it was, I'm surprised your girl made it out of there. She must be something!"

Jack grinned, and James gave Beth's hand a squeeze and continued his narrative, "We gotta plan for the future. Shit's fucked, but we got a little one on the way and I want to build something for him or her. The way I see it, we can build something better for the next generation, shit was falling apart without all the dead roaming the street, if we get the chance, we can make things a damn sight better."

"How bad have things been around here then?" Jack asked.

"Greyholt has been quiet. Because we all got together so quickly, that Roger is a wily old cat, we were prepared to take those fuckers down if we came across them. Anyway, Strongborough is pretty bad, they were caught out, so is Ripon, basically anywhere with a large population seems screwed.

"I assume you've seen the state of the A1? It's full of those ugly bastards. That's less than a mile from here, but if we stay under the radar and don't make too much noise, they should waltz right past us. That's the plan anyway, these things can't go on forever without food, they'll starve and as long as we can get by until that happens I figure we'll be alright. Assuming the disease doesn't mutate so that it becomes airborne, but then we're all fucked so no point worrying about that."

"When did you become a science buff? Mutating diseases, I remember you in set two for science." Jack said enjoying being with his friend again.

"Remedial science, in-it." James said laughing.

"Have you heard from Andy or Scott?" Jack asked about their two other close friends.

"Not from Andy, as you know he was in Manchester and I'm not hopeful, but no news is good news I guess. Scott is here though; he cycled over from Harrogate and managed the ten miles without getting his legs bitten! He's working for the group and staying in the cottage over the road. He's on lookout with a rifle in the far field. He's good physically, but his Mum and Dad didn't make it unfortunately. It's a shit state of affairs. You know Scott though, doesn't say much or open up, we're keeping an eye on him." James said gravely.

"Yeah." Jack said, thinking about his friend Andrew who had a wife and three kids. He lived and worked in Manchester and wasn't the best under stressful situations, Jack couldn't help but think of the worst.

The three of them sat and talked for a while and Jack listened as James explained exactly what they'd done and what they were trying to do in Greyholt with their grand plans for survival. After a couple of hours James stood up and said he needed to get on or he'd be lynched by the community if he shirked his responsibilities. Standing, leaning against the back of the chair, James looked serious and said to Jack, "You, Lucy and Chloe should come here and be part of the project. I mean it. There's a house a couple of doors down, John never came back from Leeds, it's empty and would make a good home. We could do with some young blood around here, not that you're young of course, but you're a damn sight younger than the rest of these lot. Besides, you're on your own in Eastloch, come on, you know you want to. Power in numbers my friend."

"You're right, I do want to, but I'll need to convince the girls, I'm sure they'll be okay with it." Jack said thinking that this was what his new family needed.

-

Jack arrived back in Eastloch without incident. He jumped over the back gate and found Lucy and Chloe sitting in the garden chatting quietly. Upon seeing Jack, Chloe ran to him and gave him a hug around his waist, "I'm so glad you're back." She exclaimed with joy.

Lucy walked over to Jack and stroked his hand smiling at him, "Hi you."

"Hello ladies, what a wonderful sight to see my two favourite girls." Jack said enjoying the attention.

"How did you get on?" Lucy asked.

"Really good. I saw James and his wife Beth, I forgot to tell you that she's pregnant. She's looking really well. They're building things there, come on inside and sit down, I want to discuss a few things with you."

"Lead the way Jack, judging by your smile, I'm eager to learn more." Lucy said smiling at him.

Sitting around the table Jack cut straight to the chase, "I think we should all go over to Greyholt to live. There's a house there for us and they're building a community." He stopped and gauged their reaction.

Chloe was first to speak, "Okay, if we all go together."

"If you think it's for the best, then I'm in too." Lucy said.

Jack was taken aback, he thought he'd have to do a hard sell, but realised he was the only one attached to the house they were sitting in, it was his childhood home, it was just another house to Lucy and Chloe. He said, "Oh, that was easy, I thought I was going to have to do more of a sales pitch, let me tell you a bit more about the place anyway, I think you'll like it."

"We're all ears boss." Lucy said with a wink.

"Well, where to begin, the start I guess would be good. As you know, they have a farm and they have a community. They've been organised from the start. They're using the farm to grow food for everyone and they're working every day to build a barrier around the place to keep the dead out. James has a JCB so they're building a mud wall. They also raided the supermarket with a tractor and trailer and took most of the tinned goods they could find to keep them going in the short term and also the garden centre for fruit and veg seeds. By the sounds of it, they also have quite a few people with expertise in different areas, there's even a doctor." Jack said as he rushed through all the things that James had told him.

"Wow, this place seems too good to be true, when are we going?" Lucy said almost sounding sarcastic, but genuine in her response.

"If it's okay with you two, I'd like to go today. The sooner we start to build our future, the better. I'm going to leave a note for my mum and dad to let them know where we've gone; when they get back." Jack said, hesitating slightly.

"And a note for my mummy and daddy." Chloe said eagerly.

"Of course kiddo." Jack said.

-

Jack wrote two notes, one for his parents and the other for Chloe's parents and left them with a page of the map ripped out to highlight the route in the remote chance that Chloe's Mum and Dad were to come looking for her. They packed and were in their new home two hours later. James had a spare key from the previous owner's neighbour, who had protested a little, but eventually resigned to the fact that Mr and Mrs Chapman weren't coming back from Leeds.

The house was a sturdy Yorkshire stone building with walled gardens and was tastefully decorated, they changed the bedding in two of the bedrooms and settled down. James had said he'd come around in the evening to talk about the village plans, so Lucy, Chloe and Jack relaxed and settled into their new home.

Chapter 34 - Mixed Reception

James and Beth arrived at about 6pm to properly introduce themselves to Lucy and Chloe, bringing a bottle of wine to toast the new arrivals. The five of them didn't have long to get acquainted before James spoke up, "Sorry to catch you unawares, but I mentioned your arrival to Roger and he suggested a community meeting to get you acquainted with everyone. I thought it was probably the right thing to do, so you're going to be thrown in at the deep end."

"Oh my. I'd have worn a suit if I'd have known we were going to be interviewed." Jack said looking a little nervous.

"Don't worry, it's just a formality. Everyone is just a little jumpy, there's been quite a bit of lawlessness around here, so strangers are greeted with a little caution. I've got your back so don't worry about these old fu-" James managed to stop himself from swearing in front of Chloe.

"When and where?" Lucy asked.

"Now actually, Roger's been gathering everyone up. The meetings tend to happen in my barn. Most of them will be there now. Come on, let's get this over with and we can get to know each other properly." James said.

James and Beth led Jack, Lucy and Chloe to the barn and as they approached they could hear the low rumble of voices, looking around as they approached, Jack spotted two people holding rifles looking over the fields and assumed that they were keeping watch to ensure there were no unwanted visitors stumbling into the meeting. As they turned the corner and entered the barn the noise stopped and people turned to look, it was an intimidating situation and Chloe nudged herself close in-between Jack and Lucy, while the two adults involuntarily stepped closer to each other.

Lucy leaned into Jack and whispered, "This is a bit intense." Jack nodded and looked worried.

The group, numbering close to 60, parted as James led the new arrivals to the makeshift stage, made from pallets, where a smartly dressed man in his 60s stood waiting, smiling, Roger.

Beth joined the rest of the group near the front and James moved closer to Roger and whispered something to him as Chloe, Lucy and Jack stood on the stage, feeling vulnerable, looking out to the eager faces. There was a mixture of people, mainly 50 plus, but there were a few children and some younger faces in their 20s and 30s.

Roger raised his hands in the air and the barn fell silent, "Ladies and Gentlemen, thanks for meeting at short notice, but I thought it right to introduce you to our new guests, we have Lucy, Chloe and Jack. Jack is one of James' oldest friends and is a local boy. They've made an incredible journey across the country to come back home to Yorkshire and James has invited them to stay at the Chapman's house."

There was a murmur in the crowd and one haggard old woman looked angry and spoke, "They've only been gone a week, they could be back. It's not right that they're staying in the Chapman house."

Jack and Lucy looked at each other and grimaced.

"Please Magda, you know as well as I do that the Chapmans aren't coming back. It's not what any of us would have wanted, but you know what we're doing here, we're building for the future, so please do not be so hostile to our new guests. We've offered them the Chapman house; they haven't taken it." Roger said with a friendly authority and the lady named Magda muttered under her breath, but didn't speak again.

"Anyway, both myself and James are happy to have you here and look forward to you being part of our project to build a sustainable community that can prosper in very challenging circumstances.

"As we set out in our first meeting, we decided that if any new members were to join us, we'd do it formally and in front of everyone, to set the rules, and to remind everyone else of the rules too. We require a little order and organisation to survive and although this all seems like an awful formality." Roger was assured and commanding and people listened willingly.

Turning to the new arrivals, Roger continued, "I think it's important to put a name to a face too. So, before we begin with all the formalities, I'd like you to introduce yourselves to the village."

Lucy and Jack both looked at each other once again, Jack whispered to Lucy, "I hate this, do you want me to go first." She nodded eagerly.

"Um, hello, my name is Jack and I was brought up in Eastloch and went to school at Strongborough, I was living in a place called Westerlyn, but wanted to come back here as it is less populated and I figured, we figured sorry, that we would have a better chance of survival.

"I'm a nice guy, fairly resourceful, not afraid of hard work and a quick learner. I want to build a better future and believe you guys are on the right track for that and would love to be part of the community."

"Thanks, Jack, you can relax." Roger said, patting him gently on the back.

Lucy took a deep breath and squeezed Jack's hand and began, "Hello, I'm Lucy and this is Chloe. Chloe is with us and we've taken care of her since we found her in a house we took refuge in. I'll spare Chloe speaking in front of you all. She's seven and is a wonderful and intelligent little girl." She spoke with defiance and set out between the lines that Chloe was her responsibility and that no one should come between them.

She continued her introduction with less force, "My name is Lucy and I owe a debt of gratitude to Jack. We met after the fall of civilisation and Jack took me in, rescued me from some very undesirable people and made sure myself and Chloe were safe. I was trapped in central Manchester in my apartment, but managed to barge my way through the crowds to get out of the city. I've seen so much and like to think I've helped people in my own way. I'm fit and willing and want to be part of your futures, we need you and I hope in time that you'll see that we are of benefit to you as a group."

There were a few gasps from the group as they took stock of Lucy's escape from Manchester and a sense of awe at the fact that she was stood in front of them having come so far.

"Thank you Lucy, you three have proved yourselves quite remarkable and I think we'll all agree that we're lucky to have you here. Does anyone have any questions?" Roger turned to the group of faces looking up at the stage.

"Hi, my name is Anne, I live in the house a couple of doors down from where you're staying. It's nice to meet you. What's it like in Manchester? We've seen around here, but none of the big cities, can you let us know more?"

Lucy stepped forward, "Hi Anne, it's nice to meet you too.

"I won't sugar coat it; it was bad. I was there from the beginning trapped in my apartment on Portland Street, for those of you that don't know, that's very central. It spread quickly and by the time of my escape, a few days after the beginning, the streets were awash with the dead. In the beginning I could still see people fleeing from my window, but by the end there was nothing living left, there were hundreds and thousands of the things.

"I watched the Army come in and start shooting, but retreat when all was futile. I heard and saw so many things I don't really want to recall, especially in front of the children. I had the fortune to use my neighbours four-wheel drive car to escape the city and at one point I was surrounded by a crowd at least ten deep all trying to claw through the windows. I was fortunate, I know that.

"Luckily for me, and Jack, the main arteries out of the city were blocked so many of the dead were trapped in the city when I left, but I can't imagine they'll be penned in for long. It was dire and I can't imagine many people survived in the cities."

Anne looked extremely sad, "Gosh. Thank you, Lucy." Lucy couldn't help but feel that Anne was holding back, she had an inkling that the woman must have had friends or family in Manchester, she hoped she was wrong.

"Brian here, do you have anything we can use to help us?" Brian was abrupt.

Jack turned to Lucy and whispered, "Should we tell them about the guns?"

Hesitating in thought, Lucy whispered back, "I think so, we need to be part of this community and I'm not comfortable having them in the house with Chloe."

"Yes, we do. We stayed at a house on the way here and it appeared that the previous owner had been a gun enthusiast. We have a selection of guns and ammunition that we'll hand over to use to protect us against the dead." Jack said.

"Excellent, that'll do nicely." Brian said without ceremony.

The room fell silent and Roger stepped to the front of the stage once again, "No more questions then. Okay, let's move on and get through the formalities so we can all go about our business. First up the rules.

"Rule number one is that we're all equal here, there's no jealousy, no maliciousness and we share all of our resources, that means food and water.

"Rule number two is about noise control. We need to be as quiet as possible, that means no raucous parties or shouting in the streets, we don't want to attract the dead here.

"Rule number three is about light control after dark. We have no electricity, but if you're using candles at night be sure to shut curtains.

"Rule number four is that we have no freeloaders, everyone needs a role here so that we're all working together, I'll talk to Jack and Lucy separately about the different jobs.

"Finally, the last rule is that we're a community, be kind to one another, if you see each other, say hello and especially to Chloe, Lucy and Jack, if you see them, introduce yourself to them.

"Right, that covers everything, thanks for coming and enjoy your evening, you'll get a chance to introduce yourself to these three in the coming days. I'm going to commandeer them to go through the jobs this evening. See you all soon."

The crowd quickly dispersed, some loitering a little, but the general consensus was to get back inside as quickly as possible.

Chapter 35 - Jobs

Jack and Lucy entertained James, Beth, Roger, and his wife Sandra in their new living room. They didn't know where anything was, so struggled to accommodate for glasses as they shared a couple of bottles of wine. Beth had brought some toys over for Chloe and she sat on the floor playing as the adults began to discuss the intricacies of the journey they were on.

James opened the wine and poured some for everyone and sat down and said, "Roger does all of the talking to the group, he's been here for eternity." He smirked at the older man. "We've got a bit of a structure here for organisational purposes, otherwise there would be chaos, luckily we've got quite a talented bunch of people who have naturally fit into the different job roles and they tend to discretely lead those who volunteer for the jobs that fall under them. I obviously know and trust you Jack and from what I've heard about you Lucy, especially from Jack's rosy tales about you, you seem like a remarkable woman and we'd like you both to be part of the steering committee to help drive this community forwards. Obviously, you'll still have to work like the rest of us, but you can help us make the big decisions."

Jack was still blushing from his friend revealing his gushing praise of Lucy and she gave him a gentle nudge with her knee, he looked at James, Roger and Beth, "I can't speak for Lucy, but I'd like that, it'd be nice to be able to contribute to the village. So, go on then, tell us what jobs you have."

Roger stood up and paced a bit and then began talking, he was more relaxed and less formal in the smaller group and with a glass of wine inside him, "We've split the jobs up into different groups that we thought were important. I'll list them in no particular order as they are all imperative to the group.

"Firstly, we have food and unsurprisingly James and a gentleman called Chris head up this operation. We have a few sheep and a couple of cows that we keep down the road away from the houses and Chris tends to these as he was, or still is I suppose, a farmer, not the arable kind. The big field you see in front of the farmyard is for crops. We've already started planting some vegetables and have a schedule to give us plenty of roughage throughout the year. It's a big job as we're not using machinery as it's just too noisy.

"Secondly we have utilities and facilities. We've got running water at the moment, but it won't last. An engineer named Arthur is looking after this one and it's a tough job, it's going to take a bit of time. Firstly we're looking into water for the long term in the form of a well or maybe water towers, then there are toilets as we need a sanitary way to dispose of waste once the water stops, the last thing we need is an outbreak of dysentery or some other ghastly disease to break our community, we've had enough of infections as I'm sure you can agree. Arthur is also looking into renewable energy sources to get some power into James' barn for refrigeration and freezers to give us options for long-term food storage."

"I've got something that might help with power." Jack said, "We stopped at a great little community in the Peak District and they had solar and wind power. The man who was keeping it running wrote down some instructions, I'll give them to Arthur, it should help him."

"Fantastic. You're already proving valuable" Roger said.

"Back to the roles and responsibilities, we also have a section for education, and this is split into two groups as it's important to educate everybody in the community. We have 12 children now, with Chloe included, and Mrs. Montgomery looks after the teaching of the kids. You'll recognise her, Magda, she's a bit of a battle axe, but her heart is in the right place and she was a head mistress in the 80s. She will be teaching the children, maths, English, and a little bit of science. We also have adult classes, this is to teach the fundamentals of survival like farming, first aid, combat, mechanics and foraging."

"You hear that Chloe; you can go back to school." Lucy said smiling at the her as Chloe pulled a face at the thought of it.

"Our two most dangerous jobs involve acting as lookout and going on supply runs, we're grateful to all those that volunteer for these. Your friend Scott is actively involved, he'll be over here soon as I know he's eager to say hello." Jack didn't think the 'eager to say hello' part sounded like Scott, but knew his friend would be involved in the dangerous role that Roger explained.

"Scott and ten others, including James here, take it in turns to keep look out to ensure the village isn't caught unawares and can continue about their business outside without walking into one of the dead. The group also handle supply runs and this is where it really is dangerous. We lost two good men on our first run; that was five days ago, and the subject is not really discussed in the wider community. People don't really want to face up to the reality of what's happening, and we don't want to crush people's hope. The two we lost, and it's not much consolation, weren't attached to anyone left in the village, but that doesn't mean that the loss was any easier to take. We have runs planned for the near future as we need equipment for our long-term sustainability." Roger was looking tired and Lucy was wondering if he had to do this for every new person that joined the community, if they were allowed to join, she wondered if Jack's friendship with James gave them special privileges.

With a puff of the cheeks, Roger smiled, took a gulp of wine, and continued, "I'll run through the rest of the jobs quickly, it's been a long day and I'm sure you've already got information overload. As I mentioned, we have a doctor, Dr Green, or Ed as he prefers. He worked at the Strongborough surgery. He lives in the large house in front of the green. He's turned one of his rooms into a doctor's surgery and he's supported by Sue and Edith, Sue is his wife. Because of the aging population, Ed, Sue, and Edith are remarkably busy and under resourced.

"And FINALLY, the rest of the village are helping build our walls and barriers to keep the dead out. This is a large job and we're getting there slowly, but we need many hands to make it happen. You'll have seen the mounds of earth when you came into the village, it's a start, but we need something more permanent and we have plans for this, but we need time and time is a luxury none of us can afford." Roger stood and downed the rest of his wine as he finished, he was shattered and eager to leave, "I'm going to leave now as I'm tired and need to sleep, you guys let the information sink in and James will talk you through any questions, he's the future." With that, Roger left as Jack and Lucy watched him slowly make his way through the door followed by his wife Sandra.

After a second or two, Jack turned to Beth and James and asked, "Is he okay? He looked weary."

"He's got cancer, he hasn't got long." James said looking at the carpet, raising his head he continued, "You can see we've got a lot of work to do, what do you reckon?"

"It is a lot of work, but between 60 people it's doable. I think what you've got here is amazing. Are people buying into it?" Jack asked.

"Yeah, people have surprised me. You look at Greyholt before all this happened and people were obsessed with petty little squabbles and were generally quite bigoted towards anyone alien to them. The shit hits the fan and I expected this privileged bunch to roll over, but they didn't, they've grouped together and are working hard and believe about the whole project. In a way, it's like going back 50 years to how it used to be, apart from the dead wanting to eat us." James said with a bitter laugh. "Do you guys have any questions or want to volunteer for any jobs?"

Lucy spoke first, "I'd like to volunteer as a lookout and for the supply runs, I have the experience of being out there."

"Lucy!" Jack exclaimed, but quickly shut his mouth as she scolded him with her eyes. He tried a different tact, "Maybe we need to talk about it between ourselves and come back to you." Jack had a pleading look in his eyes.

"No worries, it's understandable, take your time. We've got a meet tomorrow morning with the heads of all the job roles to discuss supplies, come along to that to learn more and meet the rest of the team building our futures. Now, let's talk less shop and let's get pissed." James said trying to ease the tension that was building up between Jack and Lucy.

They all turned their heads as they heard the front door close. A man with short brown hair walked in with a rifle slung over his shoulder, "Now then Jack."

It was Scott, Jack's childhood friend.

Chapter 36 - Tension

Lucy and Jack argued for the first time as they settled into the first night of their new home. Jack protested Lucy's insistence of being part of the supply runs and begged her to help with educating the children or helping on the farm. He used underhand tactics to try and get her not to take so many risks like using Chloe as an excuse that she shouldn't put herself needlessly in danger. This riled Lucy further and full-blown war erupted.

Much like when Jack had argued with Amy during their marriage, the feud between Lucy and Jack ended with him making a grovelling apology which, after a period of suffering, was graciously accepted. Jack's selfish reasoning: that he didn't want to lose Lucy, was heavily outweighed by Lucy's desire to help the community by aiding them with their quest for the equipment and provisions needed to ensure its long-term sustainability goals. Lucy's selfless outlook also forced Jack to quash any plans of his own to help the community from within, he couldn't let Lucy go out there on her own. It might have been male bravado, or even simple worry, but he knew he would have to volunteer to go back out there into the wilderness to stay close to her. She was forcing his hand to turn his back on his natural cowardice.

The following morning, Jack woke in resolute mood. He was up before Lucy and spent 20 minutes watching her peaceful face while she slept; the thought of her going out in the land of the dead made his stomach churn, but it was no match for the awe he felt at Lucy's determination to help people, people she had only just met. As he sat watching her, he knew he had been too demanding of her, he'd gone against everything he'd ever felt for women, he had acted like he owned her, he was controlling, or at least attempted to be. He knew that he was acting this way out of self-interest, wanting to keep her alive, but her safety wasn't his job, she was her own woman and a person who had shown a lot more composure and thought into their survival than the panic and fear that had driven Jack on. Deep down he was scared, scared of losing her, but he'd also fallen head over heels in love with Lucy and hadn't known he was capable of such feelings and that scared him just as much. He knew he couldn't lose another love in his life and this fear turned his personality so that he became a Neolithic man, determined to keep his woman locked up and safe from harm.

Lucy stirred and opened her eyes and tensed, she relaxed when she saw Jack looking at her and smiled, "Hi there, how'd you sleep?"

"Hey lazy bones, I slept well, you?"

"Nightmares, but nothing new. Have you been watching me?"

"Guilty. It's your fault though, you look rather pretty when you sleep, what's a guy to do?"

Lucy chuckled and wrapped the covers around her, enjoying the warmth of the bed.

"Hey Lucy, I want to talk to you. Hell, I want to apologise. I know I've been a bit of a cave man recently and I've been a bit needy too. You know how I feel about you and I sometimes get a bit overcome with worry.

"I'm sorry and it's not me, I'm going to back off a little and won't stand in your way if you want to do things. I know I've been through this before and I'll probably protest again, but I want you to know, I'm not like that, it's just worry and that's all.

"I know it's ridiculous and we've known each other for five minutes. But…

"I'm in love with you."

Lucy looked happy and laughed, "I sometimes wonder who the woman is here, you're a soppy one."

"Sensitive new age man, I think." Jack said, longing to hear more from her.

"I feel strongly towards you too Jack and you need to stop apologising." She touched his hand and looked away, she was embarrassed and was finding it hard to express her feelings, like Jack, she didn't think she'd be open to feelings of love for a long time, if ever.

She met his gaze, Jack was smiling at her, "I understand why you've been like you have and I have to say Mr. that you will face a losing battle if you think you can change my mind once it's set, I'm very obstinate, but I know your protests are coming from a good place and it endears me to you.

"You do know I'm naked under here?" She said winking at him.

"I'm all too aware, why do you think I've been waiting for you to wake up, I've been wanting to jump your bones." He said as he leaned in and kissed her, feeling her soft body against his.

Lucy had evaded the subject that she feared most.

-

Later that morning, James and Scott called to the house along with Magda. Magda introduced herself properly and apologised for the frosty reception she had given them at the village meeting. Magda's main purpose for her visit was to take Chloe across to her house where she was going to be teaching the other children with the help of an elderly couple called the Robinsons. She wanted to introduce Chloe to the children and show her the ropes of her makeshift school. Surprisingly, the girl was eager to go and learn, or at least make friends with the other children.

James and Scott informed Jack and Lucy that the meeting with the job heads was in half-an-hour, in the barn where they'd had their induction, and that they'd like Jack and Lucy to come along. They accepted the invitation, eagerly wanting to get started in their new roles.

James asked, "Did you guys sort your shit out?" Smiling as he teased them, having witnessed the tension of the previous evening, "Sorry, I mean, did you discuss the roles you'd like to be involved with?"

"We had a frank discussion, but I think we're settled, I'd like to volunteer for the lookout and supply runs." Lucy said enjoying James' teasing.

"I can see who wears the trousers." James said grinning at Jack, "What about you mate? You fancy being a nurse or something?"

"It is tempting, but I've only got the PVC nurse outfit and I fear I'd give some of the residents a heart attack." Jack said laughing, "I'd also like to volunteer for the supply runs and lookout posts, I'll help out elsewhere too."

Lucy looked at Jack, he hadn't said he'd be joining her with the dangerous activities, she raised her eyebrows and said, "Are you sure, you're not just doing this for me are you? Besides, I'd quite like to see that PVC outfit."

"You're not trying to talk me out of it are you?" Jack said with a snigger; James and Scott unaware of their in joke, "I'm sure, besides, I'm not really much use for anything else, I think we've got the experience and knowhow now to be of some use, plus you can make sure I stay safe out there."

"Alright love birds, looks like you've made your choice. Fucking good job too, we need the help. Anything to add Scott?" James was evidently happy at their choice of jobs.

"You'll need some training, but me and James can help you. Good to have you both on board, I hope you're a bit fitter than when we played 5 aside though Jacky-boy." Scott said, mocking Jack from their previous sporting rivalries.

"I'm a fighting machine Scott, I seem to remember you eating my dust on the football pitch anyway." Jack said jovially.

"Right, enough of this shit, we need to get to the barn." James said as he walked out of the room.

The meeting was a lot smaller than the one of Jack and Lucy's arrival. 12 men and three women, including Lucy, sat on an assortment of chairs around a makeshift table made from a large piece of metal sheeting resting on some barrels. The newcomers were welcomed warmly, and they were impressed with the meeting of minds. It was only the fifth time the group had met like this, but it was organised, cooperative and had already achieved a lot in a short space of time. The head of each job role spoke at length about their progress and their needs, while James took notes; including a list of items that each group needed to achieve their goals. This list was then broken down and prioritised.

The priorities were ranked as such:

1. Supplies for water and toilet facilities
2. Electrical supplies
3. Diesel
4. Food

They all knew that the water supply was going to run out sooner or later and that they were on borrowed time. They needed to set up a water system to wash and more importantly, drink from. There was a supply of bottled water that would last some time, but it was agreed that this supply was to be saved for emergencies and times of drought.

Arthur, who oversaw utilities, had a plan for drinking water, water to wash with and toilets. The plan was to use rainwater, but this needed the acquisition of water tanks, however, he knew in the nearby town of Ripon, a large plumbing supply store had a quantity of 100-gallon tanks. His plan revolved around using these tanks for drinking water, with a web of tarpaulin sheets to act as a giant funnel, filling them when it rained. They already had two large tanks that were used on the farm, the plan was to connect the existing tanks to the barn gutters and catch rain water, but because the barn roof and the tanks were well used and not exactly hygienic, these would be used for showers and washing of clothes and dishes.

The toilet block was already in progress. They had designated a field away from the houses and had dug a trench latrine. It was going to be a throwback to simpler times and the once privileged community were going to have to get used to the rules of going to the toilet, namely: covering their own waste with soil after their business and then covering the trench with boards to ensure flies weren't swarming around the community. It was undignified but was better than the alternative of living in their own filth and slowly succumbing to disease.

Diesel was also high up on the list of priorities. The village had a fleet of four vans, a JCB and tractor that all ran on diesel. Vehicles weren't allowed in the village, due to noise, but exceptions were made for the JCB and tractor as they were critical for heavy lifting and creating a secure perimeter around the village, the vans were for supply runs. James did have a large tank of red diesel, used for farm machinery, but this was now only half full and wouldn't last long.

Work had started on rigging up power for the refrigeration and freezer barn, as it had been christened; there was no need to loot fridges and freezers as every house in the village contained one of each that were no longer any use. Three houses also had solar panels which were in the process of being stripped by two of the braver members of Arthur's team who were comfortable on roof tops. The power supply was to consist of a stand-alone power system using solar and wind power. Arthur had already mapped out what was needed and wanted more electricity than was required. He wanted to split the power in two so that renewable energy fed the freezers and fridges directly in the day and the excess charged a supply of car batteries to ensure power after dark and in calm conditions. Arthur was a wise man and recognised the importance of a battery reserve in the winter months when daylight is at a premium. As a result of his particular needs, Arthur had a long list of supplies that his team needed and, against James' protests, had decided to come on the supply run to save valuable time on the expedition and avoid the need to go out again when inevitably a layman would pick up the wrong parts.

The group continued their meeting of minds, discussing project needs, when they were interrupted by the sound of a loud engine as a vehicle drove carelessly into the farmyard. James looked annoyed and said to nobody in particular, "Fucking squaddies, not again." He moved towards the barn door and said, "Stay here and continue the meeting, I'll get rid of them."

Both Jack and Lucy had the same thought, as they both stood and followed James to the barn door, they peered out and watched around the corner as James marched purposefully towards a soldier who had stepped out of his military vehicle. They heard James shout, "What the fuck are you doing? I've told you about driving your noisy trucks into the village, we've got people working outside. Are you intent on bringing the dead upon us?"

"Calm down James. We made sure we weren't followed, plus we put down two on the way here so you should be thankful." The soldier responded patronisingly.

"What do you want?" James retorted.

"Have you thought about our proposal? Our men will need your support." The soldier said.

"Look Anthony, you are all capable and trained. We can't support you; we've got enough mouths to feed. Get your men organised and do what we're doing. WORK!" James was irate.

"You'll need us when we launch our attack. We could quite easily take what we need." The soldier said in a reasonable tone which went against the intended threat of his words.

"Don't fucking come here, endangering us with your 'military intelligence', threatening to take what you want. We're here working to survive, I'm not sure what you're doing, probably sat around playing cards behind your fences with your stockpiles of weapons. You want something, you'll need to trade with us. We can't feed your men and I don't want them leering at our women either. I don't trust them." James wasn't giving an inch to the soldier.

"What do you want James?"

"We will help you, but not here, you guys are too trigger happy and you attract too much attention, we're doing all we can to stay under the radar, you've seen how many dead there are on the A1 just a mile or so away, they get wind of us and we're fucked. I'm not asking for much, we'll swap our farming knowledge, you have plenty of space in your army base to grow crops, but, and it's a big but, we want guns and ammunition."

"We can't give civilians guns." Anthony held back a laugh as he said this.

"Come on man. Don't be ridiculous, this isn't the old world. We need guns, it's only a matter of time before we are faced with more than just a few stragglers, we need to protect ourselves, but I'm more concerned about the living. I know that desperate people will do desperate things and I don't want to be a sitting duck here." James possessed a certain authority that the soldier didn't like from a civilian.

"I'll see what I can do. I'll need to talk to the Colonel. I'll be back in a few days." Anthony turned and stepped into the cab of his truck.

James called out, "Next time you come, make sure you park away from the village and come in on foot or you'll get nothing from us."

The soldier grunted something indecipherable and got in the truck before the men noisily made their exit.

James walked back to the barn and Lucy and Jack met him at the entrance, Jack asked, "What was that? What did they want?"

"They're pissing me off. Didn't you recognise him?" James said looking at Jack, "That was Anthony from school, he's in the army now and stationed at the army barracks down the road."

"Shit, yeah, I didn't recognise him. He was a thick fucker." Jack was adopting James' vernacular quickly

"Well, it seems the troops stationed there are worried about their long-term supplies and want us to supply them with food. I don't know if you heard, but he was almost threatening. I don't know if that's just Ant or whether the threats have come down the command chain. Fuck knows, but they're sat in that base and they're not fighting anyone, so I don't know why they don't grow something themselves. They seem a bit rudderless." James said the last sentence to himself.

"That doesn't sound good, do you think they will take what they want by force?" Lucy asked looking vexed.

"Fucked if I know. I'll get them to trade though, we can teach them, and they can provide us with guns and ammunition. They'll give in, they need us, plus they're supposed to be fucking trained professionals, not mercenaries taking what they want.

"Anyway, keep this chat quiet, if anyone asks, just tell people they were keeping us informed about the fight against the dead. Feel free to be positive about it, doesn't hurt to keep people's hopes up.

"Come on, let's get back to the others and finish this meeting." James seemed confident of getting his way with the soldiers and walked back into the barn with purpose.

-

The meeting was practically over when they returned, it was decided that the next supply run for electrical equipment and their water needs would happen in two days. The supply run team would meet again tomorrow to discuss strategies and formulate a plan for a stealth mission and a speedy exit.

Chapter 37 - Back to the Wilderness

The next morning was an early start. Much like the day before, James came around to Jack and Lucy's new home and took them to the barn. They were the first there and James explained what the meeting was about, "We're going to plan tomorrow's supply run, I've got an idea for the best way to get in and out as quickly as possible so I'll lead, please feel free to speak up though, you two have more experience out there so we'll take onboard anything you have to say. I must stress though, we need to protect Arthur at all costs, he's the brains here and without him, we'll struggle to get power and water."

As James finished talking the other members of the supply run team started to come through the open barn door, Jack waved to Scott, who nodded, and smiled at Arthur, but the rest of the group were strangers to him. Eight men, including Scott and Arthur sat around the table, four of the team were on watch so didn't make the meeting and wouldn't be coming on the run, they were also scheduled to be on lookout during the following day's raid; protecting the village from invasion.

James started the meeting immediately after the last of the men sat down, "Right, I want to make this quick, you can all get acquainted with Jack and Lucy after the meeting, for now, I have a plan that I want to run by you.

"Jack, you know where City Electrical Factors and the Plumb Centre is in Ripon; Lucy, basically they are on the outskirts of Ripon and I don't know if you know Ripon, but it's only a small city, but it's swarming with the dead. The two places we need to go to should be easily accessible as they're on the bypass and, thankfully, in secure premises, so once we're in we should have some time to get what we need. I'll show you on the map.

"Anyway, enough of the layout, you all know it well and I think my plan will work. The priorities of the mission are fucking simple. One, nobody dies, two; we protect Arthur at all costs and three, we get everything we need and get back to base as quickly as possible"

James was interrupted by Arthur, "I'll be fine, you guys look after yourselves."

"Look Arthur, our community is reliant on your knowledge, we like you, but it's not your rosy personality we want to protect, it's your knowledge. Knowledge is power, now more than ever, so we need to keep you in the land of the living. No arguments."

Arthur looked at his feet and seemed embarrassed.

James continued laying out his plan, "So, first things first, we'll need to draw the dead away from both City Electrical Factors and the Plumb Centre and I have the perfect idea for that."

James lifted a dust sheet off two long cylindrical tubes that were attached to simple control panels and gas canisters, "These are automated scarecrows. Basically, they use gas to make a loud explosion and are designed to scare birds away. We can use these two machines and put them at opposite ends of the road, about a mile or two apart and set them to fire at random intervals. They are loud and should draw the dead away, I'm sure of it. What do you two think?" James looked at Jack and Lucy.

Lucy answered, "They sound perfect. The dead are certainly attracted to noise; we shouted to get their attention when we were out there and it worked, they came after us."

"Good. The next part of the plan is to take three vans, we need the space to carry the equipment and us. We'll drive the vans in a line with the scarecrows in the middle van, we drive the vans to two spots." James pointed at two areas on the map, "We open the back doors, unload the scarecrows and set them to go. The front and back van will park close to protect me as I set them.

"Once the scarecrows are set, we're going to go down Littlethorpe Lane and wait for an hour to ensure the dead have time to be drawn away. I'm sure our vans are going to attract attention, so we need to lay low and wait for the scarecrows to do their work.

"We'll hit City Electrical Factors first. We're going to go in from the main road, the unit is behind a wire fence, so we'll have to cut our way in. We'll park the vans in a V shape to form a barrier around the hole in the fence and make our way in. I'm sure there will be a few of the dead in the industrial park so this is where we'll have to get our hands dirty. We need to fight quietly though so hand weapons only, guns should only be used as a last resort, they are too damn loud.

"I'm sure we'll have to break into the unit, but once we're in we need Arthur to be quick and get what's on the list.

"We leave the way we came and then head off to the Plumb Centre. I'm hoping this will be easier for us. The place is surrounded by a tall steal fence. I don't know if the gate is open, but we'll break in if we need to, once in, we'll use the vans to barricade the gate. It should be easy pickings when we're inside, again we might have to get our hands dirty, but there shouldn't be too many inside.

"Once we have everything we need we'll have to pick up the scarecrows as we'll need to use them again for other runs. This is where it gets tricky and I can only see one possibility and I'm not that big a fan of this part of the plan. One of the vans will act as a diversion, we'll drive up to the furthest away and get the dead's attention and slowly drive down the main road drawing them to follow, the van will continue past the other scarecrow and do the same again. One other van will follow, some distance behind, and pick up the scarecrows. The last remaining van, with Arthur and the essential equipment, will head straight back to the village after the Plumb Centre.

"That's it, I think I've covered everything. Any questions?" James looked at everyone in the eye and waited.

The barn was silent as the group digested the information relayed to them, Scott was first to speak, "Sounds like a good plan. Nice one James. What time do we go?"

"8am sharp. The vans are ready and fuelled and in position outside of the village." James was quick in response, "Any other questions?"

There were none, the plan was well thought out and the consensus agreed.

-

Jack woke at 5am the following morning halfway through a familiar nightmare, he shook the pieces of the broken dream out of his head and sat up and looked at Lucy. Just the sight of her calmed his nerves, but he was still feeling trepidation at the day's plans. They didn't have far to go, they should be able to do everything in a few hours, but if he was honest with himself, he didn't want Lucy out there and he didn't want himself out there either. He was keeping these thoughts to himself and wasn't prepared to rock the boat with Lucy anymore, he had no control over her, and rightly so, but that didn't mean he was happy about the risks they were taking.

8am came and both Lucy and Jack were ready, they had their weapons, Lucy's bat, and Jack's hammer. Lucy felt good with her bat and liked having it back in her possession. Jack not so much with the hammer. Magda had called to the house half-an-hour earlier and taken Chloe to her house, ready for school. Chloe had gone willingly, and it seemed that behind the battle-axe exterior, the old woman was gentle and had a caring heart that Chloe saw and liked.

Jack and Lucy didn't wait for James this time; they made their way to the barn and found the rest of the group carrying equipment to the vans parked a couple of hundred metres up the road. The vans were loaded with the scarecrows, bolt and wire cutters and a number of guns, Jack recognised the pump action shotguns and rifle from their find; what now seemed like an age ago.

Jack and Lucy were in the first van with a man named Tommy, James, and Scott in the second van and the other raiders rode in the last van protecting Arthur. Each van had a handheld radio and James relayed a message to Jack to lead the team the back way to Ripon through a village called Sharow. James explained to Jack that they had cleared the road with the tractor to ensure a clear route into Ripon a few days earlier.

As Jack approached the small city, he drove up to the first of many roundabouts on the bypass and the dead were visible, not in huge numbers, but the closer they got to the centre, more started arriving on the scene, through streets, gardens, from every direction. James radioed to turn left at the second roundabout and to stop, leaving space for the three vans.

Jack pulled to a stop and the dead were waiting, looking in the mirrors he saw the second and third van pull up as the dead approached. Hands, faces and bodies soon started to strike the side of the van and time seemed to slow down as the banging and moaning intensified, drawing more of the dead from their hiding places. Jack saw the second van's back doors open and watched as the third van inched closer to ensure no gaps allowed the dead to attack James as he set up the scarecrow. A horn sounded from the van behind to signal it was time to move shortly before James' wild radio commands, obviously shook up from being just a sheet of metal away from hungry mouths. Jack put the van into first and edged forwards, carefully pushing past the dead, he knew better than to cause damage through recklessness.

The second scarecrow drop was another smooth operation with Lucy, Jack, and Tommy all commenting about the perfection of James' plan. Tension still filled the air as the dead were swarming with purpose around every corner. They let James' van overtake them after successfully dropping the scarecrows and let him lead the way to Littlethorpe Lane. As the van went past, Jack heard the first explosion and relaxed a little, after initial confusion, when he realised it was the noise of the scarecrows doing their work.

The three vans pulled to a stop down the single-track road and they waited. They could hear the bangs of the scarecrows, set to go off at five-minute intervals. It was a frustrating wait as they had no way of knowing if the plan was working. Time seemed to stop as the hour passed painfully slowly with ten men and Lucy stood around keeping look out for anything lurking behind the bushes.

An alarm sounded on James' watch which signalled that it was time to move, the group were quick to get back in the vans, eager to get the mission over with and return to the sanctuary of the community.

"You ready?" Lucy asked James exhaling as she asked the question.

"As I'll ever be." Jack said without humour.

Driving in silence, Jack staring at the van ahead, the baseball bat and hammer rested on the middle seat, jolting with the bumps in the road as if willing themselves into action. There were five people in the leading van, a larger group, including Arthur, to keep him safe. Tommy, Lucy and Jack travelled in the middle van, with James, Scott and a man named Patrick bringing up the rear, they were to act as protection, while the first two groups got through the City Electrical fence, before making their way in. Jack worried that his own incompetence would put the group at risk, but battled valiantly to keep his doubts at bay.

As the group made their way back to the bypass, they saw that the large numbers of dead that had been following the vans had now disbursed with only a handful still visible. The turning from the narrow lane was close to City Electrical Factors and the first van quickly pulled up to the fence, Jack parked behind and the third completed the vehicle blockade. Everyone disembarked the vans quickly and started working in silence. Keeping noise down was key, although the dead in the small industrial park didn't follow the same rules. Upon seeing the 11 people approaching the fence, the dead worked their way over and started to pull on the wire and shake the noisy metal interlinks whilst moaning for their share of the flesh. Scott stepped forward and pulled a large hunting knife from a sheath on his belt, he signalled to one of the other guys who did the same. The two men tied cloth over their mouths and noses and with efficient speed, penetrated each of the dead's skulls with their knives, dropping them with stomach churning gore and a wet squelch with each stab. Jack had to look away, he wanted to vomit, Lucy stood and watched seemingly unmoved by the horrifying scenes.

Once the dead were taken care of, Patrick began to work with a pair of large bolt cutters. Within no time, the fence was cut enough to enable the group to get through one at a time, clambering over the limp bodies of the true dead.

Upon entering the small industrial park, which only contained four units, James was quick to issue orders, "Scott, Tommy, you two go to the other side and make sure the gates are shut. You four", pointing at Lucy, Jack and two men that stood

with them, "Circle Arthur and make sure he stays safe."
Arthur pulled his face and began to speak, but James was
quick to combat this, "No arguments Arthur, this is my
watch, do as I say, you can boss me around when we're
helping you with the facilities.

"The rest of us will ensure this place is clear before letting
Arthur in to pick up his electrical supplies. Everyone clear?"

The group nodded in unison and Scott and Tommy ran to the
other side of the industrial park but were quick to return.
Scott turned to James, "There ain't no gate, it's open. Never
was a gate."

"Shit, I was sure this place was secure. Okay, Scott and
Tommy, you guys stay out here and look after Arthur with
these guys then. It's probably best to stay out of sight so hide
behind one of the skips over there until we signal you.

"John, Patrick, Eddie, you guys follow me, we'll fucking
secure this place for Arthur's looting spree."

The four men went into the unit through the trade counter.
Luckily for everyone, the door was open. The unit consisted
of a trade counter, back office with facilities, warehouse with
the electrical supplies organised throughout rows of racking,
and finally a large loading bay. The trade counter was quiet
and the electric bell to signal a customer entering remained
silent as the door swung open.

Whispering to his team, James told Patrick and Eddie to
check the loading bay while he and John would go and check
the rest of the building. The pairs split up, but Patrick and
Eddie joined James and John almost immediately finding the

door to the loading bay locked, they searched the offices and warehouse, it was empty, eerily quiet and very dark, only their torches providing illumination. Patrick and Eddie found another door leading to the loading bay which was unlocked and quietly tip-toed in. They searched the back of the building where more shelves held further electrical supplies, again there was nothing. Moving to the front of the loading bay, they shone their torches and saw the coast clear. Patrick called out to the other two still looking through the shelves of the warehouse, when suddenly there was a noise. A loud thud sounded and then a crack, the torch Patrick was holding fell to the floor with a crash, shining its light on to the bare breezeblock wall. Eddie called out, "Patrick?" But no answer came, only the garbled sound of something that made the hair on the back of his neck stand on end. He ran to the torch to pick it up, but stood on something wet and squelchy, he slipped falling to the floor knocking the torch so that it spun on the floor. The circling light briefly lit up the scene before falling to a halt on a large set of roller shutters. He knew his eyes hadn't misled him during the brief light, Patrick was dead, his head caved in on the concrete floor and on top of him, one of the dead, its teeth had torn through Patrick's throat and was gnawing away strings of ligament and flesh, it wasn't clear how this had happened, the room was clear.

Eddie panicked and tried to get to his feet, but a hand grabbed his ankle, he screamed and kicked frantically in the dark, but kicked out at thin air. The moaning increased as the dead creature moved from its feeding to the living pray. Eddie couldn't see, but the dead sensed and didn't need any further motivation, it lurched forwards and bit into Eddie's leg. He felt the pain shoot through his body and wriggled free, finally managing to kick the creature in the head and crawl away.

James and John came running, but it was too late, Patrick was dead, and Eddie was bitten. James swung the torch light to the body and saw Eddie backing away into the corner. He saw the dead thing crawling to its feet and without a moment's hesitation darted towards it and struck it with a short-handled axe, powerfully smashing through the skull and destroying the brain. It fell to the floor with the axe still lodged in place. James lifted the light and shone it on Eddie and saw that he was bitten on the lower leg, "Oh Eddie. No Eddie."

"It's okay James. I can be with Emily now, it's okay, just leave me here." Eddie was remarkably calm, shock was setting in.

"We can save you Eddie, let us take your leg off, it might not have spread. We can take you to the Doc, you can survive." James was desperately looking for ways to save the man he had once despised in the old world, but had now become quite fond of.

"Fuck James, that's going to hurt. Fuck it. Do it." Eddie saw a glimmer of hope at the chance of survival.

Turning to John, James said quickly, "Go outside, get everyone in the office, we'll need a few people to help with Eddie. Then go to the van and get the big axe." John made off quickly, James shouted after him, "Just be fucking careful!"

James and Eddie waited in silence, James knew that time was against them and surveyed the loading bay, shinning the

318

torch, he saw that it had a mezzanine floor. The dead creature must have been up there and fallen onto Patrick, it looked as though Patrick had taken the full force of the fall and smashed his skull on the hard floor. It was of little comfort that Patrick would have felt no pain, Patrick was dead, and he was a good man.

A few minutes later, John came rushing in with the axe, closely followed by Jack, Lucy, and Scott. Eddie was already lying down, staring into the air in dreaded anticipation of the axe amputating his leg. Scott got down on his knee, handed Eddie a bit of wood to bite down on, and tied a belt around Eddie's thigh, "This'll stop the blood."

It seemed as though there was an unspoken understanding between everyone, Lucy and John had knelt either side of Eddie, ready to steady him. James took hold of the axe and glanced at Eddie, who had two torches on him. Eddie gave him a nod and James brought the axe up and with all his might severed the leg just below the knee. The blood rushed out quickly and Scott pulled the belt tighter. The sound of Eddie screaming through the bit between his teeth and the sight of the leg coming away would stay with them all for the rest of their lives.

The plan had changed, Lucy and Scott lifted Eddie, blood was still coming out at a rate of knots. James looked at them and said with urgency and a grave face, "Get him home now, go straight to the Doc, we'll do the other run and meet you back."

Lucy, Scott, and John carried Eddie as quickly as they could out of the building. Jack was left there with James, he wanted to go with Lucy, but knew his protests were selfish and would be met with scorn from all parties. He was part of this mission which had turned sour very quickly and they had to get the supplies.

"We'll have to leave the scarecrows." James said to himself.

"Are you okay mate?" Jack asked, looking worried as James stared at the floor.

"Fuck no. Fucking world. It's fucked." James said letting the swearing vent his disgust at the situation.

"We need to get Patrick wrapped up and give him a proper burial. What am I going to say to his wife and kids? Shit." James was close to tears, something Jack had never seen before. He put his hand on James' shoulder which seemed to give him back a little composure.

-

The remaining seven managed the rest of the supply run without any casualties and were silent and efficient as the events of the day had been forced to the back of their minds by the tasks at hand.

The two remaining vans pulled up to their parking spots outside of the village. With Arthur returned safely and the supplies for the various projects secured, James asked Jack to accompany him to the Doctor to check on Eddie, he wanted the company and was bracing himself for bad news. The chances of survival were slim; the risk of bringing an infected person into the community could be catastrophic. James asked the rest of the guys to get some help to unload the raided goods into the barn.

Jack and James sprinted to the Doctor's house and ran into the room. The Doctor was running through supplies with a note pad and pen, he turned and smiled at them. James relaxed a little, it was a good sign.

"How is he?" James asked out of breath.

"How's who?" Ed asked.

"Eddie." Jack said, realising that the Doctor might be confused with his answer due to the Doctor having the same name.

"Eddie was bitten on our run, so we cut off his leg, Scott, John and Lucy brought him here!" James was shouting, not at the Doctor, but due to the strain that had built up inside him after a day from hell.

"Nobody has come to me James. You're the first back as far as I can tell." The Doctor's smile had vanished and he looked on, confounded and concerned.

"Oh fucking hell." James fell into a chair and put his head in his hands.

"Lucy." Jack muttered under his breath.

Chapter 38 - Command

"You did what?" The Colonel asked Captain Anthony Rogers.

"You said improvise sir." The Captain responded meekly.

"We need these people on our side, we should not be threatening them. We need them as much as they need us, maybe we need them more." The Colonel said and stayed silent as Anthony stood to attention and waited for further instruction.

Captain Anthony Rogers had changed a lot since James and Jack had known him at school, tours in Iraq and Afghanistan and over 15 years serving in the Army had provided him with training, guile, and intelligence. The 16-year-old boy who lacked the brains to amount to much had been shaped by the forces and was a rounded and respected soldier whose men would willingly follow his orders and die for him on his command. He wouldn't put his men in needless jeopardy though; he was a keen tactician and would not undertake unnecessary risks. He wasn't sure the same could be said of the chain of command and nagging doubts had been eating away at him as to whether he would follow orders if he disagreed with them. For now though, he was careful to toe the party line.

"That will be all Captain, you're dismissed." The Colonel said to Anthony as the latter saluted and swiftly left the Colonel's office.

The Colonel was worried. He hadn't heard from command in three days and had limited communication with other units.

He had radioed frequently, but the radio silence was a worry he was carrying alone. Many of the troops under his command were inexperienced and young and they were being carried by a sense of purpose, waiting, and preparing to fight back in a coordinated and strong response to the uprising. The radio silence, the Colonel knew, was bad news, and even with his twenty years' experience in a variety of warzones, he felt rudderless and unable to make a decision. For now, he'd try and keep things going as normal and continue to attempt to raise a response from command.

The Colonel, Daniel Stone, was public school educated and very smart. He had seen a lot in his 49-year existence, he'd seen the best and worst in humanity in the forces, from the enemy and from within his own ranks. Quite often, war was far from black and white and the immense stresses on the human psyche made people irrational and dangerous. He had never been the type of boot camp instructor to shout and holler at his men, although he did need to be autocratic due to the nature of the army and his elevated rank, but he understood the human mind well and realised that continual denigration of the soul is counterproductive, and people need to feel some love in order to perform at peak levels.

Daniel had become disillusioned with the army about 10 years earlier, but it was all he knew and was a part of him, so soldiered on despite himself. He had been part of the invasion of Iraq that was justified as part of the weapons of mass destruction lie. He commanded 120 soldiers as Major in that war and was responsible for many deaths as Saddam Hussein's forces fought in vain to keep their land. Overall there were about 460,000 deaths, many civilians in that number, and the fight was all for a lie. True, Saddam Hussein was a despicable person responsible for atrocities, with over 250 mass graves suspected to be down to the dictator's orders. The man wiped out up to 100,000 Kurdish people using chemical weapons and was ruthless and evil in equal measures, the list of his crimes against humanity were long and gruesome. Had Daniel and his men been sent to war to dispose of this evil leader, he would have gladly accepted that, but the politics and lies behind the invasion along with the lack of foresight into the power vacuum left behind made him question the validity of the armed forces when led by such fallible people. It wasn't just the lies and the inept leadership; it was the lack of action too. He was tired of seeing children suffer, such as in Syria where war was raging, and a once beautiful nation had been turned to ruins with barely any action from the UK. It was the apathy to the whole conflict that angered Daniel more than anything, the Government bickered over minute policy details and was not concerned about the children that were being bombed and subjected to weaponised chemical attacks. The public weren't outraged either, they were concerned with the banal, the latest reality star's outfit or the latest millionaire footballer's new house. Daniel, however, was still a soldier, so put his thoughts to the back of his mind and followed orders and carried on regardless.

Today's war was far from black and white either. His troops might see it differently, living versus the dead, a fight to extinction. Daniel knew this wasn't the case. This war wasn't about extinction, it was about survival, and he didn't have enough men or fire power to take the fight to the dead. He'd seen his peers attempt aggressive tactics in the early onset of the outbreak and that ended in bloodshed and contributed to increasing the number of dead roaming the streets. Yes, he was certain that the war was about survival and creating a sustainable plan to help foster a future for his unit and their families.

Daniel's wife and two teenage daughters live on the compound, many of the men and women in the ranks also have family who had moved into the complex thanks to the foresight of Daniel. It was cramped and living conditions weren't ideal, but they were together, and keeping loved ones close and under the army's protection meant that the men and women enlisted were much more efficient and determined soldiers.

Although a leader, Daniel was still a human being and still subject to the same anxieties and stresses that the current existence created, and although his exterior showed nothing but composure, deep inside he was worried about what the radio silence meant. Of course, command could have equipment failure, they could be entrenched, fighting off the dead, but in reality, Daniel knew that these options were unlikely. Somebody would have fixed the comms by now or if they were fighting, there would be some sort of communication to provide an update. Daniel knew deep down that command was dead. He didn't know what was happening above that, he knew there was a skeleton Government making decisions, but he wasn't even sure if they were in the same location as command. He had been given only the information needed for him to do his job; he was in the dark about a lot of things.

He'd already made his decision on his unit's next move, but wanted to delay any actions, including telling Anthony and his men what his thoughts were. He wanted to wait another week to ensure that command was permanently silent before he enlisted the trust of their neighbours.

Daniel had been monitoring the community a couple of miles away and had been marvelling at their industry and organisation. In many ways, they were lightyears ahead of the army, having nothing but survival as a goal, whereas his responsibility had initially been fighting, and then, when that proved futile, waiting for the coordinated response from the chain of command. The community had already put in place plans for facilities, food, education and were working together in harmony to make it happen. Daniel was in awe and knew that he and his men, women and their families would need to pull together in a similar fashion for their long-term survival, maybe for humanity's survival.

Ironically, the Colonel had joined the army for peace. He wanted to be in a position to halt evil and provide a foundation for peace to prosper. He was still as idealistic as when he first joined the army, and this was why his plan involved establishing trust and eventually joining forces with the community to build a bigger, more organised, and more secure group. Thanks to Anthony and his superior attitude towards civilians, this task had been made all the more difficult. Not impossible, but challenging. Daniel, however, enjoyed a challenge and rarely failed.

Chapter 39 - Remains

Jack and James sat in silence, neither of them knew what to say or do. Something had gone wrong, but neither of them knew what, the only fact they were faced with was that Lucy, Scott, John, and the injured Eddie were not back and there was no sign of the van.

Having gone back out in the van again to search for the missing group immediately after visiting the doctor's house, Jack and James had returned to the village once more when the day's light started fading.

"We've got to go out and look for them. I can't lose her." Jack said, almost pleadingly to James.

James looked at his childhood friend with sympathetic eyes, he knew how much Jack had lost already in his life and had seen his friend looking happy for the first time in years, which was incredible considering the devastation of the world.

"We haven't been back long, and we'll attract too many of the dead if we take the van in the dark, but if you want to go, we'll go together." James said with resignation, he couldn't stop Jack from going and although he couldn't face any more tragedy for one day, it was a challenge he couldn't shirk.

"How?" Jack asked simply.

James was silent for a short period trying to understand what Jack meant and then flickered in understanding, "I've got a couple of bikes, it's a clear night so we should be able to see in the moonlight."

"Okay, can we get going now?" Jack said eagerly.

-

They cycled hard to get to the main road and traced the journey that the missing van was supposed to take, having already done so only an hour or two before. It was the only lead they had and was the only way to go.

The moon light gave the night a silver glow as the two cyclists freewheeled, stood on peddles like children exhilarated with the gentle pleasure of their bikes. They weren't enjoying the ride however; they stood on the peddles to peer over hedge backs and obstacles to take in the rolling fields with their silver shimmer, to look for signs of the missing people and of course, the ever present dead.

The road was quiet, no doubt the scarecrows that were abandoned earlier that day were continuing their bangs luring the dead towards them, until they eventually ran out of gas or the battery ran out.

"What's that down there, there's a break in the hedge?" Jack asked as he kicked with added oomph to close the gap. James followed suit and caught Jack and brought his bike to stop with a wide skid whilst dismounting the bike.

"What is it?" James shouted.

"The van!" Jack shouted as he ran out of sight behind the hedge. The van was on its side and muddy trails showed that it slid some distance. They rounded the skittled vehicle and moved to the back doors that were lying open.

James uttered a curse under his breath. Jack peered in and quickly looked away. There was blood covering the interior, more blood than feasibly possible in Jack's view. Slumped against the van wall, body crumpled with a gaping wound on the right side of his temple, laid Eddie. From the grisly view, it looked like Eddie had turned, and turned quickly.

"It's bad isn't it?" Jack said feeling lost,

"Not as bad as it could be, the others aren't here. We should be able to get a trail through the field though. We'll find them mate." James said summoning up all the motivational sway that he could muster.

They spread out around the van and were quick to find trampled crops showing that Lucy, Scott, and John had come this way. They followed the trail, the moonlight ample enough to illuminate enough detail. Just over the brow of the field, James stopped, grabbing Jack's arm to halt his progress, motioning for Jack to be quiet as he crouched, Jack followed suit, "Look over there, the house, there's got to be ten or 15 of the fuckers surrounding it." James whispered in a tone that was urgent, but also meant the whisper was just as audible as his normal tone.

"They've got to be in there, they must have taken shelter." Jack said, ready to ambush the house.

"Fuck, look." James' face startled Jack as he turned to see what had caused the expletive. Jack followed James' look and saw, crumpled in one of the field's troughs, a body. They worked their way to the body, making themselves as low as possible to avoid attracting the hungry guests outside the house.

"No - John." James said as he looked down at the body.

"That's not right." Jack said puzzled and horrified in equal measures, it was clear to him at first glance.

"What?"

"Look, he's been-" Jack stumbled on the words and then blurted, "Murdered. Look." Pointing to John's chest. A large dark stain, that looked black in the moonlight, covered John's chest. James leaned forward and lifted John's jumper, he grimaced as he looked at the wound and saw what looked like a puncture, a knife wound.

"You're right, some fucker's stabbed him. The dead don't do that. Some fucker's killed him." James' voice was almost a frenzied shout and the dead were beginning to notice their presence. James looked up at them and pulled out his knife, "Come on, let's kill those fuckers and get them out of the house."

Jack unsheathed his own knife and they charged with their knives held above their heads, civilisation completely washed from their constitution.

The day had been long, exhausting and stressful, but James and Jack fought with a source of electrifying energy, driven by the injustice of the day, each blow to the dead lightening the feeling of remorse and replacing it with a satisfying sense of vengeance. The dead were quick to die, blood sprayed, bones cracked, flesh tore, and cartilage snapped as the two childhood friends ruthlessly and determinedly sliced, stabbed, and smashed at the dead with eager relish.

The last of the dead fell and the two men stopped, looking at each other, panting heavily from the rigours of the fight, both covered from head to toe in the gore of battle. They turned and made for the front door.

The door was poorly barricaded from inside and with a shoulder barge, James forced it open and they hurried inside. The room was dark due to the boarding on the windows, but everything was still and calm inside, Jack called, "Lucy", but there was no answer, or movement.

They split up and Jack reached the kitchen at the back of the house, the back door was open, and he inched closer to the opening and the scene came sliding into view.

"No. No. Nooooooo." Jack whispered to himself in despair, looking out to the field stretching off the back of the house, he saw Lucy. It was her. She was walking away from the house, but Jack was not filled with joy, no, he recognised the way she moved, the unnatural way she was dragging her leg as she stumbled away. Jack was too late, he looked on and slumped his weight onto the kitchen counter as the energy sapped from his body.

Chapter 40 - Old Friends

James found Jack with his head in his hands sobbing uncontrollably like an immature child deprived of its favourite toy.

"What is it?" James asked.

"Look, out there, we were too late. Look at her, she's already dead." Jack said struggling with his breathing and slumped motionless in grief.

James walked out, checking for any predators, and looked at the figure moving away, he couldn't be sure from the distance, but it looked like Lucy. He walked towards her. Closing the distance, it was undoubtedly Lucy.

Jack followed James outside and watched on. James pulled out his knife and looked back at Jack, he understood what James was implying and nodded. He knew Lucy would not want her body roaming around devouring the living; she would have done the same for him. It wasn't something that they'd talked about, it was an unspoken understanding between them.

James walked on in slow pursuit of Lucy's spiritless body, moving closer he stepped on a twig that audibly cracked. With the noise, Lucy span, she was wielding a small axe, her baseball bat no longer with her, she wasn't dead. Spotting the knife James held, she raged in fury.

"Lucy, it's Jack!" Jack screamed in a delirious cry as he started running through the field towards her. James lowered his knife and it was only then that Lucy saw who was pursuing her and relaxed her hold on the axe, her body swayed as she balanced awkwardly, she was in pain and had injured her leg. She grinned, but it was a little maniacal. Jack approached her and held her steady asking, "Are you okay, Lucy?"

"I've twisted my knee, but other than that and a few bruises I'm okay." She said wincing.

Jack put his arms around her, and she let him hold her weight as they embraced in silence. She whispered, "I thought you were him."

"Who? What happened?" Jack asked looking concerned.

James sensed this as a time to intervene the lovers' embrace and said, "Let's talk about this inside, we're not safe here."

Moving back into the abandoned building, James closed the door, and darkness engulfed them, "I think we're going to have to stay here tonight. I don't think you should be on a bike with that knee of yours. I'll go at first light and get a car."

"He knows we're here." Lucy said clearly opposed to James' plan.

"Who? What happened Lucy?" Jack repeated his earlier question.

"Where's Scott?" James added as Jack felt worry and guilt in equal measures, he hadn't thought about his friend, finding Lucy had consumed him.

"Okay, let me get this straight in my head. It's been a bit of a whirlwind." Lucy began trying to put the different fragments of a long day together, "We left you to take Eddie back, we crossed the river, Eddie wasn't doing very well, he was in and out of consciousness, so John was driving fast. We turned a corner and someone stepped out into the road, John swerved and lost control, I remember careening through the hedge and the van flipping on to its side. It must have been a minute or so until the dust settled and my senses returned. I hurt my knee in the crash. I undid my seatbelt and clambered into the back. Scott was unconscious, he'd been thrown about in the back and had knocked his head. Eddie was dead. I tried for a pulse, but it was no good, that last trauma was one too many for his body to handle.

"John joined me in the back of the van and Scott began to come around. He was groggy, but seemed okay. John suggested we should get out of the van quickly as Eddie could turn at any moment.

"We didn't even think about the cause of the crash, we were concerned about being locked in a van that was smeared with a lot of infected blood and a body that could reanimate at any moment. Scott got the doors open and we got out as fast as we could. He stayed behind and did what he needed to do." Lucy looked thoughtful for a moment.

Lucy continued, "Scott knew about this place as he'd come across it a couple of times during his wanderings. We were walking at a slow pace due to my leg, trying to figure out what had happened. We weren't paying attention; we were trying to take stock of the situation. From nowhere somebody ambushed us; it was one of the gang Jack! The one who chased me, the one who broke into your house and the one who was one step away from gutting you. He's here!"

Jack took a little time to comprehend and when understanding struck him he felt it like a lightning bolt, "How? - Are you sure? - How can that be?" Jack was rambling and firing questions as his mind whirled.

"I just don't know, but I've had some time to think locked up in this house; I think he's been following us." Lucy said.

James, growing impatient with the half-told story, said, "We can talk about what ifs later, what happened to Scott and this fucking gangster?"

"Sorry, it was a big shock, but you're right. Anyway, this guy jumped us and it was too late for poor John, he was stabbed before any of us knew what was happening. Scott charged him and pushed him off John. Scott faced the attacker with his axe and threw me his rifle, his words still ring in my head, 'shoot the fucker'.

"I hesitated, and he saw the intent in Scott's eyes. By the time I'd cocked the rifle and took my shot he was too far, and I missed. We tried to help with John, but it was too late. He died quickly.

"The sound of the rifle attracted the dead and they were zoning in on us. Scott said he was going to find the murderer and took the rifle and left me with the axe. He told me to bunker down in the house and he'd send help. I told him not to go, but he was determined, he obviously isn't a man of words, but I could see the pain in his face as he looked down on John's body. It looked as though a small part of Scott died.

"Anyway, I managed to get inside, but I attracted quite a few of the dead and they surrounded the house. They are very patient. I was silent, but they didn't stop trying to get in. I heard you guys outside, but couldn't see out, I thought it was him so waited until it was clear to make a break for it."

"Holy shit. That's fucked. Who is this twat?" James asked as he clenched his fists with ferocity.

Lucy explained to James how she had first met the gang on her escape from Manchester and how they'd followed her to Jack's house and that it appeared that at least one of them was still in pursuit.

"I think we've led them here Jack. They broke into your home when we had our journey mapped out on the living room table, they must have known where we were going. We then left notes at your parent's house for your mum and dad and Chloe's parents. With. An. Address." Lucy shook her head, feeling the responsibility of a needless death.

Jack realising the same thing said, "Oh Christ, I'm so sorry James, this is all my fault. My plan to come back to Yorkshire, to track you down and all I've done is bring back a psychotic maniac. I'm so sorry."

James laughed, not really the response the other two were expecting, "I can't believe you didn't think of making sure you weren't being followed by a gang, who you didn't really know about during the rise of the dead, with civilisation falling around you. That is schoolboy stuff, rule 101, you two are nothing but fucking rookies. I check for following gangs as part of my morning routine, everybody does."

Lucy and Jack looked on in confusion. James continued still bitterly laughing, "You are not responsible for someone else's actions. How on earth could you predict to be entangled in some halfwit's cross-country vengeance mission?

"Okay, stop feeling sorry for yourselves; I guess we need to go then. This fucking murderer is obviously deranged and dangerous. We'll need to find a car and get out of here. You two wait here and I'll go and get us a vehicle. We could do with getting back and getting the security guys together for a briefing. We need to find and eradicate this scum."

"Agreed." Lucy said with purpose.

Chapter 41 - Favours

It was past midnight when James managed to get the full security detail together, the exception being Scott who was still missing and the permanent removal of Eddie and John. The men knew it was serious as everyone, including those on watch and off duty were summoned. They would have a meeting with everyone in the village the following morning at 10:00am.

James sombrely explained to the awaiting men what had happened and gave the bad news about Eddie and John. There was visible anger in the group as James talked about the killer roaming the area who had indiscriminately taken John's life. He expressed the urgency of the situation and the importance of finding and taking this man down. For the moment he had left out the part of the gang following Lucy and Jack, it didn't seem important right now.

"Are you saying we should kill him?" One of the men asked.

"Yes." James said without hesitation.

The man responded, "We're not killers, how can we kill a living human being? Anyway, why would this man come here and kill again?"

"What do you suggest? This man is a killer and from Lucy's account he targeted them and is likely to kill again. We have enough fear and worry in our current existence; we don't need this shit hunting us. It's our only option. There is no other way."

"We could lock him up." The man said limply.

"Where? How? Who's going to make sure he doesn't escape, who's going to feed him, who's going to change his shit bucket? We can't take prisoners, people would die because of it, people will die, people have died because of this man." James was insistent.

"He's right Gil, we need to kill him, he's already killed John. It's the only way." A burly man named Harold backed James up and Gil didn't raise any more objections, but his face didn't appear happy with the decision.

"Thanks H." James said patting him on his back, "We're all going out tonight. We need to do a sweep around the village. We'll go in pairs and sweep in a circular motion expanding our area as we go. Lucy will describe him as she's been up close to this fucker. Lucy, please describe as much as possible so the boys here know who they are looking for."

Lucy described the short stocky man with a big nose and pock marks. He was short but powerful and wore a dark hoodie and dark trousers. He had a knife. It was a short description, but all Lucy had, there was no use in emotional scorn in her description, it wouldn't help.

She added, "This guy is dangerous and will not hesitate to kill you. Don't take the chance in reasoning with him. I want to come out with you, but my leg would slow me down and put you in danger.

"I know this is a big ask, but if you can; end this tonight."

"I plan to." Everybody turned to see Scott who had walked into the meeting. He was caked in mud, but looked unfazed.

"I tried to catch him, but I lost track. I'm coming too, if I find him. He is dead."

-

Each pair was assembled, outside and armed with guns. There would be no chances taken when it came to fighting the living. Guns were to be used as a preference, noise a secondary concern.

They had four handheld radios between them, they needed more, but they hadn't been a priority in supply runs so it's all the group had between them. Communication would be difficult, but they were scouring the perimeter in a circle so each group would turn around when they encountered the group to their left and right. The theory meant that they could relay information around the whole circle as they expanded their search.

Jack was feeling dead on his feet. It had been a long day and with each step he could feel a dull ache in his arches, he turned to Scott who he had been paired up with and asked, "How are you bearing up?"

"I'm fine." Scott said, typically not letting much out.

"Come on mate." Jack said.

"It's one thing after another fucking thing. It's tiring constantly having to face some sort of battle. I sometimes just want to take a bottle of whiskey and go and sit in merry ignorance, but I can't, I always have to fight." Scott expanded on his feelings.

"Mate, it's never ending is it? Surely it's going to get better though, we're in the early struggles, we'll get better, more self-sufficient and stronger. We've got to keep trying and fighting, I believe it'll get easier." Jack was surprised with the veracity of his own response.

"Yeah. It's just tiring is all." Scott muttered.

The search was long and arduous. There was no boredom however, the constant tension saw to that; sometimes animals in the bushes startled the men, other times they came across the dead who had to be dealt with. Many nerve shredding encounters kept blood pressure high, but there was no sign of the man they were looking for.

After about three hours, James radioed that it was time to stop the search and make it back to base. Those who didn't have radios were contacted through sight and sound and eventually everybody got the message.

There was still no sign of Richie. The group were told to try and spiral their return journey to ensure that each square inch of terrain was covered on the way back to the village. Harold and Gil were paired together and were walking silently. Gil veered off directly for the village, Harold called to his friend, "Where you going Gil? We need to *spiral*, remember!"

"We've checked it once, he's not here. I need my bed so I'm going straight home." Gil said.

"Suit yourself Gil, I'm doing as told." Harold said as he walked further away from Gil, leaving the smaller man alone, immediately missing his larger friend by his side. *Just go straight home, nice and quick.*

Harold was now lost from view as Gil walked through trees silently, a noise behind him quickened his pace.

The noise was a gasp, a loud expulsion of air, the last breath. Richie appeared from a hiding place and stabbed once, twice, three times, four; quick, powerful, and deadly. Looking down at the blood flowing from puncture wounds, Harold spat blood and fell to the floor; Richie turned him over, crouched and drove the blade under Harold's jaw and into his skull, leaving the big man completely lifeless.

The noise Gil heard as he scurried away frightened, was the sound of his friend being killed.

-

The pairs had planned to meet back together when they returned from the search for a short debrief and sort the watch for the rest of the night. When Gil and Harold didn't return, worry spread. Jack and Scott had seen them on the way back, but hadn't seen either of them for the last 40 minutes of the return walk.

"Do you think they'll have gone straight home?" Jack asked.

"Gil probably would, H wouldn't though. Scott, can you go to Gil's and see if he's there please?" James said.

Scott returned about 10 minutes later, Gil followed sheepishly.

"Gilbert, what the fuck?" James questioned.

"We searched the area, I just wanted to get back and go to sleep. I did my job, ask Harold." Gil said defensively.

"Harold isn't here." James said.

The colour in Gil's face vanished, "He's not back yet?"

"No. He is not." James said with anger clearly simmering under the surface. "Come on, we're going out again to look for him. You know the route, so you lead."

They found the body about 20 minutes' walk from the village. The group of six who had gone out almost tripped on the body that was slumped in the exposed roots of a tree. James saw Harold first and looked at the body is dismay. He inspected further and saw that the gentle giant Harold had been brutally murdered.

He stood up and felt dizzy, Gil walked closer and saw the body, James couldn't hold his anger any longer and struck Gil fiercely with right hook, knocking him to the floor, James spat his words angrily, "You little fucking weasel. You shouldn't have left him."

James walked off, ashamed of his outburst and feeling pain in his knuckles. Walking back to the group, he said, "We need to get Harold back. We need to set up a proper watch on the village. We'll let him come to us."

Walking together silently carrying Harold's large frame home, the group were mourning the fourth loss of the day. James was low, but he was worried, he knew that Harold was in possession of a rifle which was no longer with his body. That meant the intruder was now armed with a gun capable of picking off long distant targets.

-

That night James barely slept, there was nothing more they could do for the time being. They set up a perimeter and could only hope that they wouldn't be surprised through the night. He got up around 6am the following morning, groggy and achy from the previous day. He went to the radio that Arthur had set up a few days ago and dialled to channel 11 and spoke into the microphone, "This is James at the Greyholt community, I'd like to speak to whoever's in charge there. This is an emergency. Over."

Chapter 42 - Meeting of Minds

James had left Roger, who was now looking quite sick, and Scott, to conduct the emergency meeting and go through the previous day's events and the threat to the community. He instructed Roger and Scott to be honest and laydown the brutal facts that there was an unknown person who had killed two of the village's own and was still at large. Everybody needed to remain vigilant. James wanted chores to be at an absolute minimum and for people to stay inside for the next day or two.

The reason James didn't attend the community meeting was because he had a meeting with the Colonel arranged and wanted to go alone. The Colonel spoke to James over radio and was eager to speak with James in person and made himself available at 9am at a place of James' choosing. James decided to go to the barracks, away from the village.

James arrived early and was let in via armed guards through a set of double gates. This was the first time he'd been to the base and was impressed with its security. He was escorted to a large grey, undistinctive building, where he got out of the car and was greeted by the Colonel himself.

"It's nice to meet you James. Please call me Daniel." The Colonel said amiably offering a hand as James got out of the car.

Shaking his hand, James said, "Nice to meet you too Daniel, I don't mean to be rude, but time is of importance so could we start the meeting ASAP?"

"No problem, I like your efficiency; follow me."

The guards left the two men at the building entrance. James followed Daniel to a small room with a table and two chairs. Daniel sat down and gestured for James to do the same.

"How can I help?" Daniel asked.

James was out of his depth, so decided to plunge straight in, "We have a deranged lunatic who has already killed two good men. We've searched for him, but don't have the skills or resources to flush him out. We need to eliminate him before more innocent lives are lost." James tried to focus his speech to patterns that military people might appreciate in the hope that the Colonel would help, but he feared the cost of the assistance.

"Goodness, I knew there would be some bad apples showing up now and then, but this person sounds dangerous." Daniel paused in thought as James sat and waited, "We'll help you, we will need a full description, locations seen and any other intel you might have. We'll also need your security details to fall back so there are no friendly fire incidents."

James let the words sink in, it all seemed a little too easy, "Thank you, it's appreciated. Are there any conditions? Catches?"

Daniel laughed, "Maybe one catch, I'd like to begin discussions with yourself and any other of your, how should I put this, leaders; to talk about working together with us, the army, these people." Daniel gestured with his arm to indicate the soldiers and families under his watch

"Discussions?" Jack asked.

"That's all I ask, civilised and constructive discussions about a bigger, stronger and more secure community. For our future, all of our futures." Daniel said with conviction.

James was finding that he quite liked Daniel despite his best efforts. He'd assumed he'd be some sort of bumbling army caricature offering platitudes and clichés, but he seemed smart and driven.

"What if HQ decides a path for us that we don't like?" James asked, testing Daniel to see if this pleasant mood was just a veneer covering something uglier.

"There is no HQ. As of four days ago, I have been unable to reach them, so I am no longer in the army, I am part of a group of people who will need to work together to build a sustainable future.

"Please keep this information to yourself as only you and I know." He added as an afterthought.

"You've got yourself a deal." James said offering his hand, he wasn't fazed by the news of failing command lines, he'd assumed there was no rescue long ago. Daniel shook James' hand and stood.

"Right, we should get organised, we'll go and see Captain Rogers and enlist some men to your service."

Chapter 43 - Routine

There was surprisingly little resistance to the military aid. James had thought the security guys would take issue with their noses being pushed out of joint, but there were no ill feelings. The community was still in shock at losing four people in one day. Four exceptional people. The mood was low and the worry about a potential sniper or someone lurking in the shadows to garrotte an unlucky passer-by added an almost unbearable tension to the air.

The army's presence lifted the weight off the community, it had started to show cracks under the strain. Gil remained vilified by a large part of the group as gossip flowed about his desertion of Harold. A victim of circumstance, in both cases.

Life went back to normal, as the army kept up their search for the hidden menace. People were busy, planting, tending to animals, constructing facilities, life was simple and because of that good.

Jack, Lucy, and Chloe settled into a routine. Jack and Chloe had tried to play housemaid to Lucy while her knee recovered, but she soon got sick of the fuss and loss of independence, so she got involved in the running of the community. They were happy, life was simple, they'd work, sleep, eat and play. Chloe had become more outgoing under the tutelage of Magda and had taken fondly to family life with Lucy and Jack. She still had bouts of sadness and depression over the loss of her parents, but as time passed she talked more and the process of mourning unfolded to enable the little girl to cope with traumas one so young shouldn't have had to handle.

Jack and Lucy were woven together more than ever, the time they spent together was natural and cherished by both. Their personalities and experiences had meshed them together perfectly and they felt as though they'd known each other all their lives. They also felt as though this new world was all they'd ever known; they didn't miss the trinkets and needless luxuries of the old ways.

Talks between the community committee and Colonel Daniel Stone and Captain Anthony Rogers took place to discuss a larger community. They were constructive; shared power, joint decision making, an integrated and equal society. The plans almost sounded utopian. Both parties were pushing for a future based on the same principles. Even Anthony had softened his earlier arrogant view on civilians and offered expertise where it mattered.

The army patrolled the area surrounding the village for three months. There was no sign of the aggressor, but they swept away anyway. The mission evolved in this time with the foresight of Daniel and Arthur to include a comprehensive survey of the surrounding land to establish natural boundaries, places to secure and testing the feasibility of building a perimeter around the village.

Roger finally gave in to his ongoing and cruel battle against cancer. The village took the news badly and it hit James particularly hard. He was like a mentor to James and his passing also meant more responsibility. Roger was the unofficial Head of State in the village and people were drawn to him, he was an excellent leader whose strength of personality and common sense made him well liked and he'd been supported unanimously. James may have been the driving force behind the scenes, but it was Roger who commanded their loyalty, and James would now need everyone to share their loyalty with him.

Beth was now eight and a half months pregnant and was really showing. The Doctor kept a close eye on her, but he was pleased that everything seemed to be going perfectly. Beth and James' son or daughter would be the first born after the breakdown of society and there was much excitement in the community. Lucy and Beth had become close and they enjoyed the excitement of preparing for the arrival.

Water did eventually run out, but Arthur had overseen the construction of a large structure that caught rainwater. So far, it was working perfectly, and people were able to take water centrally. Shower blocks were created from the barn drain off so people could shower, albeit in cold water, but most people just showered in the rain. Hygiene was more relaxed and was one of the biggest changes that people actually noticed.

The solar panel system had been a success too. Using car batteries, solar panels, and a solar inverter, they had transformed one of the farm's outbuildings as a fridge and freezer room. The batteries stored the excess energy generated in the day and kept an assortment of fridges and freezers from the community's homes running. They had the ability to keep food fresh which meant a great deal not only to the group's wellbeing, but their moral too.

Scott kept himself to himself mostly, reading and occasionally joining Jack and James at one of their houses for food and drinks.

Quite a few of the community had started brewing their own alcohol and batches kept turning up in the storeroom for people to help themselves to. Food worked in a similar fashion, people took what they needed, but where there were limited supplies, they were boxed into equal portions for the community to take. People were generally honest, there were occasional petty squabbles, but infrequently. The disaster had instilled a togetherness that meant people were really concerned by their neighbour's wellbeing. Army personnel who had family started to move into vacant properties and they were welcomed with open arms as the army and community's edges blurred.

The dead were still an ever present, but in the three months that the army patrolled the village's surroundings there were none to enter the village. The army were quietly and slowly whittling down the dead. They were an ever-present trickle, but it was manageable.

Jack still held hope for his parent's return and occasionally made trips to his childhood home to check for signs of life, but with each passing day, his reservoir of hope emptied a little more.

Jack and Lucy were quite different people from the ones they had been, as was everybody else. They had an edge to their personality now, their primal instincts sharpened with the uprising of the dead. Life was simple and their needs basic, they no longer planned too far in the future, they cherished the here and now and made sure there were no lapses in concentration. It was tiring, always being on guard, but it became second nature, even Chloe left the house with a hammer attached to her belt. Survival was everything; any luxuries on top of that were an added bonus.

After three month's patrolling and no sign of Richie, it was assumed that he had met a grizzly death at the hands of the dead, the decision was made that the threat no longer warranted army resource which would allow them to switch focus. The plan was set to start building a bigger community. It would take time and the two groups would still live separately as the work took place, but it was the beginning of a new chapter that took three months shaping.

It was a time of change, change for the good.

Chapter 44 - Awake

The instant he sat up; Jack knew something was wrong. The noise woke Lucy a fraction of a second later, as Jack was clambering out of bed, rushing to the window, Lucy was a breath away and joined him to look out onto the village's main street.

The sound was unmistakeable; Jack, and especially Lucy, had heard the dead, not just the stragglers, the crowds, the moving beast flowing like an ocean of one; the living like the moon to the dead ocean tide. They knew what was happening before their eyes confirmed it. The village was under siege from the dead, a huge hungry horde.

-

Richie had seen the army draw into the village while he was watching three months earlier. He wasn't a fool and knew if he hung around, he wouldn't be able to deal with trained killers. Richie wasn't a smart man in the old world, but he was a long way above average now that the dead had reset the base.

During his long walk across the country he had learnt a thing or two about survival. He had killed living and dead and could not distinguish a feeling of remorse for either. He is a man on his own and a master of his own destiny, no friends, just enemies. Nothing and nobody stopped him from his wants, he takes and has no issue killing for it.

He also learnt about the dead and how to use them. He identified with the dead more than the living and watched them with curious eyes. He found that he could herd groups together and lure them towards him, he was the carrot on a stick. The first time he experimented playing carrot, he didn't know if the herd would continue their pursuit to eternity. Through trial and error, Richie learnt that if he amassed a crowd, he could get ahead of them and hide, they would continue their pursuit, but after a few hours would either simply forget what they were chasing or would give up. Whatever the reason, Richie saw that the dead would remain in inertia where they stopped, in unison like a hive mind, until someone or something caught their attention and got them moving again.

Having seen the army, Richie decided to move away from the area for a period of time and plan. He wanted war, a fight against the village, to eradicate them, his hatred for every retched being kept him focused. He was going to raise an army of the dead and unleash hell. After observing the creatures with morbid fascination, Richie had decided to use them as his allies, and he revelled with intense focus as he set to work on building his army.

He worked for close to four months building his plan. Richie chose to use the A1 motorway as a funnel. There were thousands of dead littering the carriageways and the road ran a stone's throw away from the village. The first thing he did was find a new hideout, somewhere he could hole up between his dead rustling. He liberated a small and secure bungalow from an old couple who had stocked up on tinned goods in a bid to survive. They were no match for his killer instincts and weren't given a choice about whether to flee or die, Richie chose the path with least complication and killed them both before they had time to realise their peril.

He then began the riskiest part of his plan. He had to go close to the village where the A1 ran past the farm's fields and create a roadblock to divert his soon-to-be army into the heart of the community. It was a risk for two reasons; it was close to where the army were patrolling, and the road was filled with the dead. Ideally, Richie didn't want to have to kill any of his resources, but needs must. He planned to use vehicles to block the road to cause the herd to change course. He reasoned that because of the dead on the road, the village and army patrols would stay clear to keep a low profile. He was correct and was aided by the fact that there was a multiple vehicle crash blocking the road already. He had very little to do, so he cut the fence posts lining the field boundary, not cutting them down completely; he used a saw and cut most of the way through each post so they'd topple with a little force. He didn't want to draw attention before he was ready.

Over the weeks that followed Richie herded and repeated his days. He started some distance from his planned attack. Some days he had to work further away from his growing army and take down the dead in large numbers as he worked tirelessly to clear obstacles in the road. He couldn't have the herd disband before it reached its destination. He took many risks and came close to being bitten on several occasions. With each escape, Richie's feeling of invincibility grew as he darted around the countryside pulling the strings of his growing force of darkness. There were numerous times he left the crowd to rest the night and return the following day to find they had been drawn away by something in his absence, these setbacks didn't hamper Richie's determination and focus, it slowed him down, but if anything, his spite grew with each disappointment.

Time passed as Richie prepared for attack, surviving purely for his act of evil. The throng of foul-smelling rotting corpses was close to the village, undetected, motionless, and waiting for their next meal. Animals had learned to stay clear of the area as their own instincts sharpened to the new world. Even birds wouldn't fly over the dead; it was as if nature was all too aware of the stench of death. Richie slept that day having devoured a tinned delicacy of an all-day breakfast, stewed steaks and minced beef and onions. He awoke after midnight and set off, taking the rifle, he had acquired from Harold, and a hunting knife that yearned for blood.

The time was nigh as Richie drew the crowd onwards and walked only meters in front of their reach. Picking up the pace, he walked up the embankment of the motorway and kicked the fence posts to topple the fence leading onto the farm's field. He lit a fire he had placed inside the field and walked on, lighting smaller fires as he headed towards the village.

The watchmen saw the fires and their unwanted visitor arriving, the first shots fired towards him, but he ducked for cover and crawled in a ditch, watching as the dead swamped the field, alert to the sound of gunfire and a bigger prize to the prey they'd been following.

Chapter 45 - The Ocean

The horde moved across the field and drew the attention of two watchmen, Scott and Dave, spread out at opposite ends of the field. They had fired two shots as Richie had lit the first few fires, but quickly realised their mistake upon seeing the huge crowd amble up the motorway verge and through the open fence. They saw it was futile so made their escape. The two men ran through the farmyard and into the village, it was deserted as people slept. Scott ran straight to James' house to raise the alarm. James had the radio and they needed help from their new friends at the barracks, the army. Dave ran home to warn his wife and kids. As part of their training, something that the whole village took part in, they ran through the back gardens and secluded spots so they could run undetected in the event of an incident like their current predicament.

Scott found James in his kitchen, James was a light sleeper and had heard the gun shots and was about to come running, he was in the process of putting on shoes when Scott's harassed face pressed up against the window. James motioned for Scott to come in.

"What's going on?"

"We're in trouble. There's a huge crowd of dead and it is heading this way. It's minutes away. Someone led them here, they came in from the motorway and started lighting fires. I took a shot and they went down, but I don't think I hit him, it was difficult to see."

"Come on, we need to go and warn Lucy and Jack. Hang on a second, I'll be back." James disappeared upstairs and told Beth to lock the door and stay upstairs. He grabbed the handheld walkie-talkie that Daniel, the Colonel, had given him and joined Scott downstairs as they fled through the backdoor.

-

The dead had seen Scott and Dave run and followed in pursuit; they were swarming the village like the ocean overcoming flood defences. They filled every route into the village, taking roads, paths and pushing through bushes, gardens, and the farmyard. The streets were filled with all manner of decomposing creatures, some faring better than others, open wounds, missing limbs, and other body parts added to the stench that accompanied the mass of bodies. It was the noise of the stirred-up crowd that woke the village, the moans intensified as the sheer numbers of dead created an alien echo across the Vale of York, attracting more from the surrounding area.

People started to wake and rushed to their windows to see what was happening. Fear caused panic as many ran to their windows without caution. The dead were quick to sense the movement of the living and the commotion amongst them intensified as they pushed their way to the houses where people were trapped. It isn't known if the dead communicated, was there a change of pitch in their moans, or did they share a telepathic connection? Those that spotted the living and changed course attracted others to follow them, the reasoning behind this change of course was of little importance to anyone pinned in their homes, as the fact remained that the dead surrounded them en masse, cutting off any escape.

The strength of the community was quickly becoming its weakness. The sound of broken glass could be heard in contrast to the low moan, the dead were getting into houses, the numbers that pushed and jostled found weaknesses in the fortifications of houses and began to stir the residents into action.

Claudia Schmitz lived in a large house overlooking the main road as the scenes unfolded. She was 56 and lived alone, her husband had worked overseas, but she'd not heard from him since the world turned on its head. She was one of the first to her rush her window and was seen by the leading pack. It took the dead a short amount of time to topple over the low garden wall and break the windows in the front of the house. The first of the dead leaned into the house unable to climb in, but as others joined from behind, those at the front pushed their legs against those bringing up the rear enabling them to slowly tumble in through the windows.

Claudia was sitting at the top of the stairs clasping a hammer in both hands when she heard the glass break. She walked down the stairs and peeked into the front room to see the dead leaning in, the smell and the noise made her want to turn and run, but she stayed put and watched. She saw in horror as the monsters reached in through the broken windows, loud bangs at her front door startled her as she watched her peril escalate. Fear gripped her when the dead started to fall in through the window. Backing away, she watched as the foul beasts toppled onto the white plush carpet, leaving bloody and greasy stains as they clumsily rose to their feet. Claudia had seen enough; she backed into the hall and ran into the kitchen at the back of the house. Glancing back at her home, she left through the backdoor in a panic clutching her hammer.

Clambering over the garden wall, Claudia didn't have a plan; she was moving in a blind frenzy. She had sat through the training that every member of the community was expected to attend, how to fight, escape routes through the village, but she'd taken these classes for granted, sitting and daydreaming throughout. Turning a corner, an alley ran between two stone cottages and she headed down the narrow passage. Picking up the pace, she ran into the open and was immediately surrounded. Claudia screamed.

Claudia's scream ensured that the entire village was awake. The terrified scream adding urgency to those that watched on, bringing them out of the safety of their houses to help their neighbours; the strength of the community was now a weakness in danger of killing it.

-

Jack and Lucy had seen enough, they were trying to figure out what to do, "We need to get out there, we have to fight, there's no other way." Lucy said staring intently at Jack.

He nodded, "We need to raise the rest of the security guys, army included."

They moved into Chloe's room; she was still sleeping. Gently shaking her, Jack help up his finger to shush her as she woke up startled, looking concerned.

Whispering, Lucy said, "Chloe, honey, we've got a problem. There are lots of monsters outside, but you're safe in here. I want you to get under your bed and stay there. Don't make a noise, even if someone walks into the room. We'll come back for you, only answer to our voices. Do you understand?" The intensity in Lucy's tone caused as much reaction from Chloe as her words, the little girl nodded, sat up and wearily hugged both Jack and Lucy.

She got off the bed and crawled under it, clutching a teddy. Bending down, Jack whispered, "We love you and we'll come back for you. Do as Lucy said, we'll see you soon."

They left via the back door; pump action shotguns holstered on their backs. Precision shooting wasn't needed, she chose the weapon that would make the biggest impact. After trying to raise James and Scott, they moved on to Dave's house and found him running towards them with a couple of soldiers, who had moved into the village with their families.

Dave was first to speak, "We're in deep here. Scott and James have gone somewhere, I can't find them. What do we do?"

"We need to draw them away from the village. I heard a scream; people are getting hurt. You guys." Lucy pointed to the soldiers, "There's a tall wall at the end of the village by the fork in the road, can you two get on top of it and attract the dead, you can take them down one at a time from up there, do you have knives, they should be easy pickings?"

Lucy was taking command to the relief of those that stood and listened. The soldiers nodded and also showed the army issued Glock 17 pistols that they'd smuggled from the barracks. The army was over, but the establishment rules still lingered as the Colonel had forbidden military weapons to be taken to the new homes of the troops that had moved into the village. His reasoning focused around potential integration issues and a lack of social boundaries; he didn't want a village shooting to shatter the plans they were building. Unfortunately, he had taken the dead for granted and left the village short of firepower for a horde of this size.

"Me and Jack will head to the road that forks left, Dave, find someone to help you and take the right-hand road." Pointing back at the soldiers, Lucy continued, "Just draw the dead towards you, they'll gather under the wall to try and get you. We'll get in place down the two forks in the road and once we're there, you guys split up and join the two of us to draw them out. We need their attention so they follow us. Do you understand?"

There were nods all round.

The group ran together in silence before splitting off in smaller packs. Dave went to try the houses of some of the security crew, the soldiers ran with seasoned fitness to the tall wall, being careful to remain hidden from the crowds of dead on the main road.

Jack ran alongside Lucy, relieved to be doing something and happy to have the decisions made for him. Mostly he was grateful for being by Lucy's side.

-

Claudia had run blindly into her front garden and straight into five of the dead who had fallen into the garden over the waste high wall. She skidded to a stop across the grass as the five creatures swung around sensing their opportunity, stumbling backwards, she tripped, falling on to the soft turf and screamed once more. Scrambling back, her palms gathering soil, she managed to spring to her feet and push one of the dead away as it lunged. The counter force of her push sent her into the grasp of a badly decomposed elderly woman. Claudia managed to wedge her hammer under its chin and push the creature's jaw away from her, but she was in its embrace with the others closing in.

The elderly corpse's grip abruptly loosened as its body fell limply away. Claudia cleared the hair out of her eyes to see Gil; he was pushing the dead away. He turned and hurriedly shouted, "Get out to the back of the houses, remember the training, stick to the hidden routes and get out of the village. Get away from this crowd!"

One of the dead lunged at the two of them and Gil pushed again, his fingers sinking into decomposed flesh; he had a knife, but waved it wildly, carving chunks of flesh away, but doing little to stop the unrelenting beasts.

Claudia hesitated, as Gil shouted, "Go!"

She fled to the back of the house.

Another carcass launched at Gil, but he saw it from the corner of his eye and swung his arm around and pierced its skull forcing the blade deep, the creature fell, but the knife wedged and took Gil tumbling to the ground as he held his grasp of the knife. One of the dead sensed its opportunity and fell on Gil willingly. It bit his face, tearing his cheek, Gil found strength and pulled the knife from the skull it was lodged in and took down the creature chewing on his face, it fell on him as he felt himself being eaten alive by two others. He screamed and cried out in agony and thrashed wildly with his blade, he tore through throats, torsos and covered himself in a sea of red. He killed the remaining dead who were piled on his bleeding body, his face, torso, and arms were badly bitten, and he was losing blood quickly. Gil looked at the garden wall as more of the dead were in the process of falling over it. He was gone. Sitting silently, tingling from the loss of blood, he watched as two more of the dead fell clumsily onto the grass.

Gil looked down at his knife. He didn't want to be like them. He counted down; three, two, one.

Gil breathed heavily; he couldn't do it.

Coward.

Gil drove his knife powerfully under his chin, slicing through skin, cartilage, and muscle, finally resting in his brain. He fell to the side, in peace, as the dead devoured him.

Chapter 46 - Futile

The two soldiers scaled the wall Lucy described, leant over and started shouting at the top of their voices. The dead nearest took the bait and more were soon to follow. The wall was too high for the uncoordinated husks to climb and they soon gathered around underneath the soldiers, reaching up, desperately stretching their arms to reach the fresh meat. Continuing their shouts and whistles, the soldier's training took over and they began fiercely piercing skulls with their razor-sharp blades, dropping them efficiently.

Despite the soldier's bravery, efficiency and deadly accuracy, the plan was failing. People had come out of their homes to take the fight to the dead and help those in trouble. They were in plain sight and were making large numbers of the dead stay right where they were. Lucy's lure could not work whilst the community continued to fight in the open.

Lucy and Jack, along with Dave and a young guy called Chris, were unaware of the situation unfolding in the village and moved to their positions ready to draw the dead away from the soldiers. They had seen the soldiers begin their part and waited in the wings for the dead to surround them. It was an infuriating wait as they watched, motionless, occasionally having to fight off small groups that came their way.

It quickly became apparent to Lucy that the plan wasn't working. The dead were moving towards the soldiers, but the pack had split with the vast majority staying in the main part of the village. She was quick to understand the cause, she knew that the people had come out of their homes to try and take the fight to the dead.

"Fuck!" Lucy exclaimed.

Jack still catching his breath from butchering a nearby wanderer asked, "What's wrong?"

"They're not following. People must have come out of their houses. We need to get them out of there or at least back inside, otherwise we have no hope of luring them away." Lucy said briskly, knowing that if they didn't get the horde moving every single member of the community would be doomed.

"I'll go and see what I can do. Stay here and be ready to start making a big noise! I'll be back once I've managed to get people to go back inside. Stay safe." Jack looked at Lucy and placed a hand on her face whilst gently kissing her.

"Jack?"

"Yes?"

"It doesn't matter." She knew what she wanted to say.

He ducked and ran behind the houses, looking for a safe vantage point to see what was going on.

Lucy watched her surroundings alertly when she heard distant gun fire. Hearing a whistle and feeling the air move close to her, she took a step sideways. She heard another shot and her brain's logic clicked into gear, realising that someone was shooting at her, just as the bullet struck. Lucy fell to the floor.

-

Jack ran around the back of the house with the tall wall at the front, where the soldiers shouted and killed. He bounded around the back of the large house and startled Dave and Chris as they raised their weapons and then relaxed upon recognising Jack.

He explained to Dave and Chris that the crowd wasn't moving, and it was likely that people were in the village fighting; making it impossible to lure the dead away. Dave told Chris to wait where he was, and joined Jack as they sped off to try and remedy the issues of good people doing good deeds.

They came to the centre of the village and looked for a way to the main road. Climbing a fence, they found a side gate and passage to the front of a house facing James' abode. Peering over the gate, they saw the crowds, most of the dead were in the road, but many had managed to get into gardens. They could see the Doctor out in his garden batting the dead away, he was taking them one at a time as they came over his dry-stone wall. The Doctor wasn't in immediate danger, but down the road Jack could see Magda, she was also in her garden and was pushing the dead away with a broom. She was old and tiring rapidly, looking destined to succumb to the never-ending desire of the dead.

Jack saw Magda and thought of Chloe and the affection the girl had for the old woman. He told Dave and that he was going to help Magda and that Dave should try and get the Doctor inside. Disappearing behind the houses again, Jack frantically tried to find a way to cross the main road to reach Magda. The woman had two orphan children living with her that she had taken in during the early stages of the outbreak. She had known the children all their lives and it seemed natural that Magda should assume responsibility and she did

it with delight, the children igniting a force in her that had
faded over a decade before. The dead had been breaking
panes of glass in her house and she had told her children to
hide in the attic, she should have done the same, but her
motherly instinct forced her outside to fight for her adopted
children's futures.

Jack turned the corner and saw a gap in the crowd. He didn't
stop to think, he ran with all his might, weaving around the
grasps of the dead as he leapt onto and then over a garden
wall. He jumped two walls of neighbouring houses and found
himself in with Magda and the group of dead. He continued
at pace and struck a former man, wearing just boxer shorts, its
skin mottled yellow and grey, two more were lurching
towards him and a couple more were being held by Magda
and her broom. To buy himself time, Jack kicked the closest
of the dead in the chest and sent it sprawling backwards, he
noticed that more were falling over the wall and joining the
pursuit, they didn't have much time. He dealt with a former
teenage girl, it was slim, but badly cut up and ripped apart; he
marched towards it and smashed his hammer into the side of
its skull.

Magda's strength was giving way, she now held the broom
outstretched and was trapped between it and the door as she
pushed in vain, her head tilted back to keep two chomping
jaws from reaching her, only inches away as the tension in
her muscles loosened with each breath.

Jack jumped and kicked the first of the dead in the ribs from
the side, it flew into its partner and they both tumbled to the
floor, three more were bearing in. Turning to Magda he said,

"We need to go, we're trying to lure them out of the village, but you need to get inside and hide."

She was quick to understand, "My girls are in the attic, they're safe, but I can't stay here, they'll get in."

"Come on, we need to go." Jack pulled Magda by the hand and ran to the edge of the garden, they were slow, he tried to pull Magda along, but she was a 73-year-old woman and no longer built for speed. Jack picked her up and lifted her over the adjoining garden wall and placed her on her feet, jumping over himself and then leading her on. He batted a couple of the dead away with ineffective blows and lifted Magda over a second wall. They slowly ran around the corner leading to the back of the houses.

Turning to Magda, Jack said, "Go to my house. Chloe is there, she's under her bed. Wait with her there. Just please be careful and quiet getting in."

"Thank you, Jack." Magda trotted away while Jack kept watch for her safe passage.

It was time to get back to Dave, and then to Lucy.

-

Doctor Edward Green was a retired Doctor; he retired six months before the outbreak so was still well versed to take over the community's medical needs. He was well known throughout the area due to two decades as General Practitioner, and because of his exotic choice of footwear, which caused great amusement to his patients. Because of his standing, he had seen a great deal of the disease early on, and had assumed the world was doomed long before it became evident that it was. He was called to houses of friends to check up on loved ones and was confused by the fever and injuries, the bites. He managed to survive these times by chance, he was never present when one of his ex-patients turned, which was just as well as he had no idea they would try to eat him.

By the time he realised what was happening, the world was awash with the dead. The ex-patients and friends he had seen that were bitten were already doomed. He did conjure up the courage to check on a friend, and came across scenes of a massacre. Blood was everywhere and there were signs of an epic struggle, he wandered to the back of the house and saw his friend and their son stood in the garden, they were bedraggled and bloody. They sensed him, turned, and began to approach. Ed slid the patio door shut and walked out of the house. The dead eyes of his friend and her son irreversibly changed the Doctor.

As the weeks and months unfolded Ed saw more and more of the infection. He lost people he knew; he had to pierce the brain of reanimated friends. As a Doctor with considerable experience, he had learned a long time ago how to cope with death, but this new infection had brought a whole new meaning to the word dead. Doctor Edward Green hated the dead.

The dead had started to break into the Doctor's house after seeing his wife Sue looking from the bedroom window at the commotion. Ed told Sue to stay in the bedroom and to lock the door. She didn't argue with him, she saw the look on his face and knew not to attempt to dissuade him from his wants.

He had sat and watched discretely as the dead started to approach the house. It took ten to 15 minutes for them to start banging at the windows and a few more minutes for the windows to break. He zipped up his leather jacket, picked up a kitchen knife and axe and headed for the front door. As the windows cracked, so did Ed's fragile resistance to wreaking havoc upon the dead.

Striding out of the door, kicking it shut as he left, he swung wildly with pure animal aggression and sliced, chopped, and battered the walking dead into submission. With the dead in his garden handled, he walked the walled boundary hitting as he pleased, striking the axe into the heads of those trying to make their way over.

Dave watched from the sides as the Doctor wildly killed the dead. He had a crowd of more than 200 concentrated around his property with more joining it, some were busy with the soldiers and with Magda's battle, but the Doctor was getting more than his fair share of attention.

Dave saw it happen; the front of the crowd toppled forwards onto each other in a great pile. The wall collapsed under the concentrated weight of so many bodies pushing, and the dead started streaming into the garden. Dave didn't wait, he made a dash for it, ducking and weaving like a child playing tag. He made it to the far wall of a garden and jumped his body onto it. Kicking a couple of grasps from him, he rolled into the garden and scrambled on his hands and knees to his feet missing the clutch of another hand.

Ed was fighting admirably for a man of his age, but there were too many, he was attempting to create space between himself and the house to provide room to quickly attack the mob, but with so many dead, he was being overrun. Dave came jumping into the garden and stood beside Ed giving him a nod. Stood together, they began to fight as the dead continued forwards. Dave moved back to the door and tried it; it was locked. He shouted, "The keys Ed, throw me the keys."

"There are no keys, leave me. It's a fight to the death; these profane beasts need to die."

Dave stood motionless; it was too late to run. He had to fight. Moving alongside the Doctor, they began hacking and stabbing as the numbers closed in on them. They were surrounded and fighting. A huge beast lunged at the Doctor and grabbed him around the shoulders, mouth gaping. Dave flashed his knife towards its skull, but the angle was wrong, and the blade rebounded off the bone. Another creature seized the moment and tore its teeth into the soft flesh of Dave's forearm. He screamed in pain and withdrew his arm as the skin ripped away. Losing grip of his knife, he pushed frantically, but it was too late. Hands pulled Dave forwards and down, he fell to the floor as the dead dropped on him, too many hands and teeth to fight, they tore and shredded as Dave died in pain. The Doctor lost his battle with the large corpse who was straining its neck forwards, held off only by Ed's ebbing strength, his head pressed back against the door as far as it could go. The creature sunk its teeth into Ed's nose, the cartilage popped with excruciating pain as the end of his nose was ripped from his face. An ever-present supply of the dead followed the big one's lead, they pushed Ed against the door, the force of the mass pinned him upright whilst he was devoured.

-

Jack returned to the point where he'd left Dave and couldn't see him or the Doctor. He surveyed his surroundings but couldn't see any sign of them and assumed Dave had got the Doctor away. He left the scene and returned to Chris telling him to stay where he was and that the plan was still going ahead, assuring him that Dave would be back soon. Carrying on, he visited the soldiers on the wall next, safely behind it, and told them to keep up their good work and that they should join up with Chris and Dave when the main bulk of the crowd got to them.

Finally, he ran with everything he had to get back to Lucy. He returned to the spot he left her, but she was gone.

Chapter 47 - Best Laid Plans

Jack was in panic, but he resisted any action. There were many reasons for Lucy's absence, he needed to focus, she'd come back to him soon. She was better out in the wild than Jack. He clung to positive thoughts.

The soldiers screamed and shouted, they stabbed and extinguished, and the dead finally started to group together, focused only on the soldiers with the rest of the village quiet. The plan was working as the group of dead moved together as one, gathering against the wall, they were soon standing on the bodies of the fallen and becoming a trouble for the soldiers, who's stomach muscles ached with having to hang over the wall and avoid the flailing hands. With their work accomplished, the soldiers lowered themselves down and fled towards Chris who waited alone.

Chris and Jack had been diligent when the soldiers made their departure, on seeing them vanish behind the wall, they began firing their weapons into the horde. Jack pumped the shotgun and shot the three shells at three second intervals. He reloaded his gun and did the same again. He remained still as the dead started to move towards him. Chris was doing the same with his rifle, the soldiers were quick to join Chris and began firing their pistols, each taking it in turns to fire to make their ammunition last, they needed to draw them out and guns got attention.

The plan was working, the horde was splitting at the fork in the road, some were following Jack, and the larger group were following the soldiers and Chris. They were siphoning out of the village.

The village watched on, whilst all the commotion happened outside, eyes peered through windows, watching in horror as fear drove them to inertia. They watched as the crowd moved away, a similar thought struck many who watched the departing mass; now was the time to escape.

Panic purged logic and seven residents took flight. Panic eradicated training, common sense and thought as the seven blindly ran from their houses away from the departing pack. They were loud and clumsy in their escape. Seeing the departing corpses, the seven ran for their lives, two of the fleeing villagers ran into the dead as they peered at the mob behind them. They rebounded with a scream escaping narrowly, but in doing so attracted more of the dead to follow. They scurried away, but the hunt was on. The dead were moving back into the village once more.

Jack, Chris, and the soldiers all saw what was happening from their different vantage points, as the back of the pack split off. They were committed with the dead that they had drawn away and were now stuck with the path they had taken. The pack had split once again, but there was nothing that Jack, Chris, or the soldiers could do as they moved away from the village with a barricade of dead blocking them from the heart of the community. The plan was falling away.

The roar of a large diesel engine took the failing plan out of the minds of the four people attempting to lead the dead away. At the other side of the village an aging New Holland combine harvester turned into the village, James sat in the cab grinning as he lowered the cutting bar and headed into the back of the crowd. He saw people running away from the village and hoped that Scott wouldn't shoot them. Patrolling behind the combine, Scott took up the flanks with an army issued assault rifle, the negotiations and agreements with the army had come with a few perks that were kept secret from most of the village.

James ploughed forward and hit the crowd, the blades were turning with their old teeth crushing and shattering skulls in continuous motion. The combine rattled and shook as the dismembered bodies got maneuvered by the machine to the thrashing drum in the back. James knew that the old combine would give out eventually, it wasn't meant for the harvest of skin and bones, but he didn't see any other alternatives, he could climb on top of the machine if he got stuck.

Although the combine was nearly the same width as the small road that ran through the village, Scott was kept busy picking off those that managed to escape the blades.

Over the sound of the engine and the constant moan of the dead, Jack was startled by a voice he recognised. It was Captain Anthony Rogers, who despite his initial opinion, had grown to like.

"You need to hang back Jack, let us deal with this." Anthony said adding with a grin, "Good to see you're still with us."

Jack looked around and saw at least 20 soldiers dressed for night-time combat surrounding the perimeter. A simple hand gesture from the Captain had them inching forwards in formation towards the horde, they had some sort of silencer on their weapons as they began to open fire, single shot rounds placed accurately, the echoes of their silenced shots were not quiet, but lacked the explosive shock, it gave the approaching soldiers a coordinated elegance, like they were part of a well-choreographed dance troop. They fired in groups, providing their brothers and sisters in arms time to reload, taking time with each shot.

More soldiers approached the village and provided Scott and James with reinforcements. The village and army began to merge further as they worked together and squeezed the horde from all sides, raising the body count into the thousands.

Jack watched feeling helpless as the army and horde fought a moving battle zone, the soldiers pushing forwards and being driven back in equal measures like magnets pushing each other apart. He had been tasked with a couple of junior recruits to sweep the back of the soldier's formation to ensure they weren't taken by surprise. It was pointless, there were no dead to be fought, his thoughts went back to Lucy, *where was she?*

Desertion was an army term, Jack thought as he left his post in search of Lucy. He had other concerns and wasn't needed so jogged off with mild guilt rankling at him as thoughts turned to Gil leaving Harold. This was different. This was noble.

Chapter 48 - Searching

The only place Jack could think to look was home. He ran, killing two of the dead as he went.

Chloe and Magda heard the door creak open downstairs and then footsteps. They had been sitting on top of Chloe's bed as Magda said it would be alright. Hearing someone in the house made them cautious so they crawled to the floor and under the bed. Magda felt the weight of the day as she dragged her tired body under, she wrapped her arms around Chloe and they waited, breathing shallow breaths.

The footsteps paced around downstairs and then came slowly up the stairs. Checking the master bedroom and then the bathroom, the footsteps approached Chloe's room. Looking from under the bed, Magda watched as muddy boots came into view, the person stayed motionless.

Richie looked around the room; he inhaled through his nose a deep breath, the room smelt different to him, like the air was fresher or disturbed. He didn't register any meaning from it and turned on his heels and left the room, headed downstairs and out of the house.

A few minutes later, the back door opened again with gusto. This time Jack bounded up the stairs and called to Chloe. The girl wriggled free from Magda and was out from under the bed before Magda could stop her. The old woman followed more slowly.

Jack embraced the girl as she ran towards him, he looked at her and asked, "Has Lucy been here Chloe?" Forcing a casualness to his tone.

"She's with you, where is she?" Chloe didn't respond casually.

"We got split up, I'm sure she's fine, we're winning!" Jack said rubbing the girl's hair, but feeling worry build inside his gut. He didn't know where to look.

Magda rubbed Jack's arm and smiled at him, "Someone was here just before you. I don't know who it was, we were under the bed. They were looking around the house, I mean every room." She glanced down at Jack's shoes, "It wasn't you."

He stood back and tried to think. He knew James and Scott were tied up in the fight, he couldn't think of anyone else who would come into his home the way Magda had described. The army might have done a sweep, but they were fully focused on the ensuing battle outside.

"I don't like this." Jack said to himself.

Worry intensified to panic. Had the threat been eliminated, or if there was some evidence of his death, Jack might not have thought of their historic foe. Surely it was paranoia, but something felt wrong to him.

"Can you two hide please? I'm going to get Lucy. Don't respond to anyone you don't know. Just stay hidden."

"Of course." Magda said, seeing the worry etched into Jack's face.

He left them and went to look for Lucy.

Lurking in the shadows, waiting for an opportunity, Richie moved in the darkness searching too. He was intent on revenge and domination, his only drivers during the previous months. He had seen Lucy fall, but lost her after disposing of a group of dead that had attacked him.

Tracking was impossible in the darkness and with the chaos ensuing all around, so Richie settled for prowling around the backs of the houses and waiting in the shadows until opportunity presented itself.

Jack ran to James' house, he knew that Lucy and Beth were friends, so reasoned that she could be ensuring that Beth, who was over eight months pregnant, was okay. He entered the back door quietly and shut it behind him. He edged through the house, darkness hindering his way, he whispered, "Beth, it's Jack, is Lucy here?"

He listened and heard footsteps, the door to the lounge opened and candlelight flickered through the gap. Beth stood there, looking very pregnant and motioned impatiently for Jack to come in.

He jogged to the open door and went in, Beth quickly closing the door behind her. The lounge had expensive blackout curtains, so the light wouldn't betray them. Surveying the room, Jack's eyes rested on some legs on the sofa, he instantly recognised who it was, he rushed to the sofa and crouched by the side so he could see her face.

"Hey." Lucy said, she was burning up with a fever, she looked pale.

"Hey you. What's happened?" Jack said as tears formed in his eyes, she was a shade of grey that scared him.

Lucy began to speak, "It's him again."

Beth shushed her and said, "You just rest Lucy, you're weak.

"She's been shot. Not bitten. I think she's in shock, but I also think she's going to be okay. I've stopped the bleeding and it looks like the bullet passed straight through her just above her collar bone. I've checked her breathing and there's no blood, so it looks like her lungs are okay.

"We need to get her medical help, but it's a bit crazy outside, so while we wait, we'll give her lots of water, make her rest, keep her wound clean and make sure the bleeding has stopped."

Jack nodded. Stunned into silence, he held Lucy's hand. *How could anyone shoot someone so perfect?* He knew the answer to his question. The person who did this was obvious to Jack and he had to be stopped, but right now, he needed to put vengeance on the backburner.

"I'm going to get Chloe and Magda, are they okay to stay here? Our intruder is back, and he knows where we live." Jack asked Beth.

"You don't need to ask."

"It's more risk if this madman is back and looking for me and Lucy."

"We're in this together, for one and for all."

"Thank you."

Beth half patted Jack on the arm and half pushed him to get going. He took the hint and left quietly out of the back. Quickly getting Chloe and Magda, the three of them scurried to James and Beth's house and bunkered down. Jack carried

Lucy upstairs and put her into bed and asked Beth, Magda, and Chloe to stay with her. He was intent on going hunting.

-

In the corner of the garden, in amongst the bushes, hidden in the shadows, Richie watched. He saw the child and the old woman return with Jack and heard the girl ask about Lucy. *Lucy.* He would wait and finally put an end to his plan. He was the master of the dead and he wanted control back from the woman who had inflicted more pain to him than anyone since his childhood. It felt like a climax to him, like he was a fisherman battling a legendary fish, finally getting it into his net. It felt right and just.

Chapter 49 - House of Horrors

Lucy's condition didn't change during the night, she remained in pain, just paracetamol providing any relief, the fever still raged, and her wound still bled. Jack checked on her periodically and spent a couple of hours pacing around downstairs and around the house, listening for noise. The battle outside still raged on and he wanted nothing more than to shut his eyes, open them and for normality to return. He was tired, he was scared, and he was angry.

Jack felt useless pacing around the house waiting for the fight to come to him, he was a sitting duck if the aggressor was to approach in darkness, he decided it was time to be proactive and hunt the psychopath down. He picked up an axe and shotgun and went outside.

Immediately, Jack bumped into Scott and his heart missed several beats. Composing himself, Jack asked, "How are things going out there?"

"Aye, not bad, the worst of it is dying down. The military are sweeping the area and taking down any stragglers." Scott's face turned sour as he stared at his feet, "It looks like we've got a few casualties. It was him, all this, it was him. He's back."

"Shit. How do you know?"

"Me and Dave were on look out, he brought the crowd with him."

Jack tried to comprehend Scott's words and it only intensified his desire for blood, he said, "Lucy has been shot and I need to kill him. Are you needed elsewhere?".

"I was coming here anyway as James wanted me to check on Beth. What do you need?"

"Can you stand guard here? Beth, Magda, Chloe and Lucy are inside, and I need to find this madman and put an end to it."

"You can count on me. Be careful" Scott said with little ceremony as he left and made his way to James and Beth's house.

-

Whilst Scott and Jack talked, Richie saw the opportunity to leave his hiding space. Only metres away, but hidden by the garden wall, Richie slipped out of the bushes and quietly walked into the open house. All was quiet as he slipped in through the kitchen door, opened the pantry and closed the door behind him. He sat in the darkness and rummaged for food, greedily eating breakfast bars. Richie loaded his rifle and ran his fingers along the sharp edge of his hunting knife. In the darkness, Richie smiled.

-

Jack walked cautiously around the chaos of the village. He was careful not to startle the military to avoid being caught in the crossfire of the fight that was still stuttering on. The problem Jack had was that he had no idea where to look. His initial instinct was to guard the house, but two hours of that bore no fruit and had tested his patience. Wandering aimlessly, clutching the shotgun close to his chest, wasn't producing any results either. Finally, he saw James who was cleaning his axe with a rag, a lifeless and limp body at his feet. Jack ran from behind the house and called James' name.

James turned and looked devoid of emotion, a shell of a man. His hollow eyes looked at Jack, the effects of adrenaline had passed, and James had seen his kingdom take a battering with many of the people under his watch falling victim to the horde. He spoke to Jack in a monotone voice, "We're fucked. Look at this mess. We can't rebuild for this to happen again, we're defenceless against these bastards."

"Look mate, sorry to sound callous, but I can't dwell on these things now. The guy who killed Harold and followed us across the country is back. He shot Lucy, she's hurt and at your place, he brought the horde with him."

"I know, Scott told me." James was lifted from his stupor and immediately anxious as he heard the news of Lucy's injury.

"Have you seen him, I mean, anyone you don't recognise?" Jack asked with urgency knowing that it was a pointless and stupid question.

"No, just locals and the military, or our allies, whatever they're called these days.

"I'll help you look."

The two of them set off trying to find some organisation in their search for someone that could be anywhere. After a careful and battling circumference of the village, James and Jack stopped in unison, frustration clearly showing on their rapidly aging faces.

James gasped suddenly as logic clicked in his brain, "Think about it Jack. If all of this is to do with him, then what does it mean?"

"I'm not sure I follow." Jack said looking confused.

"It's an assault on us, but it's a diversion for him. If all this is to do with this fuck head, it's been about creating a diversion, so he can sneak up on you and Lucy. So far, it's worked. He wants us split up, he wants us disorganised. If he's managed to somehow coordinate a horde of the dead this size, then he clearly has a plan. We shouldn't be out here, we should be back with Beth, Lucy and Chloe, he'll come looking, he's too far down in his plan to back out now.

"Come on, let's head back."

-

Beth, Magda, and Chloe were all perched silently around the bed Lucy lay on, peering at her as she slept. Scott appeared at the door and knocked gently to try and avoid frightening the women. He failed, the three of them jumped in unison, with Beth raising her rifle instinctively.

"Sorry, didn't mean to startle you, Jack sent me to stand watch, how is she?" Scott asked as he walked in the room and rested his shotgun against the wall, grateful to be relieved of its weight.

"She's okay, I'm a little worried about this fever though, she's burning up." Beth responded.

Scott didn't say anything, he just looked on. He was a man of few words, but a man with enormous emotions flowing under the skin.

"Look Scott, you don't need to stand guard." Beth lifted her rifle to indicate her meaning, "Can you find the doctor and bring him here? I want to get this fever under control."

Neither Scott nor Beth knew about Ed's grisly demise. Scott stood silent for a moment and looked at Lucy once again, "Okay, I won't be long."

He left to go find the Doctor.

Magda turned to Chloe, "You must be hungry dear, I know I could do with some breakfast. I'll get us something to eat and then I must get back home to let the girls out of the attic, assuming it's safe."

The sun had risen a couple of hours earlier as the fighting continued, gunfire becoming more infrequent as the living quelled the onrushing numbers of dead.

Chloe didn't answer, but Magda wasn't offering her a choice. The old lady stood up slowly, patting the girl gently and made her way downstairs to see what she could rustle up for breakfast.

-

Scott bound purposefully through the village, fleetingly evading skirmishes with the remaining dead. He moved stealthily across gardens and came to the rear of the Doctor's house. He peered through the windows but couldn't see Ed. *He'll be out helping people.*

He walked around the side of the picturesque York stone house towards the front and saw the street in the morning light for the first time since the horde descended. There were bodies everywhere, several were writhing and reaching, still fully focused on their need for flesh. There was no immediate danger as he could see groups of his people, both the army and community members, taking their time to destroy the brains of the still animated creatures.

Scott stood and watched. It was all too much to take. Six months ago, there wouldn't have been a soul in the street, they'd have been busy with their daily routines. Now looking out at the blood bath, he couldn't tell who the bodies were, were they part of the horde or were they people who had become his friends, who had become his family. A thought struck him, they were all people once, they were all previously loved.

He turned his head to look away from the scene and focused on the front of Ed's house. He knew immediately that Ed was dead.

He peered at the body, it wasn't recognisable, the Doctor's flesh had been eaten from his face, his clothes torn from his torso leaving the hungry dead with soft fleshy organs to devour and devour they did. They had chomped and shredded everything down to the spine. A stranger would not have been able to identify the body, but Scott knew it was Ed. Scott knew because of the shoes. Bright red moccasins.

"You didn't deserve this Doc." Scott said to himself.

A solitary tear ran down his cheek and found refuge in his beard. He turned immediately and ran back to Beth and James' house.

-

Magda was looking in cupboards for food. She found a couple of tins of soup and put them on the kitchen worksurface as an option for breakfast. She felt the women needed something more substantial. The soup would be perfect for Lucy, who needed to keep up her strength and Magda planned to force her to eat at least half a can.

Moving around the kitchen, she admired the homely nature of it whilst making her way to the pantry. Reaching for the door handle, she stopped, something caught her eye. A bottle of brandy. Still badly shaken up from her narrow escape, a little drink was needed to steady her nerves. She picked up the bottle and placed it next to the soup, found a glass and poured herself a large one. She smelt it and took a generous sip. The warm aromas whirled around her mouth, she found the familiar strength from the burning within, upon swallowing the amber liquid, a simple pleasure of the old world.

Taking her glass with her, Magda went back to the pantry and opened the door. It was dark inside, and she stepped into the shadow, holding the door with her spare hand to illuminate the shelves.

Magda felt a breath on her neck, spinning around and letting go of the door, it closed gently extinguishing the light behind. Her eyes didn't adjust, unable to see anything, with a meek voice she asked, "Who are you?"

Richie, who had been waiting in the darkness, could see clearly, his eyes adjusted to the dark and aided by the small crack of light coming in from the pantry door. He reached out and put his calloused hand tightly around Magda's neck and squeezed.

Magda tried to scream out to warn the others, but couldn't raise her decibel level with her throat squeezed shut. She swung her hand and smashed the glass of brandy into the side of Richie's head. The fine glass shattered loudly, cutting Richie's cheek and forehead, he loosened his grip and stumbled backwards as the alcohol burnt the fresh cuts.

Magda sensed her opportunity to escape, she wriggled free of his grasp and reached for the door. Richie recovered and pulled her arm and swung the frail old lady around as if she were a ragdoll. Once again, Richie placed his hand around her throat and let out a guttural noise. He flung Magda to the back of the pantry, still holding her, he smashed her against the far wall. Lifting her up, he took his hunting knife and, with a frenzy of anger, stabbed once, twice, three times and continued until the wound was just a gaping mess, entrails sagging and sticking to his arm as he calmed and slowed his motions.

Magda was dead, she died mercifully before ever being stabbed, her heart stopped in the moments before Richie began his brutal and gruesome assault.

He let go of her limp body and she fell to the floor, just a pile of skin and bones.

-

"Did you hear that?" Beth whispered to Chloe and Lucy, who was sitting up in bed sipping on water having woken.

The little girl shook her head, but Lucy said hoarsely, "I heard a smash."

"You two wait here, I'm going to see what's going on." Beth said leaving the room before any protests could reach her. She shut the door behind her and lightly tip-toed her way across the hall and down the stairs trying to make as little noise as possible.

Sneaking around in your own home had its advantages, Beth missed the third step on her descent of the staircase, avoiding the loud creak. She peeked around the wall, down the hall to the kitchen and saw nothing. She wanted to call out to Magda, but something in her bones made her remain silent. Staying still, viewing a small snapshot of the kitchen that the open door allowed, Beth held her breath and listened. There was a flicker of light followed by a noise and then, she saw him. He had blood all over him, his hands, his clothes, even his face, blood flowed from open wounds across his cheeks and forehead.

Beth lifted her rifle and took aim, but it was too late, Richie moved from view. She crept down the hallway, getting closer to the kitchen, looking down the gun sites as she inched her way forwards. Reaching the open door, she put her hand on the handle and breathed a shallow breath, with a quick survey of the room, something caught her eye. On the oven door, she could see a reflection, a reflection of a man crouched in a shooting position aiming directly at the doorway. Beth froze.

Instinct kicked in, she let go of the handle and inched away carefully.

Reaching the staircase, Beth panicked and ran up the stairs forgetting about the squeaky step. Richie heard it from the kitchen and smiled to himself. The chase was on and he was enjoying it.

Beth rushed into the bedroom and closed the door, leaning her back on it as she faced Lucy and Chloe. She breathed heavily as the exertion had taken its toll in her pregnant state. Catching her breath, she said, "Chloe, can you please get under the bed."

Turning to face Lucy, she said in an urgent whisper, "He's in the house!"

Lucy sat up, grimacing with pain as she moved, "Come on, move the wardrobe in front of the door."

-

Scott got back to the house quickly as he ran from the scenes of terror, he saw Richie through the window. He was covered in blood and looked to be aiming his gun. Scott cursed at himself, he'd left his shotgun upstairs in the bedroom in his haste to locate the Doctor. He did have a small axe that had done him proud in the past few months and in particular, hours. Unhooking the axe from his belt, he crept under the kitchen window and around the side of the house. He found that the doors leading into the living room were open, so he crept in. He heard someone run upstairs. He walked out into the hall and waited around the corner next to the staircase, down the hall from the kitchen. Scott waited and listened.

Before long he heard someone slowly walking down the corridor. He waited with his axe lifted, his back against the wall as the sound of footsteps approached, Scott was going to pounce on the intruder and stop the madness.

Richie took a couple of steps on the stairs at once and began his ascent to exact his murderous intentions. Scott leapt from around the corner, mustering all his might to close the gap between himself and the invader with as much swiftness as possible. Scott misjudged the distance, he'd planned to swoop in one motion, but had to turn a corner, find his target and then leap; Richie had time to react to Scott's ambush, pushing Scott in the chest, forcing him backwards with the butt of his rifle. With a wild swing of his axe, Scott missed Richie and was propelled backwards losing his footing on the steps.

The initial shock of the ambuscade slowed Richie down as his brain caught up with his instincts, he raised his gun and took aim at Scott. His delay gave Scott the opportunity to pounce once more, grabbing the barrel with both hands, pushing it away as the gun went off with a mighty roar, sending the bullet sailing harmlessly into the wall behind Scott. The bang left the two men in a stilted silence until Richie headbutted Scott flush on the bridge of his nose, it cracked and blood poured immediately as he fell backwards bringing Richie with him as they both clung to the rifle.

-

Jack and James were running back to the house when they heard the gun shot. They exchanged a look of terror and sprinted with lung busting effort to close the seemingly endless distance between themselves and their loved ones.

With the house a stone's throw away, they turned one final corner to run straight into the path of three of the dead, who had been lured from their hiding places by the gunfire. James ran straight into the creatures, having no time to react to their sudden appearance, hands grasped at him and he stumbled and fell trying to evade their determined hunger.

"Go, GO! Get to the house, I'll be fine." James shouted as he scrambled in the dusty path trying to get some footing to spring an attack on the dead.

Jack didn't hesitate, he knew his friend was tough so carried on running with all the energy he could muster when he heard another crack of gunfire. Skidding through the gate into the back garden, Jack barged into the kitchen and saw with horror the crumpled body of Magda in the Pantry. *He was too late.*

Checking the shotgun was loaded, Jack walked through the kitchen door and into the corridor that led to the stairs. That's when he saw the body, tiptoeing closer he gasped in horror. Laying lifeless on the floor was Scott, his face was a mess, his jaw facing the wrong direction. He'd been bludgeoned to death and lay in a pool of blood. Jack's stomach turned and could feel tears welling up in his eyes as he looked down on one of his oldest friends, he felt an abyss of despair. Scott was a good man, a solid man, principled and caring. The anger started to rise in his body, he clenched his jaw together wanting murder.

Chapter 50 - The Final Act

Scott had fallen backwards and taken Richie with him, but the advantage didn't fall with him. Richie landed on top of him, Scott's eyes blurred from the tears that had swilled his eyes with the broken nose he'd suffered from Richie's headbutt. Richie straddled Scott and began pummelling him with both fists, Scott was unconscious after a few blows, not content, Richie picked up a heavy ornament and crushed Scott's bruised face into a shattered mess of bones and skin, his features sagged without the natural support of his facial structure.

With the frenzy over and his heart thumping, Richie stood, stooped to pick up his gun and ascended the stairs, eager to finish what he started months ago. Leaping up the stairs with zest, he turned right and saw the closed door and immediately knew that behind the wood was his prize, his reason for traipsing across the dead wilderness, Lucy.

Richie approached the closed door quietly and listened. He couldn't hear anything. He had no choice, he was going in, but he wasn't prepared to rush. He'd come this far; his plan was faultless, and he was near the end. With his back to the wall, he reached for the door handle, turned it, and gave the door a shove, it creaked open.

Inside, Beth crouched behind a chest of drawers with her rifle trained on the door, Lucy sat on the floor beside Beth, she had no weapon and was in no physical condition to fight. She could only rely on her friend to fight for her. Lucy looked under the bed and could see Chloe laying in the foetal position under some blankets against the wall, she was hidden from the door by a wardrobe that Beth and Lucy had pushed across the room, unable to move it as far as the door, but far enough to give her cover should a fight unfold. Lucy knew that a fight was indeed about to unfold, she looked up at Beth and could see her tighten her grip on the rifle as the door noisily swung open.

The tension in the bedroom was palpable, Beth saw Richie poke his head from the other side of the wall to get a look at what lay in wait for him. Instinctively she fired the rifle. Richie's head moved back behind the safety of the wall before Beth's finger could press the trigger and the bullet flew through the empty door frame, lodging itself somewhere in the hallway.

Sensing opportunity, Richie, with incredible speed, scrambled into the room and slid himself in front of the chest of drawers that Beth and Lucy hid behind.

Beth watched with baited breath as she saw Richie burst into the room in a low crouch, the terror showed in her eyes as he disappeared behind the drawers, he was right in front of her, but she couldn't see him, only a few pieces of wood separated the women from the heinous man. She fumbled with the gun and loaded a bullet into the chamber and leaned over the drawers to fire.

Richie looked up and saw the barrel of Beth's rifle appear, he let go of his own gun, reached up and grabbed the barrel with both hands, using his feet for grip, he swung the gun and Beth to the left. The gun fired, the bullet again planting itself harmlessly into a wall. Beth fell from behind the drawers heavily on her side, she looked up and saw Richie holding the gun backwards by the barrel. She didn't try to move, instead curled herself into a ball and resigned herself to her helplessness.

Richie turned the gun around and aimed it at Beth. Lucy struggled to her feet and shouted, "STOP! It's me you want. Leave her alone, she's pregnant."

He stopped, turned, and grinned at Lucy. His face repulsed her, and she involuntarily stepped backwards. He approached her with his gun trained on her head, still grinning maniacally, when the sound of rushing footsteps coming up the stairs made them all stop and turn. Jack appeared, looking crazed with his shotgun ready, but Richie was one step ahead and turned his entire body and fired. Jack continued to move forward, but with each step he stumbled forwards, until he stopped, dropped the shotgun and fell to his knees, he put his hand on his stomach and then raised it to see it soaked in claret red. The colour from his face left instantaneously as he struggled for breath.

Richie walked over to Jack and kicked the gun away and pushed Jack onto his back with his foot.

"Jack. Don't. Please-" Lucy was incoherent as Richie again turned around to face Lucy, once again with his gun trained on her.

"Why?" Lucy asked.

"You should have kept your mouth shut all those months ago. You people, you good people. What have you ever done for me other than let me rot? You shouldn't be allowed to say things about me, about my life and get away with it.

"It's always been me versus the likes of you. I hate you. I hate her. I hate him." Richie said with venom as he pointed the gun at Beth and Jack, who was breathing shallow breaths.

"It's over now. Why doesn't matter. It just is, things happen just like they happened to me. You shouldn't be allowed to talk about me or my past. It's over now anyway. It's over."

Richie once again pointed the gun. Beth was still crouched in the corner, unable to move. Lucy looked down the barrel of the gun and decided to go with dignity. She straightened herself out and stared blankly at the grotesque man. She heard the click of the gun and then the gunfire, so loud, deafening, echoing in the small room. Thinking to herself in an instant that it was strange to hear the shot, assuming she'd simply fall down dead.

Her eyes adjusted to the scene, she saw Richie's face explode in front of her, pellets ripped through his skin and tore his face apart, his eyes popped as shotgun pellets shredded his skin, blowing off his whole face as it disintegrated into a shower of mush. Looking down, Lucy saw Chloe, still under the bed, clutching the shotgun that Scott had left leaning against the wall. She had crawled from her hiding spot, and from her training had managed to fire the gun directly up into the underside of Richie's jaw as he focused all his attention on Lucy. Richie's body countered the blow, rising swiftly until gravity took over, bringing his remains crumpling to the floor.

Chloe pushed the shotgun aside and crawled out from under the bed, "Jack!" She screamed as she ran towards him laying panting on his back. Lucy moved out from behind the drawers and weakly stumbled over to Jack and knelt beside him.

"Hey" he whispered hoarsely.

"Oh Jack." She sobbed looking at his complexion with grave hopelessness.

"It's over, don't look so sad." Jack said.

"Please Jack, don't speak, we need to help you."

"Don't look so sad. It's over, we can move on. Life can get better now. Don't you see it?" Jack said, mustering energy to speak as Beth joined his side followed by James appearing from the stairs.

"I'm not following you Jack?" Lucy said stroking his hair whilst Beth applied pressure to his wound.

Wincing with pain, Jack continued, "Even before these abominations rose from the grave I was lost, from despair to where? I had no idea. Not just me though, as a species we'd lost sight of what was important, we needed a catastrophe to change everything from the foundations up. We can build a better world.

"That guy," Jack looked towards Richie's gruesome form, "has done so many things to us, the horde, Scott, Magda." Chloe's eye's widened, but she remained mute as Jack continued.

"He was a man-made problem. This whole world is a man-made problem, but we've been given the chance to start again. Mankind has been reduced so dramatically that we're already completely changed from our old selves. In the few months that we've been here, you've seen how this whole community has pulled together, working for survival, working for each other and sharing everything for the common good.

"That man, we don't even know his name. He was a product of mankind. The old world. I don't know what made him the way he was, but it wasn't the uprising of the dead, it was something deep inside him, something that only the greed, envy and cruelty of the old world could produce.

"We have the chance to leave all that behind, we can be kind to the earth, leave behind material possessions, become a simpler version of man. We can use the mistakes of yesterday to guide us to a bright and brilliant future." Jack spluttered and wheezed with pain.

In the background, Beth whispered into James' ear. James turned on the spot and rapidly retreated down the stairs with a look of concentrated numb despair on his face.

Lucy continued to stroke Jack's hair, the worry and stress had somehow brought Lucy out of her fever and gave her cheeks more colour. Chloe cried gently by his side, saying nothing. The innocent girl, thrust into a world of chaos, having just gruesomely killed a man, was in a precarious mental state. She wasn't even fully aware of Magda's demise; the girl was having to deal with more than any child or adult should have to handle.

Jack looked at Chloe and smiled at her, he continued, "Chloe, James and Beth's child, this is the future. Our community, our family, this is the future. If we stick together, we can survive anything. We might be outnumbered, but these last few months have given me hope and I know we are better and stronger than the dead.

"We've shown our collective strength and how we can work together in harmony, build our futures for Chloe, for the children. A year ago, I was stuck in a bubble, the bubble around my life. My house, my job, my commute, it was all I did, and it was all I knew. It wasn't just me; it was everybody, we were all stuck in our own little bubbles while the world was burning. We were heading for disaster while we all worked to earn money to buy things when everything was going to Hell.

"We've shaken off our shackles and we're now free from the self-inflicted ills of mankind. Money and status no longer matter, we have been forced to evolve.

"Imagine; no more distasteful politics, no more corporations, no more terrorists, no more worshiping of false deities, no more vanity, no more greed, no more rat race, no more destroying the earth for the sake of convenience. Humanity needed the sorrow and loss of everything they thought was important for them to understand what really is important.

"The old world is gone and good riddance to it. We're at the dawn of a new world and I know we're not going to be focusing our futures on the pointless luxuries that drove the world insane.

"Our species and our world have come from despair to an age of hope and opportunity. We can learn from the existence that mankind had calved out for itself and use this knowledge to create something beautiful." Jack trailed off as he felt shivers of cold running through his body.

He looked at Chloe and then at Lucy. Smiling, he squeezed Lucy's hand as his eyes filled with tears, "Thank you. You made me love again."

Lucy held Jack closely and kissed him gently on the lips.

"I love you Jack."

Jack smiled and shut his eyes.

-

THE END

Printed in Great Britain
by Amazon

80152042R00230